CN
CARTOON NETWORK

STEVEN UNIVERSE

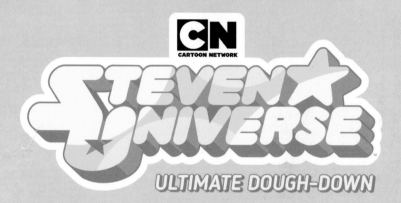

ULTIMATE DOUGH-DOWN

STEVEN UNIVERSE: ULTIMATE DOUGH-DOWN, December 2018. Published by KaBOOM!, a division of Boom Entertainment, Inc. STEVEN UNIVERSE, CARTOON NETWORK, the logos, and all related characters and elements are trademarks of and © Cartoon Network. A WarnerMedia Company. All rights reserved. (S18) KaBOOM!™ and the KaBOOM! Logo are trademarks of Boom Entertainment, Inc., registered in various countries and categories. All characters, events, and/or institutions depicted herein are fictional. Any similarity between any of the names, characters, persons, events, and/or institutions in this publication to actual names, characters, and persons, whether living or dead, events and/or institutions is unintended and purely coincidental. KaBOOM! Does not read or accept unsolicited submissions of ideas, stories, or artwork.

For information regarding the CPSIA on this printed material, call (203) 595-3636 and provide reference #RICH - 820489.

BOOM! Studios, 5670 Wilshire Boulevard, Suite 400, Los Angeles, CA 90036-5679. Printed in USA. First Printing.

ISBN: 978-1-68415-281-0, eISBN: 978-1-64144-143-8

CARTOON NETWORK

STEVEN UNIVERSE

ULTIMATE DOUGH-DOWN

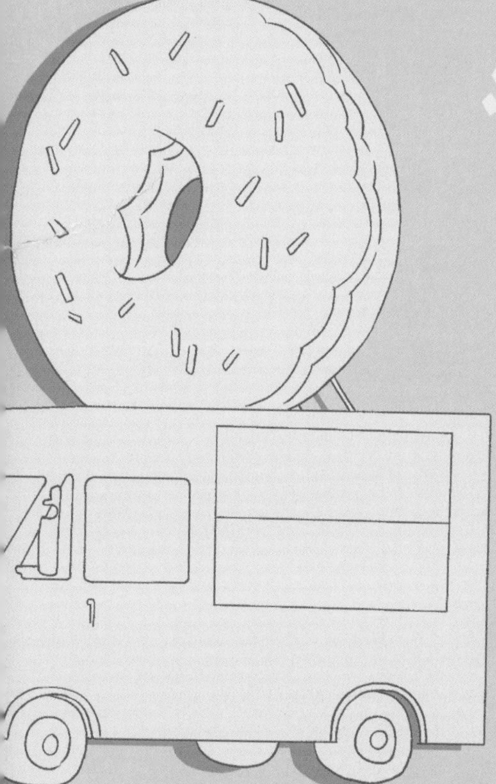

created by
REBECCA SUGAR

written by
TALYA PERPER

illustrated by
MEG OMAC

colored by
KIERAN QUIGLEY

lettered by
MIKE FIORENTINO

cover by
LORENA ALVAREZ GOMEZ

designer
CHELSEA ROBERTS

assistant editor
MICHAEL MOCCIO

editor
MATTHEW LEVINE

With Special Thanks to
Marisa Marionakis, Janet No, Becky M. Yang,
Conrad Montgomery, Jackie Buscarino and the wonderful folks at Cartoon Network.

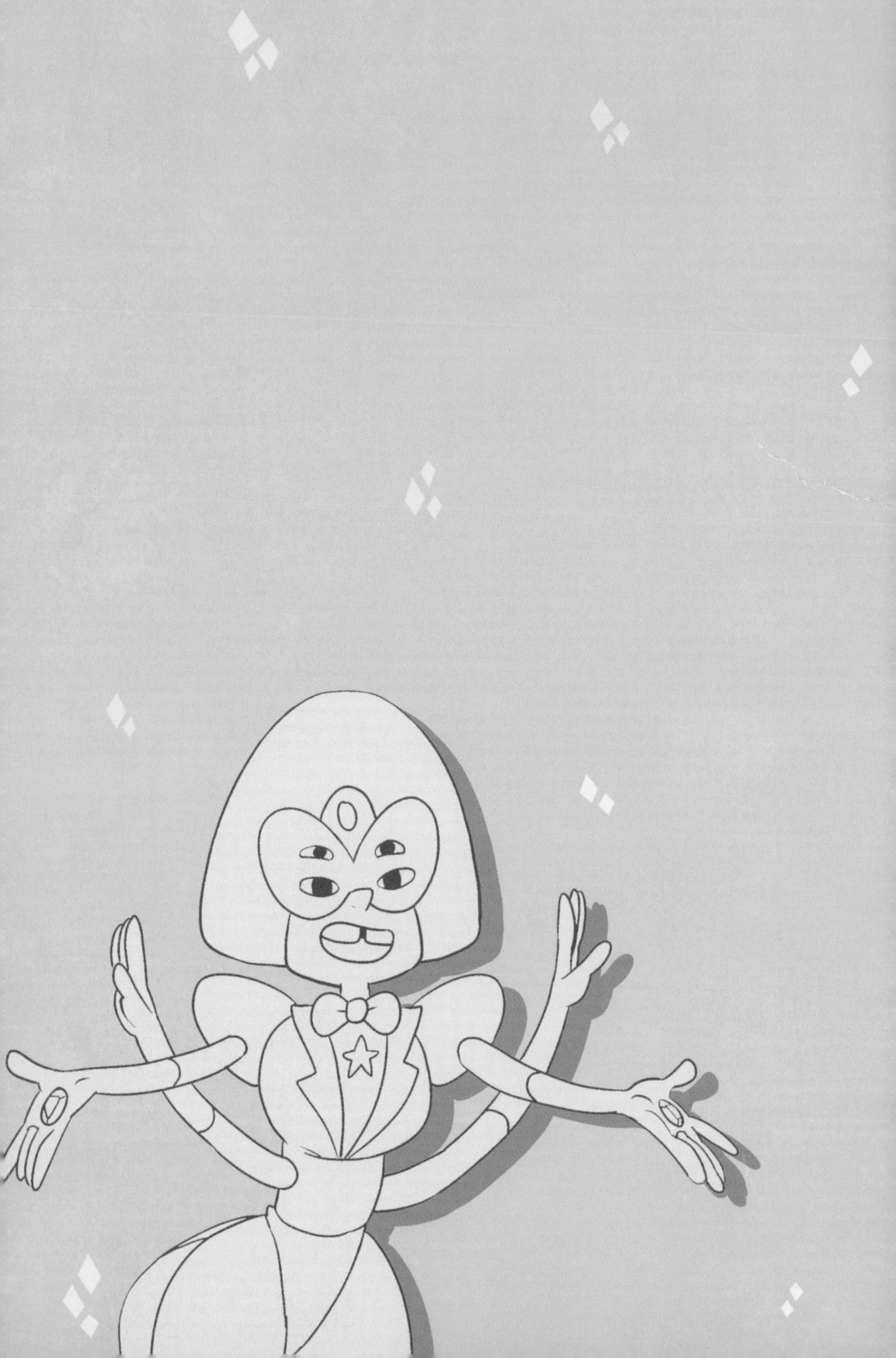

DONUTS

DAILY
SINGLE
HALF DOZEN
DOZEN
PARTY

WE ONLY
SELL
DONUTS!

COMBO

3.39

BREAKUP

6.49

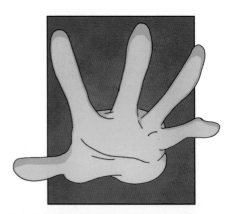

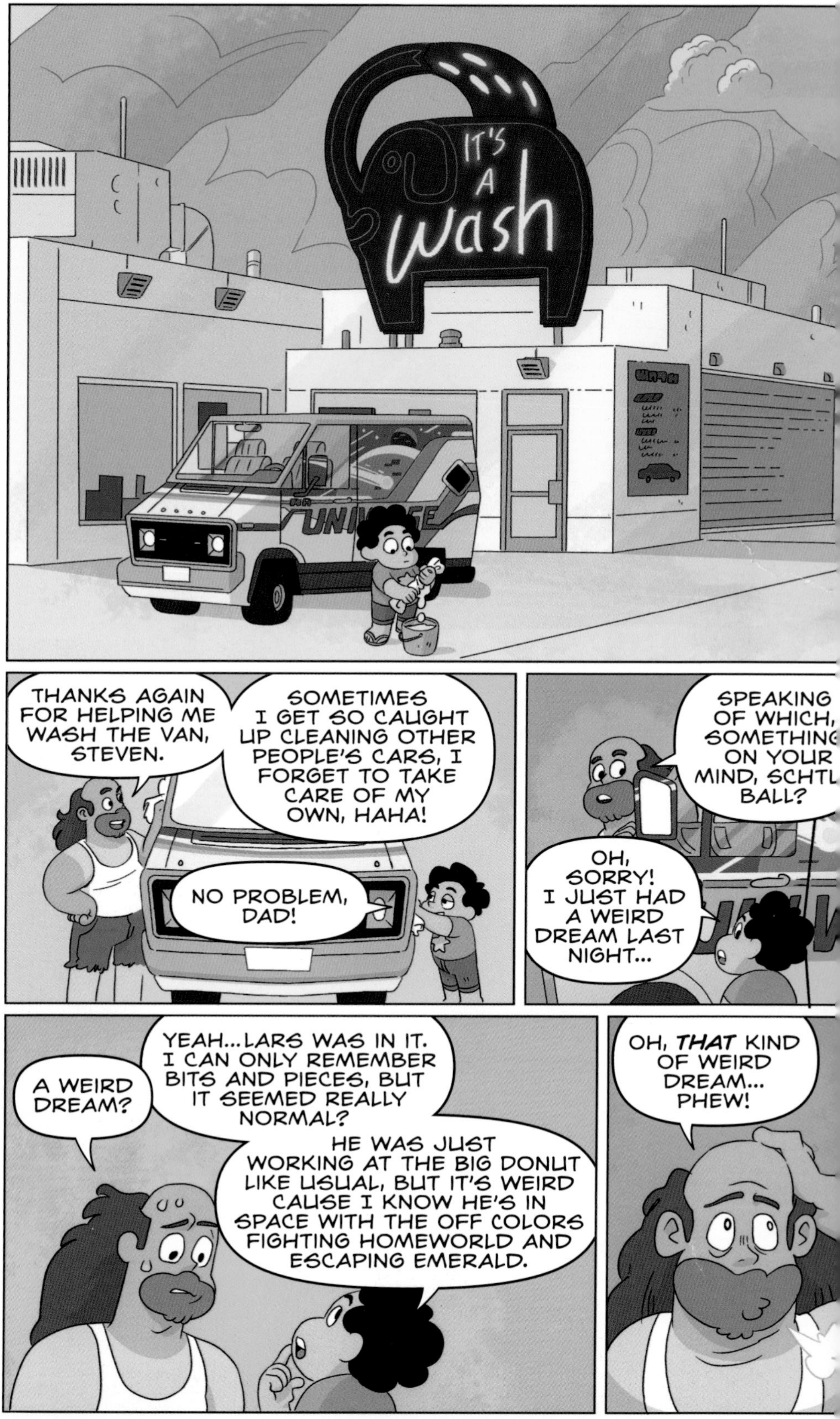
IT'S A wash
THANKS AGAIN FOR HELPING ME WASH THE VAN, STEVEN.
SOMETIMES I GET SO CAUGHT UP CLEANING OTHER PEOPLE'S CARS, I FORGET TO TAKE CARE OF MY OWN, HAHA!
NO PROBLEM, DAD!
SPEAKING OF WHICH, SOMETHING ON YOUR MIND, SCHTL BALL?
OH, SORRY! I JUST HAD A WEIRD DREAM LAST NIGHT...
A WEIRD DREAM?
YEAH...LARS WAS IN IT. I CAN ONLY REMEMBER BITS AND PIECES, BUT IT SEEMED REALLY NORMAL?
HE WAS JUST WORKING AT THE BIG DONUT LIKE USUAL, BUT IT'S WEIRD CAUSE I KNOW HE'S IN SPACE WITH THE OFF COLORS FIGHTING HOMEWORLD AND ESCAPING EMERALD.
OH, *THAT* KIND OF WEIRD DREAM... PHEW!

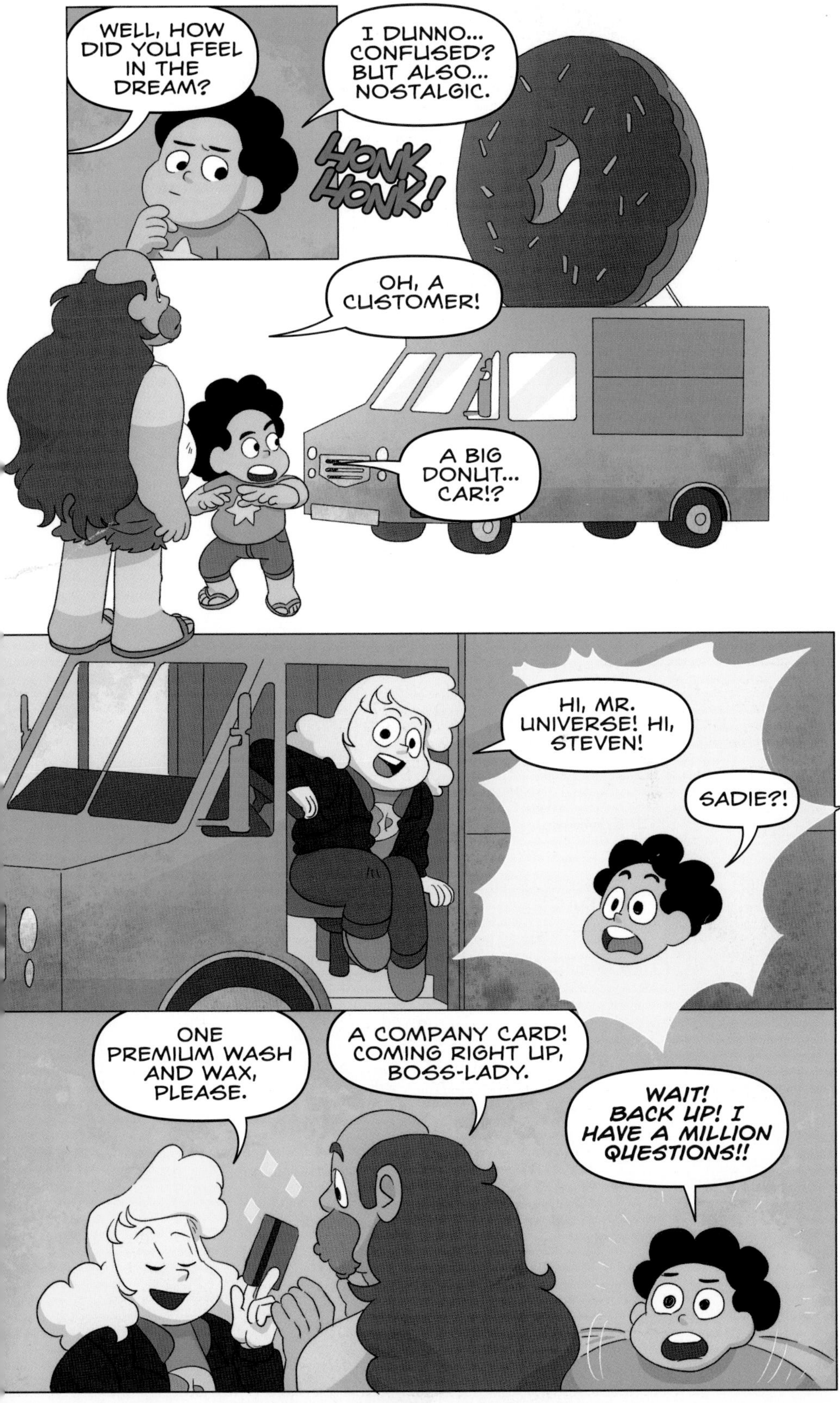
WELL, HOW DID YOU FEEL IN THE DREAM?
I DUNNO... CONFUSED? BUT ALSO... NOSTALGIC.
HONK HONK!
OH, A CUSTOMER!
A BIG DONUT... CAR!?
HI, MR. UNIVERSE! HI, STEVEN!
SADIE?!
ONE PREMIUM WASH AND WAX, PLEASE.
A COMPANY CARD! COMING RIGHT UP, BOSS-LADY.
WAIT! BACK UP! I HAVE A MILLION QUESTIONS!!

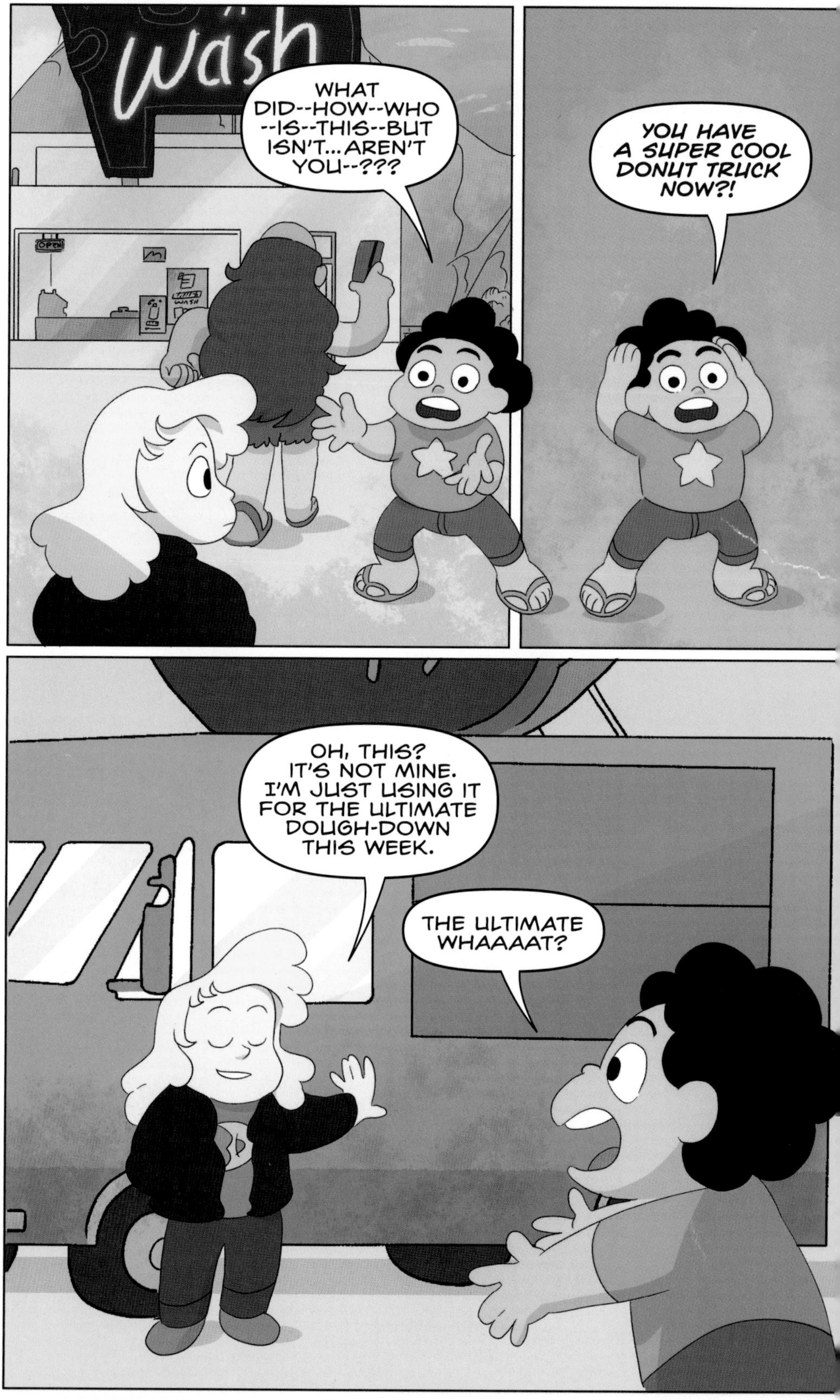
Wash
WHAT DID--HOW--WHO --IS--THIS--BUT ISN'T...AREN'T YOU--???
YOU HAVE A SUPER COOL DONUT TRUCK NOW?!
OH, THIS? IT'S NOT MINE. I'M JUST USING IT FOR THE ULTIMATE DOUGH-DOWN THIS WEEK.
THE ULTIMATE WHAAAAT?

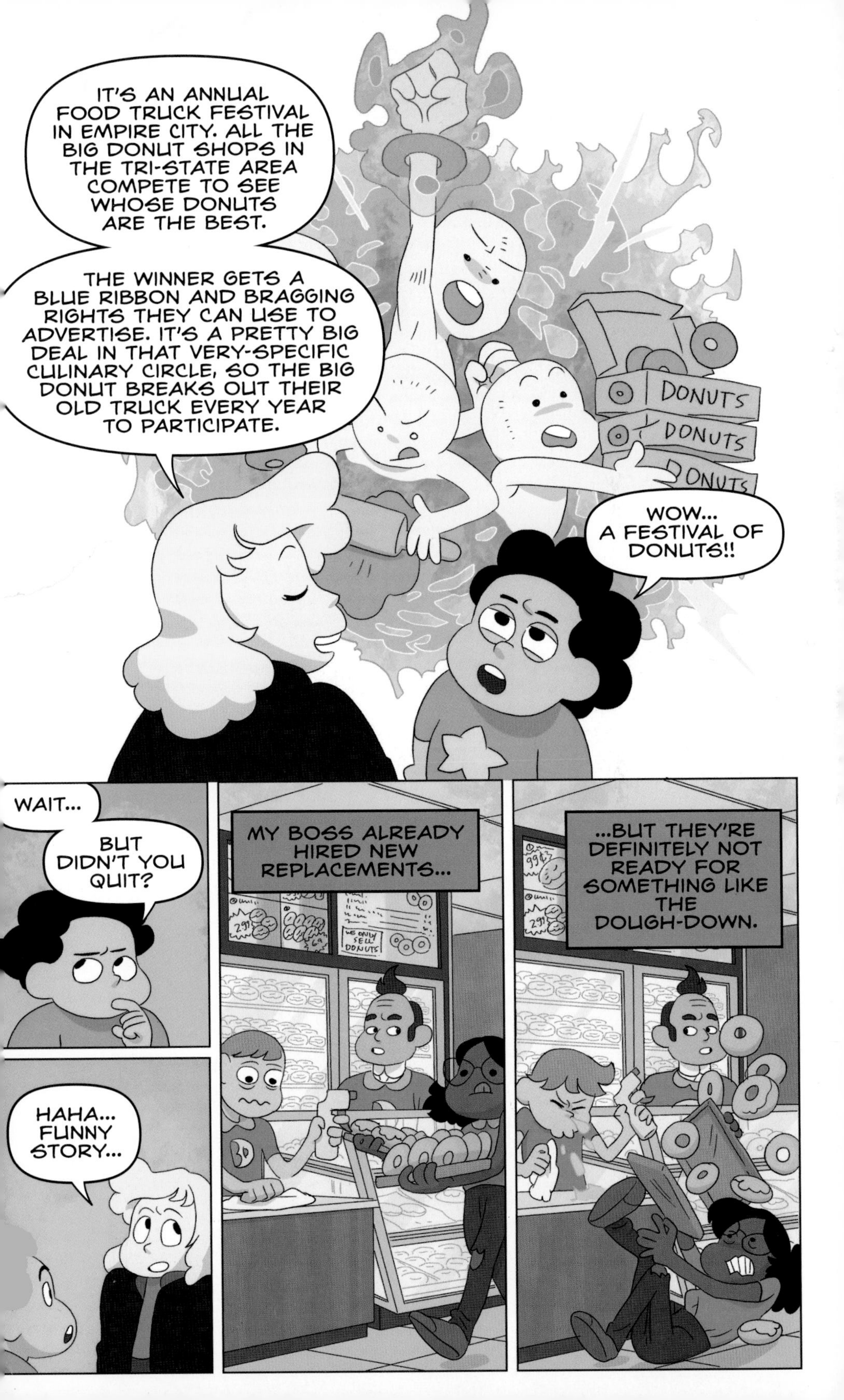
IT'S AN ANNUAL FOOD TRUCK FESTIVAL IN EMPIRE CITY. ALL THE BIG DONUT SHOPS IN THE TRI-STATE AREA COMPETE TO SEE WHOSE DONUTS ARE THE BEST.
THE WINNER GETS A BLUE RIBBON AND BRAGGING RIGHTS THEY CAN USE TO ADVERTISE. IT'S A PRETTY BIG DEAL IN THAT VERY-SPECIFIC CULINARY CIRCLE, SO THE BIG DONUT BREAKS OUT THEIR OLD TRUCK EVERY YEAR TO PARTICIPATE.
DONUTS
DONUTS
DONUTS
WOW... A FESTIVAL OF DONUTS!!
WAIT...
BUT DIDN'T YOU QUIT?
HAHA... FUNNY STORY...
MY BOSS ALREADY HIRED NEW REPLACEMENTS...
WE ONLY SELL DONUTS
...BUT THEY'RE DEFINITELY NOT READY FOR SOMETHING LIKE THE DOUGH-DOWN.

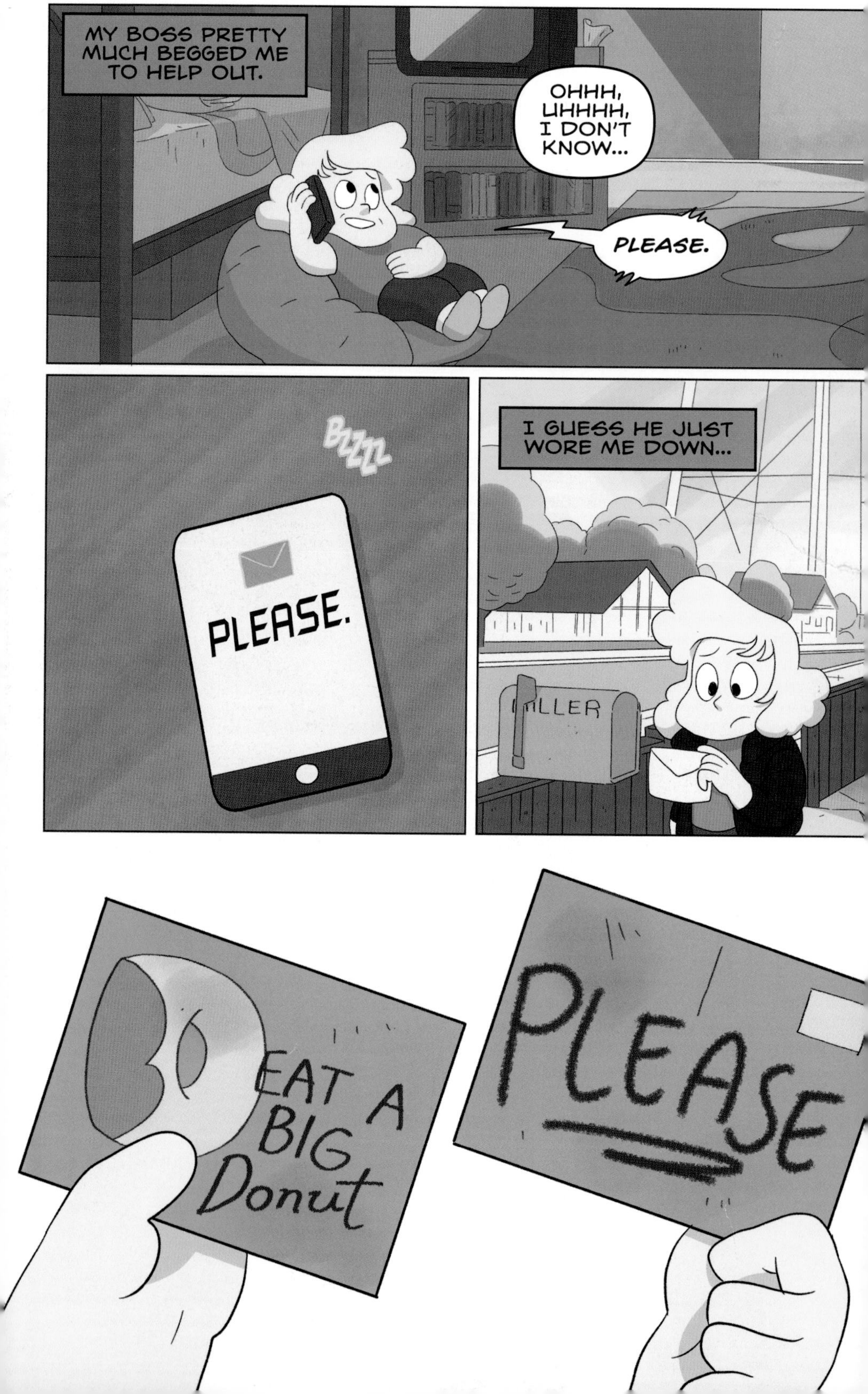
MY BOSS PRETTY MUCH BEGGED ME TO HELP OUT.
OHHH, UHHHH, I DON'T KNOW...
PLEASE.
BZZZZ
PLEASE.
I GUESS HE JUST WORE ME DOWN...
EAT A BIG Donut
PLEASE

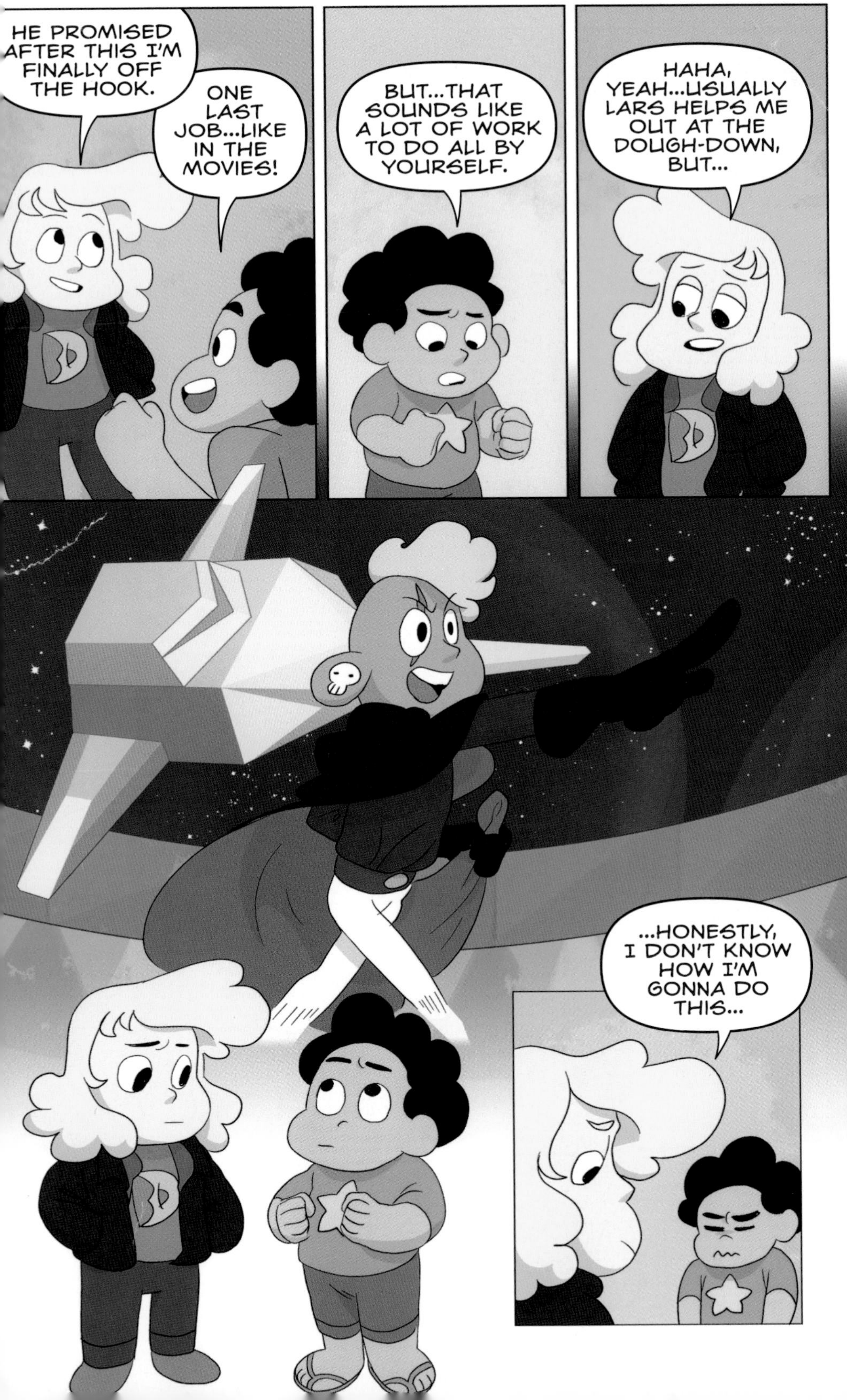
HE PROMISED AFTER THIS I'M FINALLY OFF THE HOOK.
ONE LAST JOB...LIKE IN THE MOVIES!
BUT...THAT SOUNDS LIKE A LOT OF WORK TO DO ALL BY YOURSELF.
HAHA, YEAH...USUALLY LARS HELPS ME OUT AT THE DOUGH-DOWN, BUT...
...HONESTLY, I DON'T KNOW HOW I'M GONNA DO THIS...

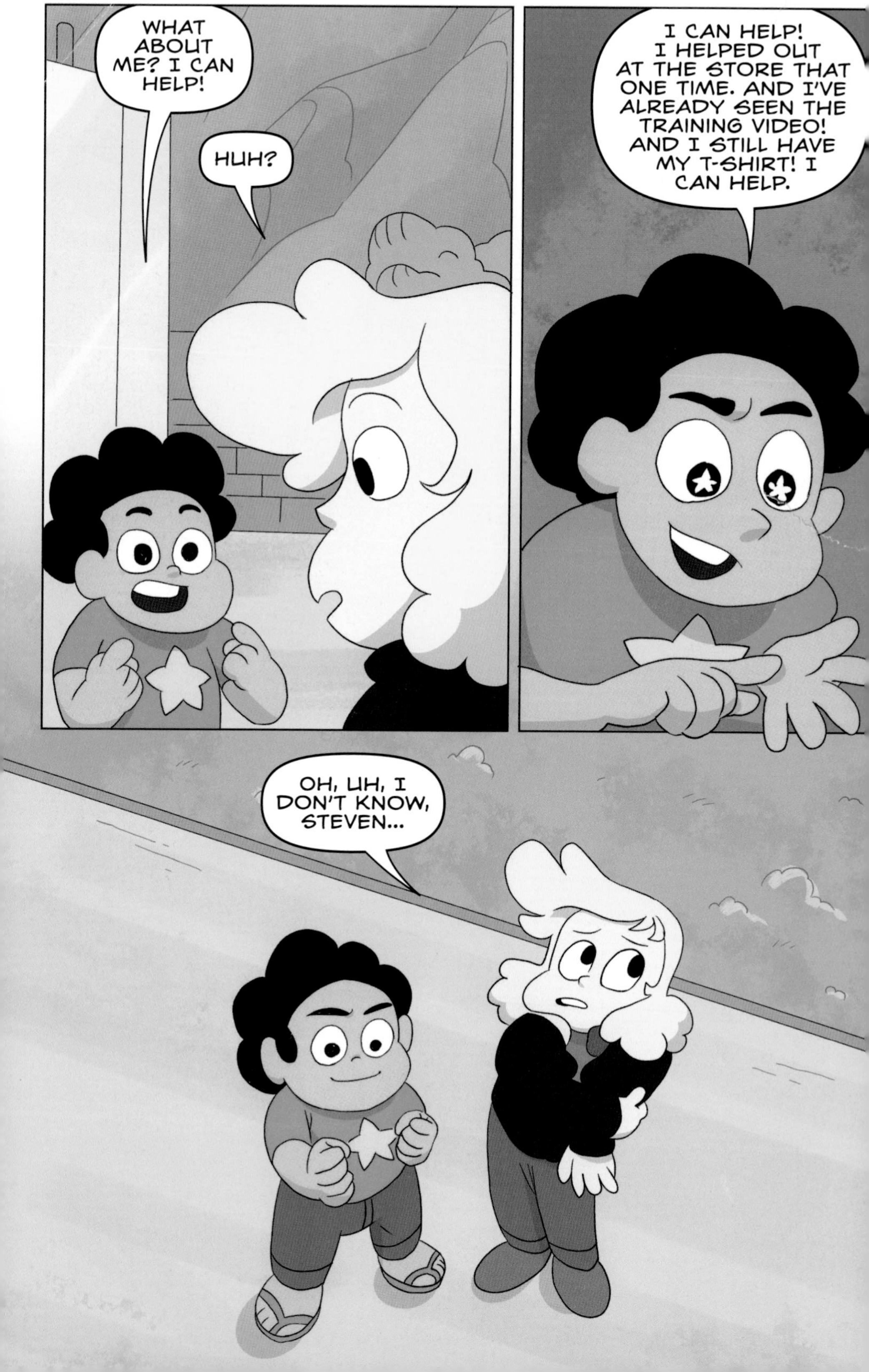
WHAT ABOUT ME? I CAN HELP!
HUH?
I CAN HELP! I HELPED OUT AT THE STORE THAT ONE TIME. AND I'VE ALREADY SEEN THE TRAINING VIDEO! AND I STILL HAVE MY T-SHIRT! I CAN HELP.
OH, UH, I DON'T KNOW, STEVEN...

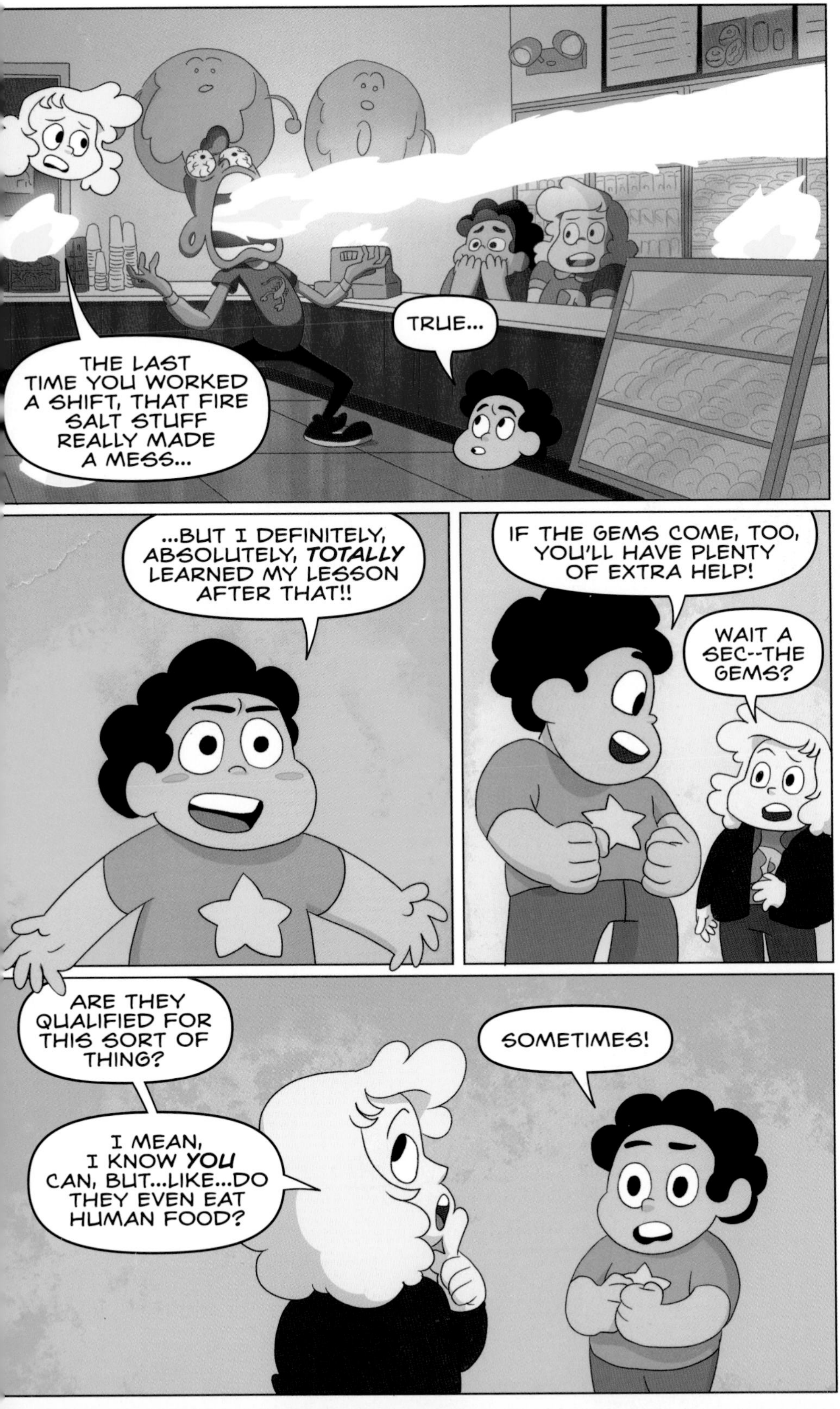
THE LAST TIME YOU WORKED A SHIFT, THAT FIRE SALT STUFF REALLY MADE A MESS...
TRUE...
...BUT I DEFINITELY, ABSOLUTELY, *TOTALLY* LEARNED MY LESSON AFTER THAT!!
IF THE GEMS COME, TOO, YOU'LL HAVE PLENTY OF EXTRA HELP!
WAIT A SEC--THE GEMS?
ARE THEY QUALIFIED FOR THIS SORT OF THING?
I MEAN, I KNOW *YOU* CAN, BUT...LIKE...DO THEY EVEN EAT HUMAN FOOD?
SOMETIMES!

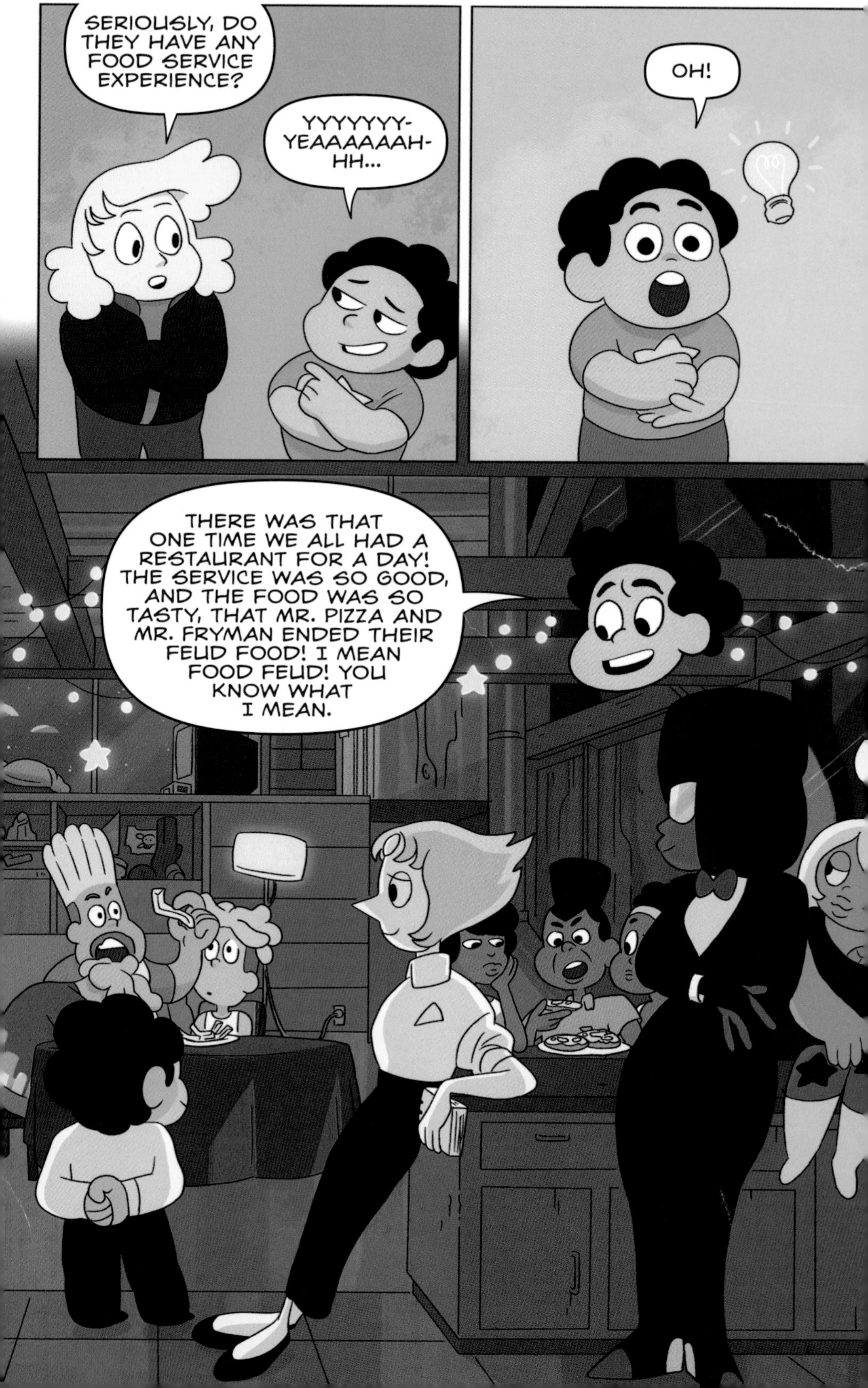
SERIOUSLY, DO THEY HAVE ANY FOOD SERVICE EXPERIENCE?
YYYYYYY-YEAAAAAAH-HH...
OH!
THERE WAS THAT ONE TIME WE ALL HAD A RESTAURANT FOR A DAY! THE SERVICE WAS SO GOOD, AND THE FOOD WAS SO TASTY, THAT MR. PIZZA AND MR. FRYMAN ENDED THEIR FEUD FOOD! I MEAN FOOD FEUD! YOU KNOW WHAT I MEAN.

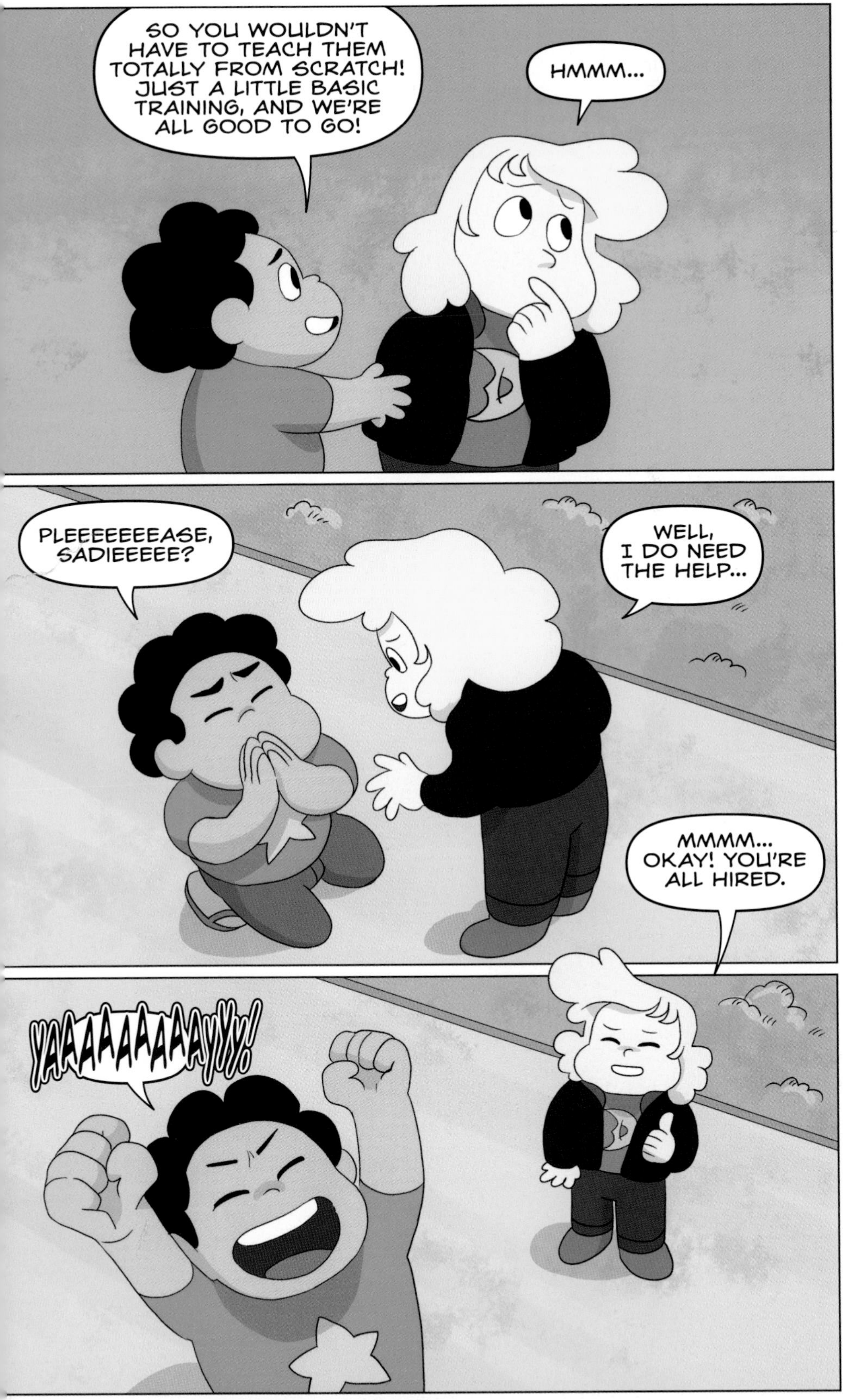
SO YOU WOULDN'T HAVE TO TEACH THEM TOTALLY FROM SCRATCH! JUST A LITTLE BASIC TRAINING, AND WE'RE ALL GOOD TO GO!
HMMM...
PLEEEEEEEASE, SADIEEEEE?
WELL, I DO NEED THE HELP...
MMMM... OKAY! YOU'RE ALL HIRED.
YAAAAAAAAAYYY!

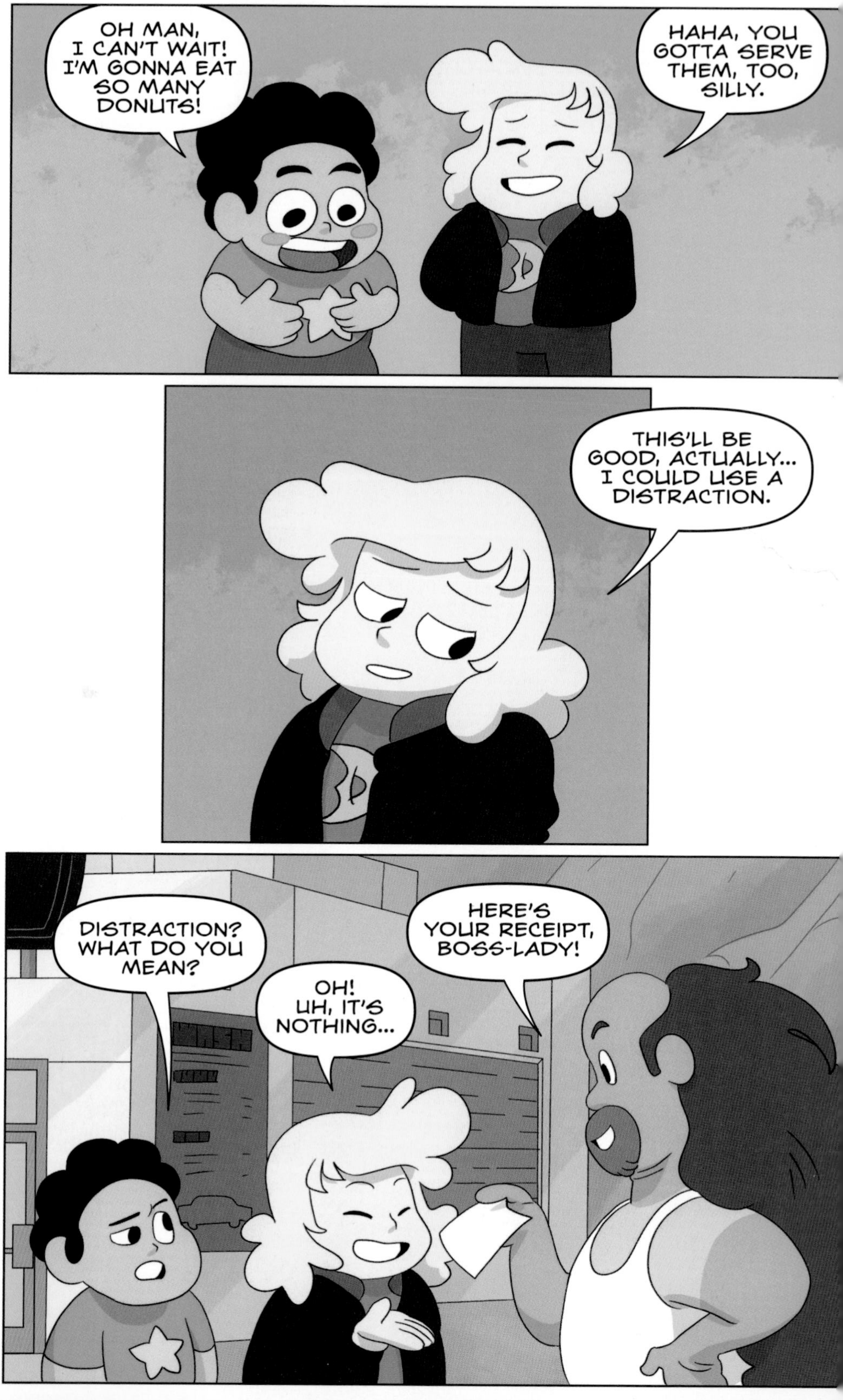
OH MAN, I CAN'T WAIT! I'M GONNA EAT SO MANY DONUTS!
HAHA, YOU GOTTA SERVE THEM, TOO, SILLY.
THIS'LL BE GOOD, ACTUALLY... I COULD USE A DISTRACTION.
DISTRACTION? WHAT DO YOU MEAN?
OH! UH, IT'S NOTHING...
HERE'S YOUR RECEIPT, BOSS-LADY!

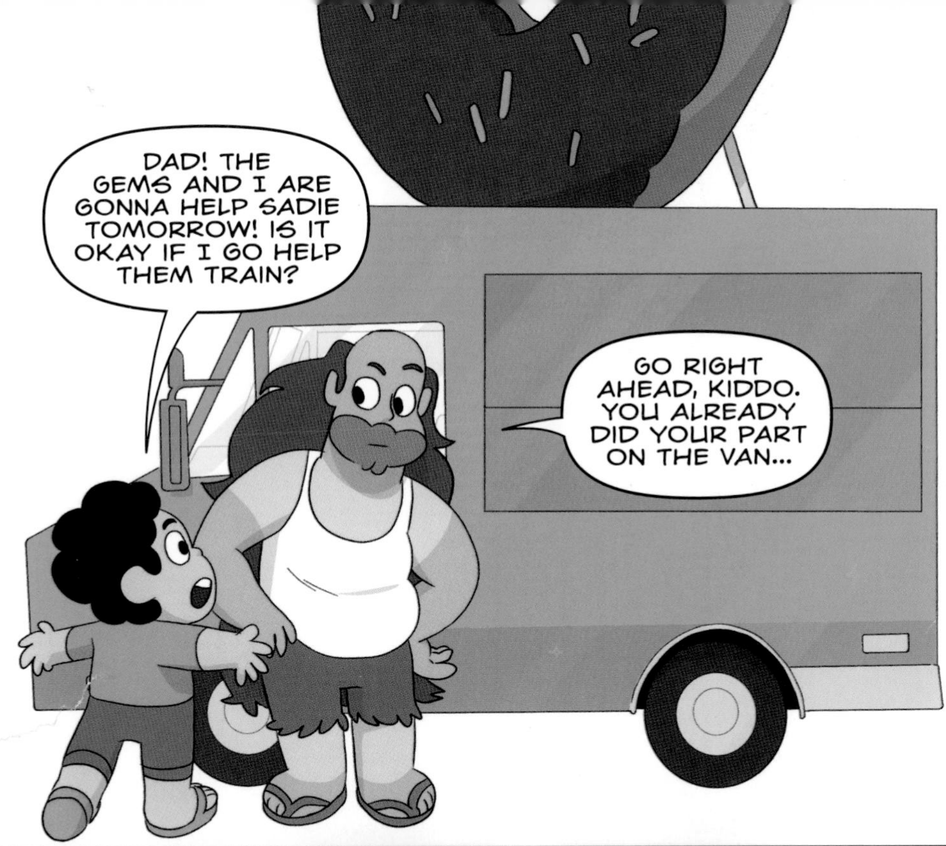
DAD! THE GEMS AND I ARE GONNA HELP SADIE TOMORROW! IS IT OKAY IF I GO HELP THEM TRAIN?
GO RIGHT AHEAD, KIDDO. YOU ALREADY DID YOUR PART ON THE VAN...

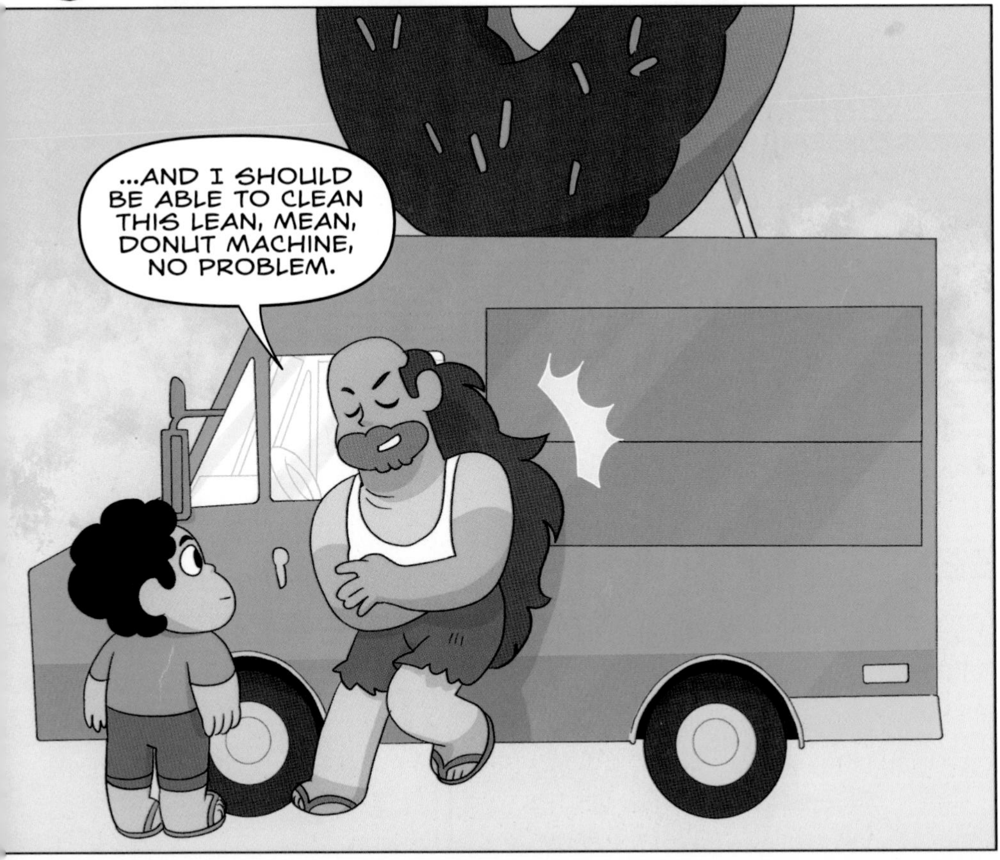
...AND I SHOULD BE ABLE TO CLEAN THIS LEAN, MEAN, DONUT MACHINE, NO PROBLEM.

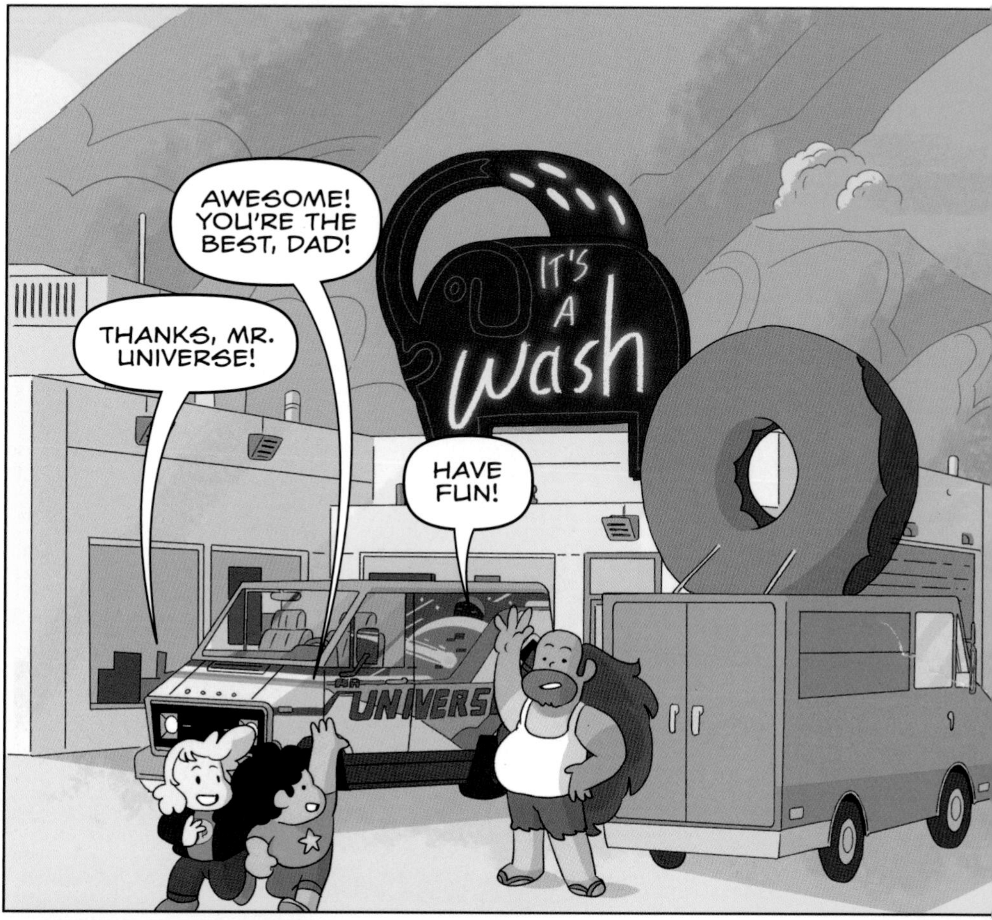
IT'S A wash
AWESOME! YOU'RE THE BEST, DAD!
THANKS, MR. UNIVERSE!
HAVE FUN!
UNIVERSE

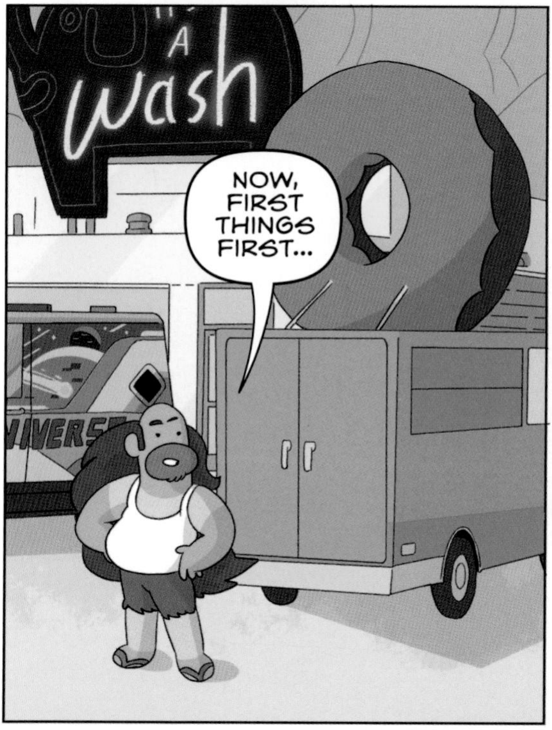
A wash
NOW, FIRST THINGS FIRST...

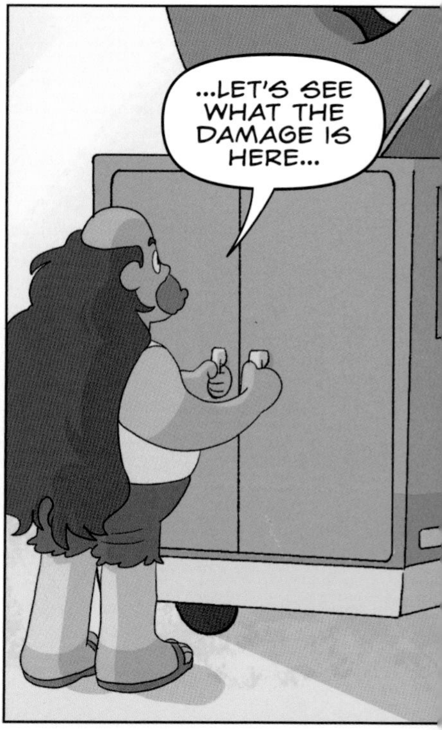
...LET'S SEE WHAT THE DAMAGE IS HERE...

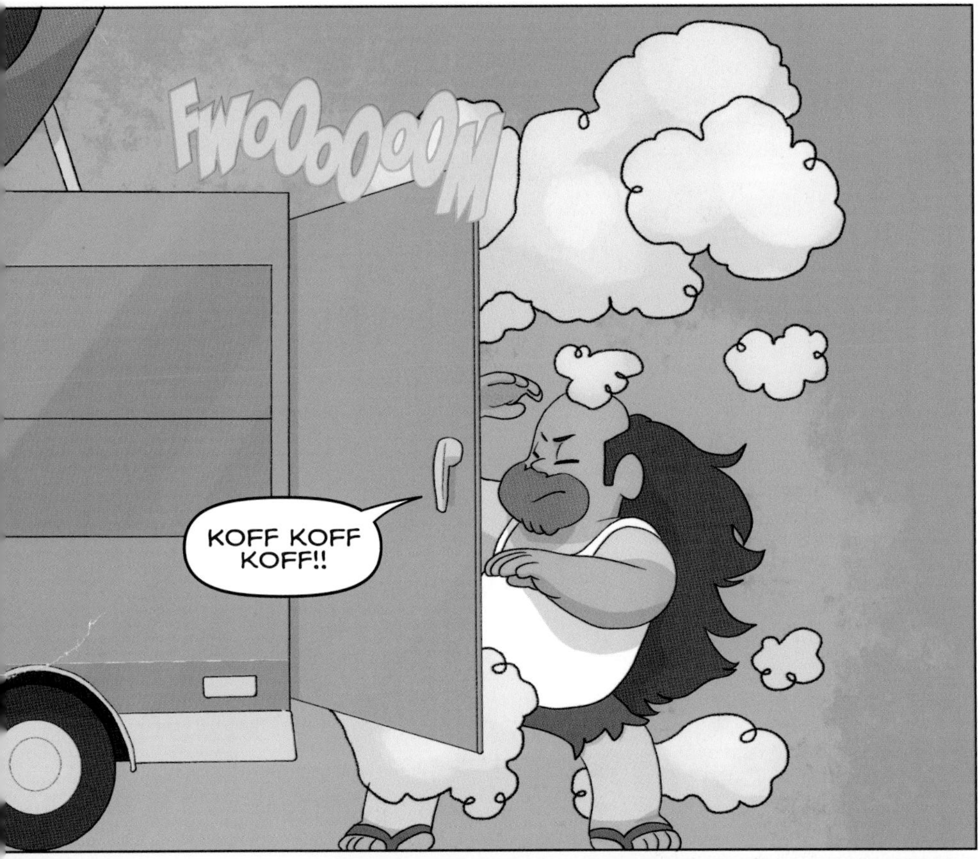
FWOOOOOOM
KOFF KOFF KOFF!!

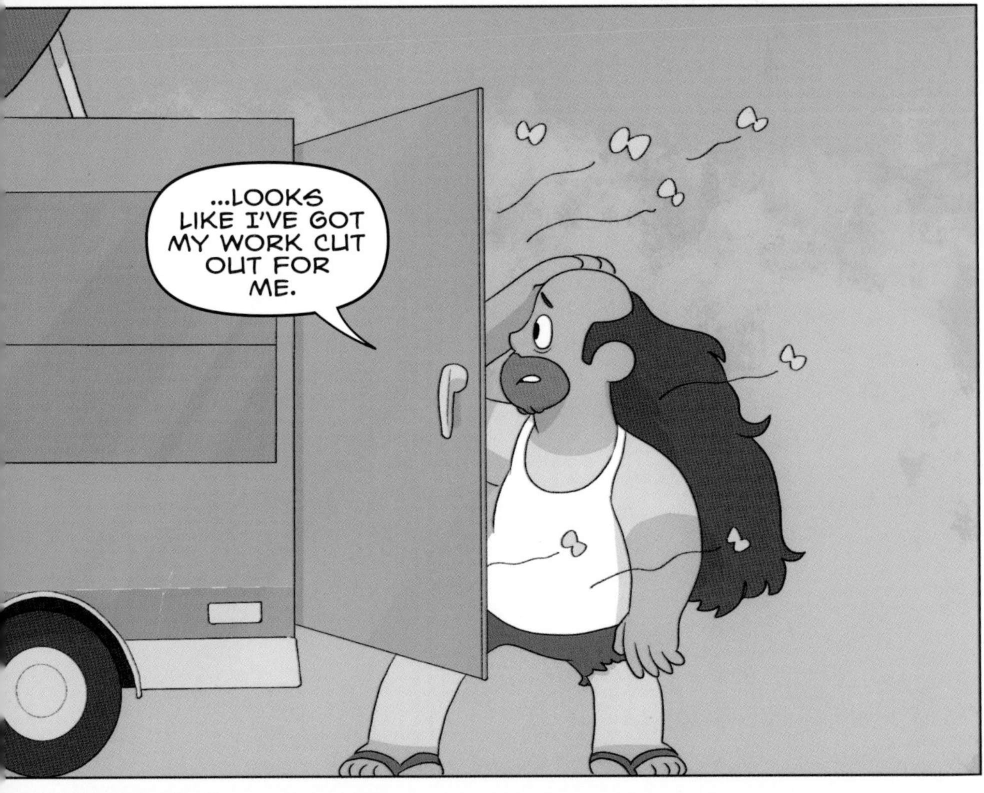
...LOOKS LIKE I'VE GOT MY WORK CUT OUT FOR ME.

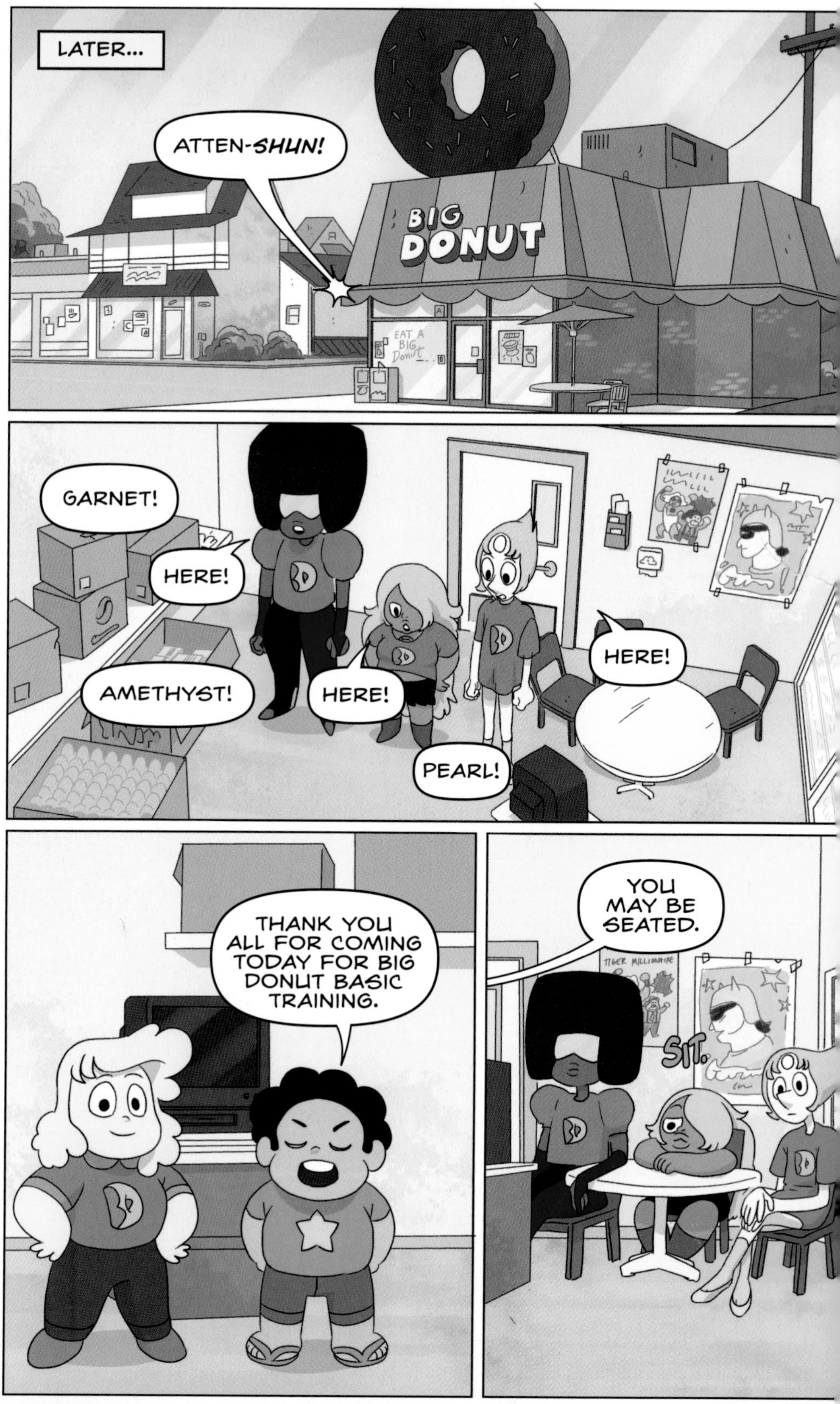
LATER...
ATTEN-SHUN!
BIG DONUT
EAT A BIG Donut
GARNET!
HERE!
AMETHYST!
HERE!
HERE!
PEARL!
THANK YOU ALL FOR COMING TODAY FOR BIG DONUT BASIC TRAINING.
YOU MAY BE SEATED.
TIGER MILLIONAIRE
SIT.

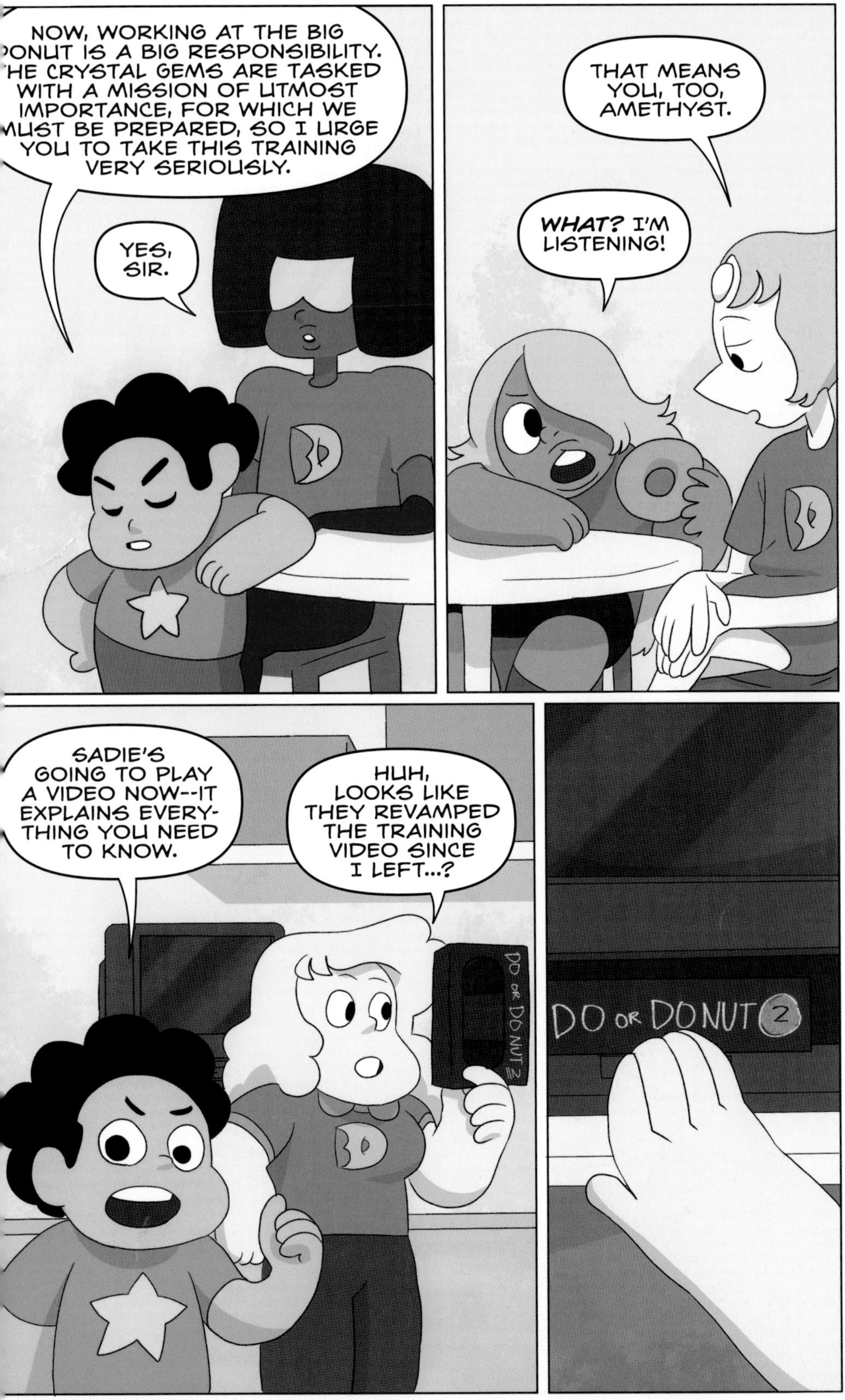

NOW, WORKING AT THE BIG ONUT IS A BIG RESPONSIBILITY. HE CRYSTAL GEMS ARE TASKED WITH A MISSION OF UTMOST IMPORTANCE, FOR WHICH WE UST BE PREPARED, SO I URGE YOU TO TAKE THIS TRAINING VERY SERIOUSLY.
YES, SIR.
THAT MEANS YOU, TOO, AMETHYST.
WHAT? I'M LISTENING!
SADIE'S GOING TO PLAY A VIDEO NOW--IT EXPLAINS EVERYTHING YOU NEED TO KNOW.
HUH, LOOKS LIKE THEY REVAMPED THE TRAINING VIDEO SINCE I LEFT...?
DO or DONUT 2
DO or DONUT 2

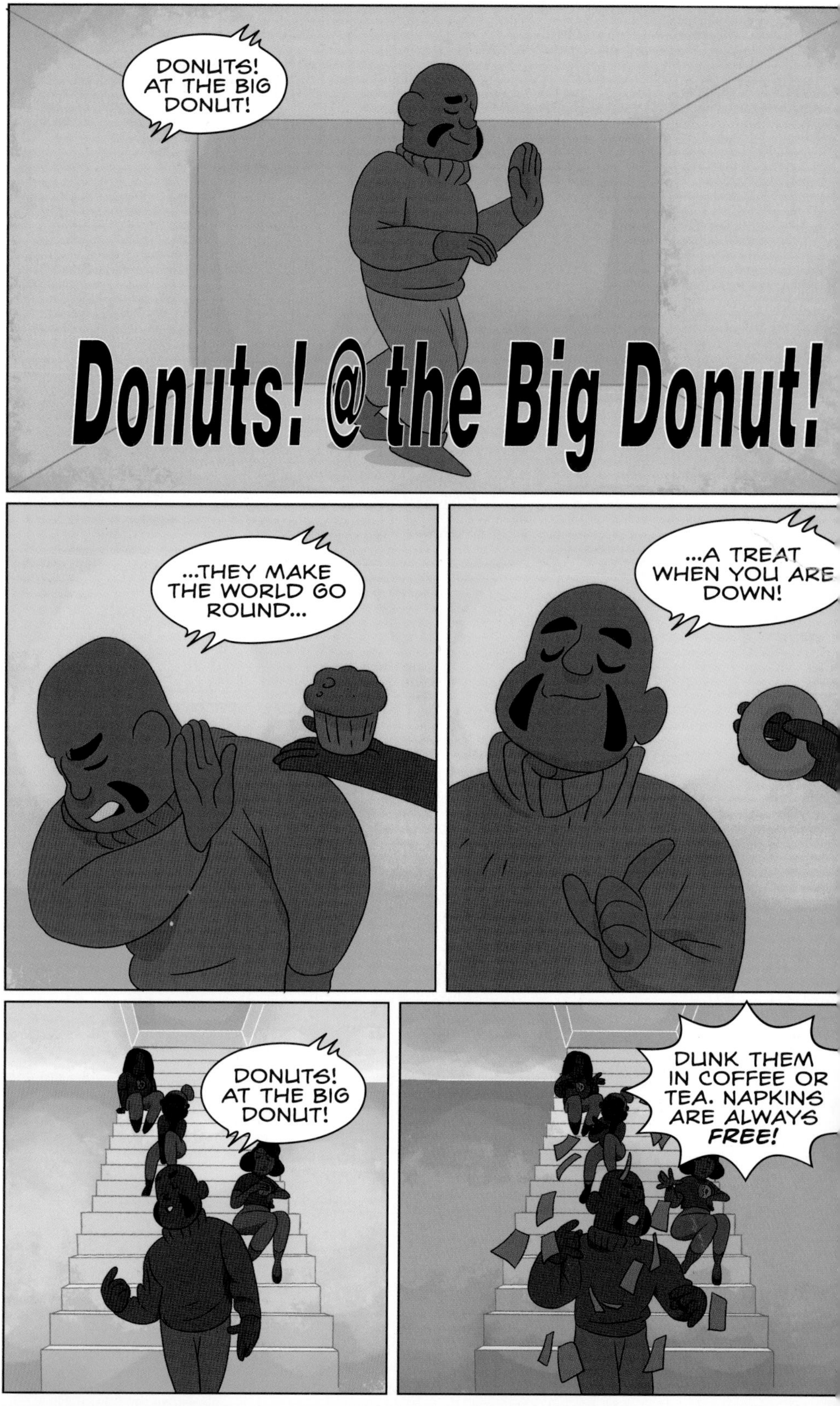
DONUTS! AT THE BIG DONUT!
Donuts! @ the Big Donut!
...THEY MAKE THE WORLD GO ROUND...
...A TREAT WHEN YOU ARE DOWN!
DONUTS! AT THE BIG DONUT!
DUNK THEM IN COFFEE OR TEA. NAPKINS ARE ALWAYS FREE!

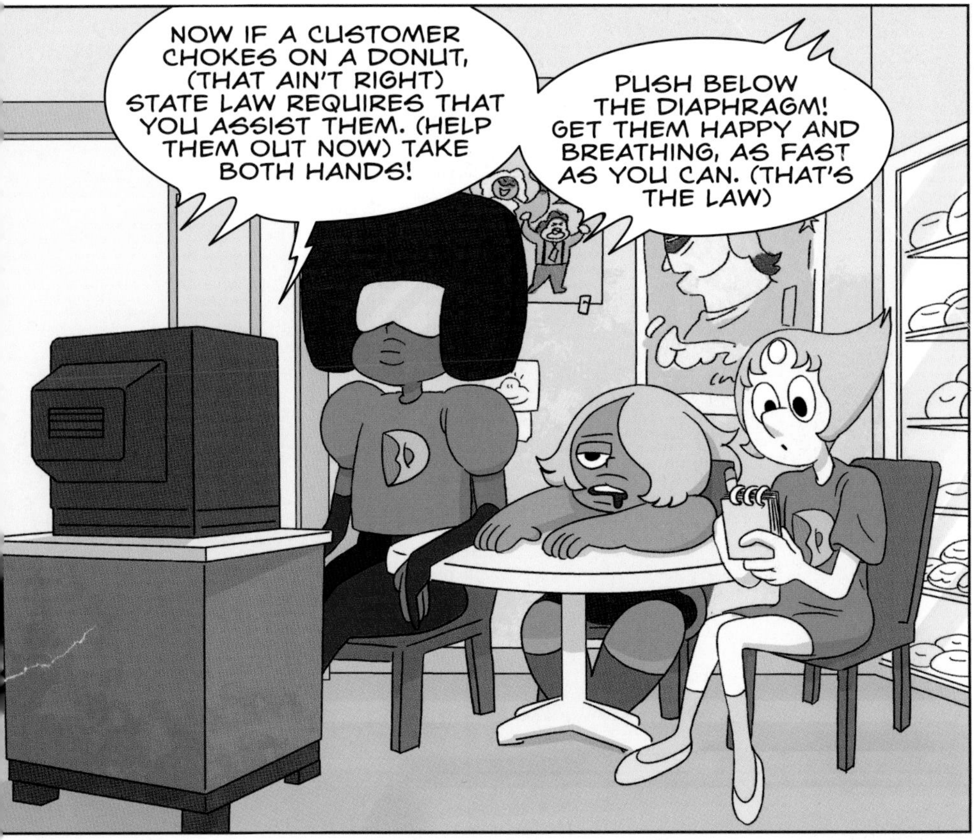
NOW IF A CUSTOMER CHOKES ON A DONUT, (THAT AIN'T RIGHT) STATE LAW REQUIRES THAT YOU ASSIST THEM. (HELP THEM OUT NOW) TAKE BOTH HANDS!
PUSH BELOW THE DIAPHRAGM! GET THEM HAPPY AND BREATHING, AS FAST AS YOU CAN. (THAT'S THE LAW)

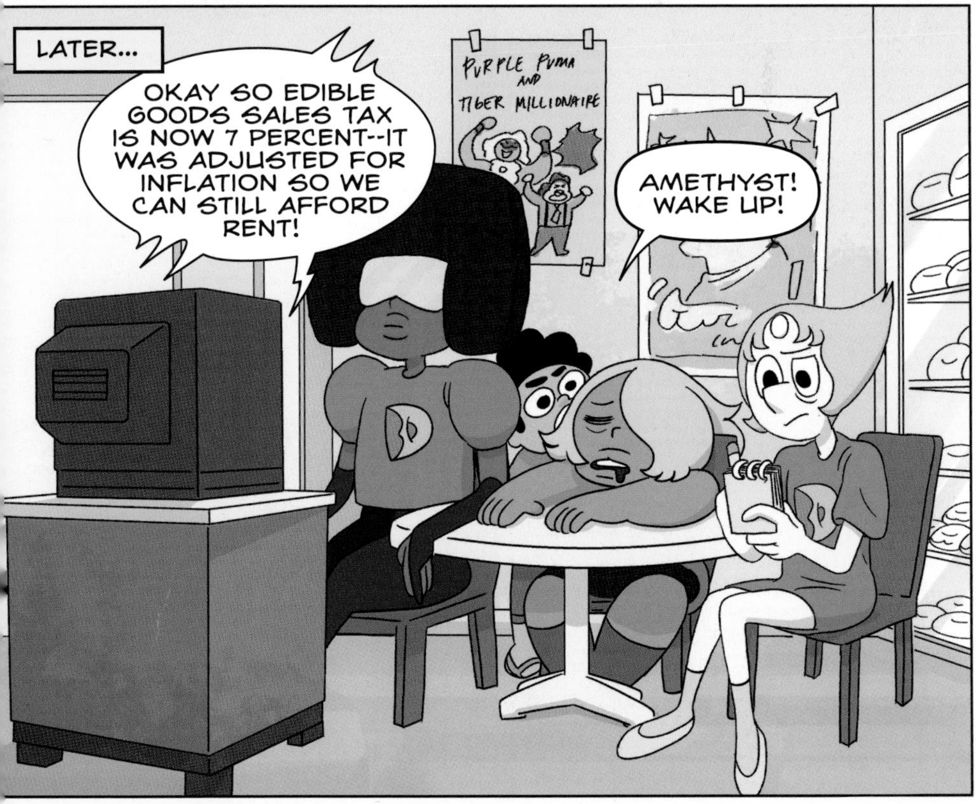
LATER...
OKAY SO EDIBLE GOODS SALES TAX IS NOW 7 PERCENT--IT WAS ADJUSTED FOR INFLATION SO WE CAN STILL AFFORD RENT!
PURPLE PUMA AND TIGER MILLIONAIRE
AMETHYST! WAKE UP!

IF YOU SEE THE HEALTH INSPECTOR MAKING NOTES WITH A FROWN, BE SURE TO KEEP HIM HAPPY SO WE DON'T SHUT DOWN!

COME ON! THIS IS IMPORTANT...

QUIIIIT IIIT! I'M LISTENIIING!

NOW CHECK OUT THIS ACRONYM IT DOESN'T DISAPPOINT, IT'S H-A-C-C-P-HAZARD ANALYSIS AND CRITICAL CONTROL POINTS.

PFFT WHAT'S THE BIG DEAL? SELLING DONUTS CAN'T BE ANY HARDER THAN FIGHTING MONSTERS...

FORTY TO ONE HUNDRED AND FORTY DEGREES IS THE DANGER ZONE FOR FOOD, SO STAY AWAY FROM IT PLEASE!

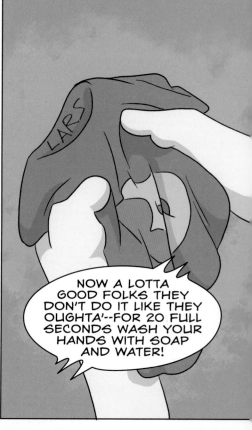

NOW A LOTTA GOOD FOLKS THEY DON'T DO IT LIKE THEY OUGHTA'--FOR 20 FULL SECONDS WASH YOUR HANDS WITH SOAP AND WATER!

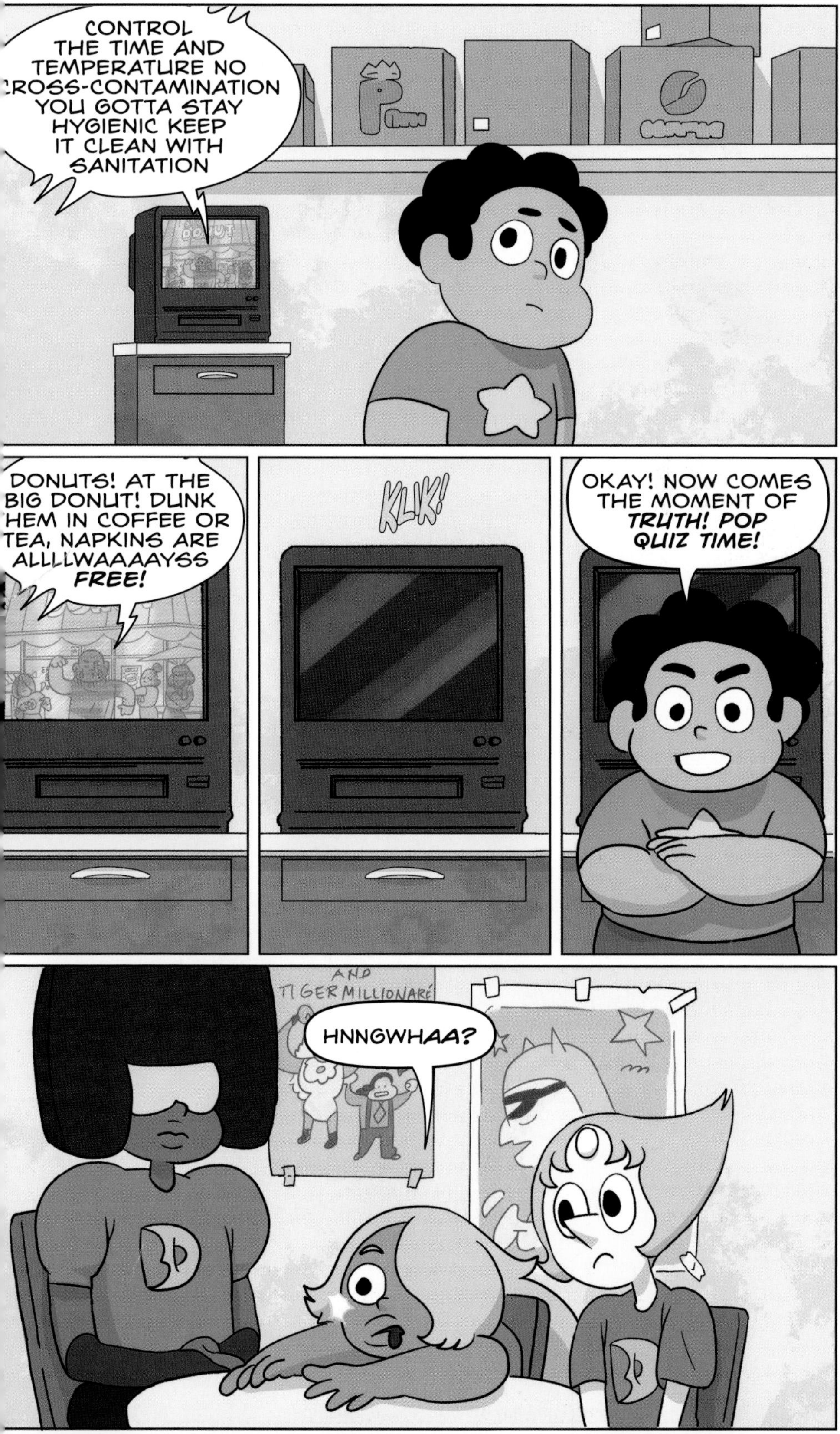
CONTROL THE TIME AND TEMPERATURE NO CROSS-CONTAMINATION YOU GOTTA STAY HYGIENIC KEEP IT CLEAN WITH SANITATION
DONUTS! AT THE BIG DONUT! DUNK THEM IN COFFEE OR TEA, NAPKINS ARE ALLLLWAAAAYSS FREE!
KLIK!
OKAY! NOW COMES THE MOMENT OF TRUTH! POP QUIZ TIME!
AND TIGER MILLIONARÉ
HNNGWHAA?

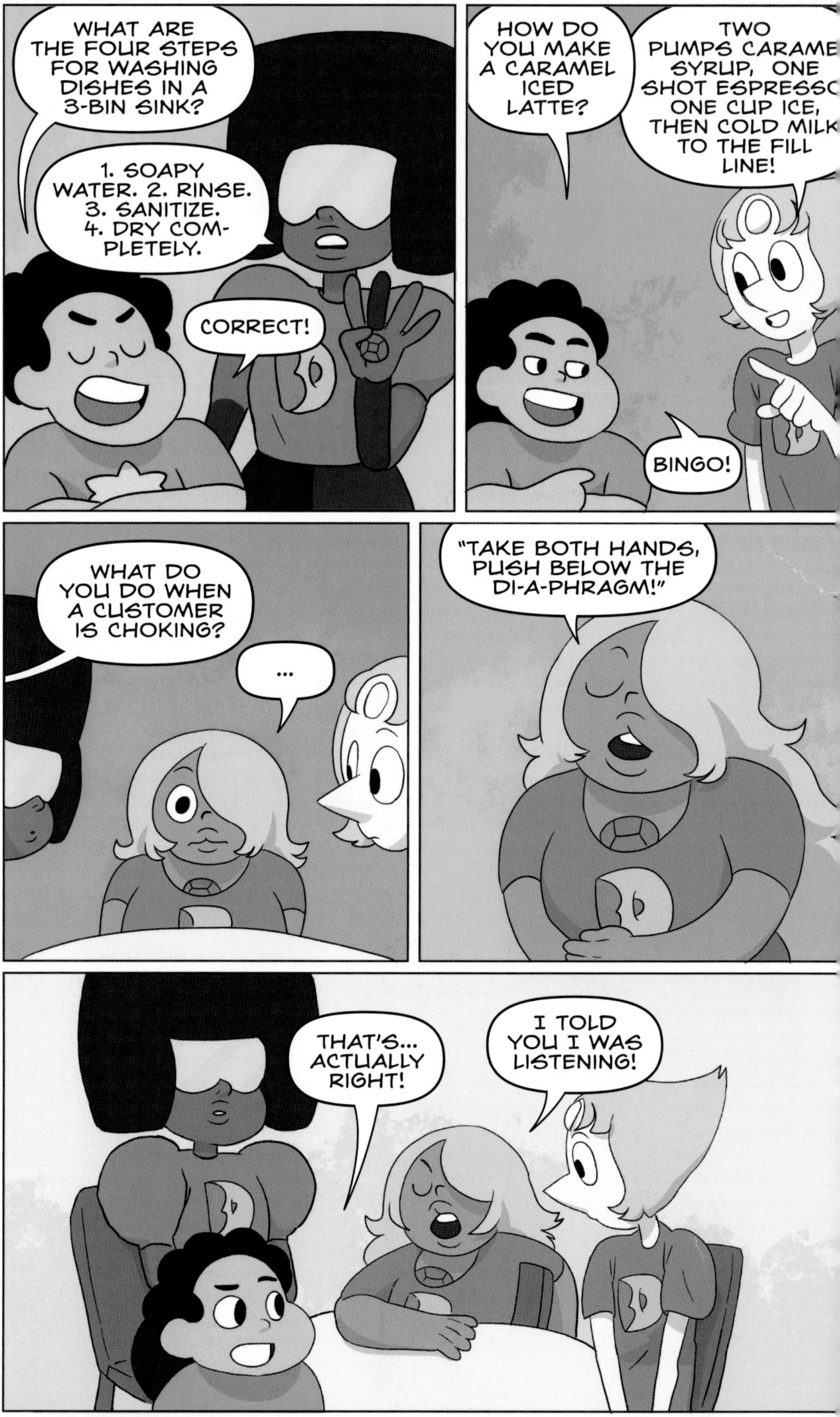
WHAT ARE THE FOUR STEPS FOR WASHING DISHES IN A 3-BIN SINK?
1. SOAPY WATER. 2. RINSE. 3. SANITIZE. 4. DRY COMPLETELY.
CORRECT!
HOW DO YOU MAKE A CARAMEL ICED LATTE?
TWO PUMPS CARAME SYRUP, ONE SHOT ESPRESSO ONE CUP ICE, THEN COLD MILK TO THE FILL LINE!
BINGO!
WHAT DO YOU DO WHEN A CUSTOMER IS CHOKING?
...
"TAKE BOTH HANDS, PUSH BELOW THE DI-A-PHRAGM!"
THAT'S... ACTUALLY RIGHT!
I TOLD YOU I WAS LISTENING!

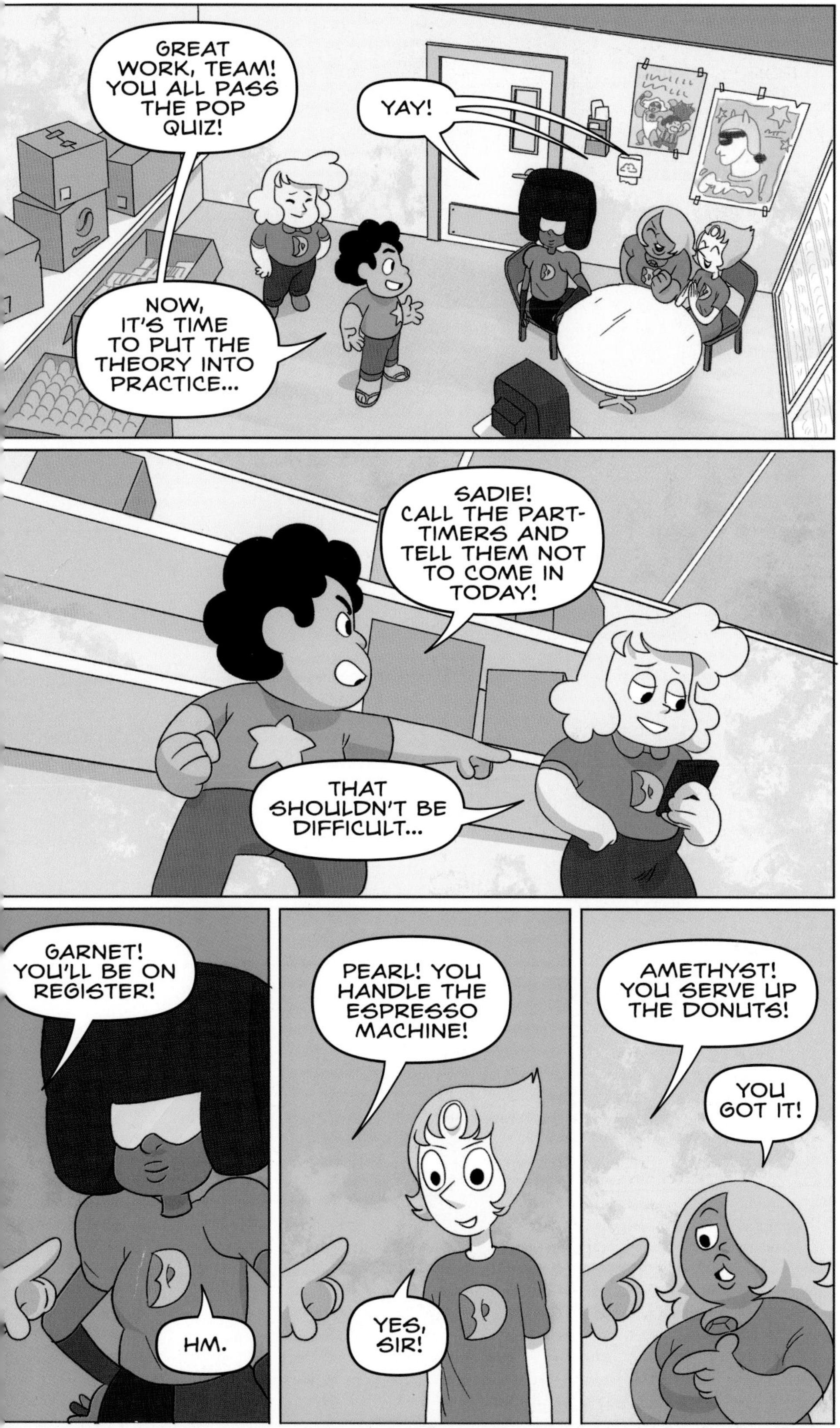
GREAT WORK, TEAM! YOU ALL PASS THE POP QUIZ!
YAY!
NOW, IT'S TIME TO PUT THE THEORY INTO PRACTICE...
SADIE! CALL THE PART-TIMERS AND TELL THEM NOT TO COME IN TODAY!
THAT SHOULDN'T BE DIFFICULT...
GARNET! YOU'LL BE ON REGISTER!
HM.
PEARL! YOU HANDLE THE ESPRESSO MACHINE!
YES, SIR!
AMETHYST! YOU SERVE UP THE DONUTS!
YOU GOT IT!

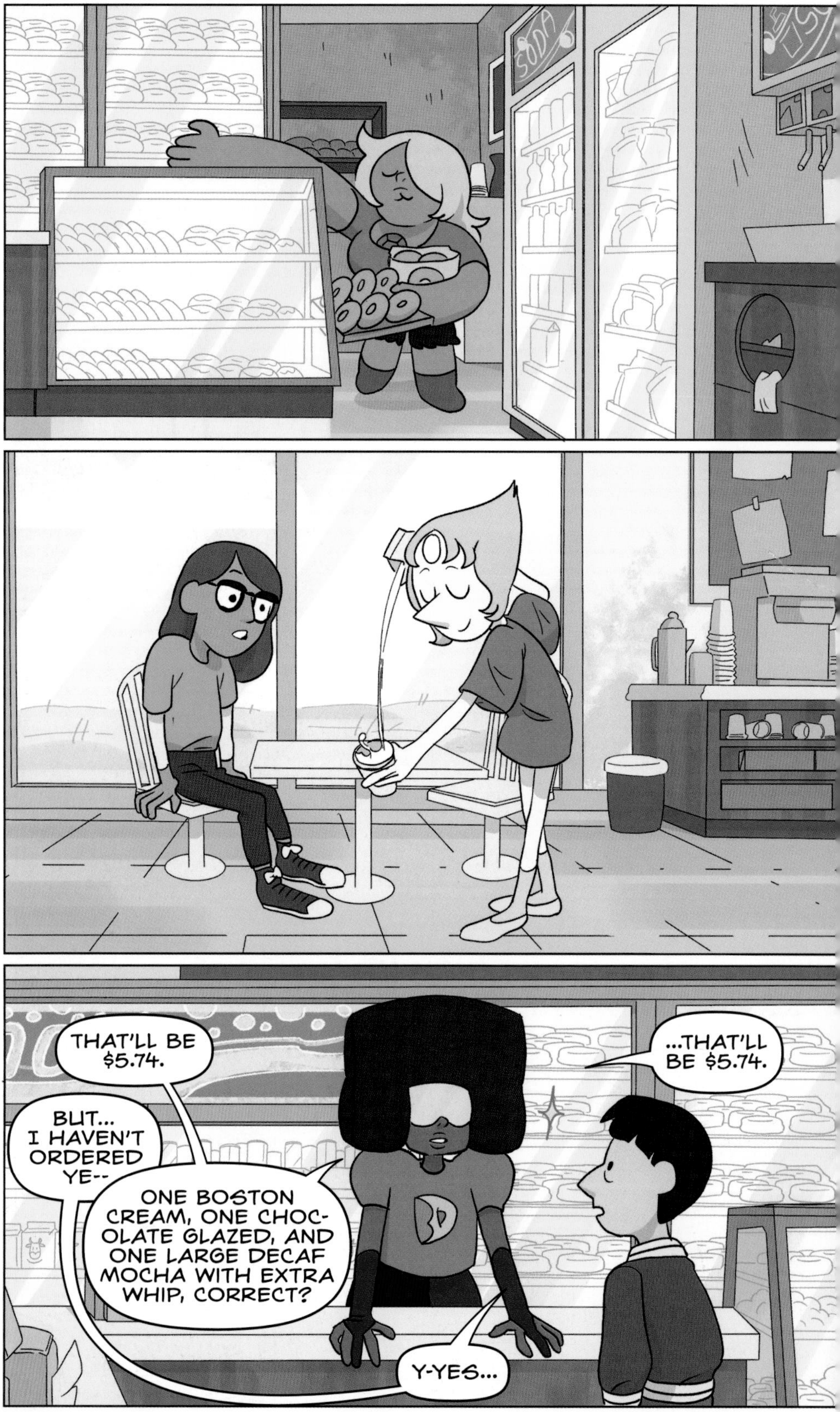
THAT'LL BE $5.74.
...THAT'LL BE $5.74.
BUT... I HAVEN'T ORDERED YE--
ONE BOSTON CREAM, ONE CHOCOLATE GLAZED, AND ONE LARGE DECAF MOCHA WITH EXTRA WHIP, CORRECT?
Y-YES...

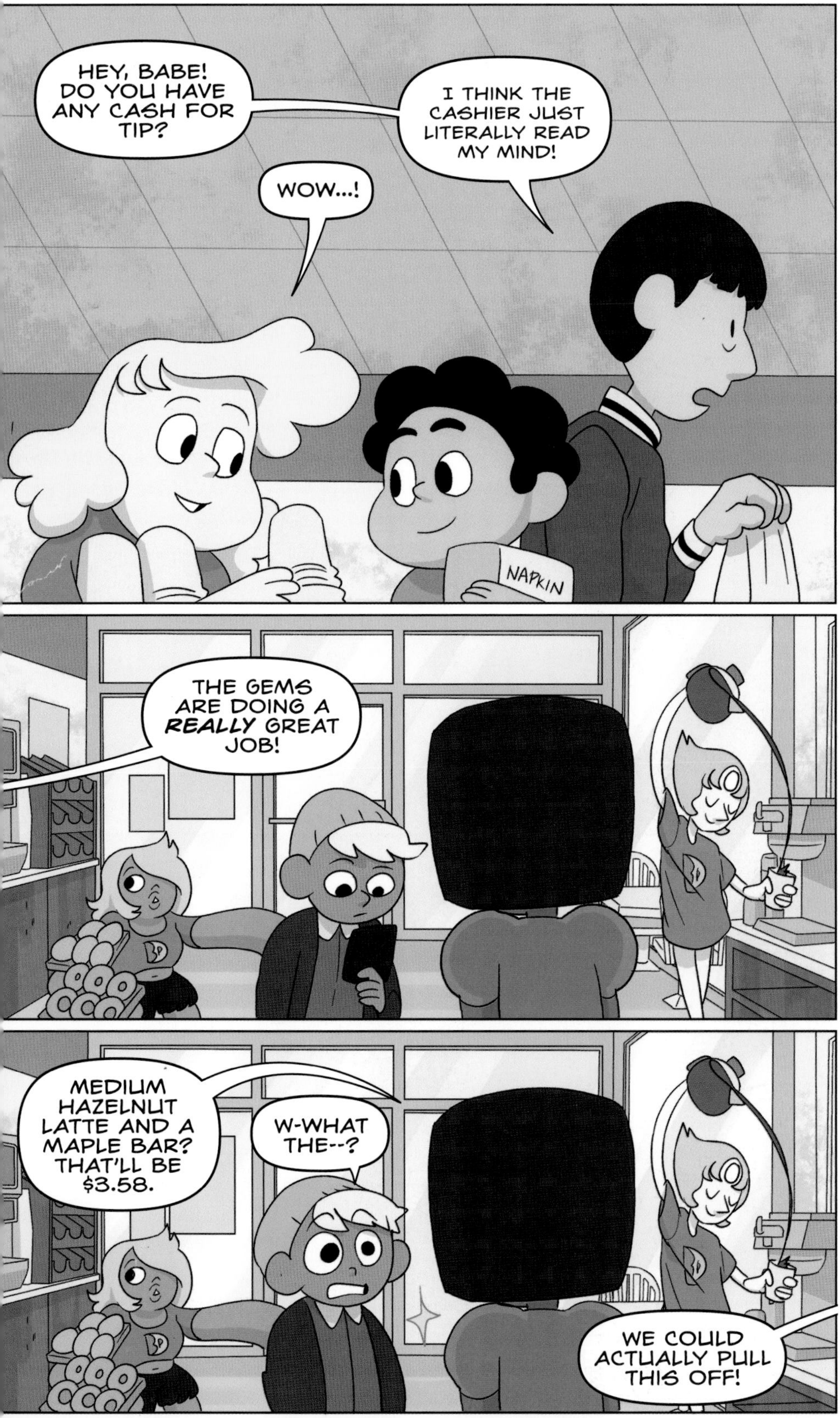
HEY, BABE! DO YOU HAVE ANY CASH FOR TIP?
I THINK THE CASHIER JUST LITERALLY READ MY MIND!
WOW...!
NAPKIN
THE GEMS ARE DOING A *REALLY* GREAT JOB!
MEDIUM HAZELNUT LATTE AND A MAPLE BAR? THAT'LL BE $3.58.
W-WHAT THE--?
WE COULD ACTUALLY PULL THIS OFF!

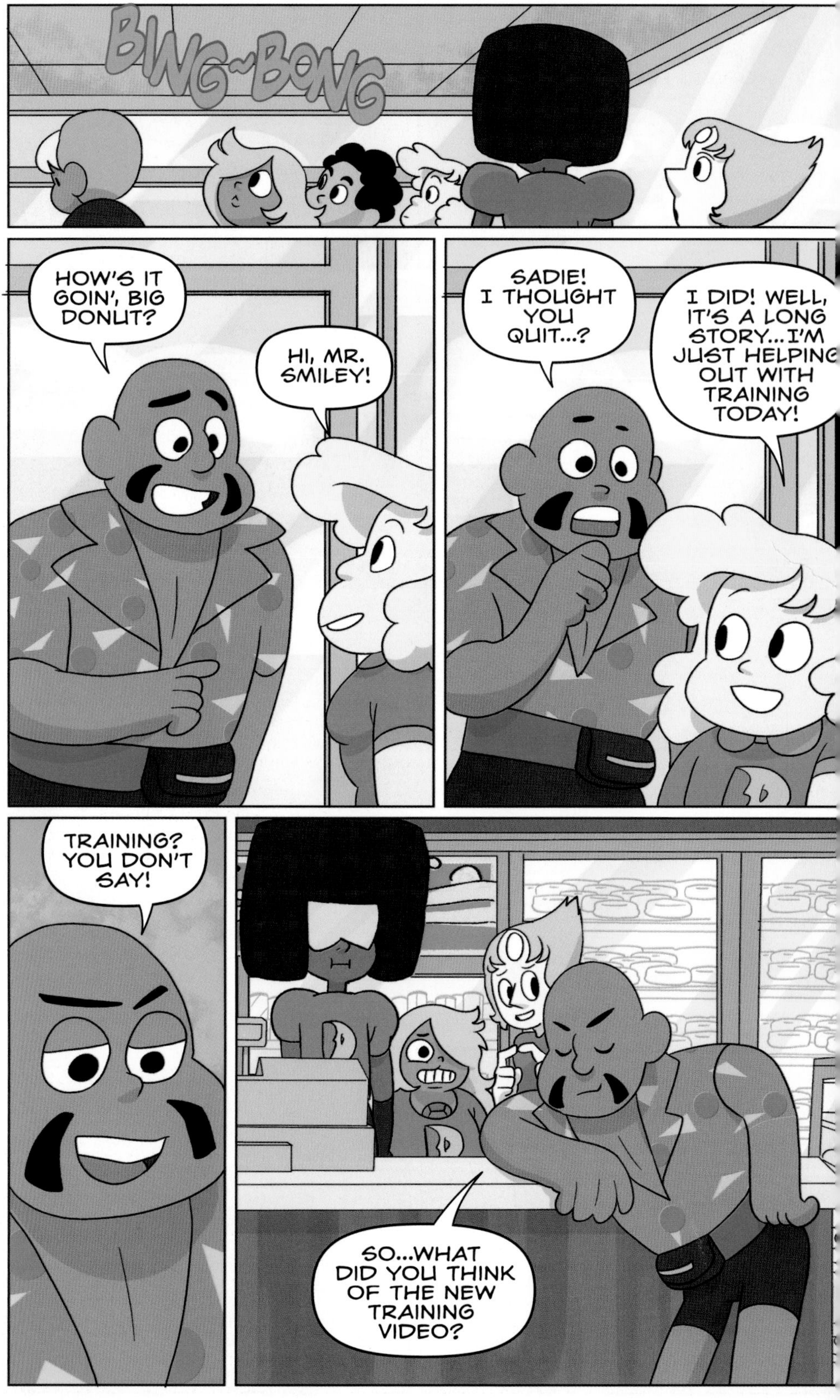
BING~BONG
HOW'S IT GOIN', BIG DONUT?
HI, MR. SMILEY!
SADIE! I THOUGHT YOU QUIT...?
I DID! WELL, IT'S A LONG STORY...I'M JUST HELPING OUT WITH TRAINING TODAY!
TRAINING? YOU DON'T SAY!
SO...WHAT DID YOU THINK OF THE NEW TRAINING VIDEO?

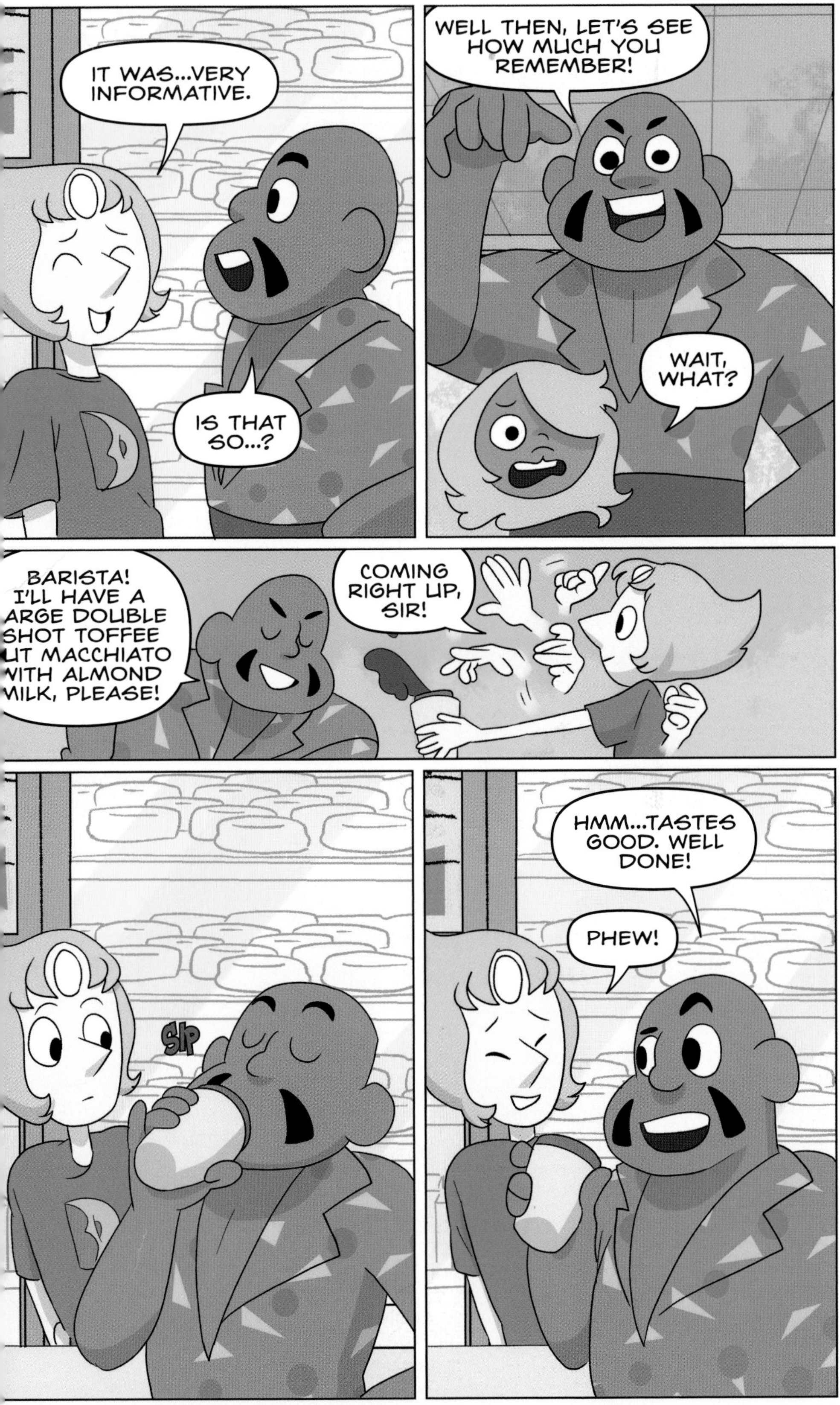

IT WAS...VERY INFORMATIVE.
IS THAT SO...?
WELL THEN, LET'S SEE HOW MUCH YOU REMEMBER!
WAIT, WHAT?
BARISTA! I'LL HAVE A ARGE DOUBLE SHOT TOFFEE UT MACCHIATO VITH ALMOND MILK, PLEASE!
COMING RIGHT UP, SIR!
SIP
HMM...TASTES GOOD. WELL DONE!
PHEW!

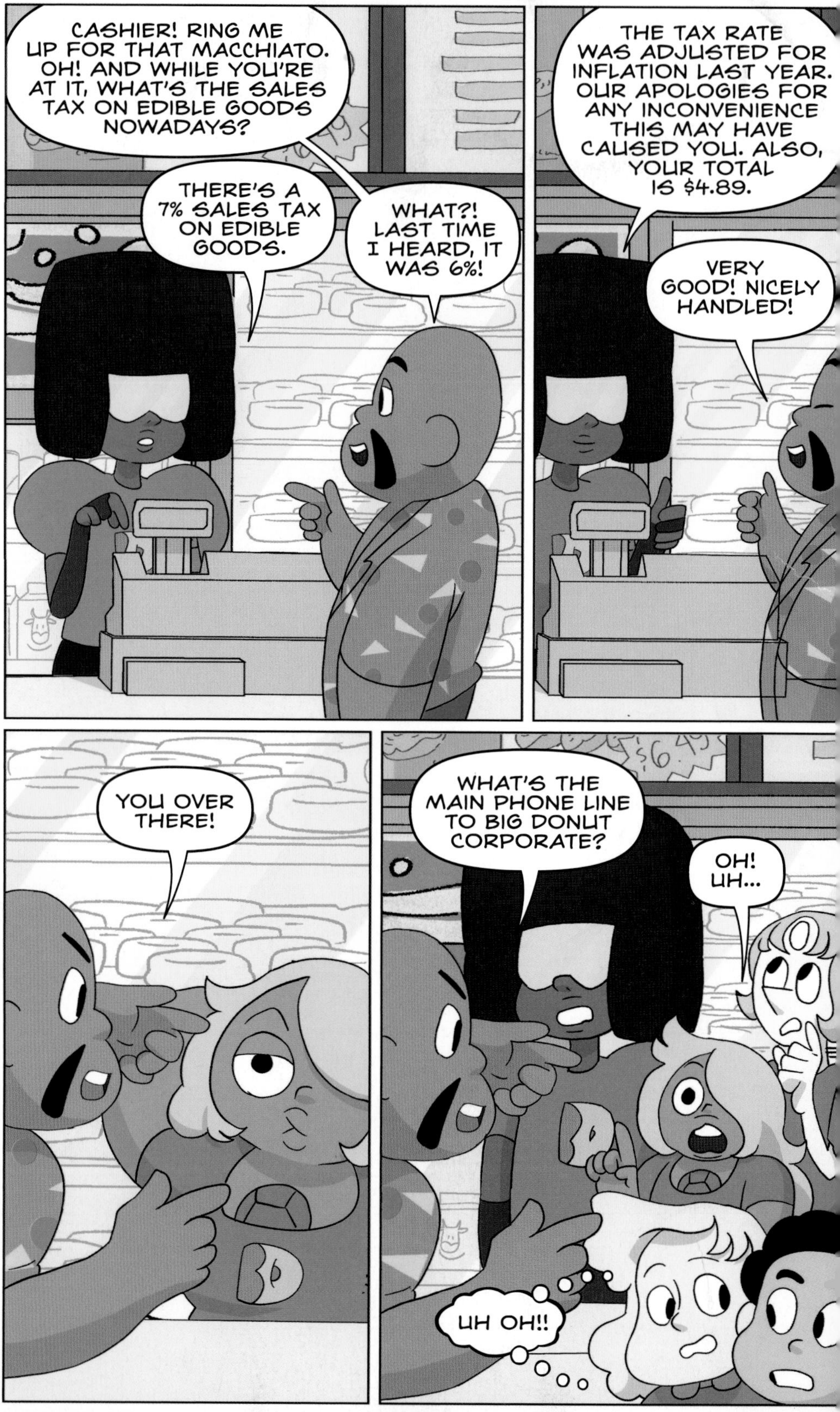
CASHIER! RING ME UP FOR THAT MACCHIATO. OH! AND WHILE YOU'RE AT IT, WHAT'S THE SALES TAX ON EDIBLE GOODS NOWADAYS?
THERE'S A 7% SALES TAX ON EDIBLE GOODS.
WHAT?! LAST TIME I HEARD, IT WAS 6%!
THE TAX RATE WAS ADJUSTED FOR INFLATION LAST YEAR. OUR APOLOGIES FOR ANY INCONVENIENCE THIS MAY HAVE CAUSED YOU. ALSO, YOUR TOTAL IS $4.89.
VERY GOOD! NICELY HANDLED!
YOU OVER THERE!
WHAT'S THE MAIN PHONE LINE TO BIG DONUT CORPORATE?
OH! UH...
UH OH!!

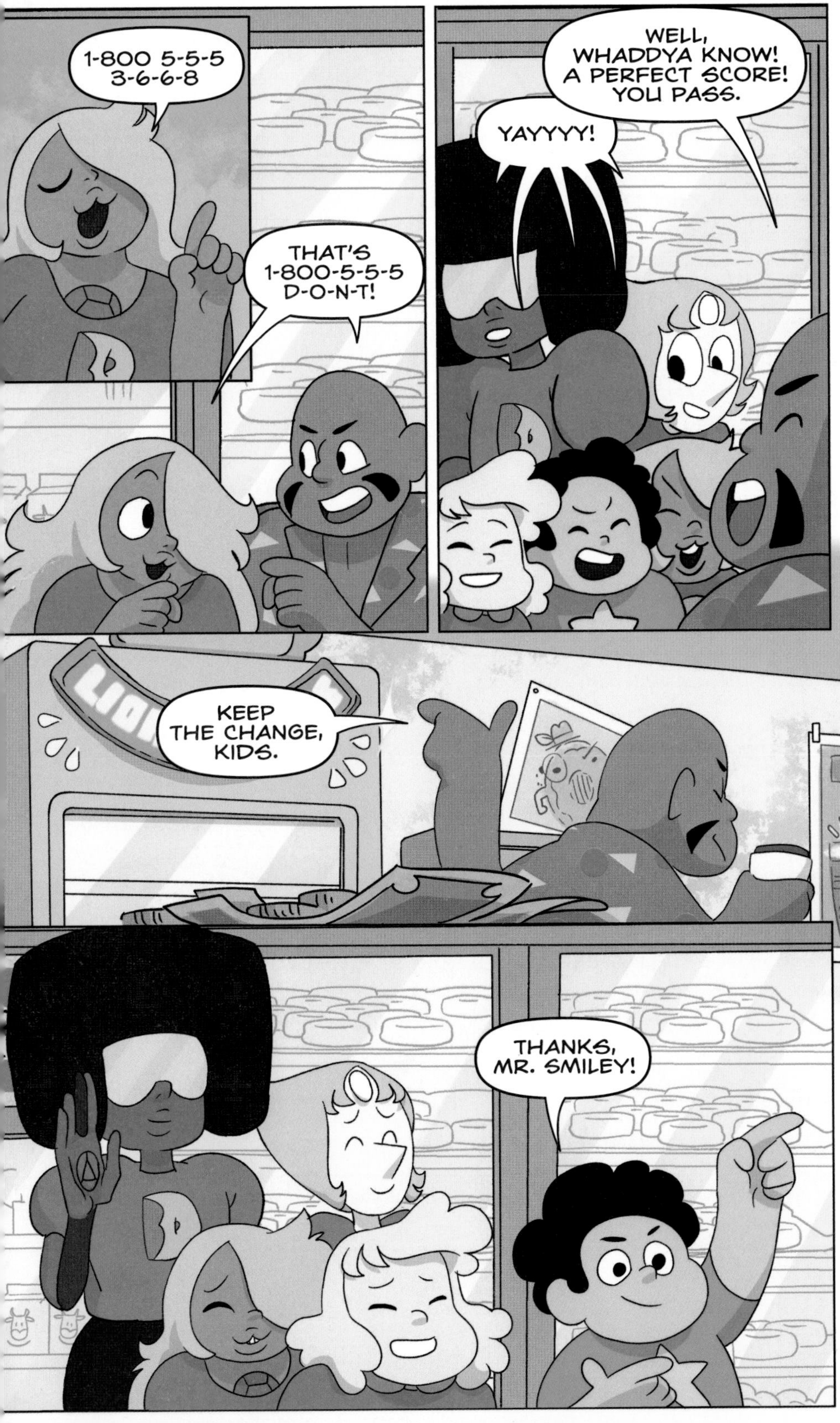
1-800 5-5-5
3-6-6-8
THAT'S
1-800-5-5-5
D-O-N-T!
WELL,
WHADDYA KNOW!
A PERFECT SCORE!
YOU PASS.
YAYYYY!
KEEP
THE CHANGE,
KIDS.
THANKS,
MR. SMILEY!

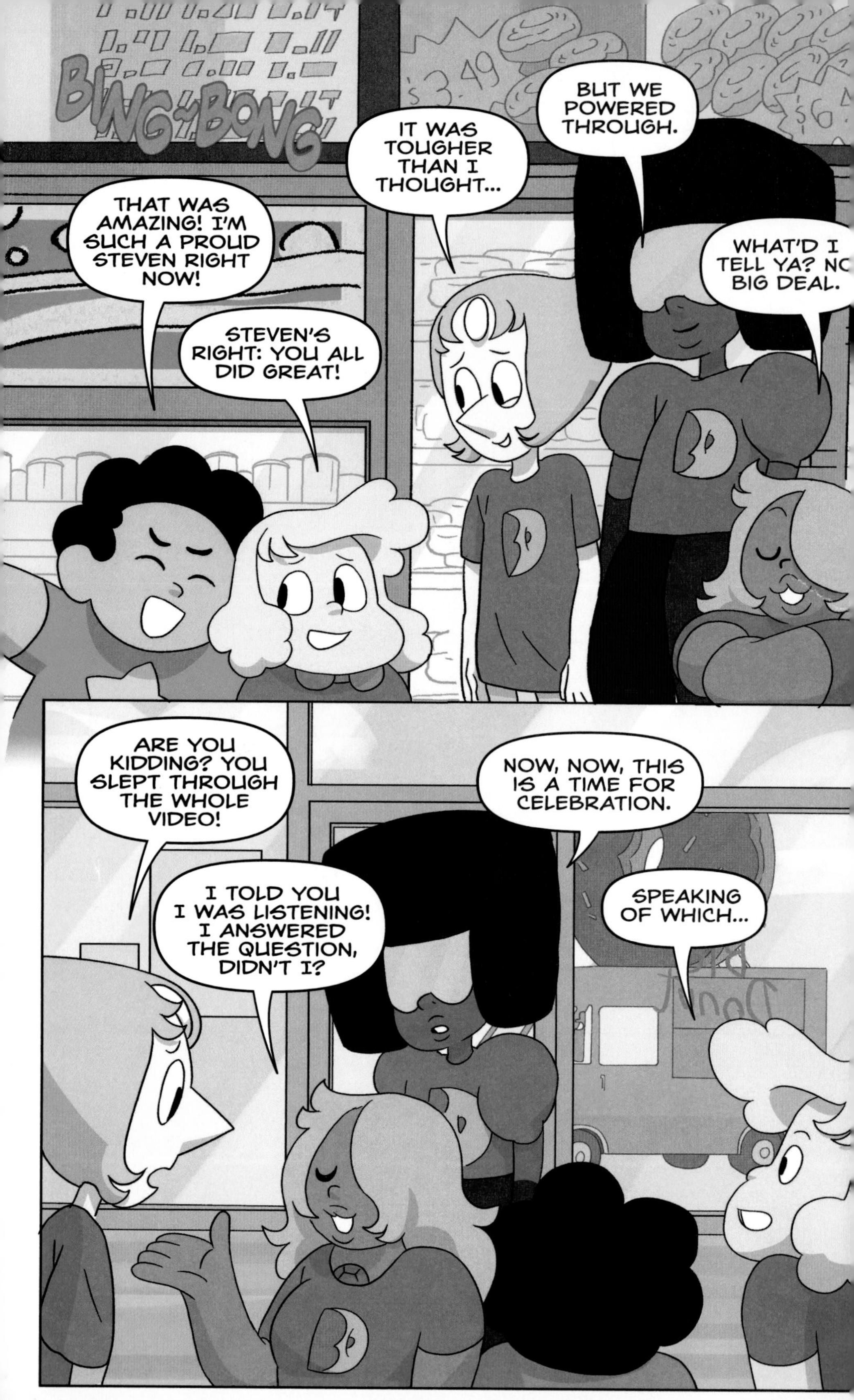
BING-BONG
THAT WAS AMAZING! I'M SUCH A PROUD STEVEN RIGHT NOW!
STEVEN'S RIGHT: YOU ALL DID GREAT!
IT WAS TOUGHER THAN I THOUGHT...
BUT WE POWERED THROUGH.
WHAT'D I TELL YA? N
BIG DEAL.
ARE YOU KIDDING? YOU SLEPT THROUGH THE WHOLE VIDEO!
I TOLD YOU I WAS LISTENING! I ANSWERED THE QUESTION, DIDN'T I?
NOW, NOW, THIS IS A TIME FOR CELEBRATION.
SPEAKING OF WHICH...

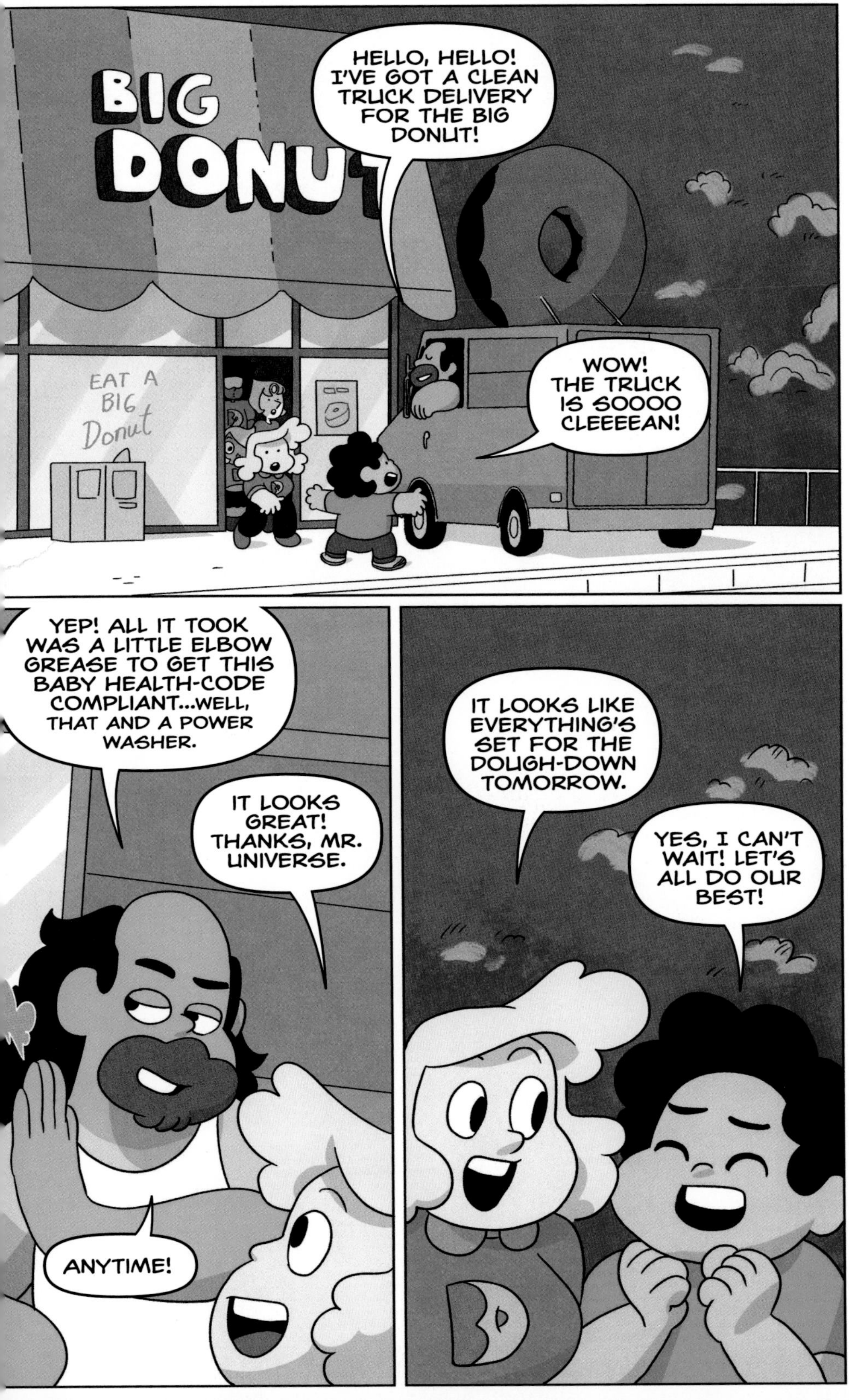
BIG DONUT
HELLO, HELLO! I'VE GOT A CLEAN TRUCK DELIVERY FOR THE BIG DONUT!
EAT A BIG Donut
WOW! THE TRUCK IS SOOOO CLEEEEAN!
YEP! ALL IT TOOK WAS A LITTLE ELBOW GREASE TO GET THIS BABY HEALTH-CODE COMPLIANT...WELL, THAT AND A POWER WASHER.
IT LOOKS GREAT! THANKS, MR. UNIVERSE.
ANYTIME!
IT LOOKS LIKE EVERYTHING'S SET FOR THE DOUGH-DOWN TOMORROW.
YES, I CAN'T WAIT! LET'S ALL DO OUR BEST!

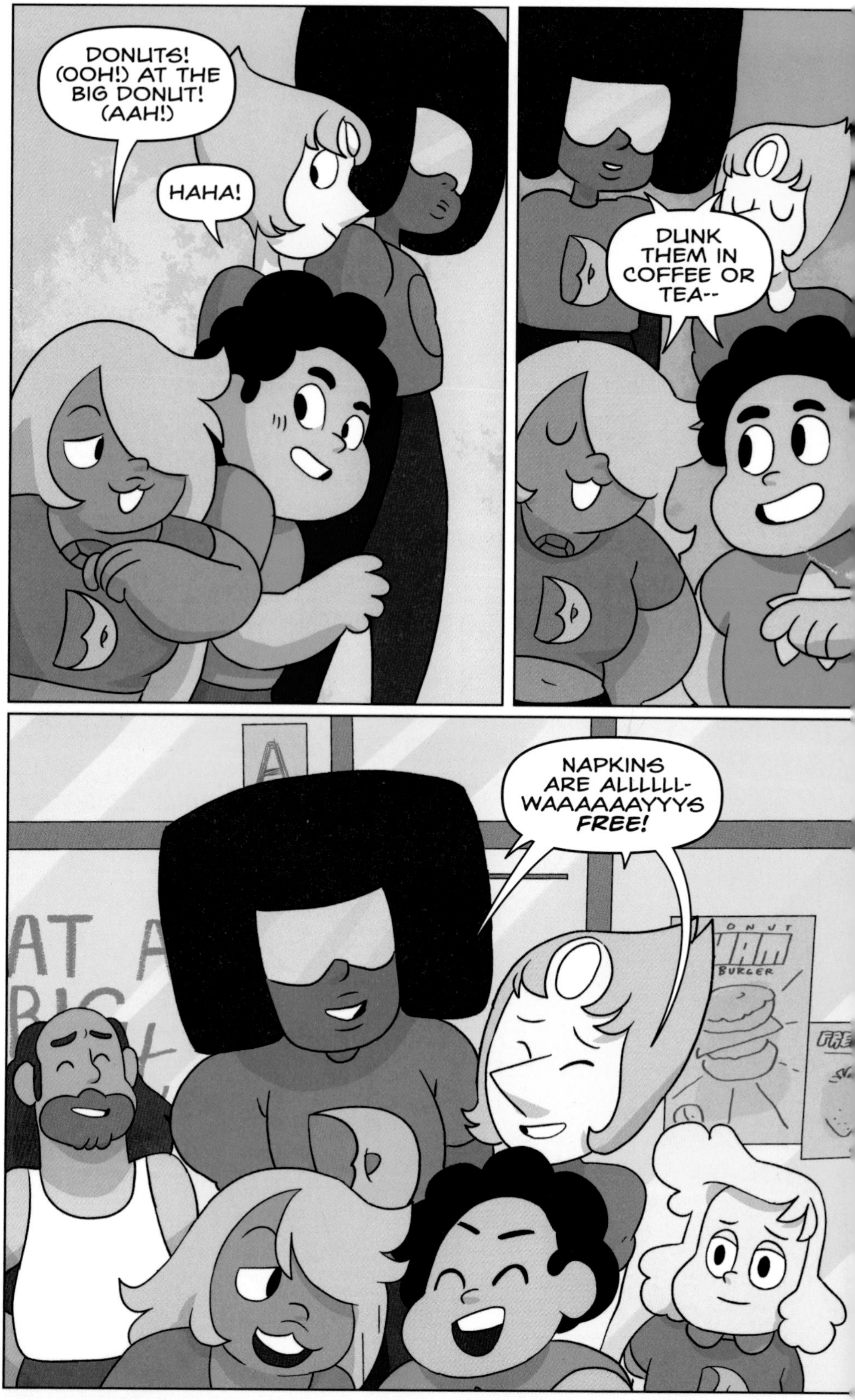
DONUTS! (OOH!) AT THE BIG DONUT! (AAH!)
HAHA!
DUNK THEM IN COFFEE OR TEA--
NAPKINS ARE ALLLLLL-WAAAAAAYYYS **FREE!**
DONUT
BURGER

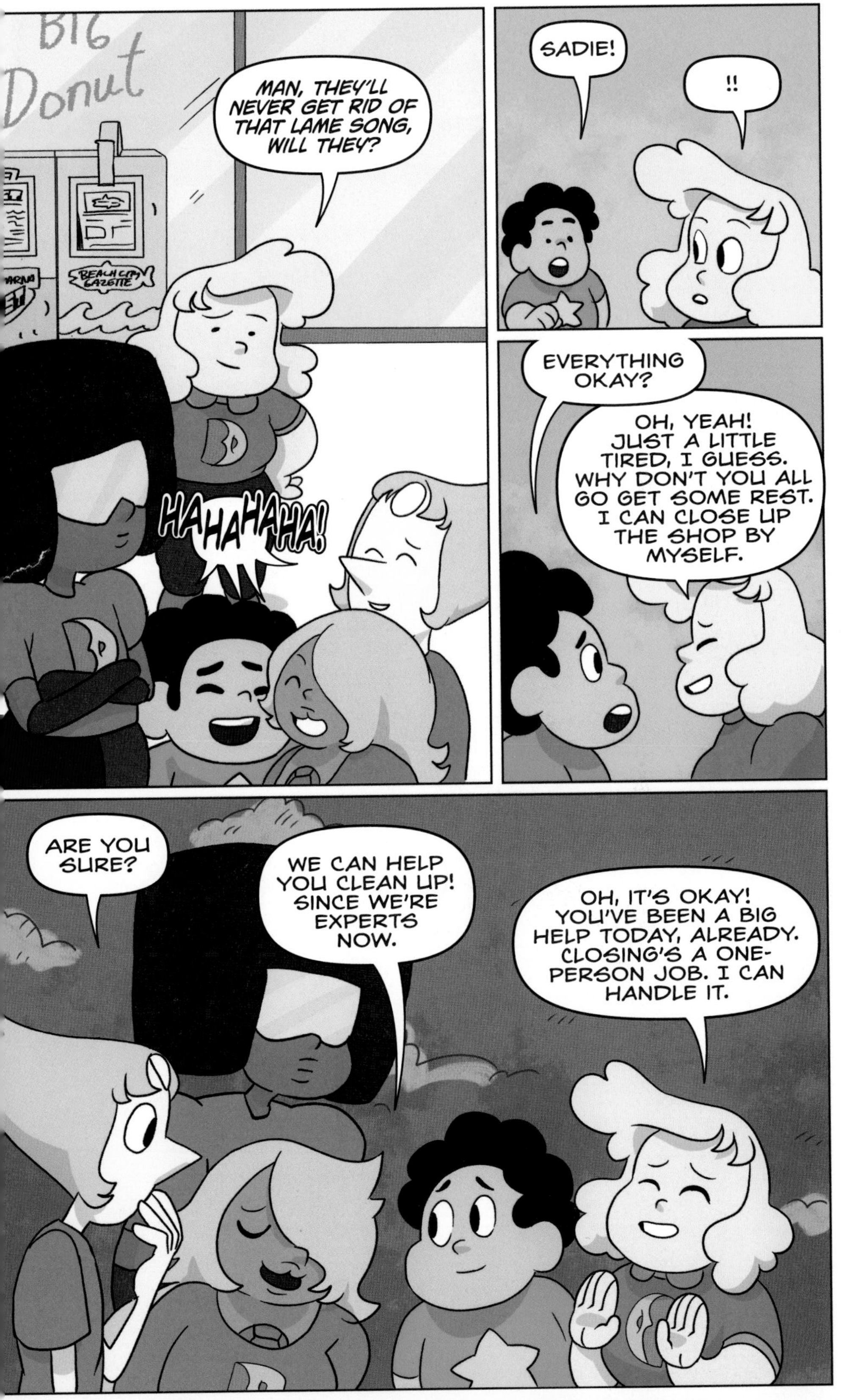

BIG Donut
BEACH CITY GAZETTE
MAN, THEY'LL NEVER GET RID OF THAT LAME SONG, WILL THEY?
HAHAHAHAHA!
SADIE!
!!
EVERYTHING OKAY?
OH, YEAH! JUST A LITTLE TIRED, I GUESS. WHY DON'T YOU ALL GO GET SOME REST. I CAN CLOSE UP THE SHOP BY MYSELF.
ARE YOU SURE?
WE CAN HELP YOU CLEAN UP! SINCE WE'RE EXPERTS NOW.
OH, IT'S OKAY! YOU'VE BEEN A BIG HELP TODAY, ALREADY. CLOSING'S A ONE-PERSON JOB. I CAN HANDLE IT.

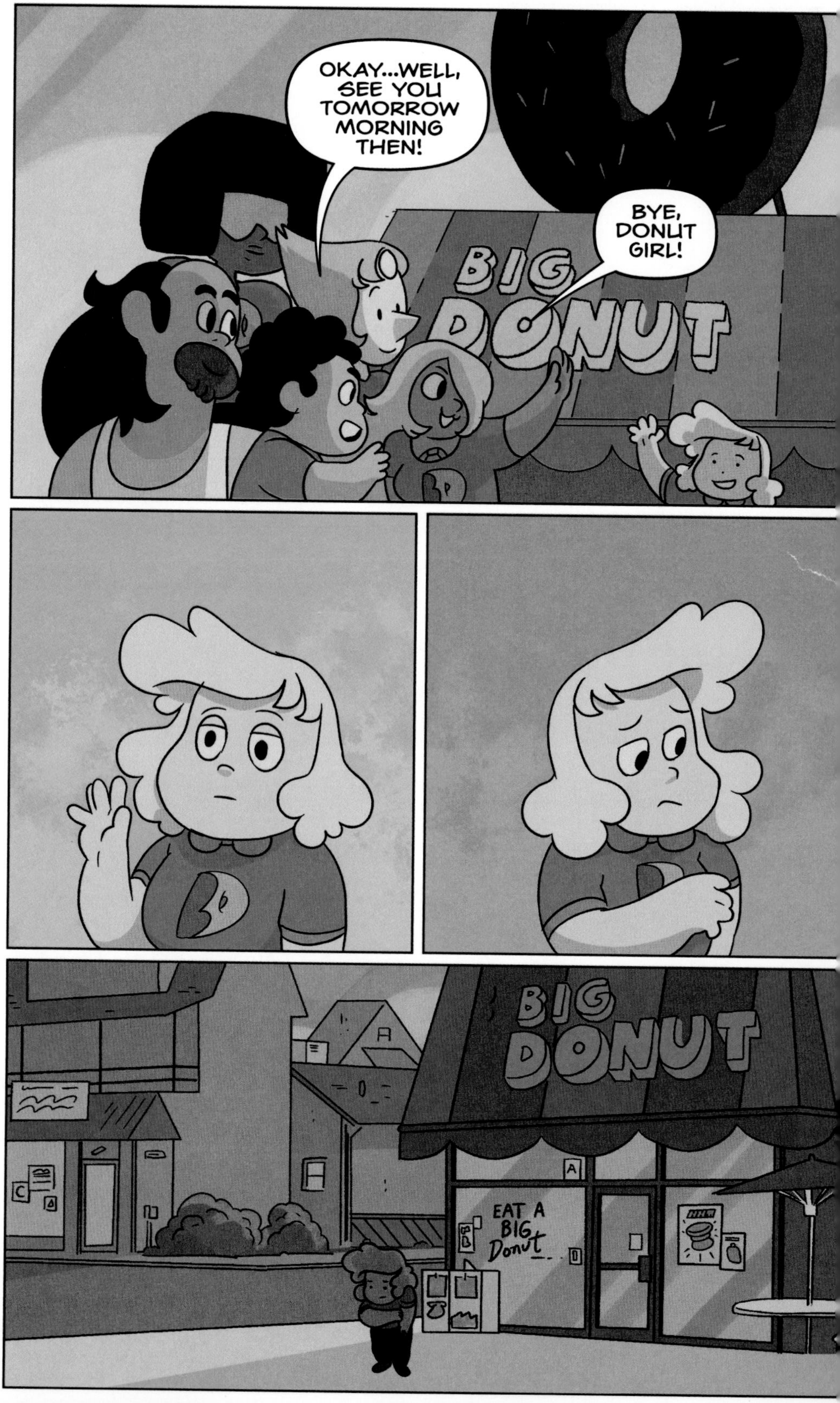
OKAY...WELL, SEE YOU TOMORROW MORNING THEN!
BYE, DONUT GIRL!
BIG DONUT
BIG DONUT
EAT A BIG Donut

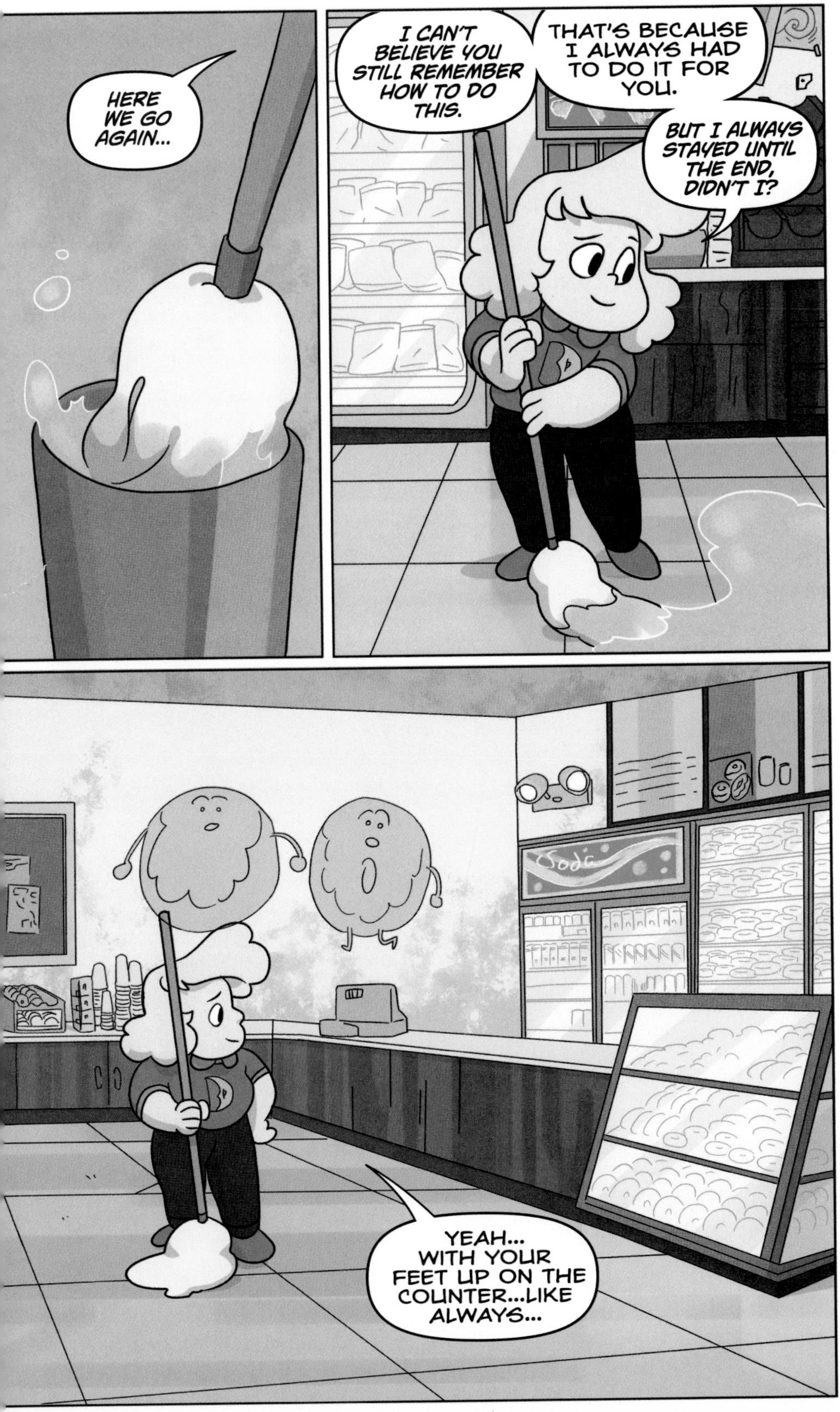
HERE WE GO AGAIN...
I CAN'T BELIEVE YOU STILL REMEMBER HOW TO DO THIS.
THAT'S BECAUSE I ALWAYS HAD TO DO IT FOR YOU.
BUT I ALWAYS STAYED UNTIL THE END, DIDN'T I?
Soda
YEAH... WITH YOUR FEET UP ON THE COUNTER...LIKE ALWAYS...

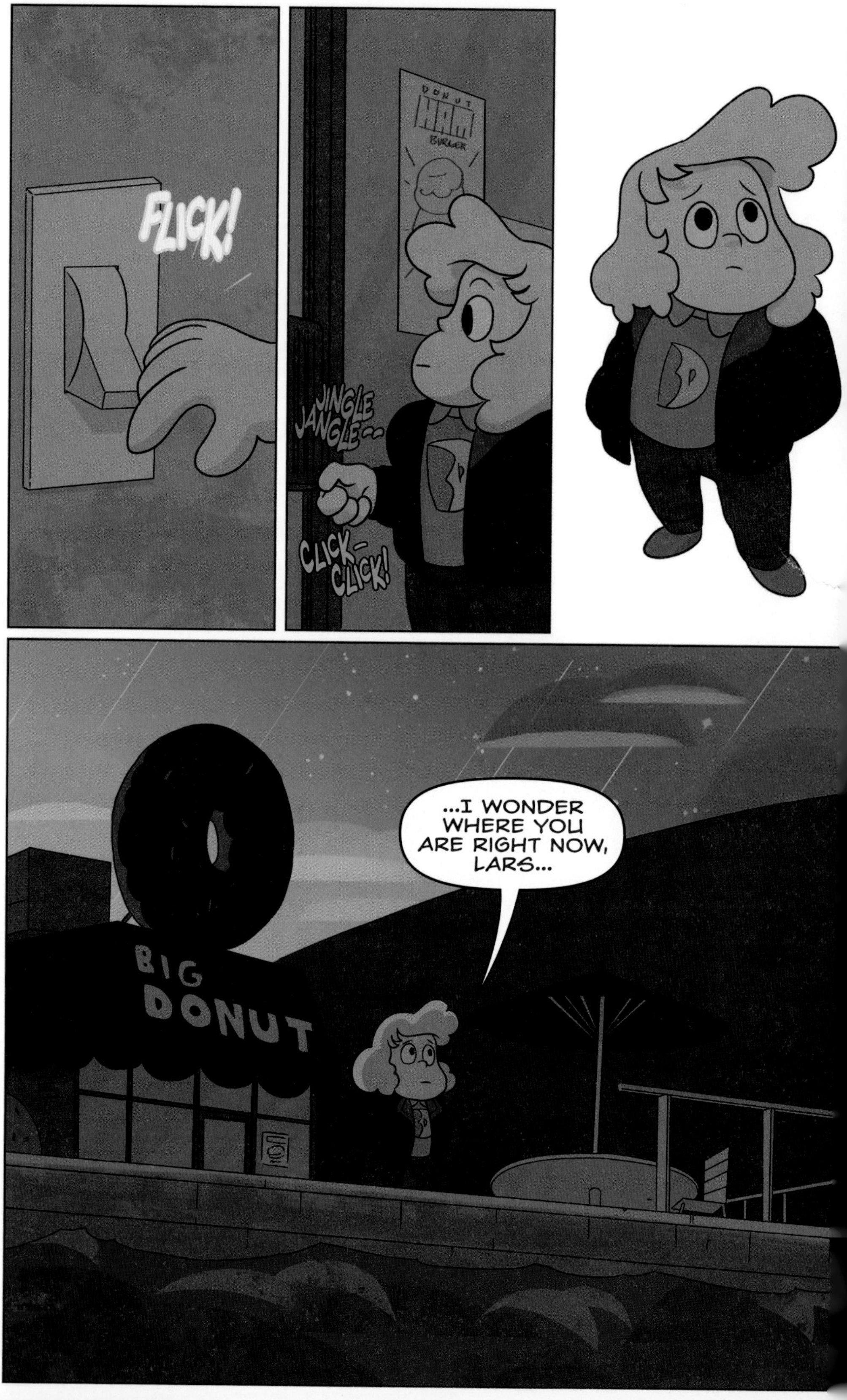
FLICK!
DONUT
HAM
BURGER
JINGLE JANGLE--
CLICK-CLICK!
BIG DONUT
...I WONDER WHERE YOU ARE RIGHT NOW, LARS...

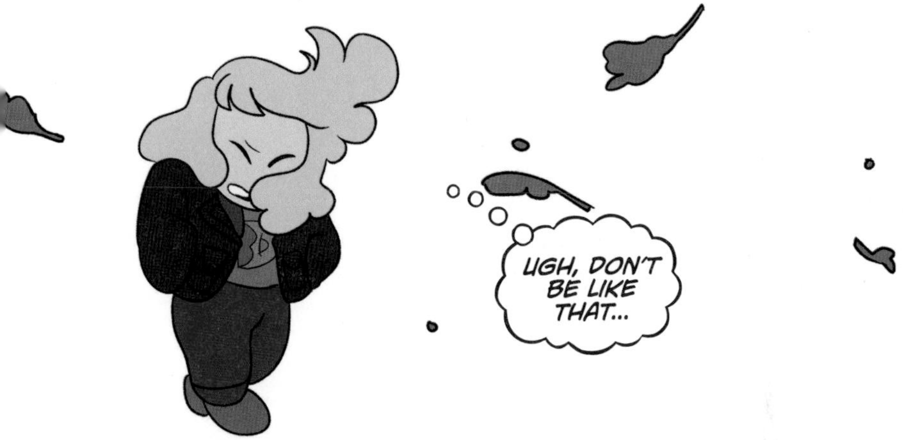
UGH, DON'T BE LIKE THAT...

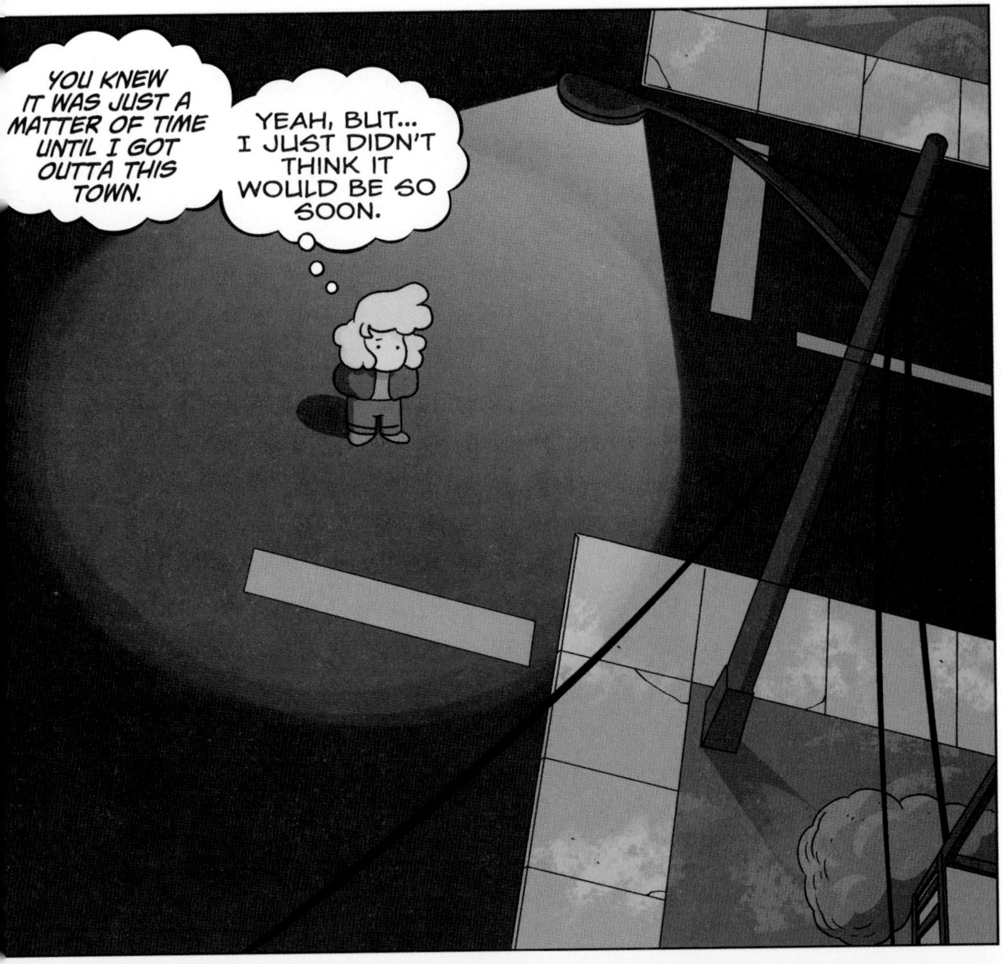
YOU KNEW IT WAS JUST A MATTER OF TIME UNTIL I GOT OUTTA THIS TOWN.
YEAH, BUT... I JUST DIDN'T THINK IT WOULD BE SO SOON.

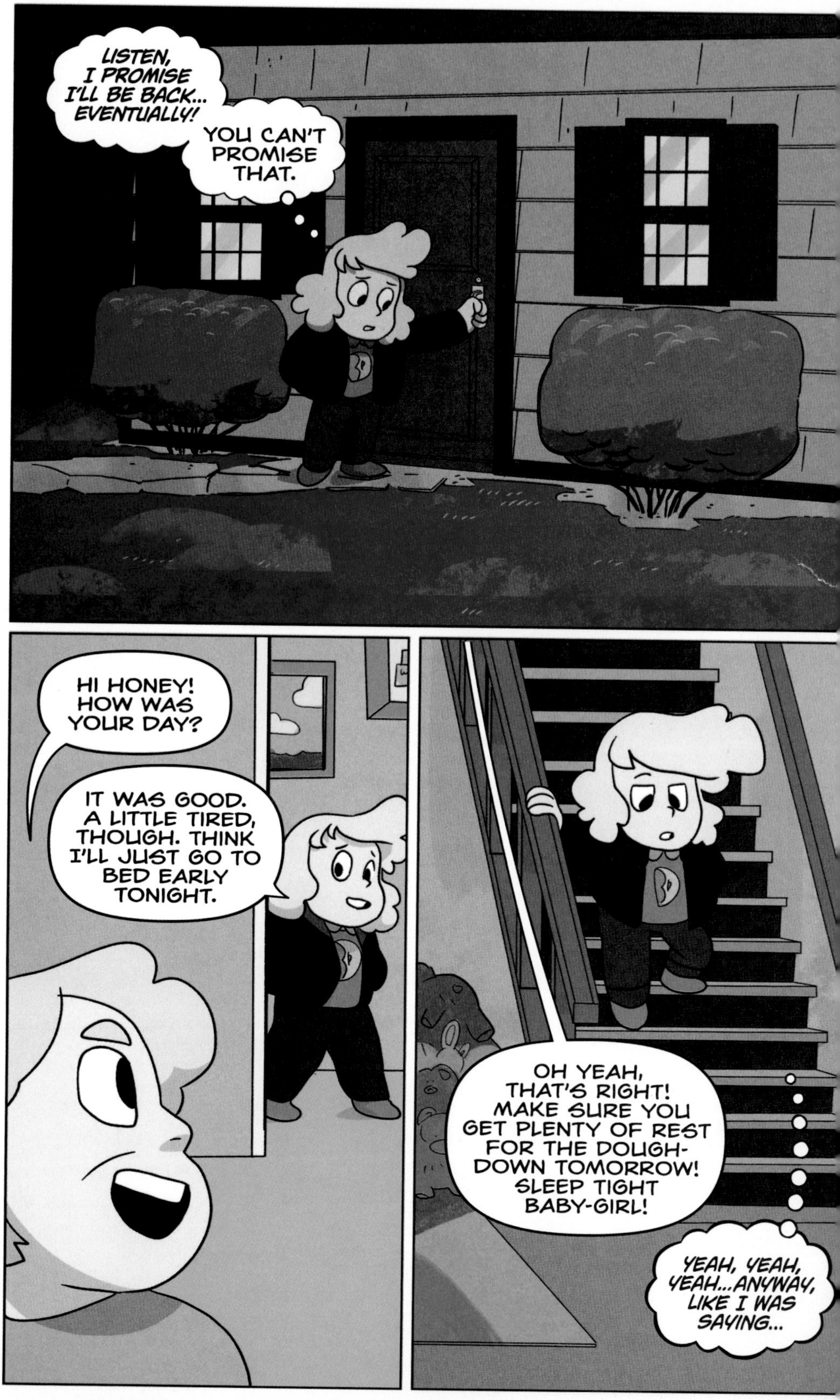
LISTEN, I PROMISE I'LL BE BACK... EVENTUALLY!
YOU CAN'T PROMISE THAT.
HI HONEY! HOW WAS YOUR DAY?
IT WAS GOOD. A LITTLE TIRED, THOUGH. THINK I'LL JUST GO TO BED EARLY TONIGHT.
OH YEAH, THAT'S RIGHT! MAKE SURE YOU GET PLENTY OF REST FOR THE DOUGH-DOWN TOMORROW! SLEEP TIGHT BABY-GIRL!
YEAH, YEAH, YEAH...ANYWAY, LIKE I WAS SAYING...

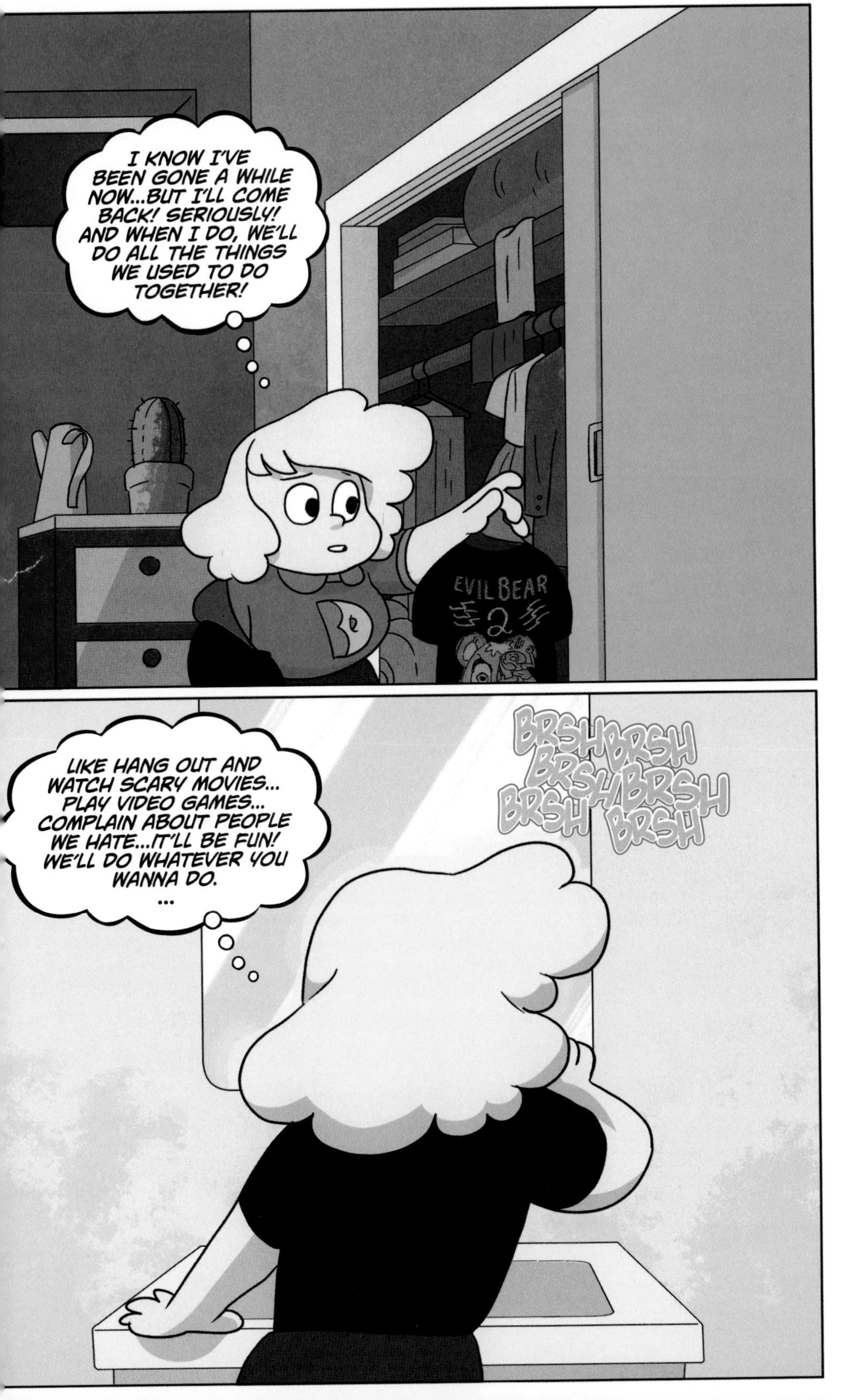
I KNOW I'VE BEEN GONE A WHILE NOW...BUT I'LL COME BACK! SERIOUSLY! AND WHEN I DO, WE'LL DO ALL THE THINGS WE USED TO DO TOGETHER!
EVIL BEAR 2
LIKE HANG OUT AND WATCH SCARY MOVIES... PLAY VIDEO GAMES... COMPLAIN ABOUT PEOPLE WE HATE...IT'LL BE FUN! WE'LL DO WHATEVER YOU WANNA DO. ...
BRSH BRSH BRSH BRSH BRSH BRSH BRSH

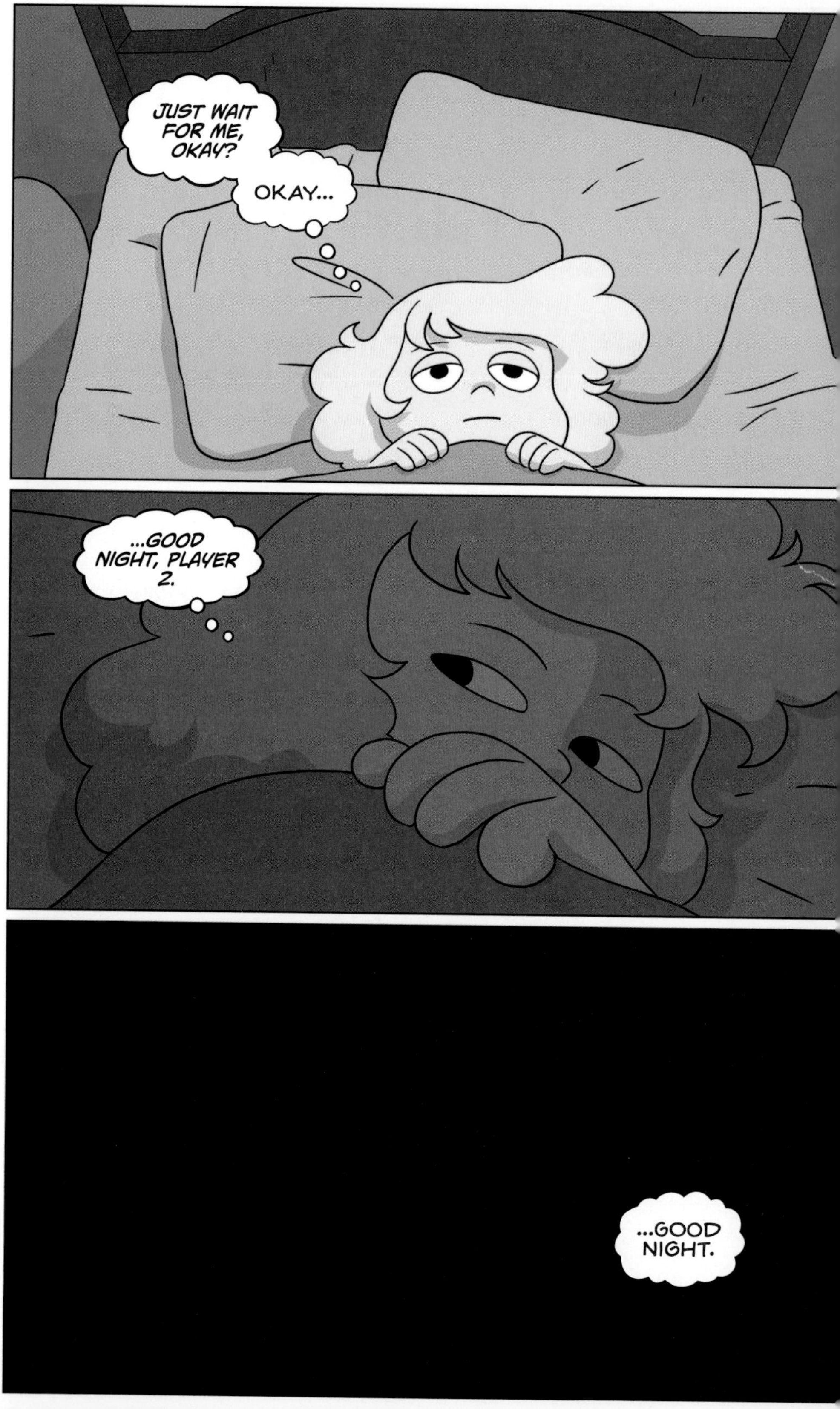
JUST WAIT FOR ME, OKAY?
OKAY...
...GOOD NIGHT, PLAYER 2.
...GOOD NIGHT.

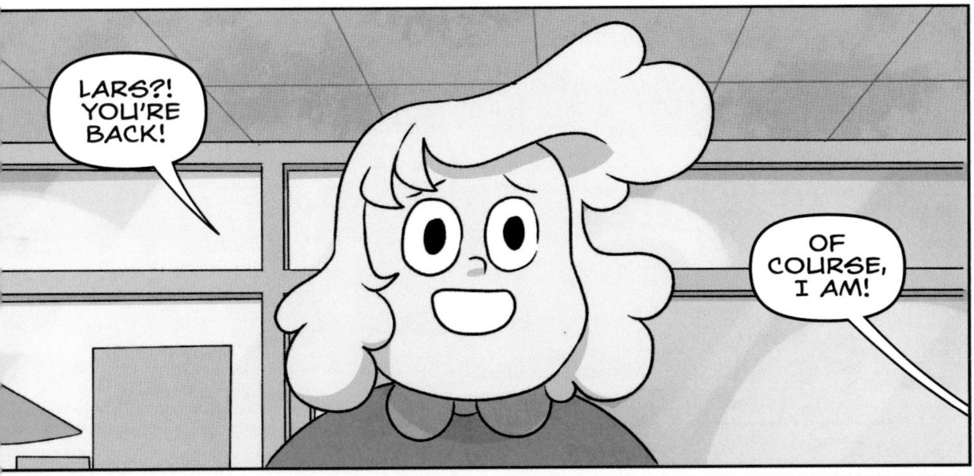
LARS?! YOU'RE BACK!
OF COURSE, I AM!

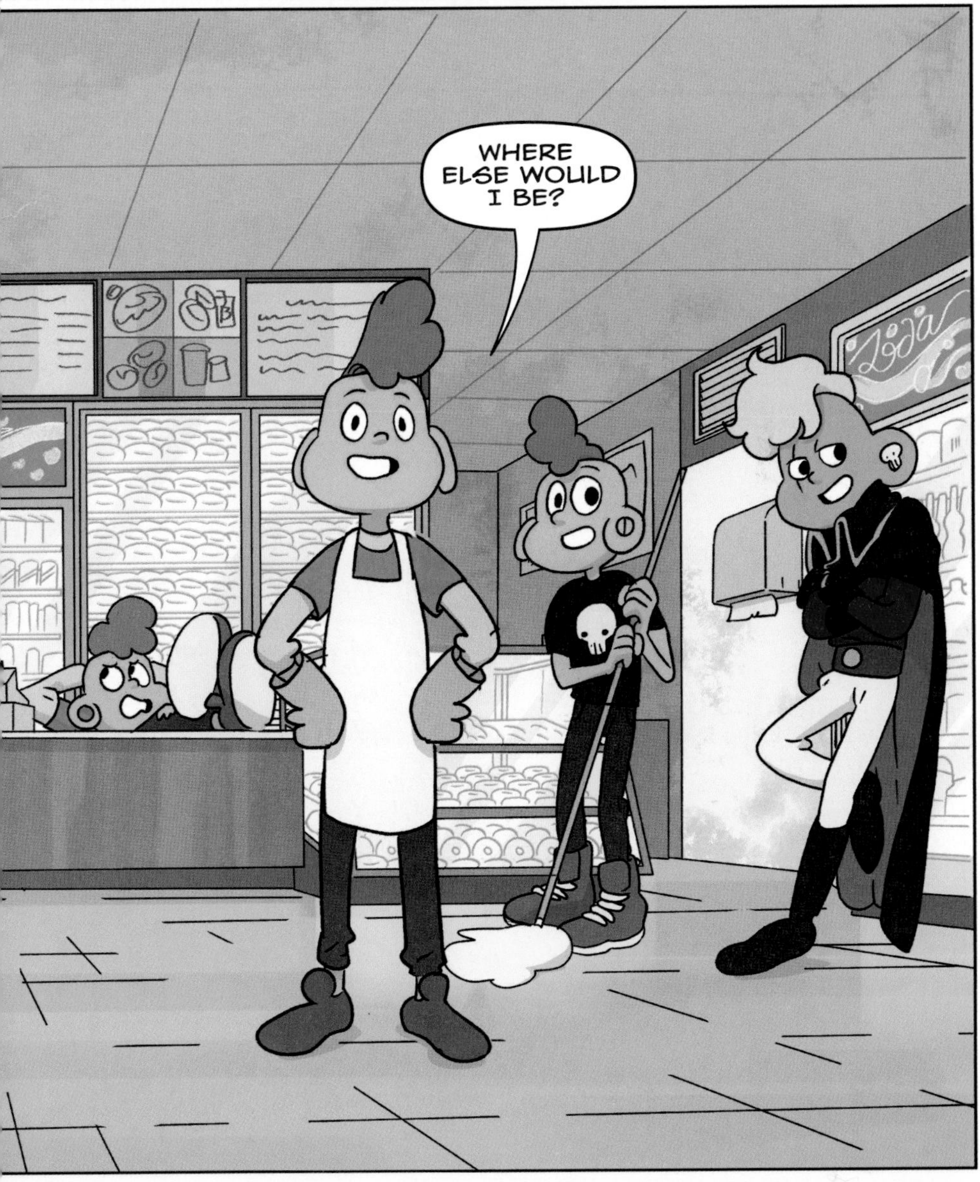
WHERE ELSE WOULD I BE?

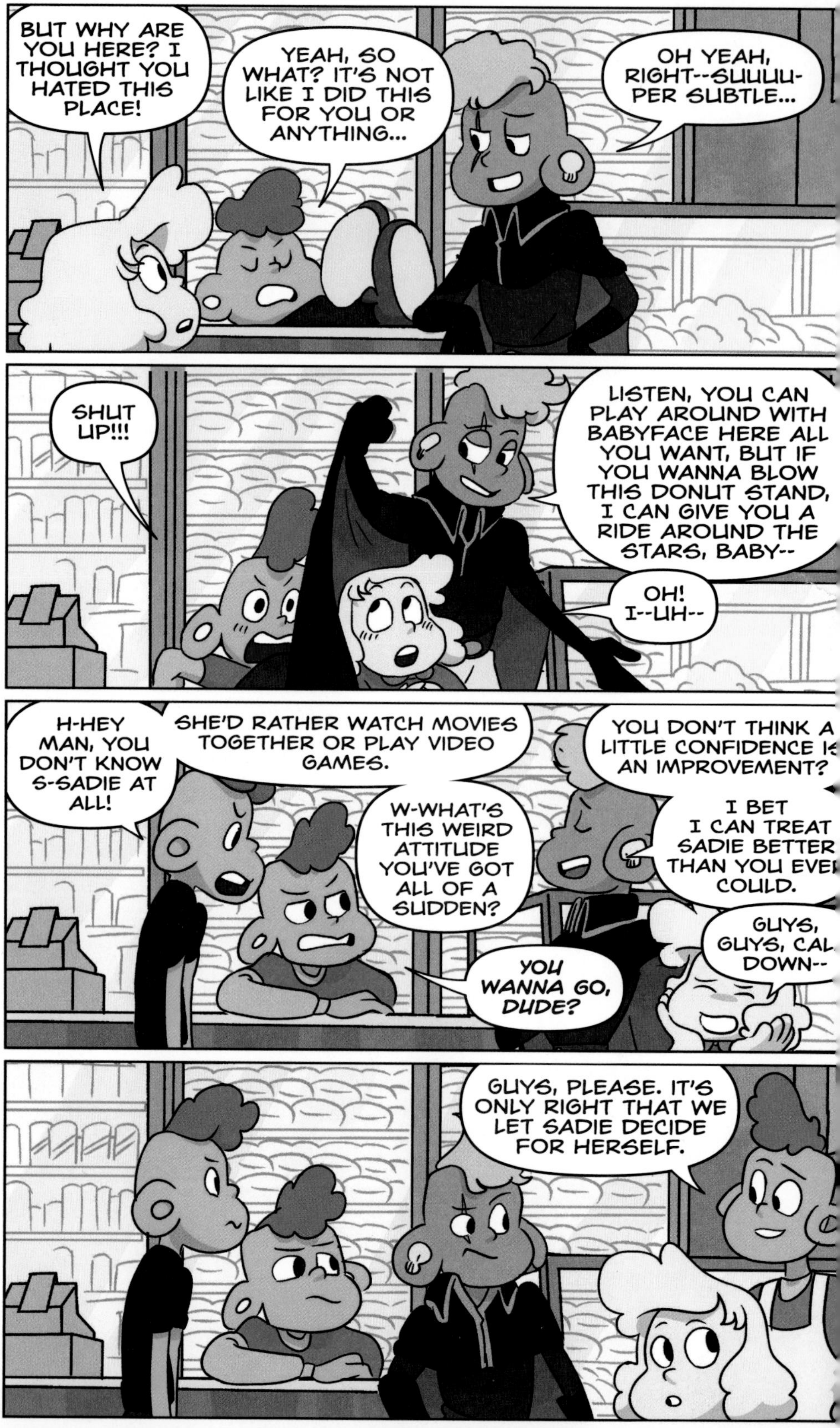
BUT WHY ARE YOU HERE? I THOUGHT YOU HATED THIS PLACE!
YEAH, SO WHAT? IT'S NOT LIKE I DID THIS FOR YOU OR ANYTHING...
OH YEAH, RIGHT--SUUUU-PER SUBTLE...
SHUT UP!!!
LISTEN, YOU CAN PLAY AROUND WITH BABYFACE HERE ALL YOU WANT, BUT IF YOU WANNA BLOW THIS DONUT STAND, I CAN GIVE YOU A RIDE AROUND THE STARS, BABY--
OH! I--UH--
H-HEY MAN, YOU DON'T KNOW S-SADIE AT ALL!
SHE'D RATHER WATCH MOVIES TOGETHER OR PLAY VIDEO GAMES.
YOU DON'T THINK A LITTLE CONFIDENCE IS AN IMPROVEMENT?
W-WHAT'S THIS WEIRD ATTITUDE YOU'VE GOT ALL OF A SUDDEN?
I BET I CAN TREAT SADIE BETTER THAN YOU EVER COULD.
YOU WANNA GO, DUDE?
GUYS, GUYS, CAL DOWN--
GUYS, PLEASE. IT'S ONLY RIGHT THAT WE LET SADIE DECIDE FOR HERSELF.

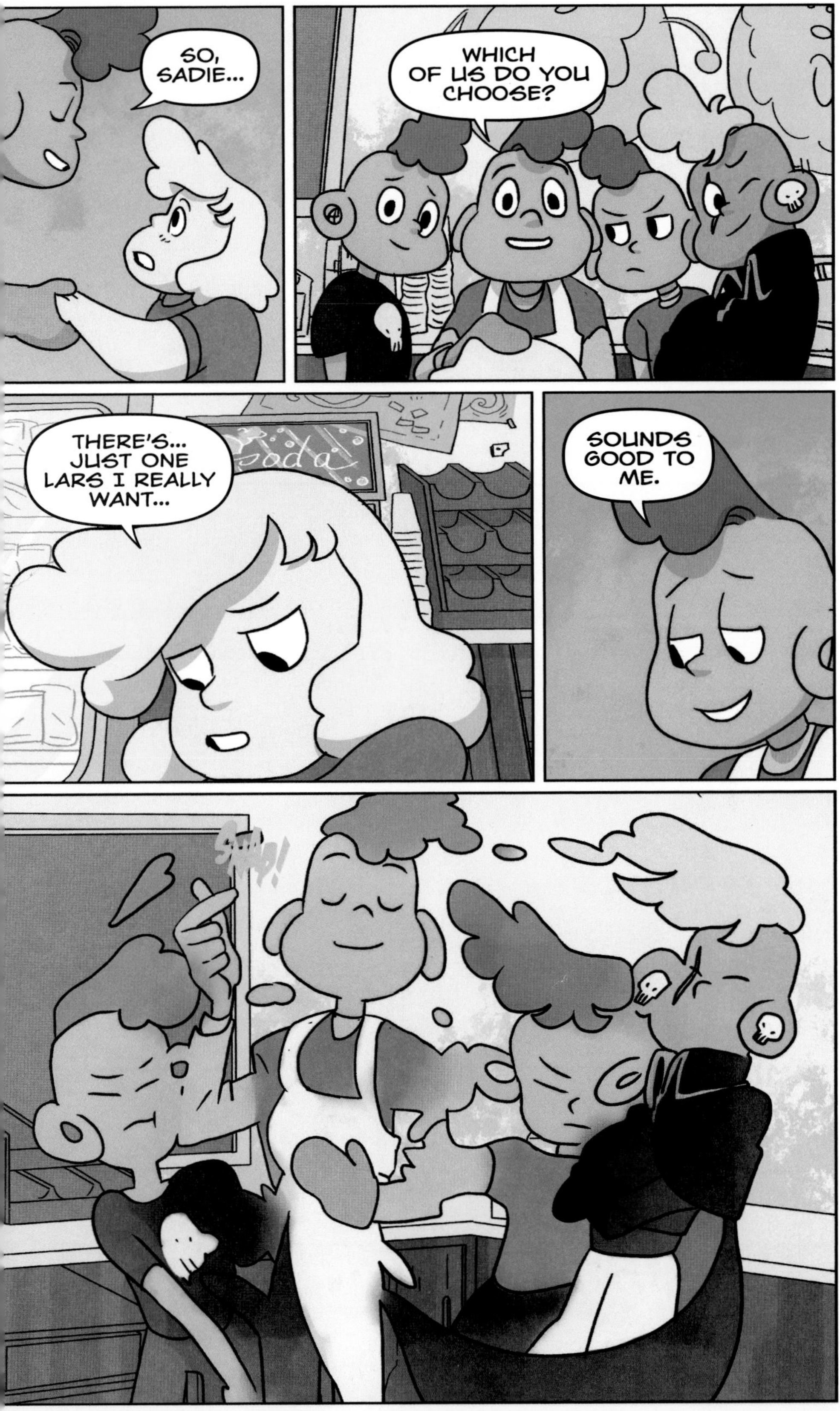
SO, SADIE...
WHICH OF US DO YOU CHOOSE?
THERE'S... JUST ONE LARS I REALLY WANT...
SOUNDS GOOD TO ME.
SNAP!

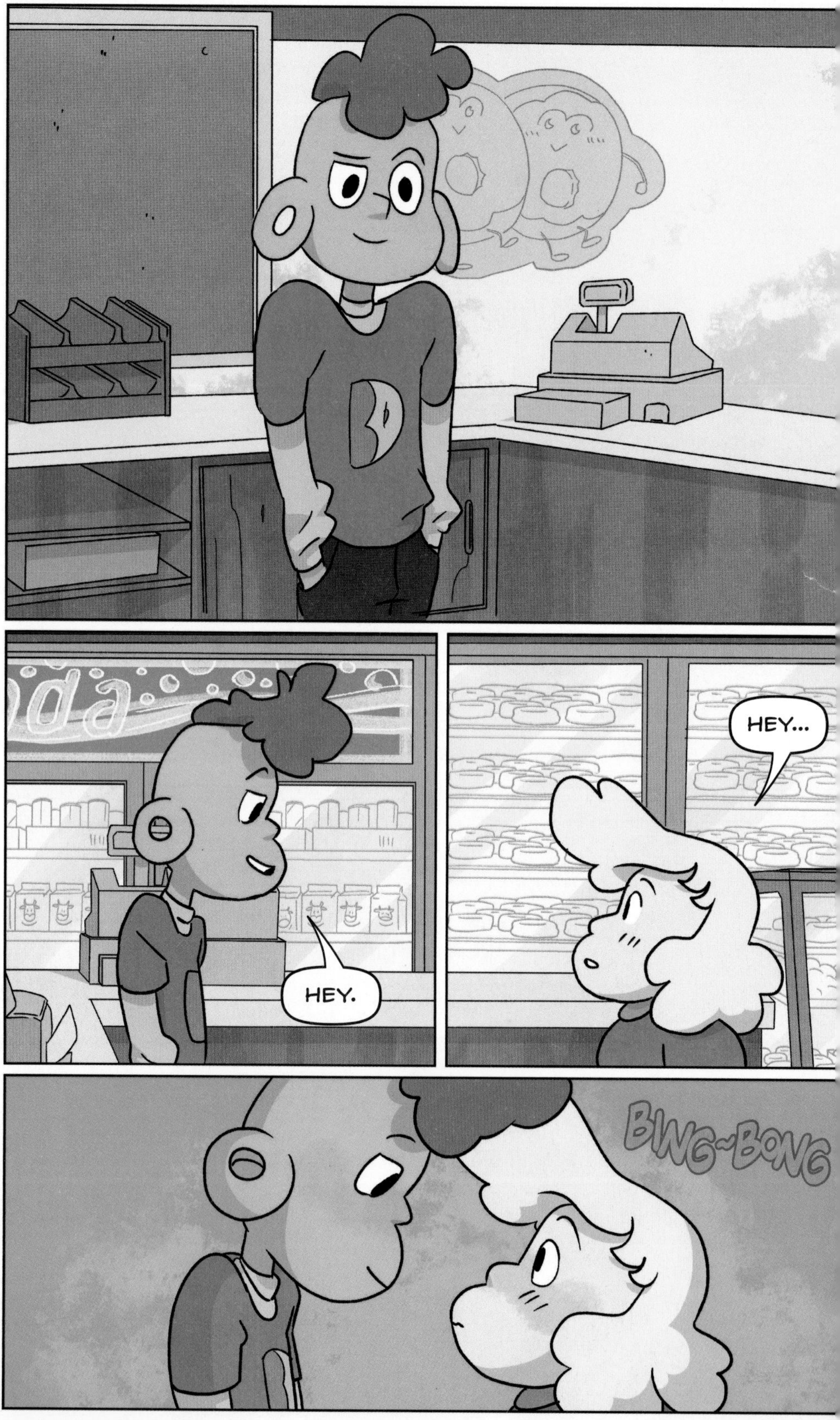

HEY.
HEY...
BING~BONG

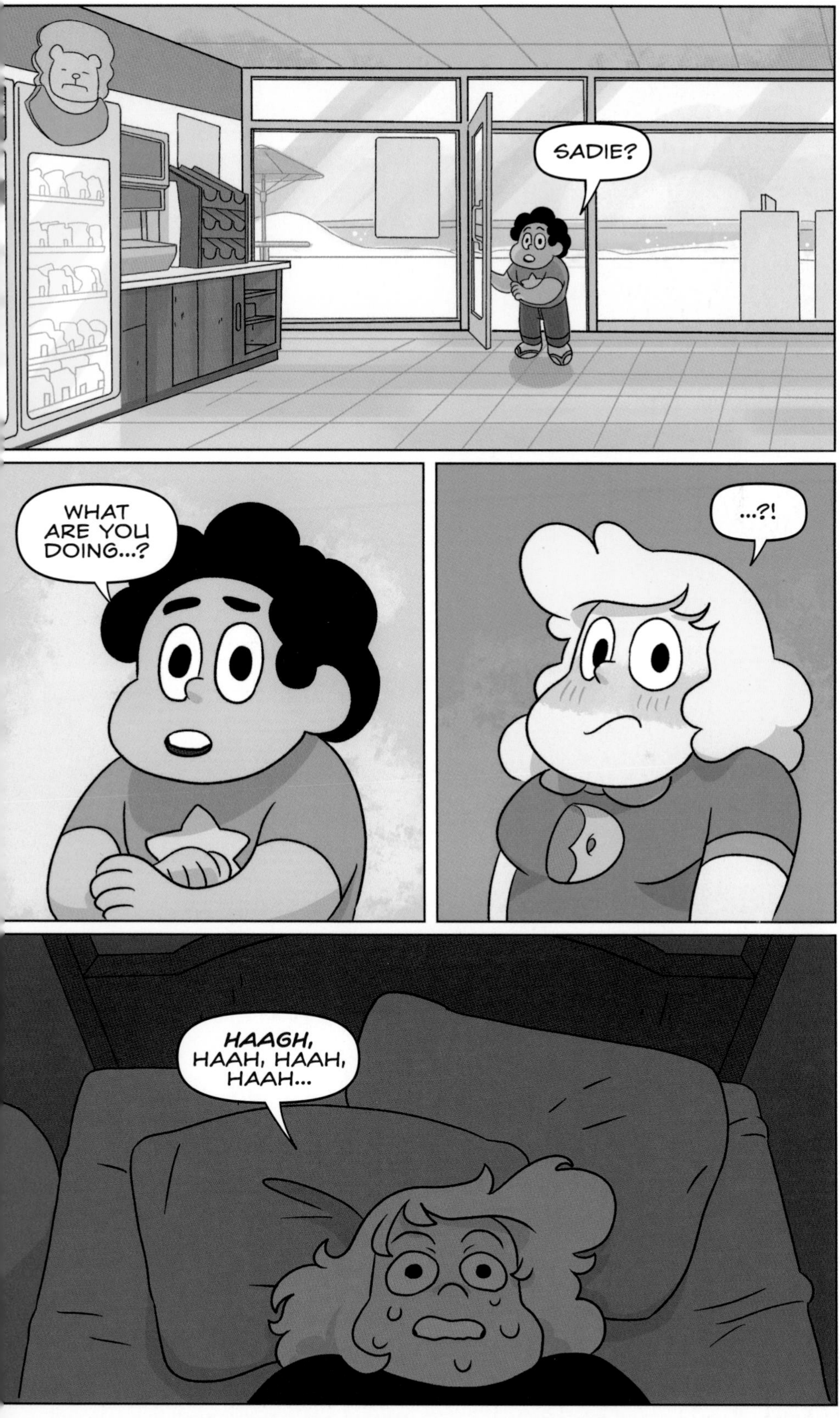
SADIE?
WHAT ARE YOU DOING...?
...?!
HAAGH, HAAH, HAAH, HAAH...

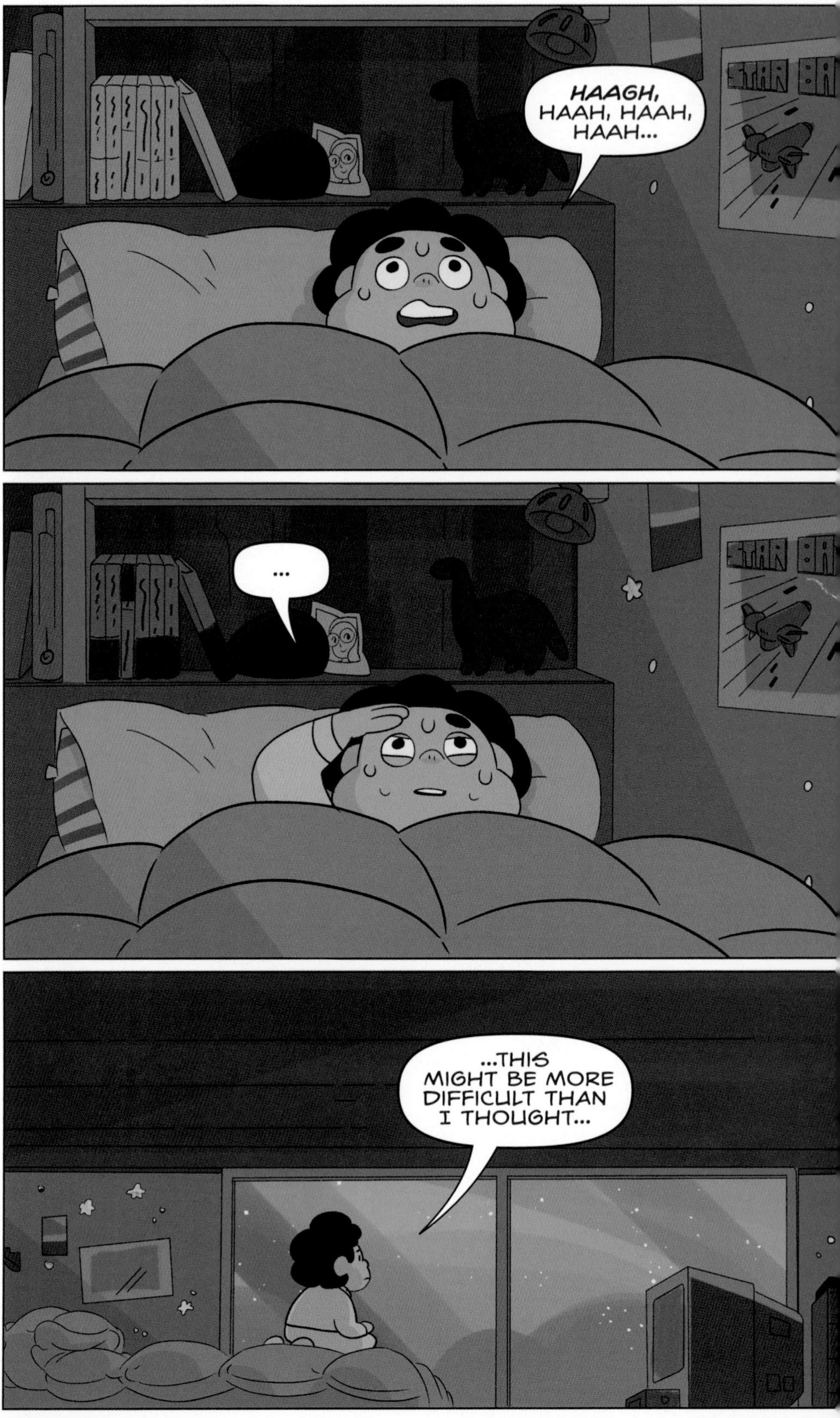
HAAGH, HAAH, HAAH, HAAH...
...
...THIS MIGHT BE MORE DIFFICULT THAN I THOUGHT...

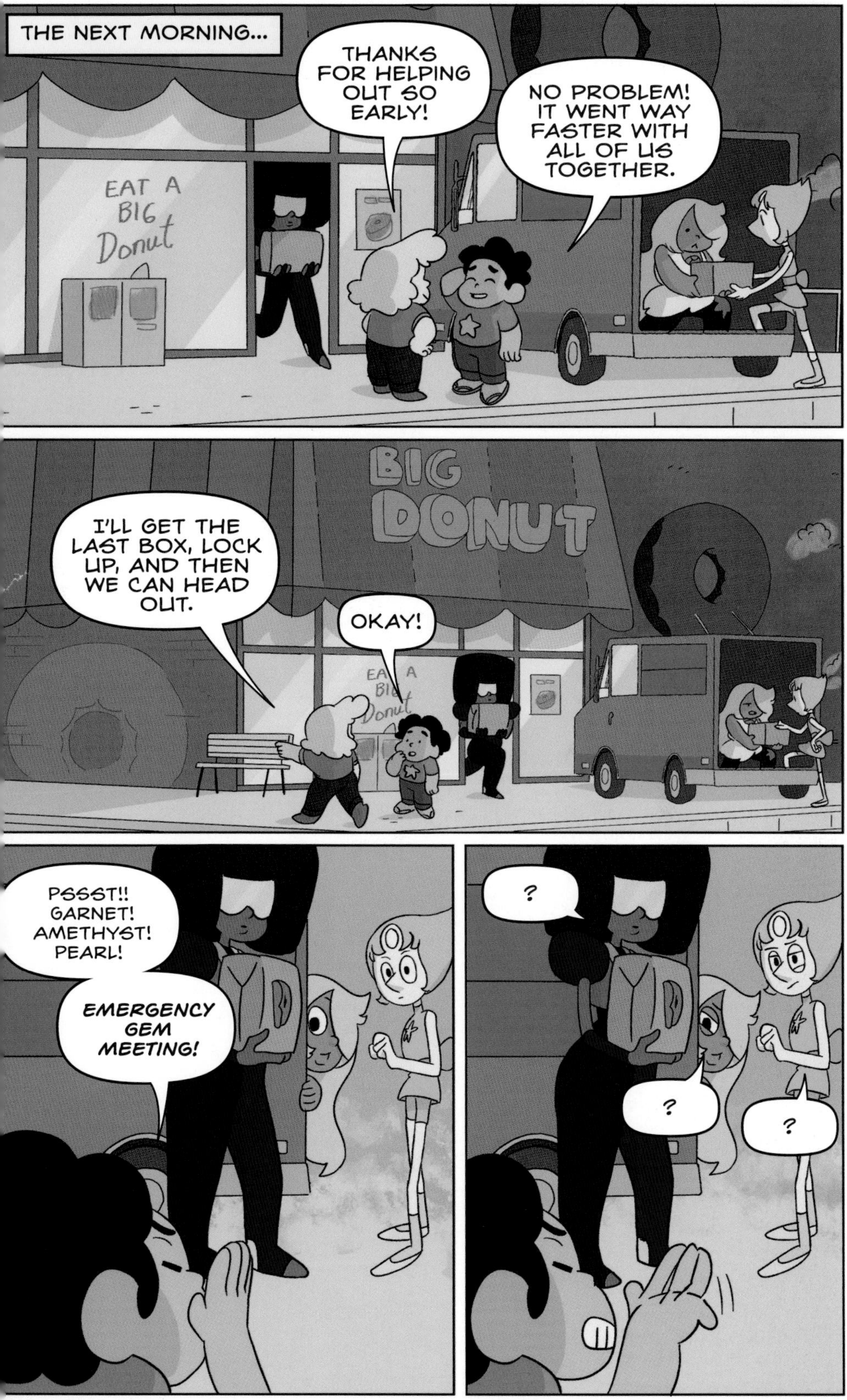
THE NEXT MORNING...
THANKS FOR HELPING OUT SO EARLY!
NO PROBLEM! IT WENT WAY FASTER WITH ALL OF US TOGETHER.
EAT A BIG Donut
BIG DONUT
I'LL GET THE LAST BOX, LOCK UP, AND THEN WE CAN HEAD OUT.
OKAY!
PSSST!! GARNET! AMETHYST! PEARL!
EMERGENCY GEM MEETING!
?
?
?

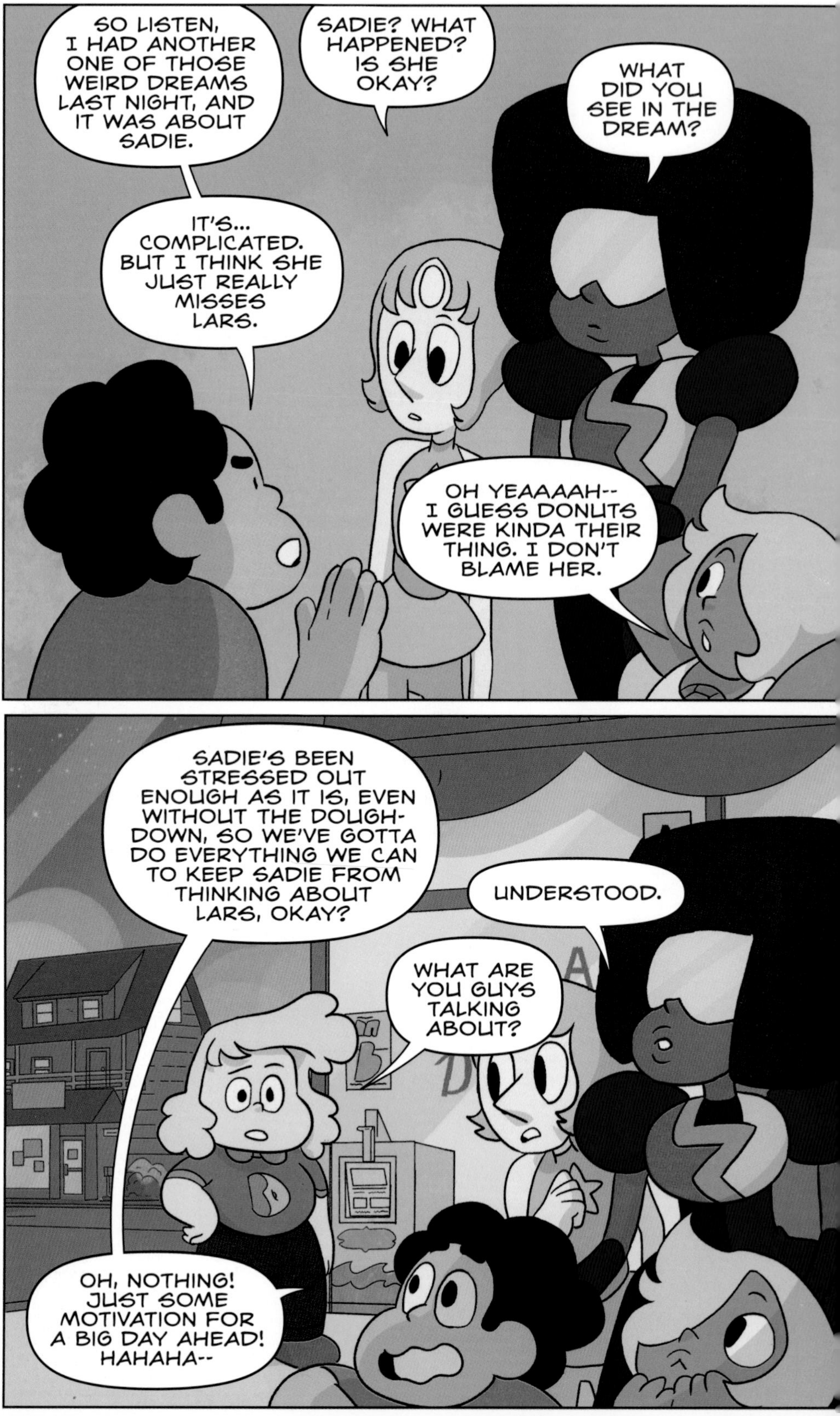
SO LISTEN, I HAD ANOTHER ONE OF THOSE WEIRD DREAMS LAST NIGHT, AND IT WAS ABOUT SADIE.
SADIE? WHAT HAPPENED? IS SHE OKAY?
WHAT DID YOU SEE IN THE DREAM?
IT'S... COMPLICATED. BUT I THINK SHE JUST REALLY MISSES LARS.
OH YEAAAAH-- I GUESS DONUTS WERE KINDA THEIR THING. I DON'T BLAME HER.
SADIE'S BEEN STRESSED OUT ENOUGH AS IT IS, EVEN WITHOUT THE DOUGH-DOWN, SO WE'VE GOTTA DO EVERYTHING WE CAN TO KEEP SADIE FROM THINKING ABOUT LARS, OKAY?
UNDERSTOOD.
WHAT ARE YOU GUYS TALKING ABOUT?
OH, NOTHING! JUST SOME MOTIVATION FOR A BIG DAY AHEAD! HAHAHA--

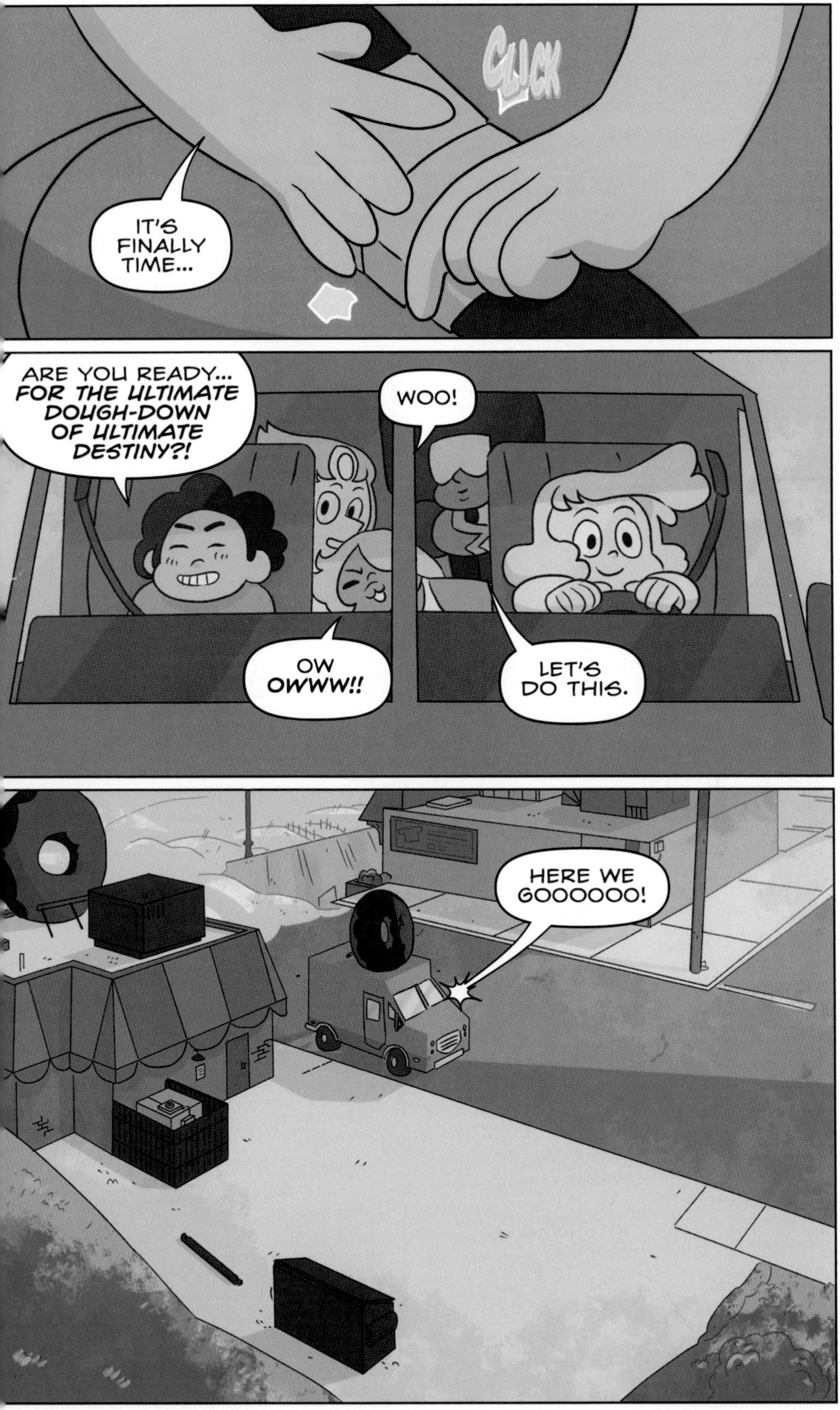
CLICK
IT'S FINALLY TIME...
ARE YOU READY... FOR THE ULTIMATE DOUGH-DOWN OF ULTIMATE DESTINY?!
WOO!
OW OWWW!!
LET'S DO THIS.
HERE WE GOOOOOO!

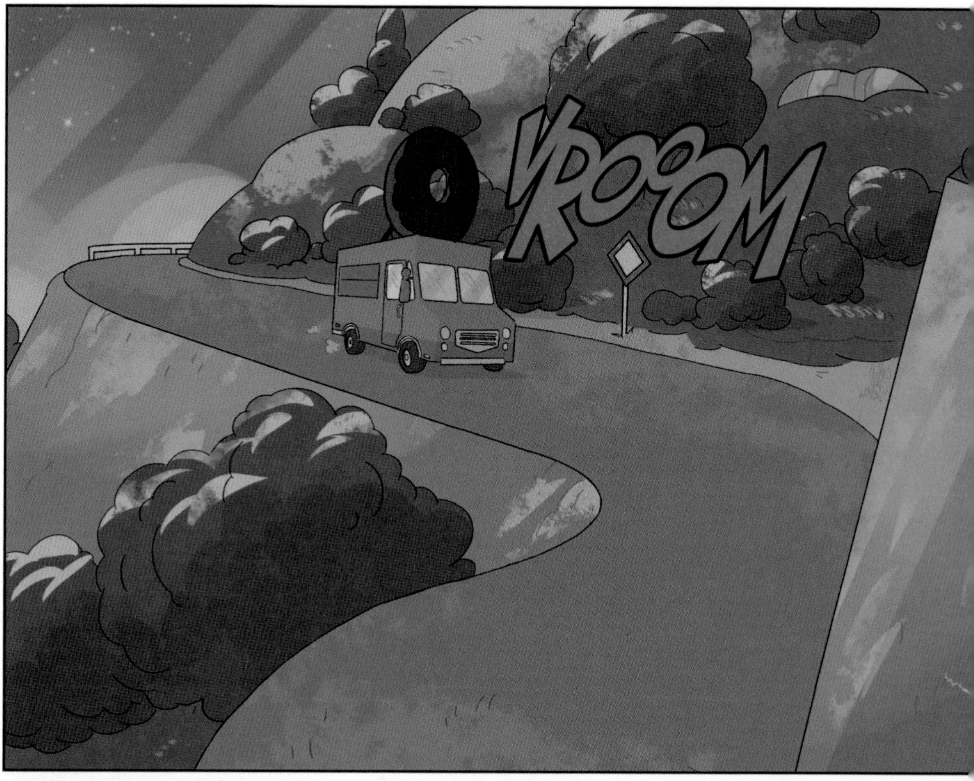
VROOOM

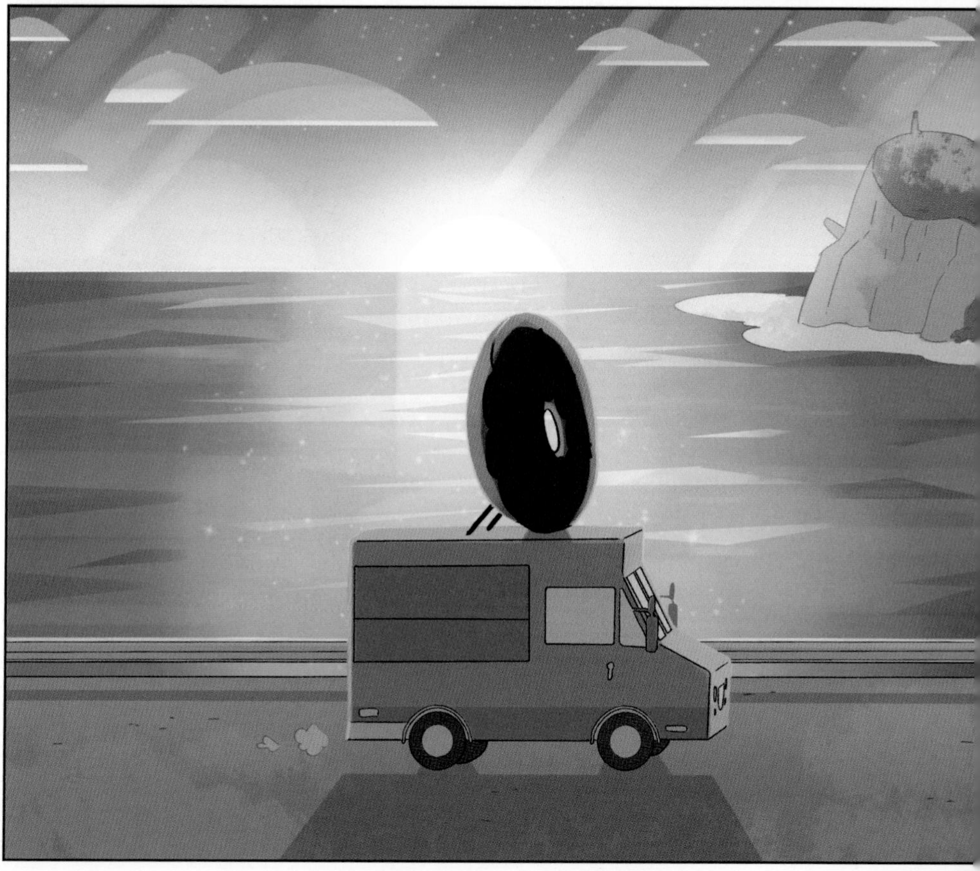

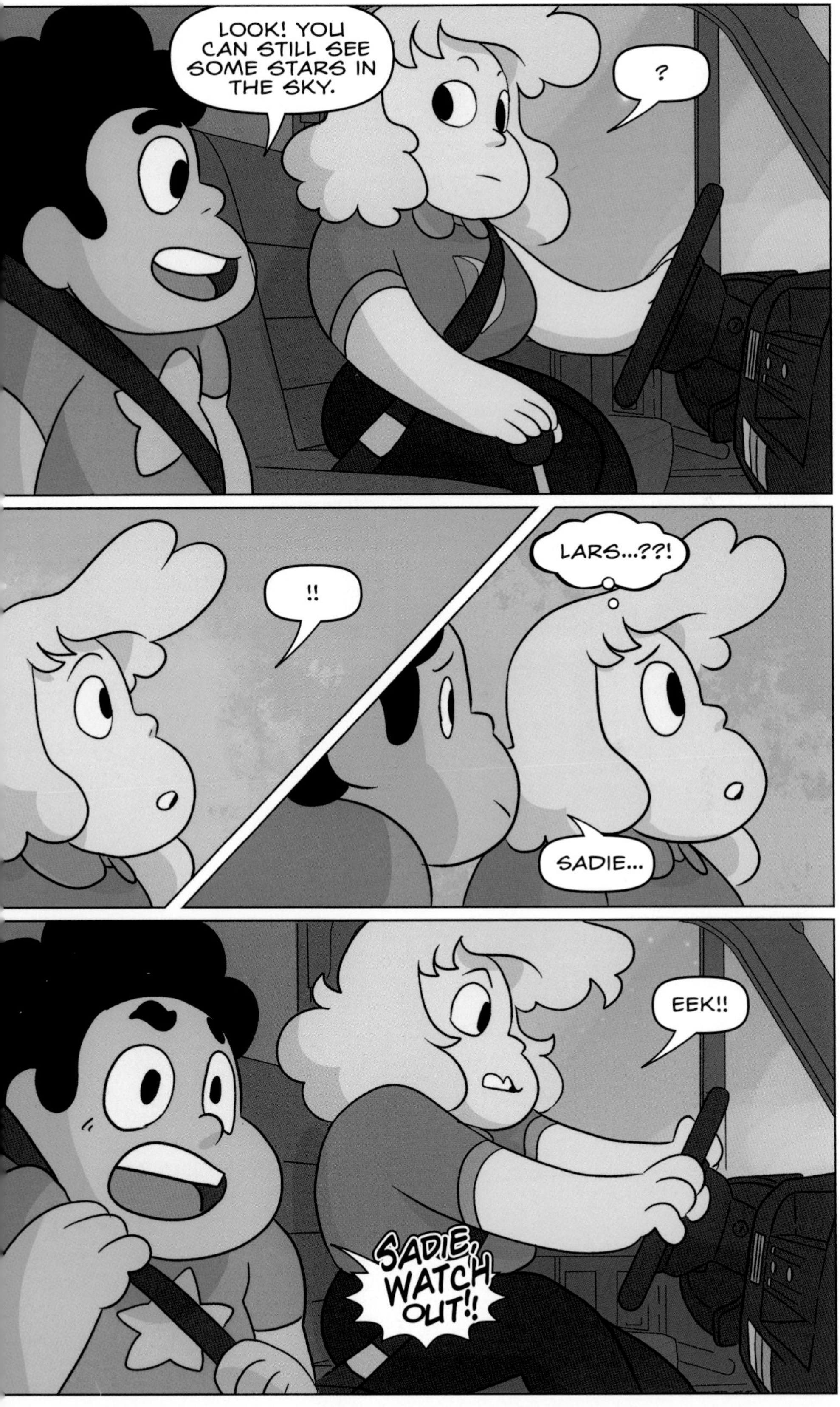
LOOK! YOU CAN STILL SEE SOME STARS IN THE SKY.
?
!!
LARS...??!
SADIE...
EEK!!
SADIE, WATCH OUT!!

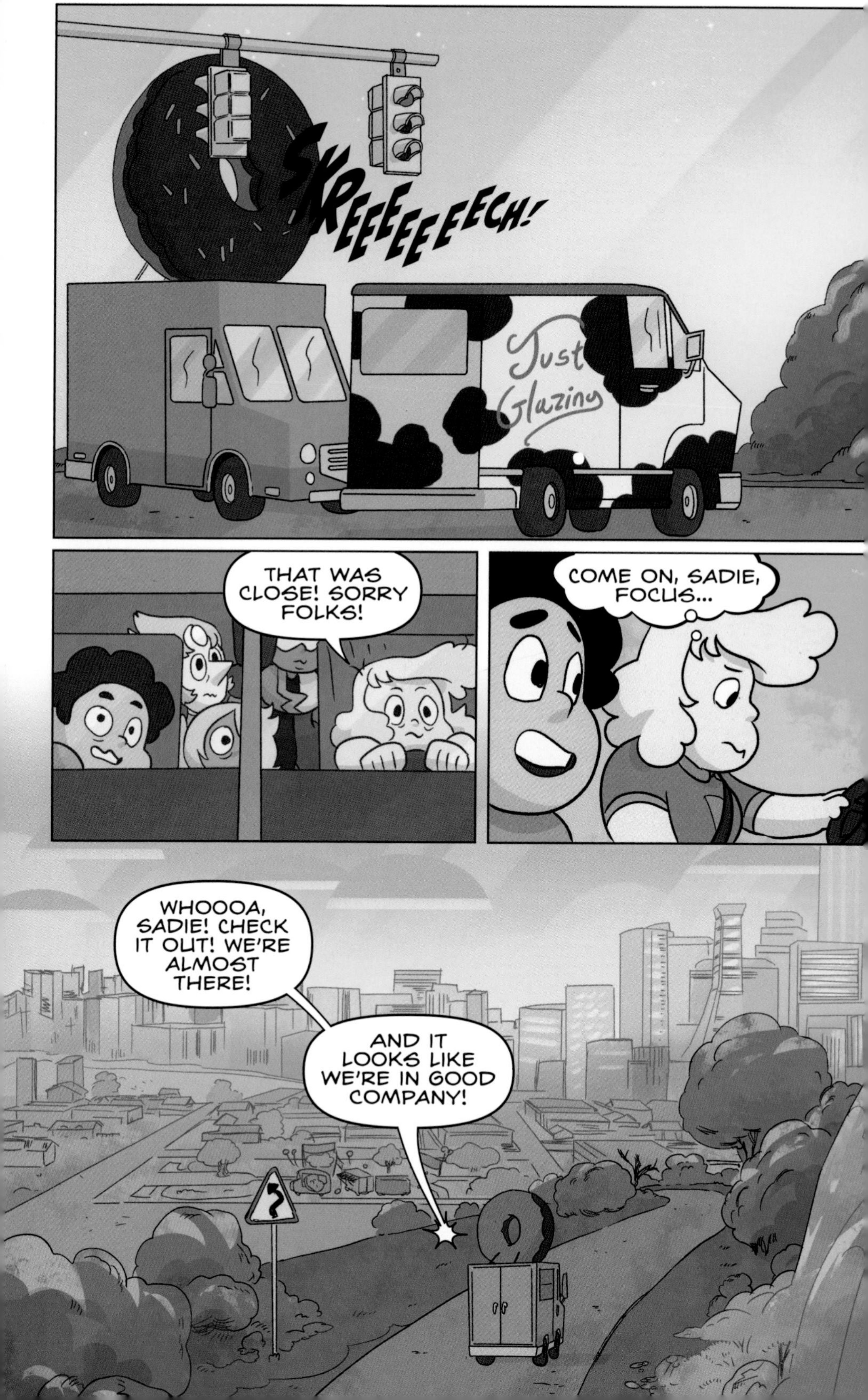
SKREEEEEEEECH!
Just Glazing
THAT WAS CLOSE! SORRY FOLKS!
COME ON, SADIE, FOCUS...
WHOOOA, SADIE! CHECK IT OUT! WE'RE ALMOST THERE!
AND IT LOOKS LIKE WE'RE IN GOOD COMPANY!

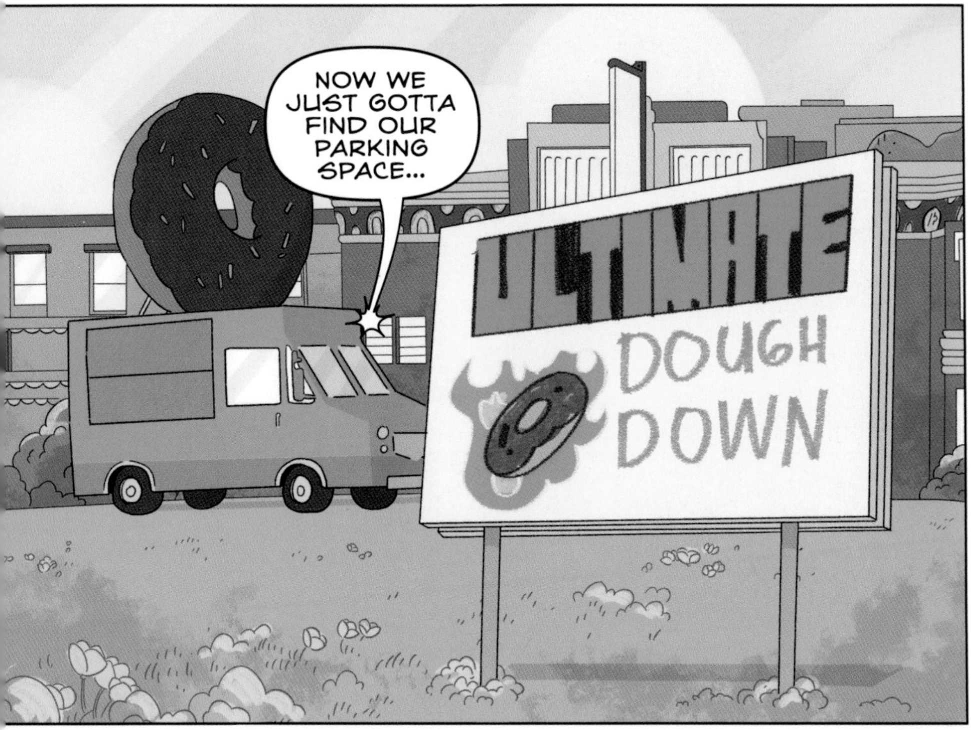
NOW WE JUST GOTTA FIND OUR PARKING SPACE...
ULTIMATE
DOUGH DOWN

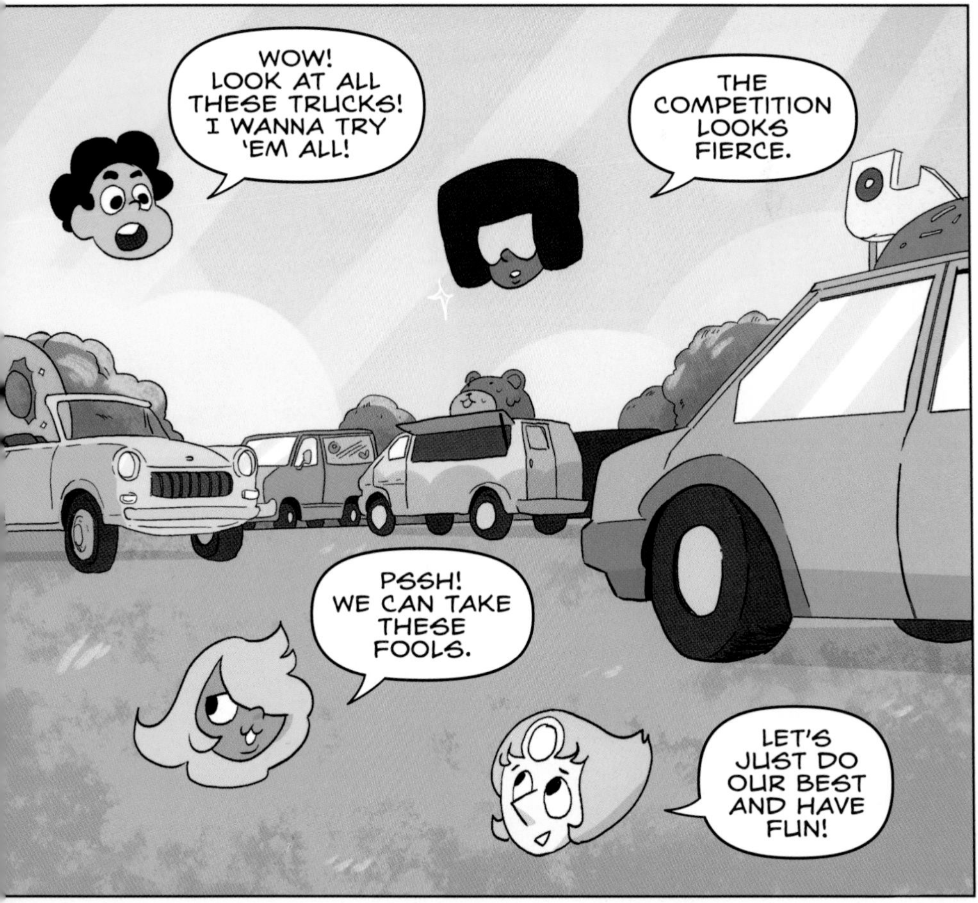
WOW! LOOK AT ALL THESE TRUCKS! I WANNA TRY 'EM ALL!
THE COMPETITION LOOKS FIERCE.
PSSH! WE CAN TAKE THESE FOOLS.
LET'S JUST DO OUR BEST AND HAVE FUN!

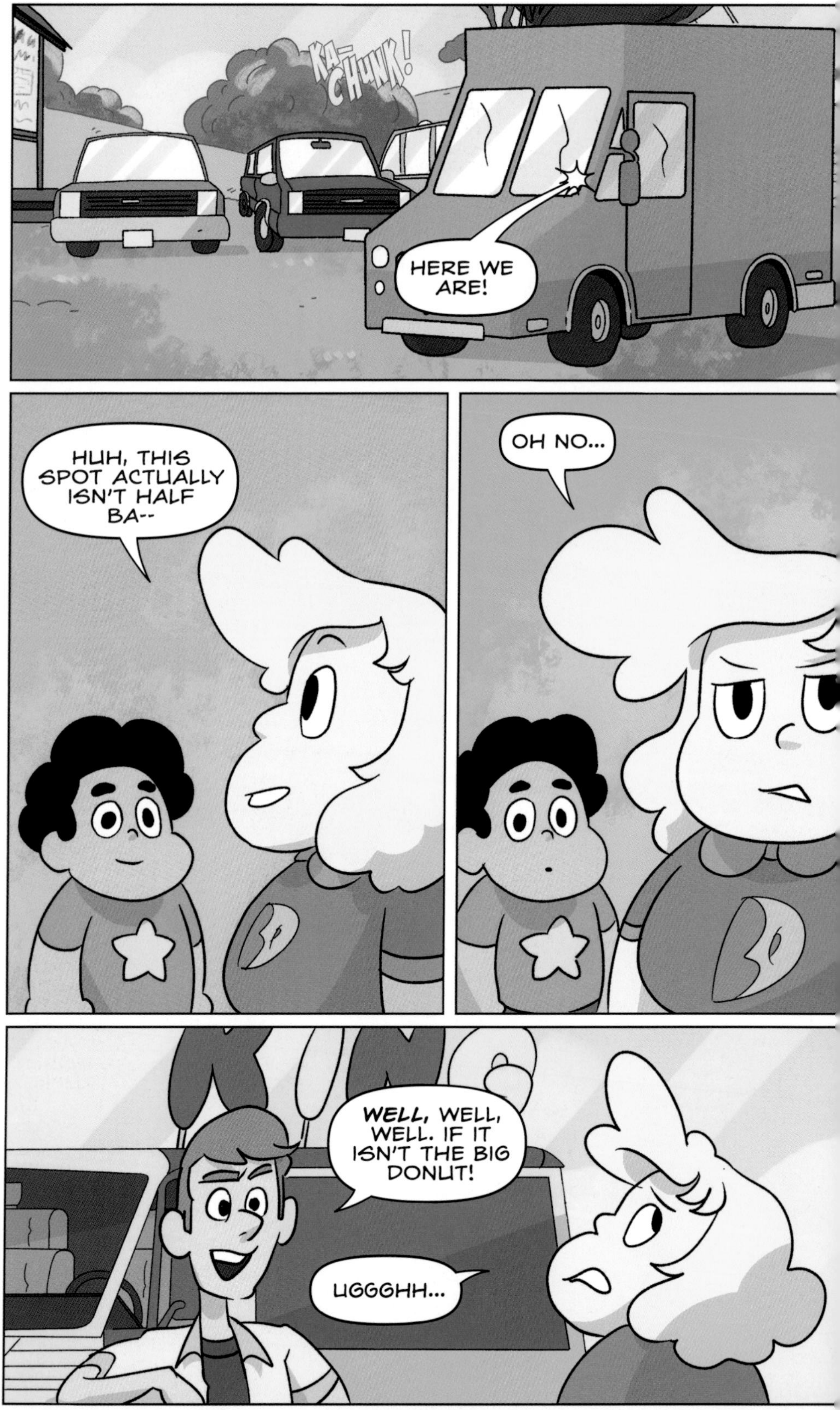
KA-CHUNK!
HERE WE ARE!
HUH, THIS SPOT ACTUALLY ISN'T HALF BA--
OH NO...
WELL, WELL, WELL. IF IT ISN'T THE BIG DONUT!
UGGGHH...

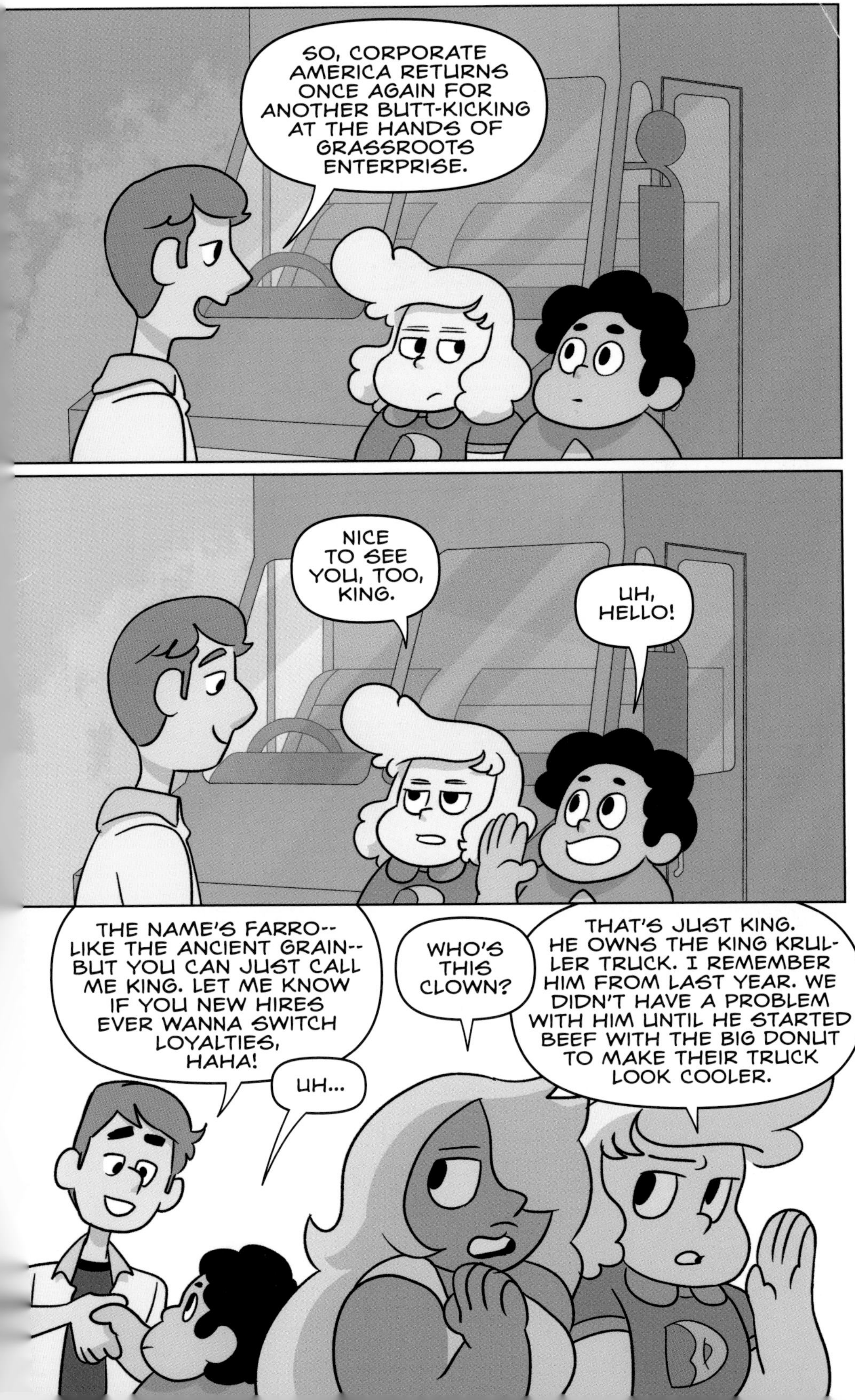
SO, CORPORATE AMERICA RETURNS ONCE AGAIN FOR ANOTHER BUTT-KICKING AT THE HANDS OF GRASSROOTS ENTERPRISE.
NICE TO SEE YOU, TOO, KING.
UH, HELLO!
THE NAME'S FARRO-- LIKE THE ANCIENT GRAIN-- BUT YOU CAN JUST CALL ME KING. LET ME KNOW IF YOU NEW HIRES EVER WANNA SWITCH LOYALTIES, HAHA!
UH...
WHO'S THIS CLOWN?
THAT'S JUST KING. HE OWNS THE KING KRULLER TRUCK. I REMEMBER HIM FROM LAST YEAR. WE DIDN'T HAVE A PROBLEM WITH HIM UNTIL HE STARTED BEEF WITH THE BIG DONUT TO MAKE THEIR TRUCK LOOK COOLER.

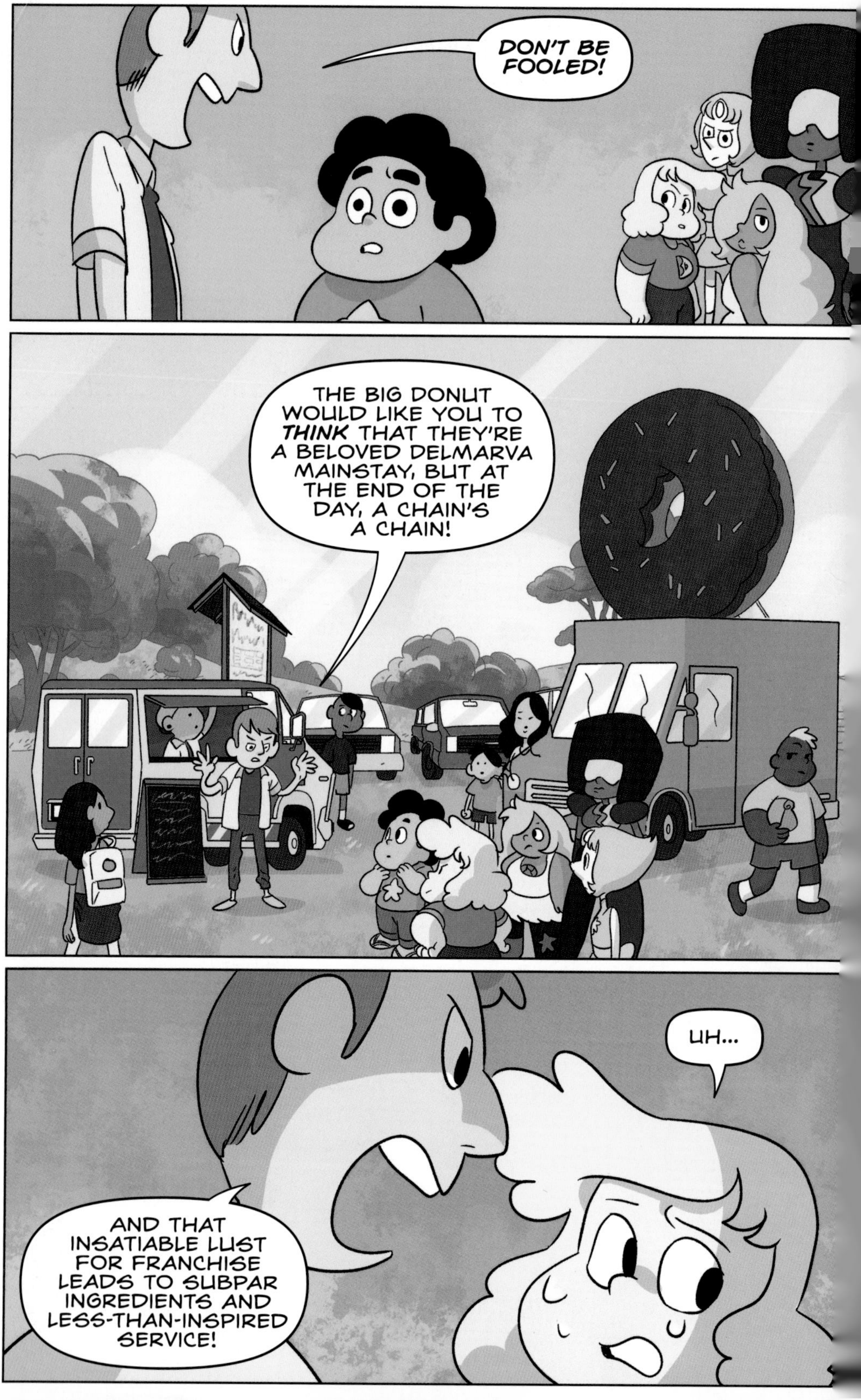
DON'T BE FOOLED!
THE BIG DONUT WOULD LIKE YOU TO *THINK* THAT THEY'RE A BELOVED DELMARVA MAINSTAY, BUT AT THE END OF THE DAY, A CHAIN'S A CHAIN!
UH...
AND THAT INSATIABLE LUST FOR FRANCHISE LEADS TO SUBPAR INGREDIENTS AND LESS-THAN-INSPIRED SERVICE!

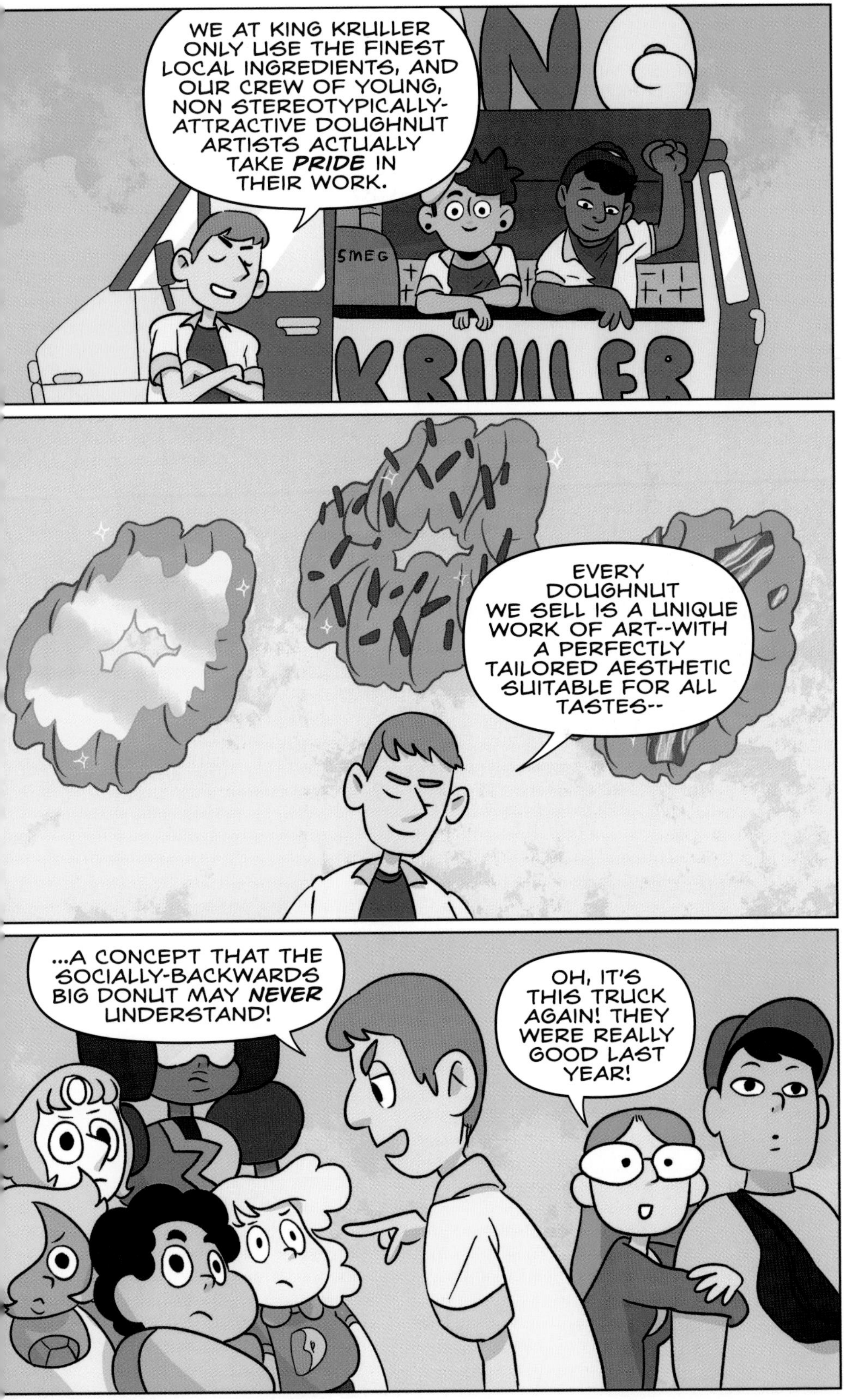
WE AT KING KRULLER ONLY USE THE FINEST LOCAL INGREDIENTS, AND OUR CREW OF YOUNG, NON STEREOTYPICALLY-ATTRACTIVE DOUGHNUT ARTISTS ACTUALLY TAKE *PRIDE* IN THEIR WORK.
SMEG
KRULLER
EVERY DOUGHNUT WE SELL IS A UNIQUE WORK OF ART--WITH A PERFECTLY TAILORED AESTHETIC SUITABLE FOR ALL TASTES--
...A CONCEPT THAT THE SOCIALLY-BACKWARDS BIG DONUT MAY *NEVER* UNDERSTAND!
OH, IT'S THIS TRUCK AGAIN! THEY WERE REALLY GOOD LAST YEAR!

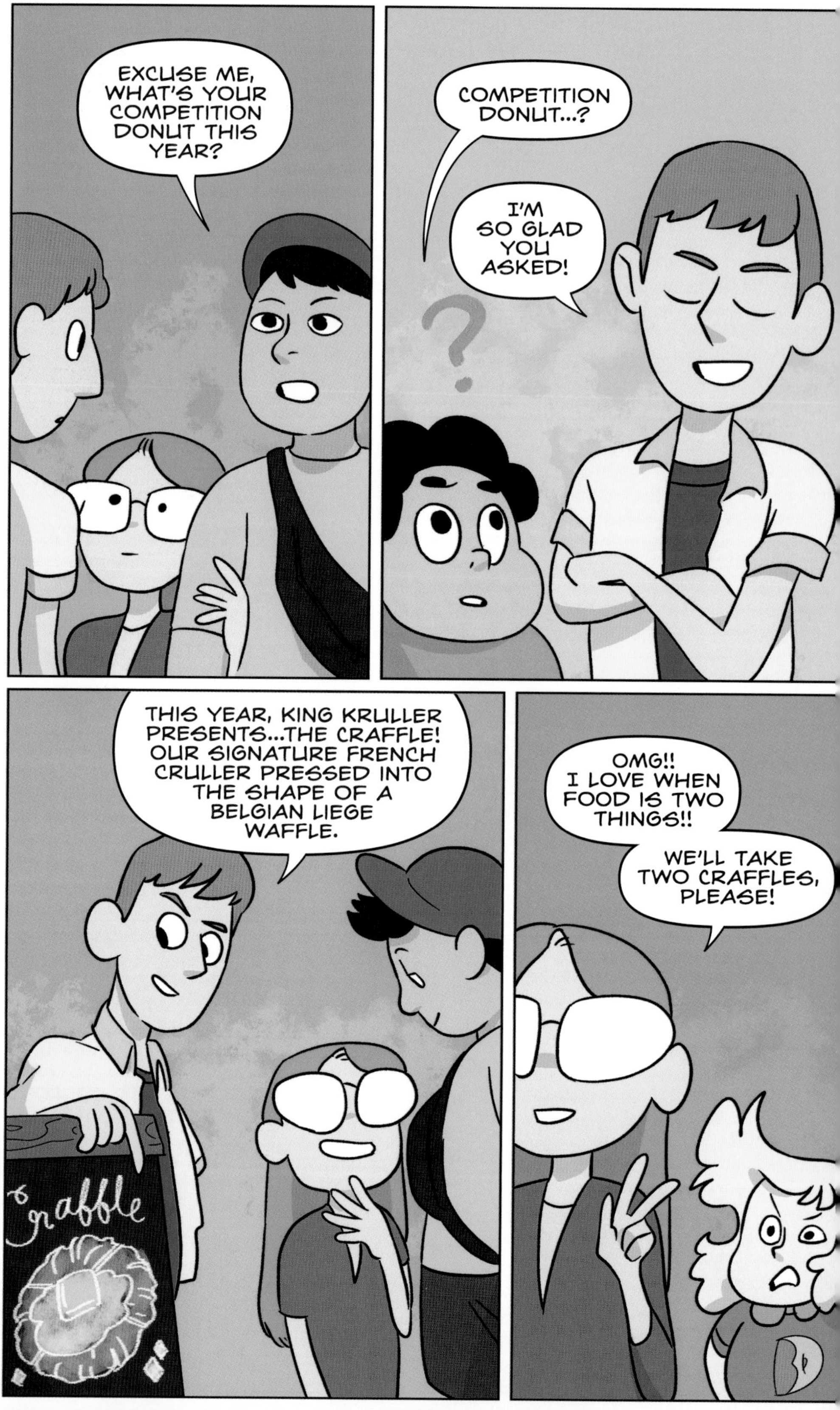
EXCUSE ME, WHAT'S YOUR COMPETITION DONUT THIS YEAR?
COMPETITION DONUT...?
I'M SO GLAD YOU ASKED!
THIS YEAR, KING KRULLER PRESENTS...THE CRAFFLE! OUR SIGNATURE FRENCH CRULLER PRESSED INTO THE SHAPE OF A BELGIAN LIEGE WAFFLE.
craffle
OMG!! I LOVE WHEN FOOD IS TWO THINGS!!
WE'LL TAKE TWO CRAFFLES, PLEASE!

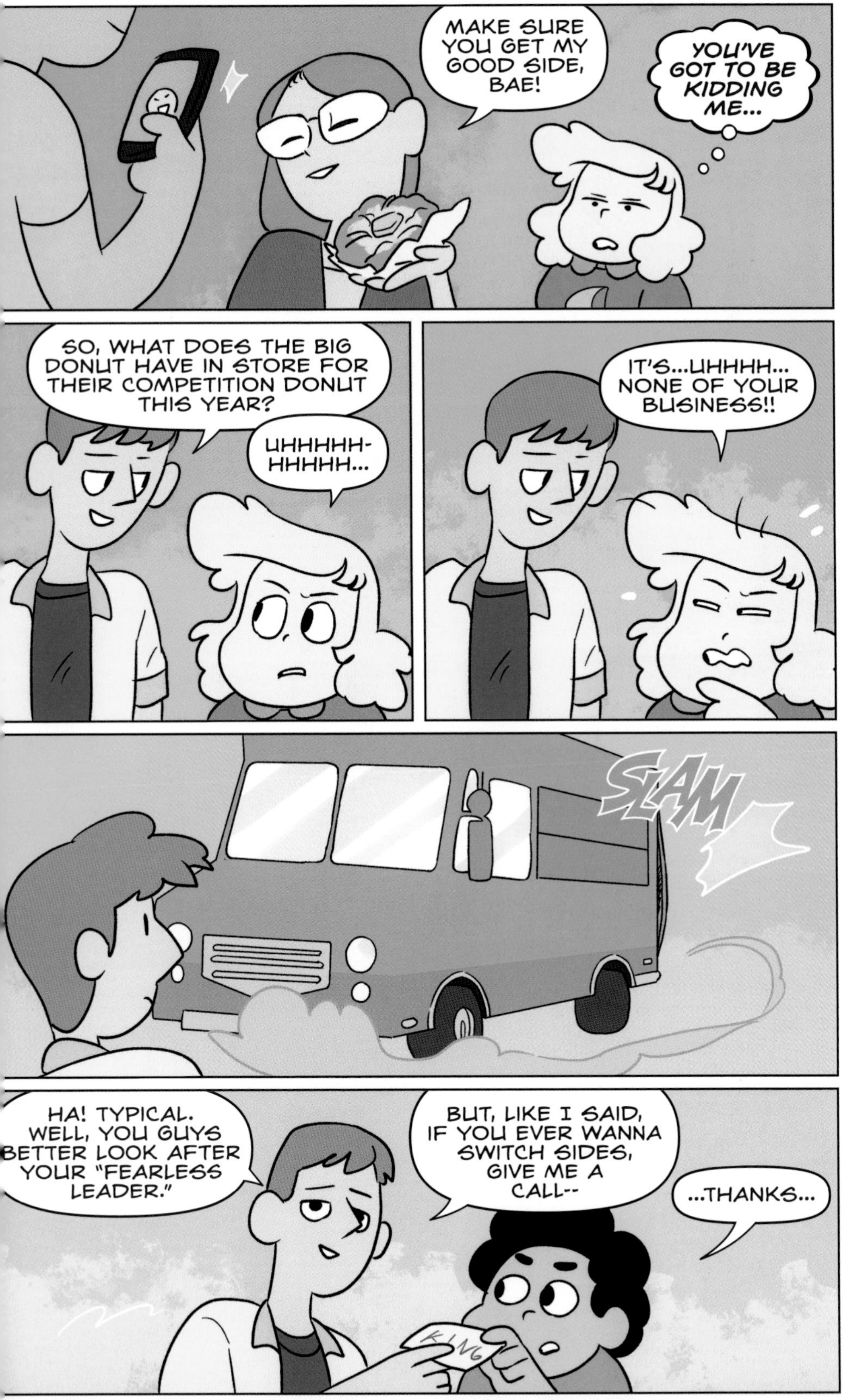
MAKE SURE YOU GET MY GOOD SIDE, BAE!
YOU'VE GOT TO BE KIDDING ME...
SO, WHAT DOES THE BIG DONUT HAVE IN STORE FOR THEIR COMPETITION DONUT THIS YEAR?
UHHHHH-HHHHH...
IT'S...UHHHH... NONE OF YOUR BUSINESS!!
SLAM
HA! TYPICAL. WELL, YOU GUYS BETTER LOOK AFTER YOUR "FEARLESS LEADER."
BUT, LIKE I SAID, IF YOU EVER WANNA SWITCH SIDES, GIVE ME A CALL--
...THANKS...
KING

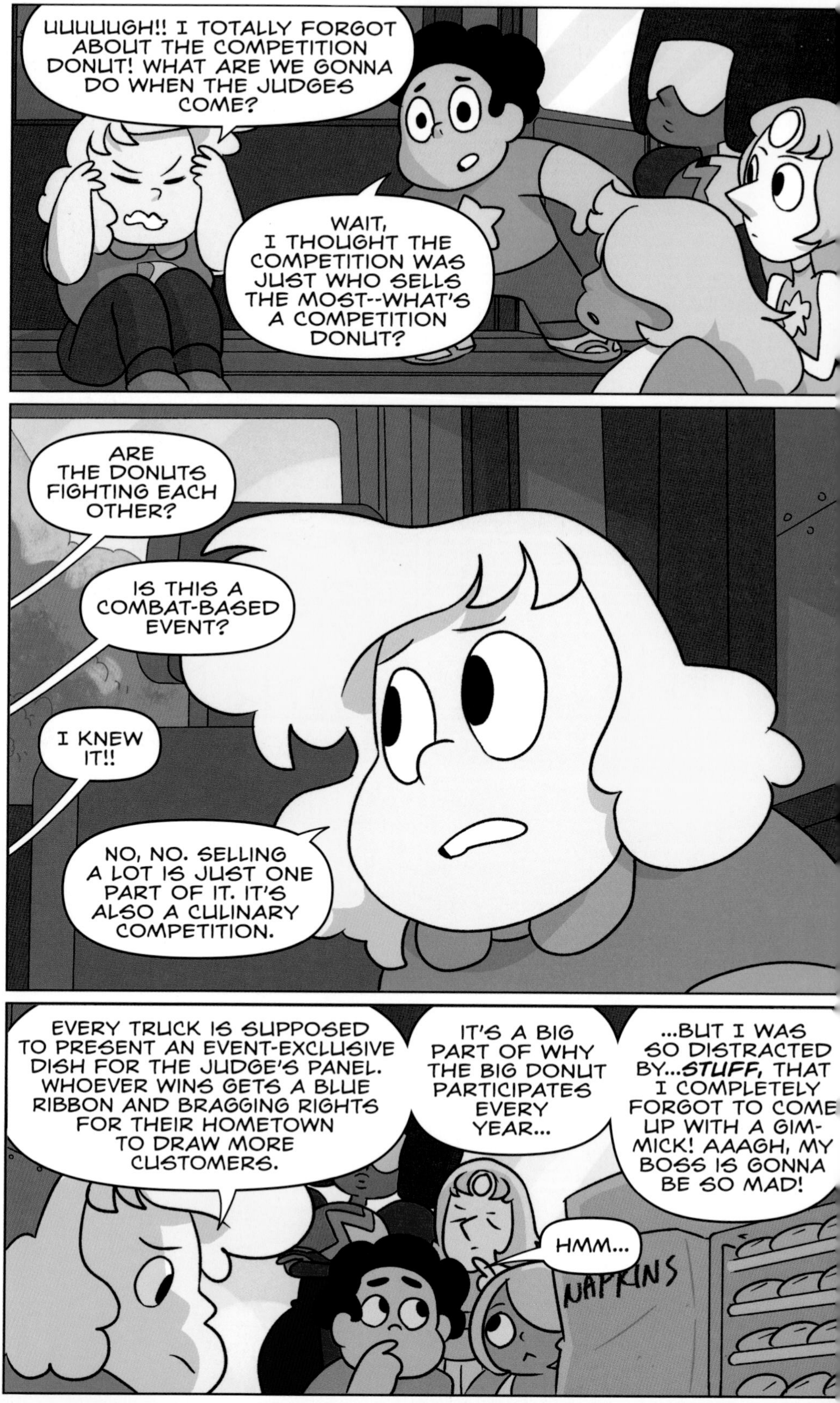
UUUUUGH!! I TOTALLY FORGOT ABOUT THE COMPETITION DONUT! WHAT ARE WE GONNA DO WHEN THE JUDGES COME?
WAIT, I THOUGHT THE COMPETITION WAS JUST WHO SELLS THE MOST--WHAT'S A COMPETITION DONUT?
ARE THE DONUTS FIGHTING EACH OTHER?
IS THIS A COMBAT-BASED EVENT?
I KNEW IT!!
NO, NO. SELLING A LOT IS JUST ONE PART OF IT. IT'S ALSO A CULINARY COMPETITION.
EVERY TRUCK IS SUPPOSED TO PRESENT AN EVENT-EXCLUSIVE DISH FOR THE JUDGE'S PANEL. WHOEVER WINS GETS A BLUE RIBBON AND BRAGGING RIGHTS FOR THEIR HOMETOWN TO DRAW MORE CUSTOMERS.
IT'S A BIG PART OF WHY THE BIG DONUT PARTICIPATES EVERY YEAR...
...BUT I WAS SO DISTRACTED BY...*STUFF*, THAT I COMPLETELY FORGOT TO COME UP WITH A GIM-MICK! AAAGH, MY BOSS IS GONNA BE SO MAD!
HMM...
NAPKINS

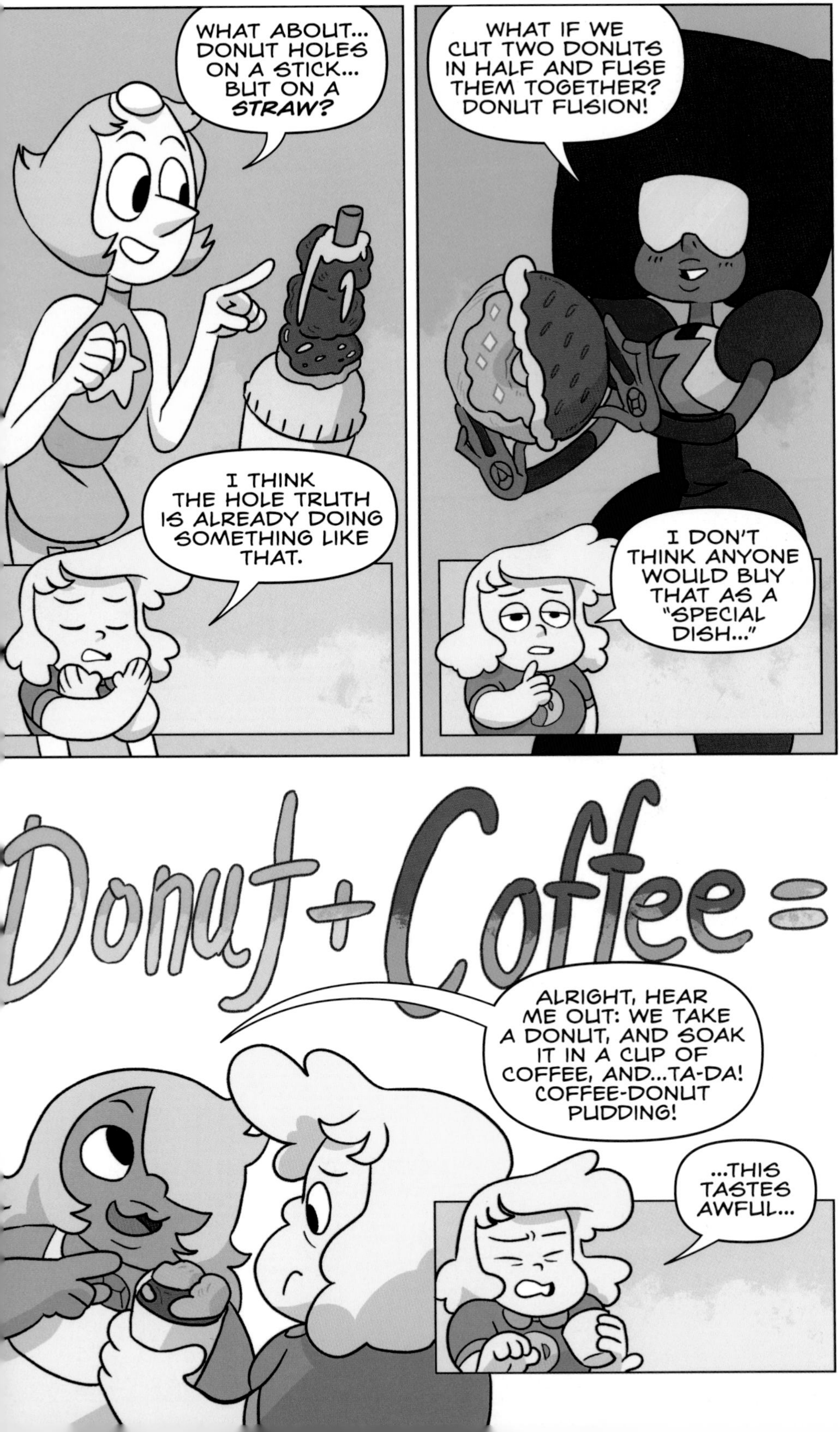
WHAT ABOUT... DONUT HOLES ON A STICK... BUT ON A *STRAW?*
I THINK THE HOLE TRUTH IS ALREADY DOING SOMETHING LIKE THAT.
WHAT IF WE CUT TWO DONUTS IN HALF AND FUSE THEM TOGETHER? DONUT FUSION!
I DON'T THINK ANYONE WOULD BUY THAT AS A "SPECIAL DISH..."
Donut + Coffee =
ALRIGHT, HEAR ME OUT: WE TAKE A DONUT, AND SOAK IT IN A CUP OF COFFEE, AND...TA-DA! COFFEE-DONUT PUDDING!
...THIS TASTES AWFUL...

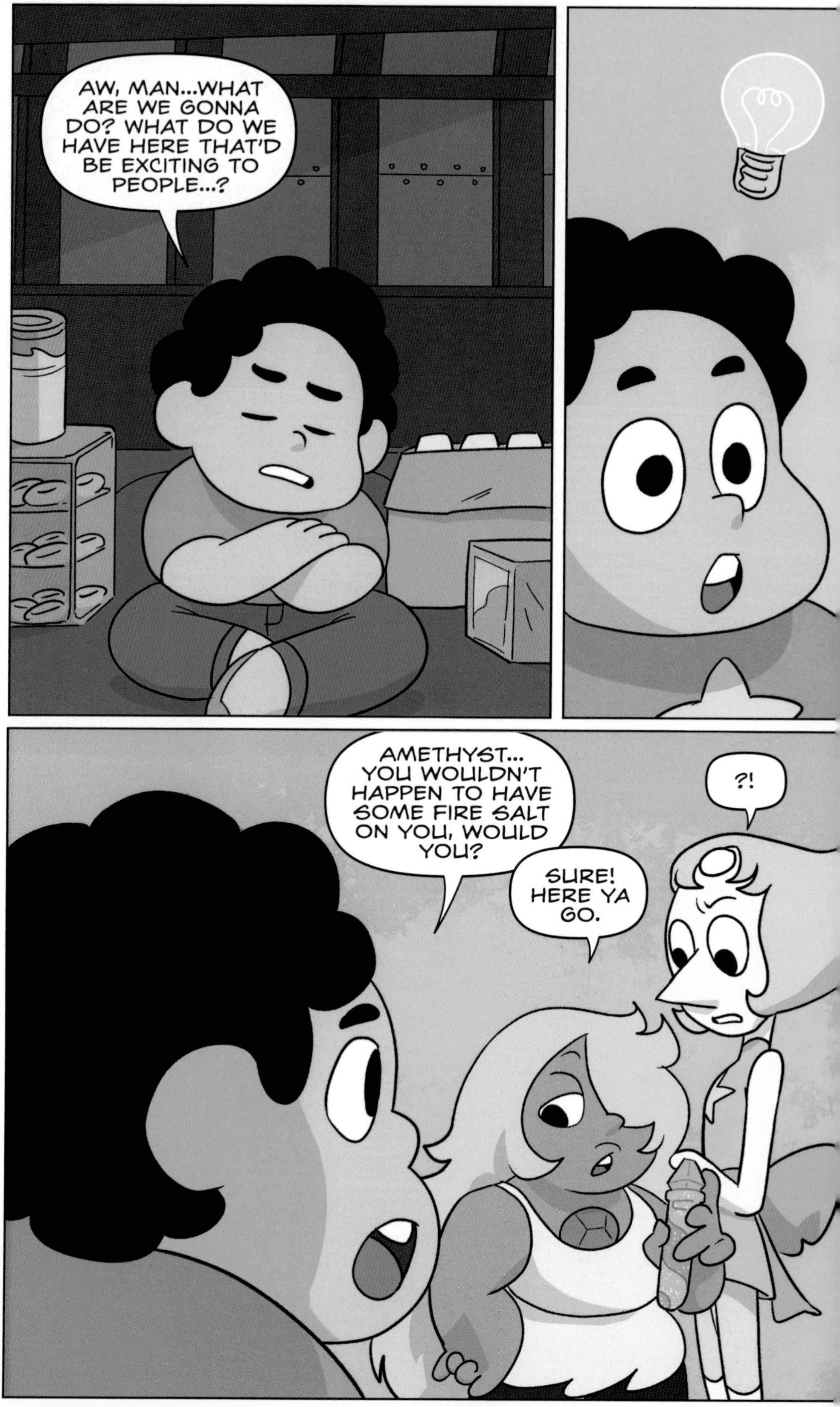
AW, MAN...WHAT ARE WE GONNA DO? WHAT DO WE HAVE HERE THAT'D BE EXCITING TO PEOPLE...?
AMETHYST... YOU WOULDN'T HAPPEN TO HAVE SOME FIRE SALT ON YOU, WOULD YOU?
?!
SURE! HERE YA GO.

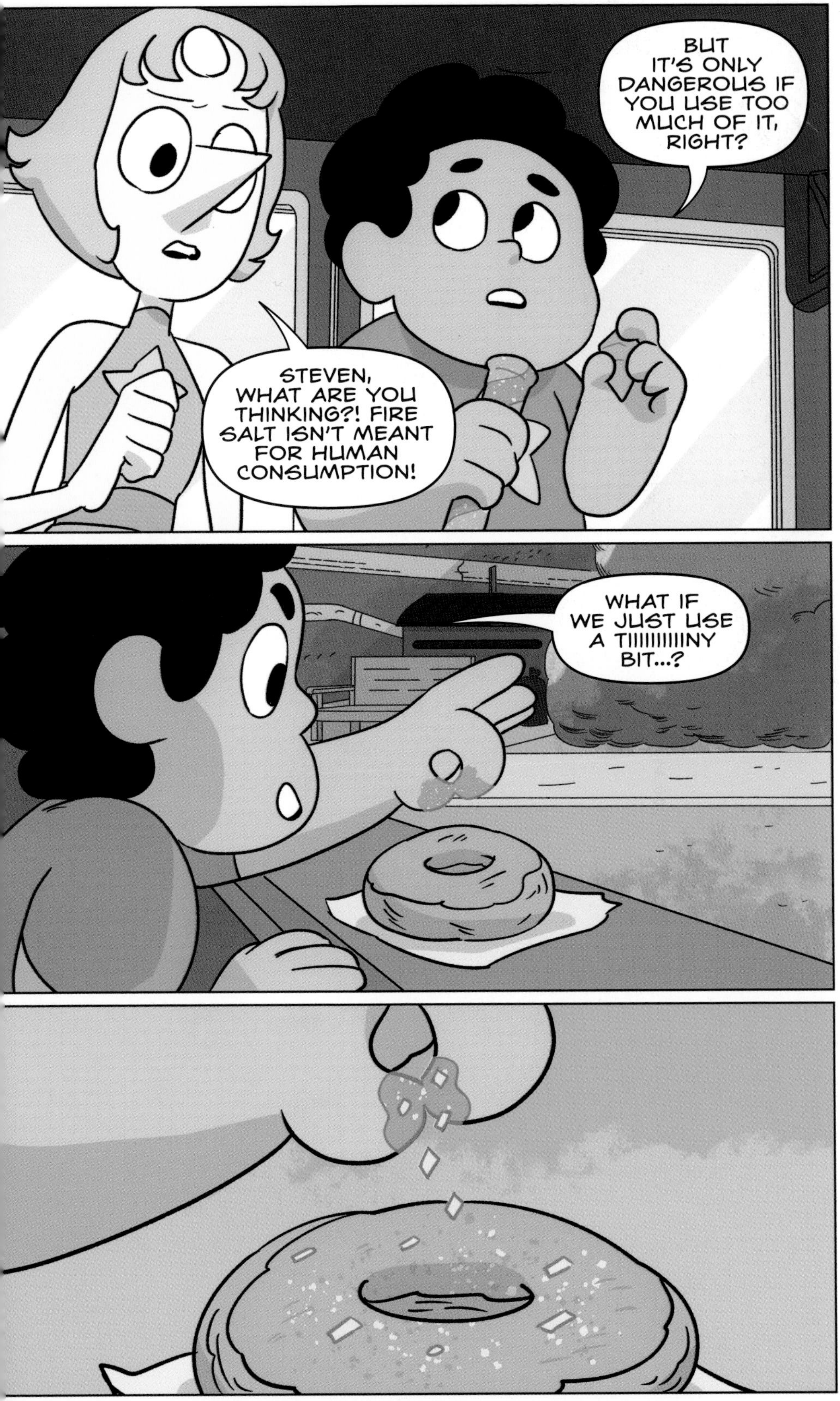
BUT IT'S ONLY DANGEROUS IF YOU USE TOO MUCH OF IT, RIGHT?
STEVEN, WHAT ARE YOU THINKING?! FIRE SALT ISN'T MEANT FOR HUMAN CONSUMPTION!
WHAT IF WE JUST USE A TIIIIIIIIIINY BIT...?

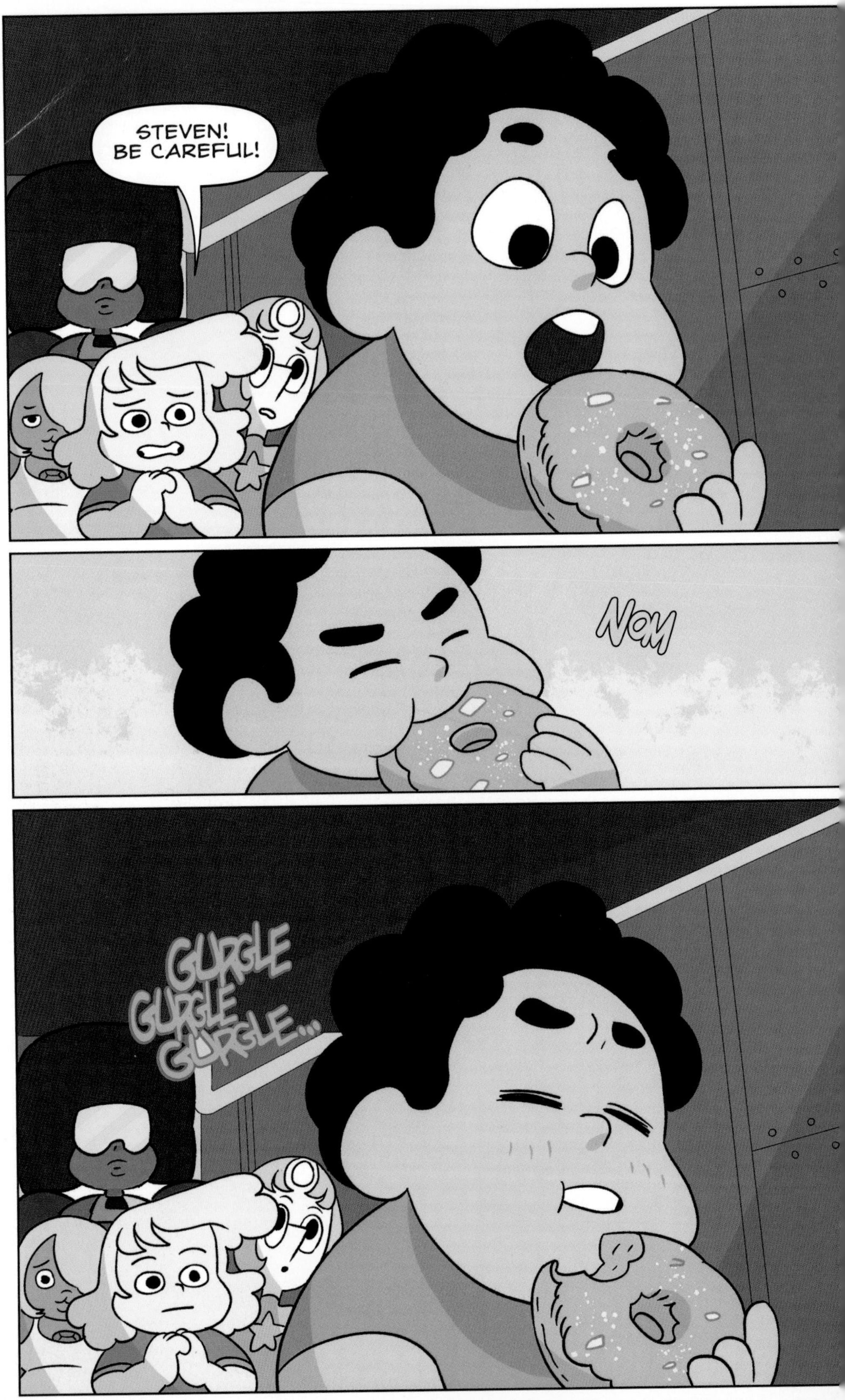
STEVEN! BE CAREFUL!
NOM
GURGLE
GURGLE
GURGLE...

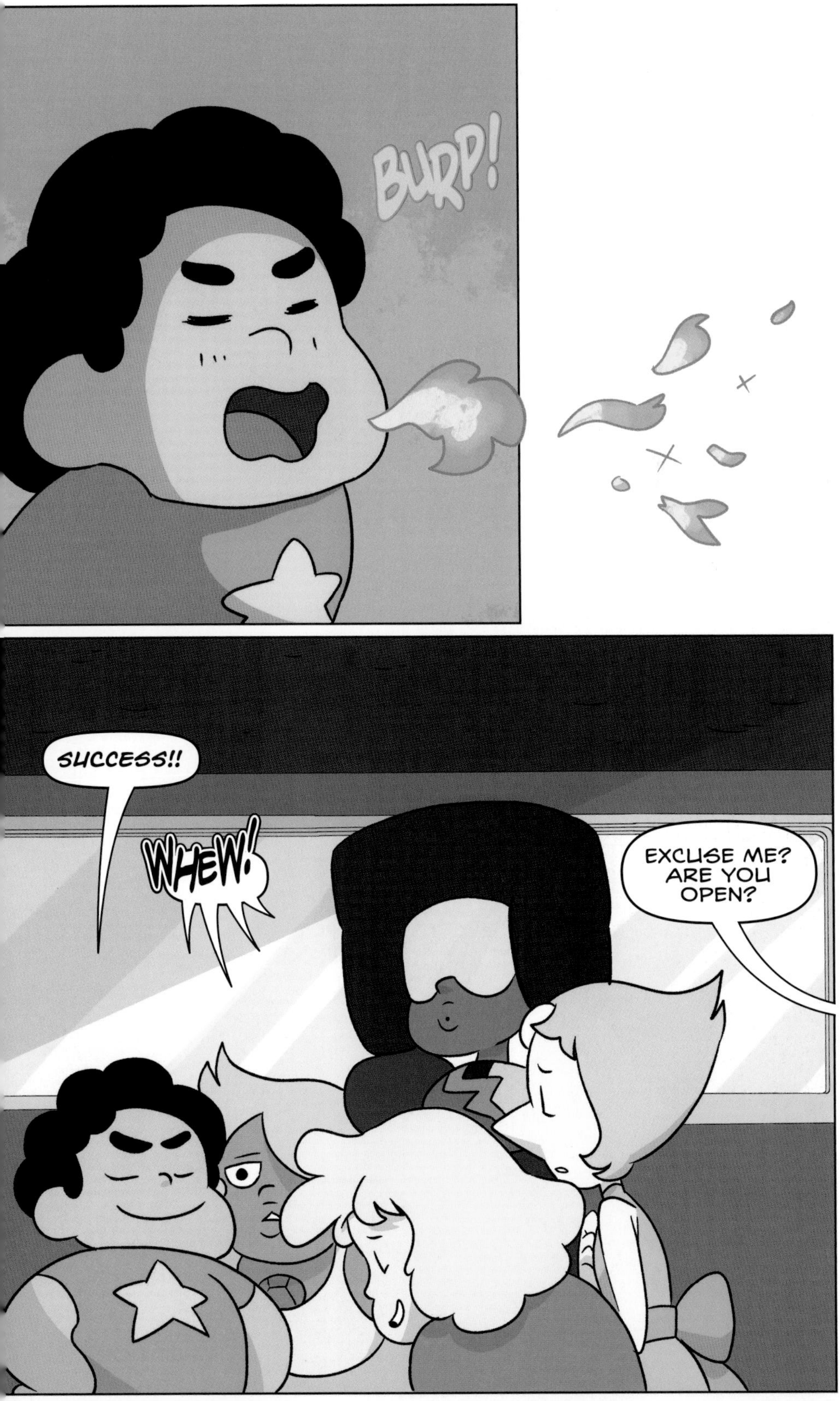
BURP!
SUCCESS!!
WHEW!
EXCUSE ME? ARE YOU OPEN?

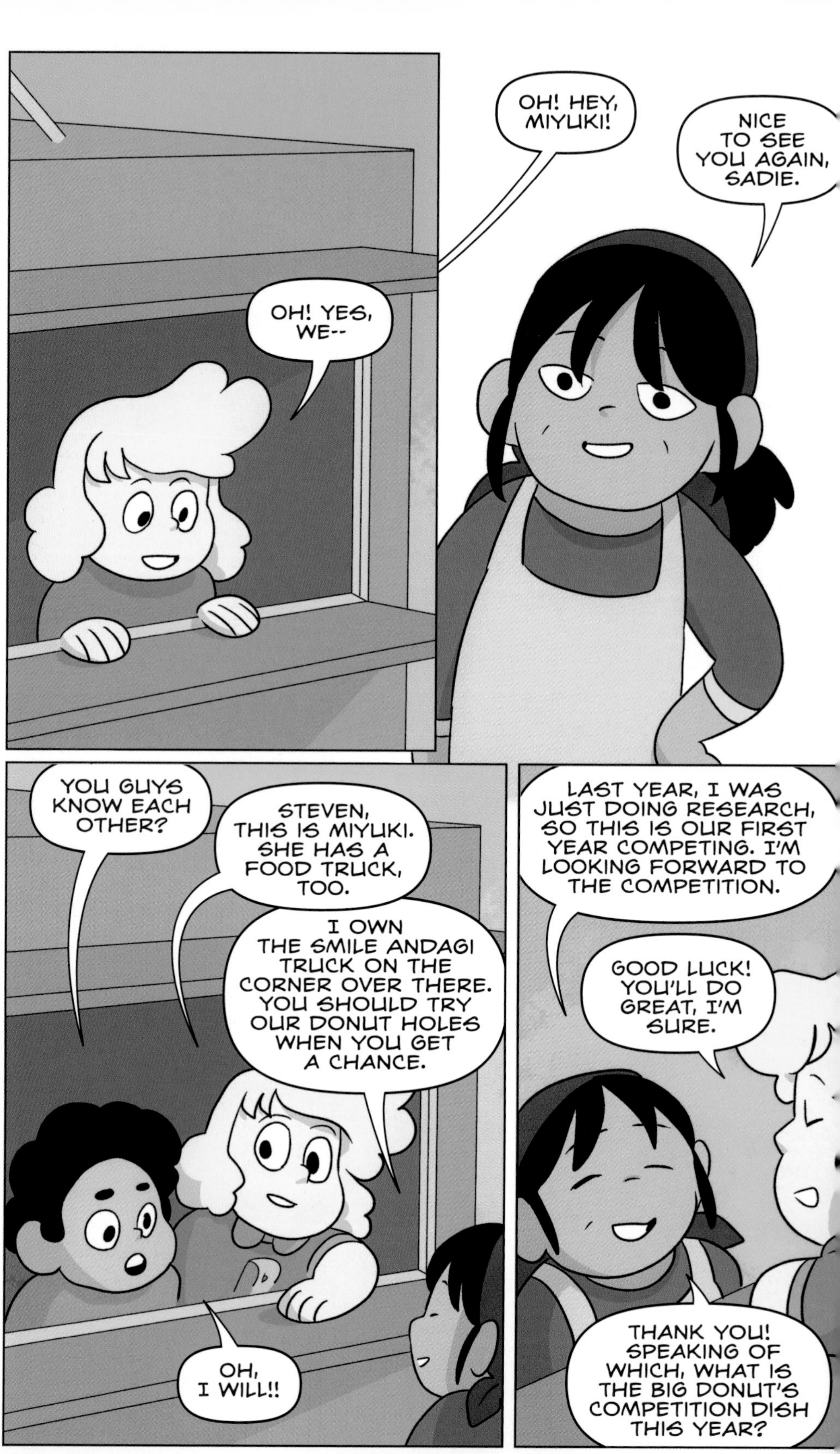
OH! HEY, MIYUKI!
NICE TO SEE YOU AGAIN, SADIE.
OH! YES, WE--
YOU GUYS KNOW EACH OTHER?
STEVEN, THIS IS MIYUKI. SHE HAS A FOOD TRUCK, TOO.
I OWN THE SMILE ANDAGI TRUCK ON THE CORNER OVER THERE. YOU SHOULD TRY OUR DONUT HOLES WHEN YOU GET A CHANCE.
OH, I WILL!!
LAST YEAR, I WAS JUST DOING RESEARCH, SO THIS IS OUR FIRST YEAR COMPETING. I'M LOOKING FORWARD TO THE COMPETITION.
GOOD LUCK! YOU'LL DO GREAT, I'M SURE.
THANK YOU! SPEAKING OF WHICH, WHAT IS THE BIG DONUT'S COMPETITION DISH THIS YEAR?

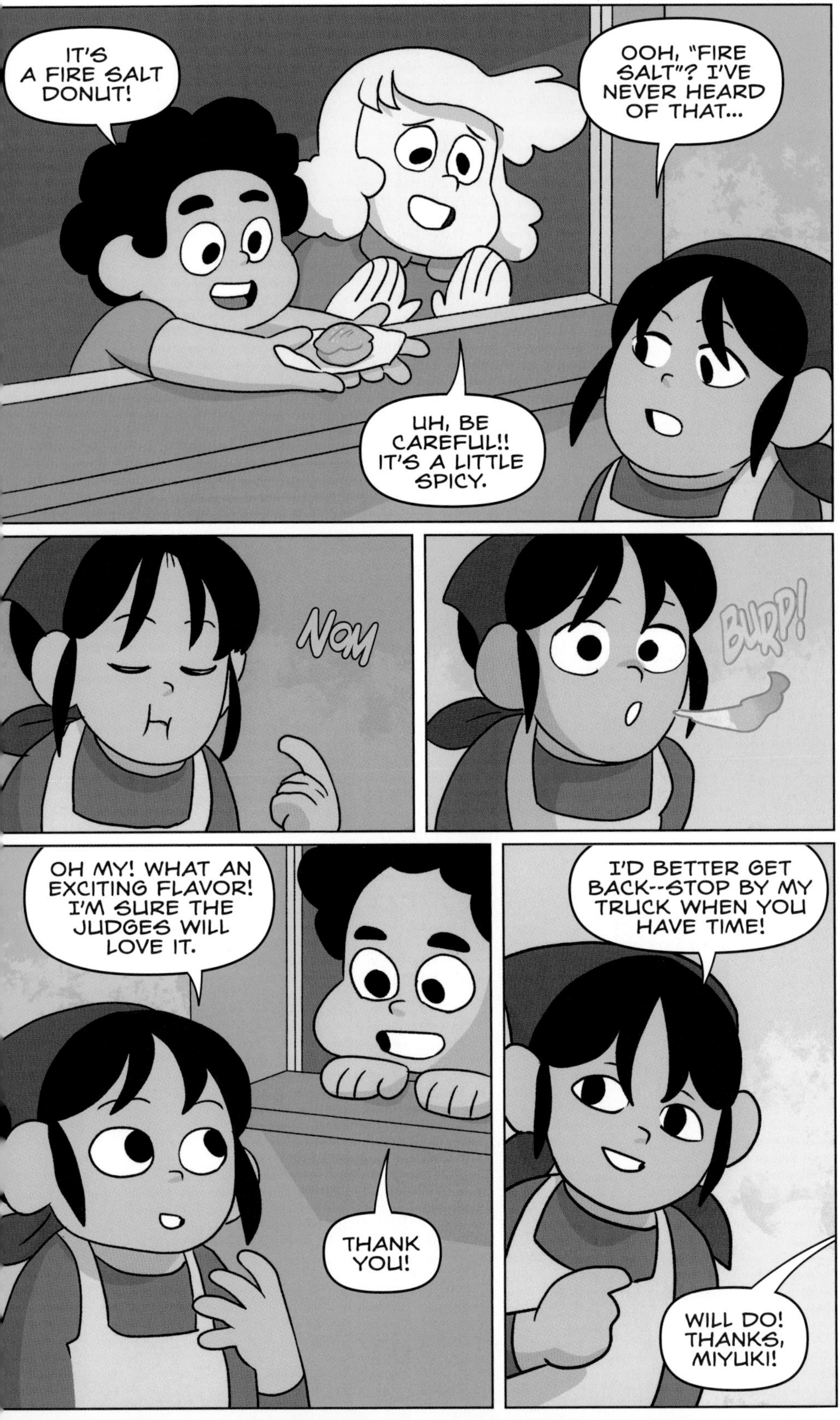
IT'S A FIRE SALT DONUT!
OOH, "FIRE SALT"? I'VE NEVER HEARD OF THAT...
UH, BE CAREFUL!! IT'S A LITTLE SPICY.
NOM
BURP!
OH MY! WHAT AN EXCITING FLAVOR! I'M SURE THE JUDGES WILL LOVE IT.
THANK YOU!
I'D BETTER GET BACK--STOP BY MY TRUCK WHEN YOU HAVE TIME!
WILL DO! THANKS, MIYUKI!

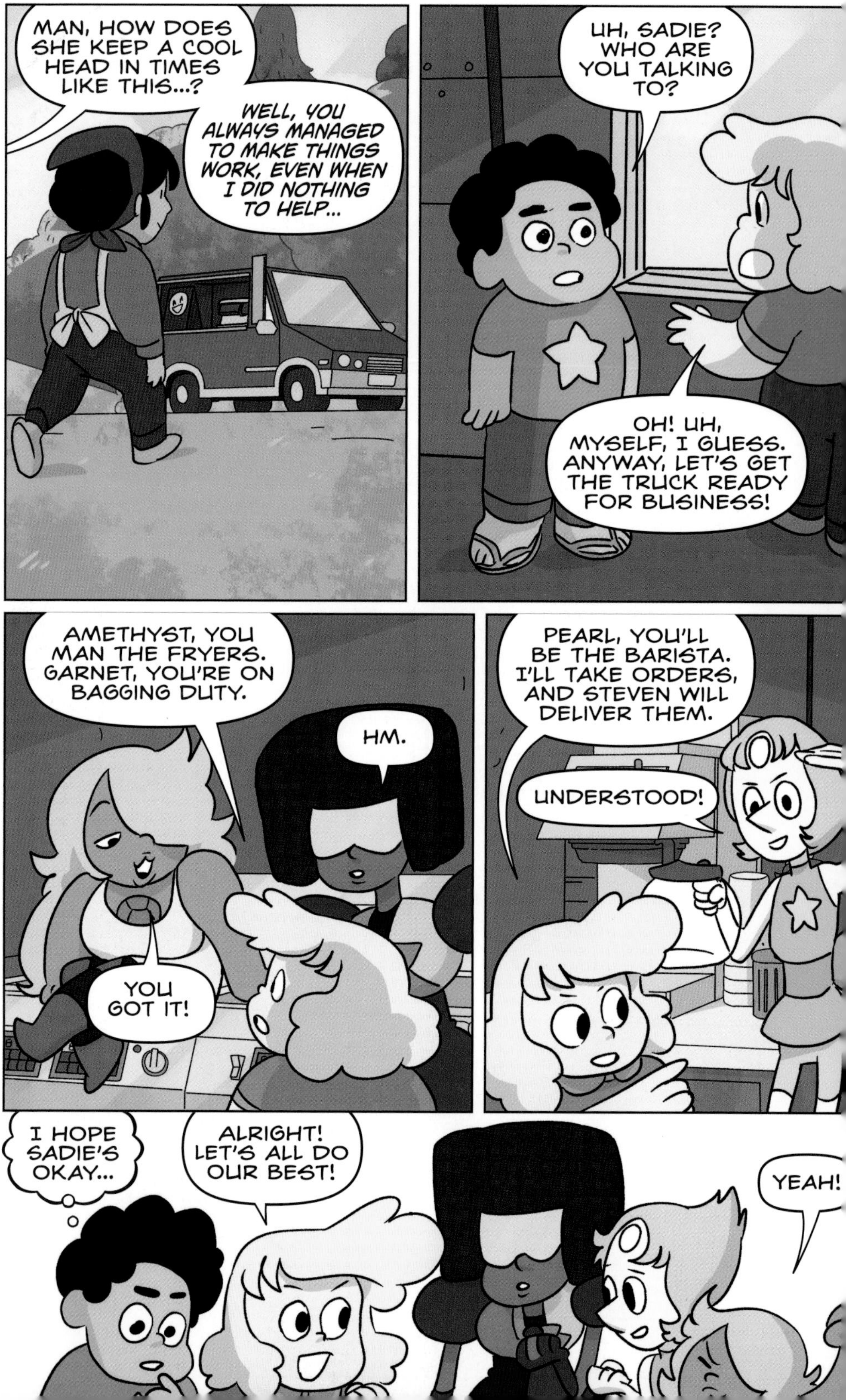
MAN, HOW DOES SHE KEEP A COOL HEAD IN TIMES LIKE THIS...?
WELL, YOU ALWAYS MANAGED TO MAKE THINGS WORK, EVEN WHEN I DID NOTHING TO HELP...
UH, SADIE? WHO ARE YOU TALKING TO?
OH! UH, MYSELF, I GUESS. ANYWAY, LET'S GET THE TRUCK READY FOR BUSINESS!
AMETHYST, YOU MAN THE FRYERS. GARNET, YOU'RE ON BAGGING DUTY.
HM.
YOU GOT IT!
PEARL, YOU'LL BE THE BARISTA. I'LL TAKE ORDERS, AND STEVEN WILL DELIVER THEM.
UNDERSTOOD!
I HOPE SADIE'S OKAY...
ALRIGHT! LET'S ALL DO OUR BEST!
YEAH!

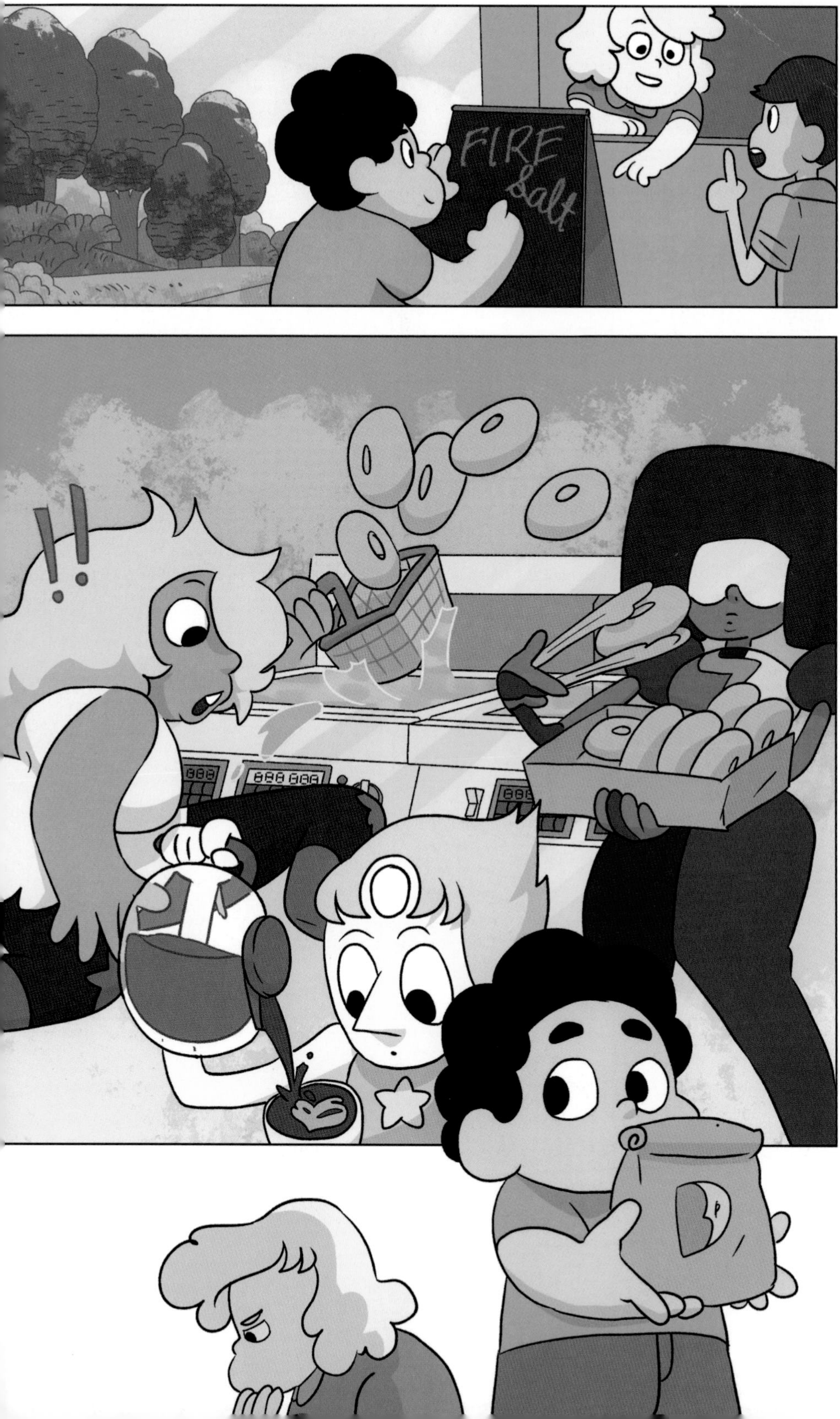
FIRE Salt

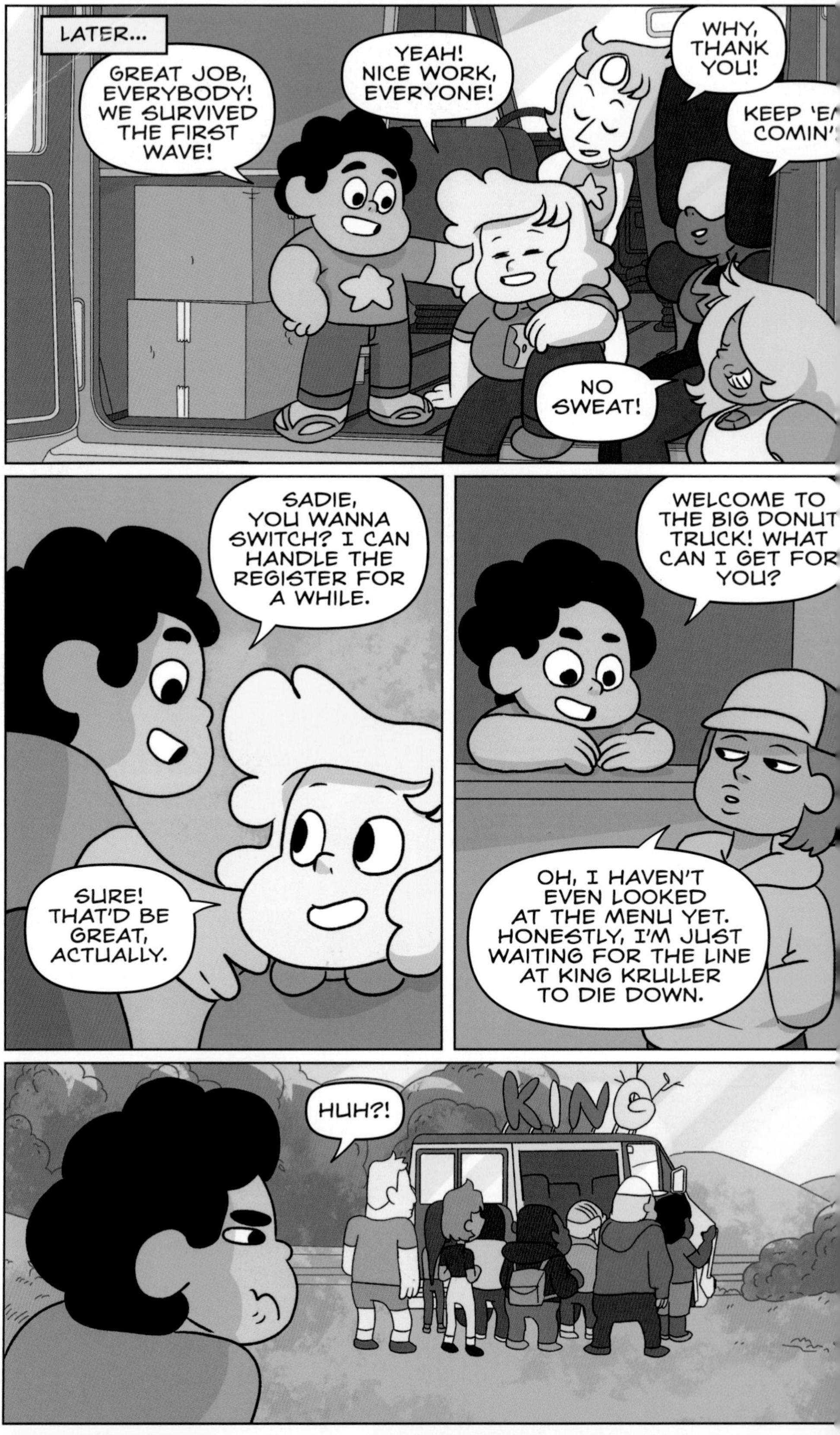
LATER...
GREAT JOB, EVERYBODY! WE SURVIVED THE FIRST WAVE!
YEAH! NICE WORK, EVERYONE!
WHY, THANK YOU!
KEEP 'E
COMIN'
NO SWEAT!
SADIE, YOU WANNA SWITCH? I CAN HANDLE THE REGISTER FOR A WHILE.
SURE! THAT'D BE GREAT, ACTUALLY.
WELCOME TO THE BIG DONUT TRUCK! WHAT CAN I GET FOR YOU?
OH, I HAVEN'T EVEN LOOKED AT THE MENU YET. HONESTLY, I'M JUST WAITING FOR THE LINE AT KING KRULLER TO DIE DOWN.
HUH?!
KING

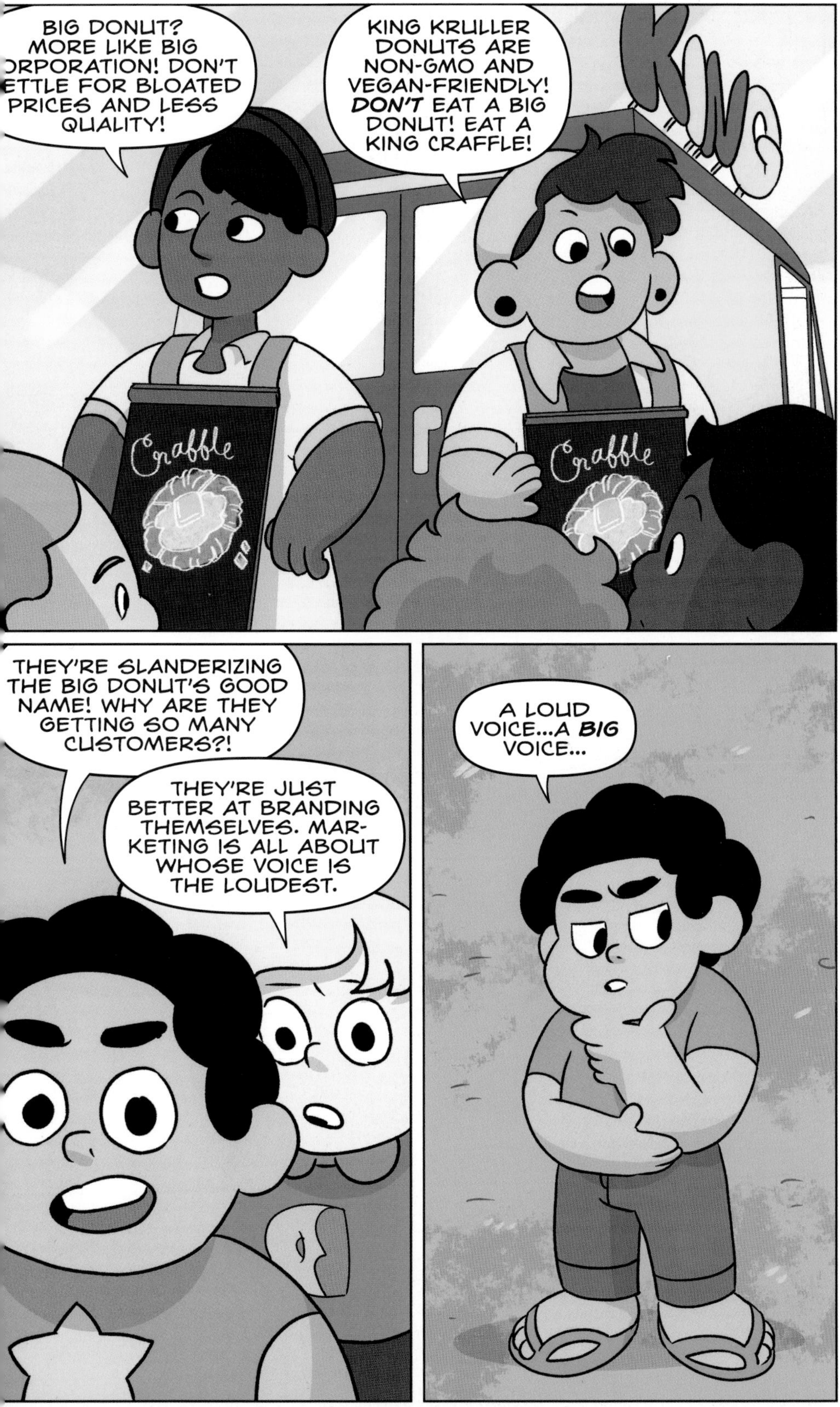
BIG DONUT? MORE LIKE BIG RPORATION! DON'T TTLE FOR BLOATED PRICES AND LESS QUALITY!
KING KRULLER DONUTS ARE NON-GMO AND VEGAN-FRIENDLY! ***DON'T*** EAT A BIG DONUT! EAT A KING CRAFFLE!
KING
Craffle
Craffle
THEY'RE SLANDERIZING THE BIG DONUT'S GOOD NAME! WHY ARE THEY GETTING SO MANY CUSTOMERS?!
THEY'RE JUST BETTER AT BRANDING THEMSELVES. MAR-KETING IS ALL ABOUT WHOSE VOICE IS THE LOUDEST.
A LOUD VOICE...A ***BIG*** VOICE...

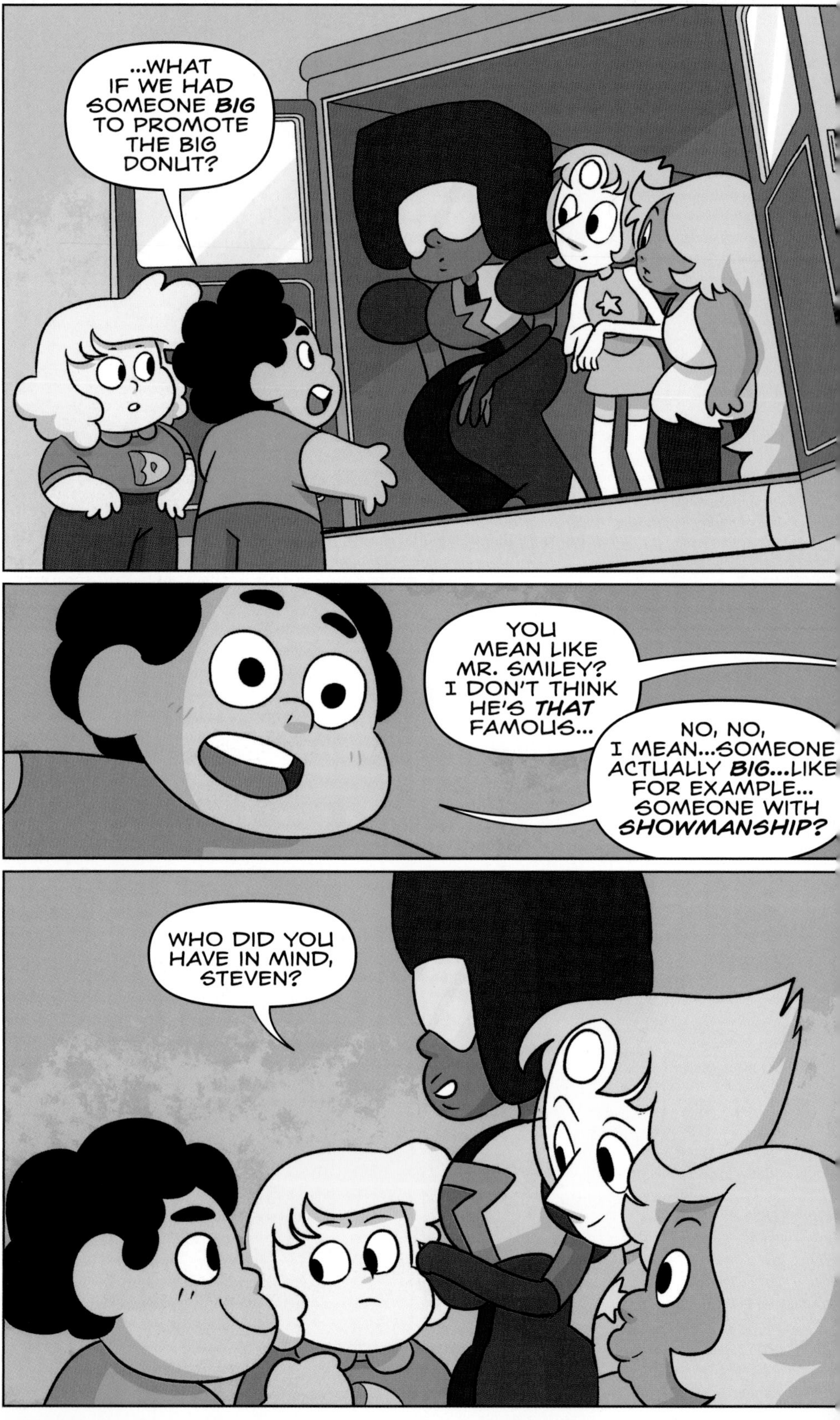
...WHAT IF WE HAD SOMEONE BIG TO PROMOTE THE BIG DONUT?
YOU MEAN LIKE MR. SMILEY? I DON'T THINK HE'S THAT FAMOUS...
NO, NO, I MEAN...SOMEONE ACTUALLY BIG...LIKE FOR EXAMPLE... SOMEONE WITH SHOWMANSHIP?
WHO DID YOU HAVE IN MIND, STEVEN?

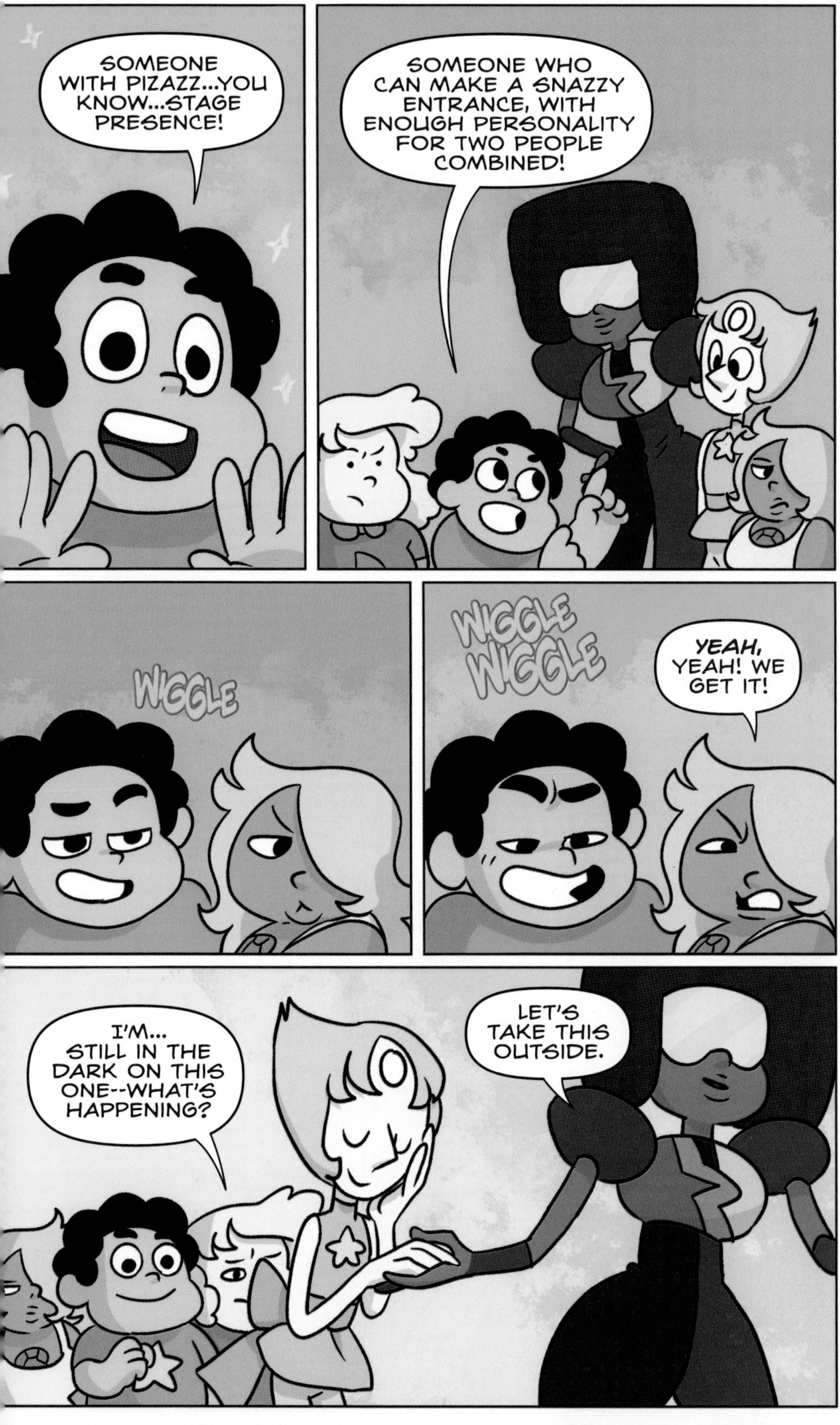
SOMEONE WITH PIZAZZ...YOU KNOW...STAGE PRESENCE!
SOMEONE WHO CAN MAKE A SNAZZY ENTRANCE, WITH ENOUGH PERSONALITY FOR TWO PEOPLE COMBINED!
WIGGLE
WIGGLE WIGGLE
YEAH, YEAH! WE GET IT!
I'M... STILL IN THE DARK ON THIS ONE--WHAT'S HAPPENING?
LET'S TAKE THIS OUTSIDE.

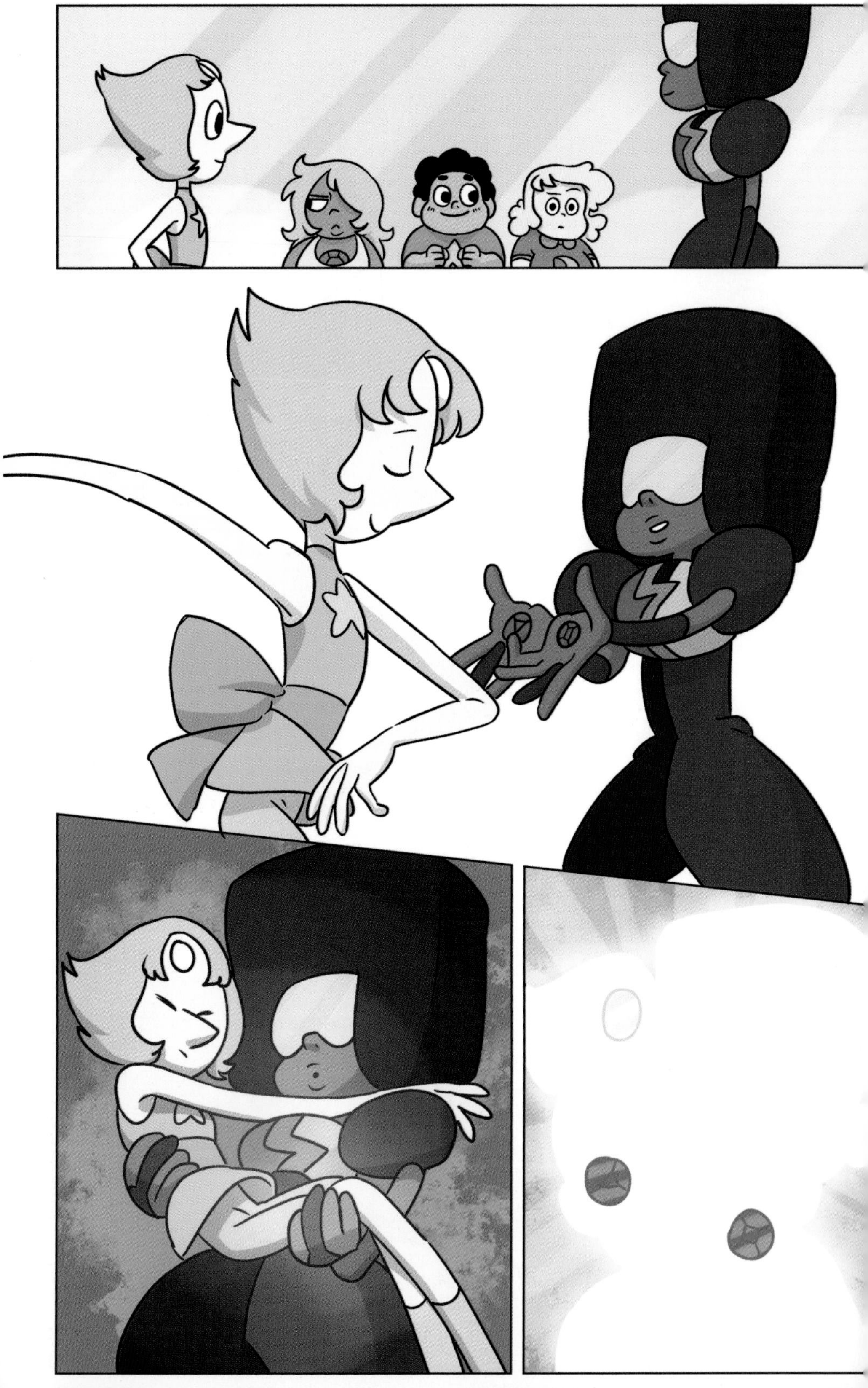

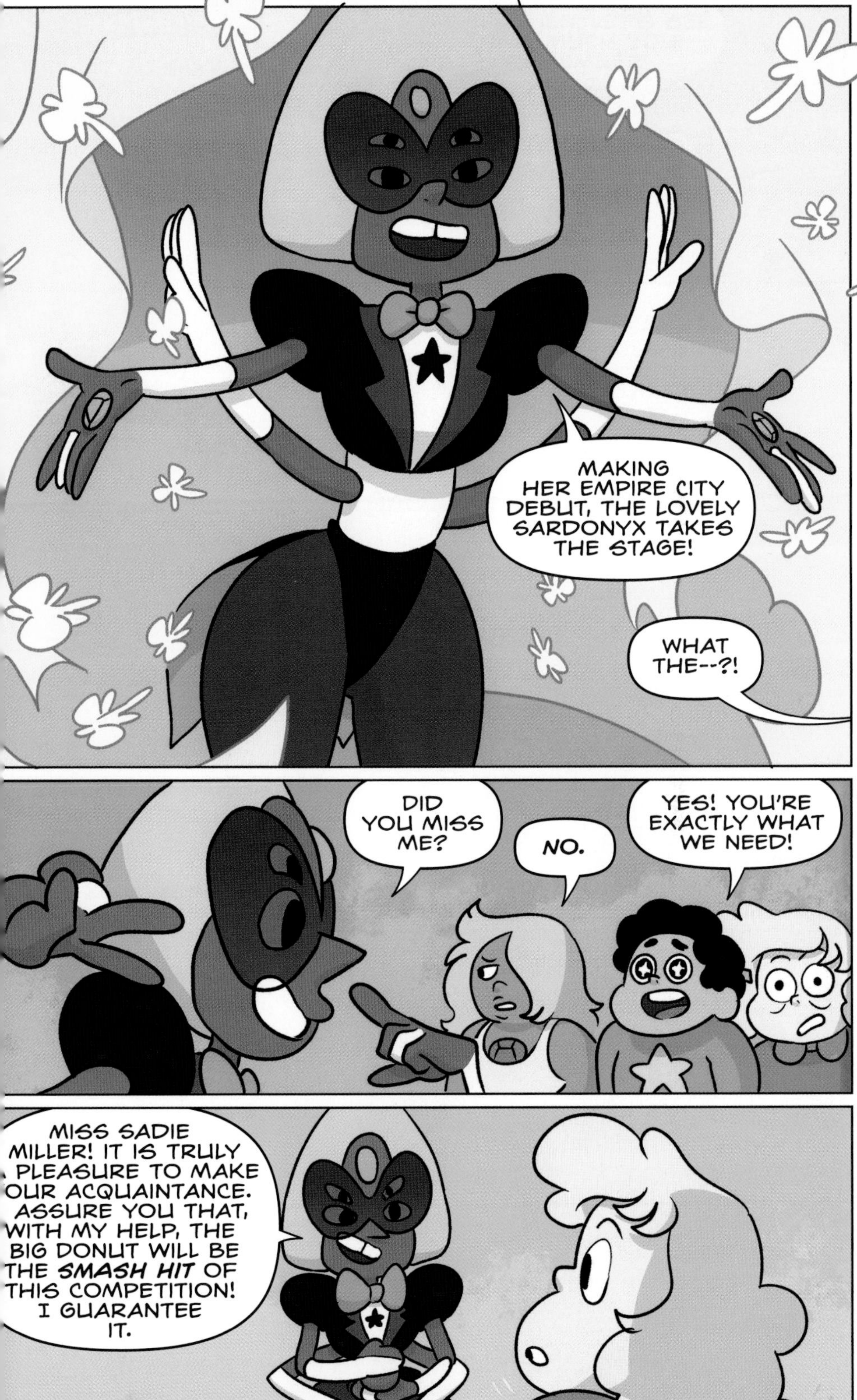
MAKING HER EMPIRE CITY DEBUT, THE LOVELY SARDONYX TAKES THE STAGE!
WHAT THE--?!
DID YOU MISS ME?
NO.
YES! YOU'RE EXACTLY WHAT WE NEED!
MISS SADIE MILLER! IT IS TRULY PLEASURE TO MAKE OUR ACQUAINTANCE. ASSURE YOU THAT, WITH MY HELP, THE BIG DONUT WILL BE THE *SMASH HIT* OF THIS COMPETITION! I GUARANTEE IT.

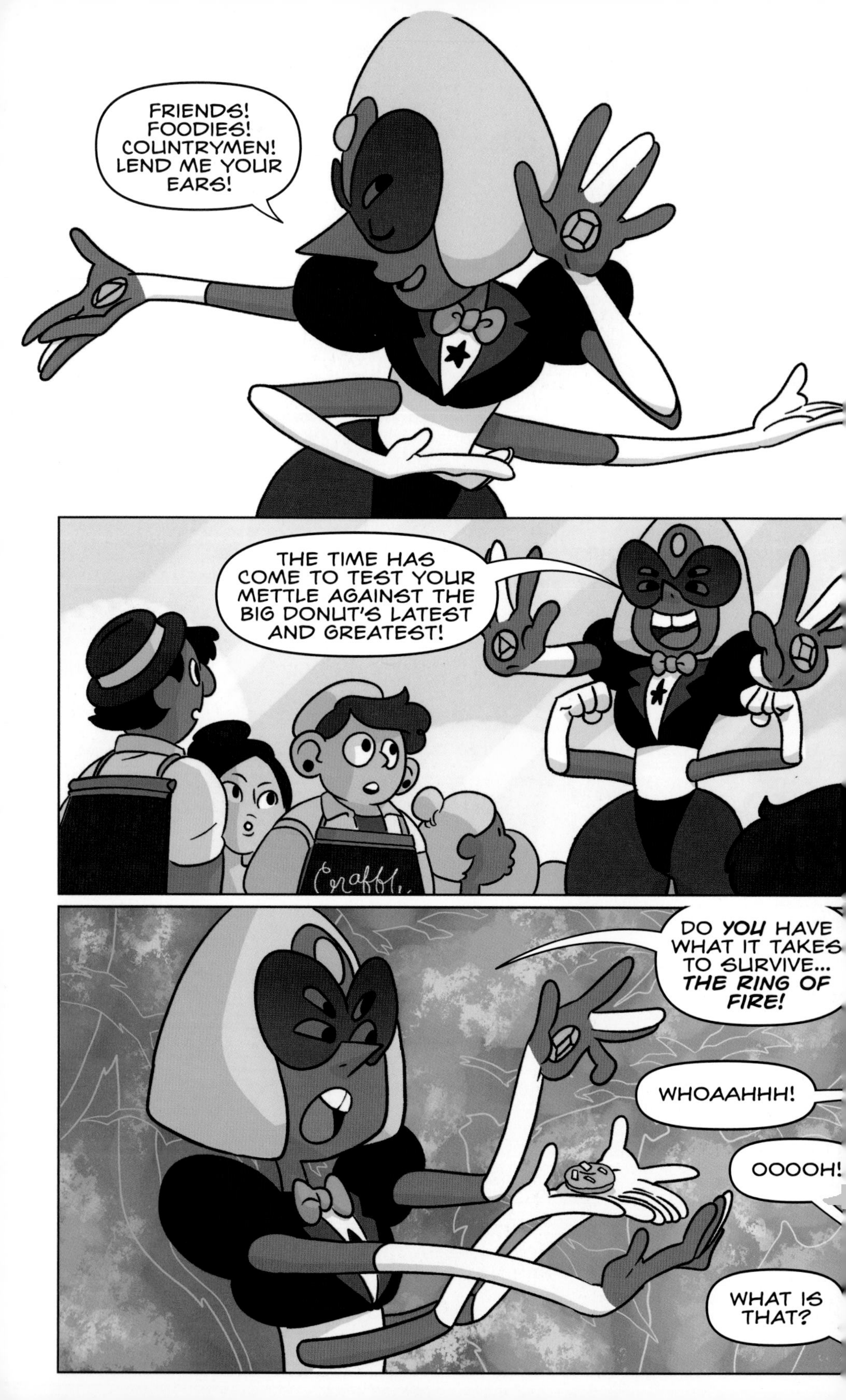
FRIENDS! FOODIES! COUNTRYMEN! LEND ME YOUR EARS!
THE TIME HAS COME TO TEST YOUR METTLE AGAINST THE BIG DONUT'S LATEST AND GREATEST!
DO YOU HAVE WHAT IT TAKES TO SURVIVE... THE RING OF FIRE!
WHOAAHHH!
OOOOH!
WHAT IS THAT?

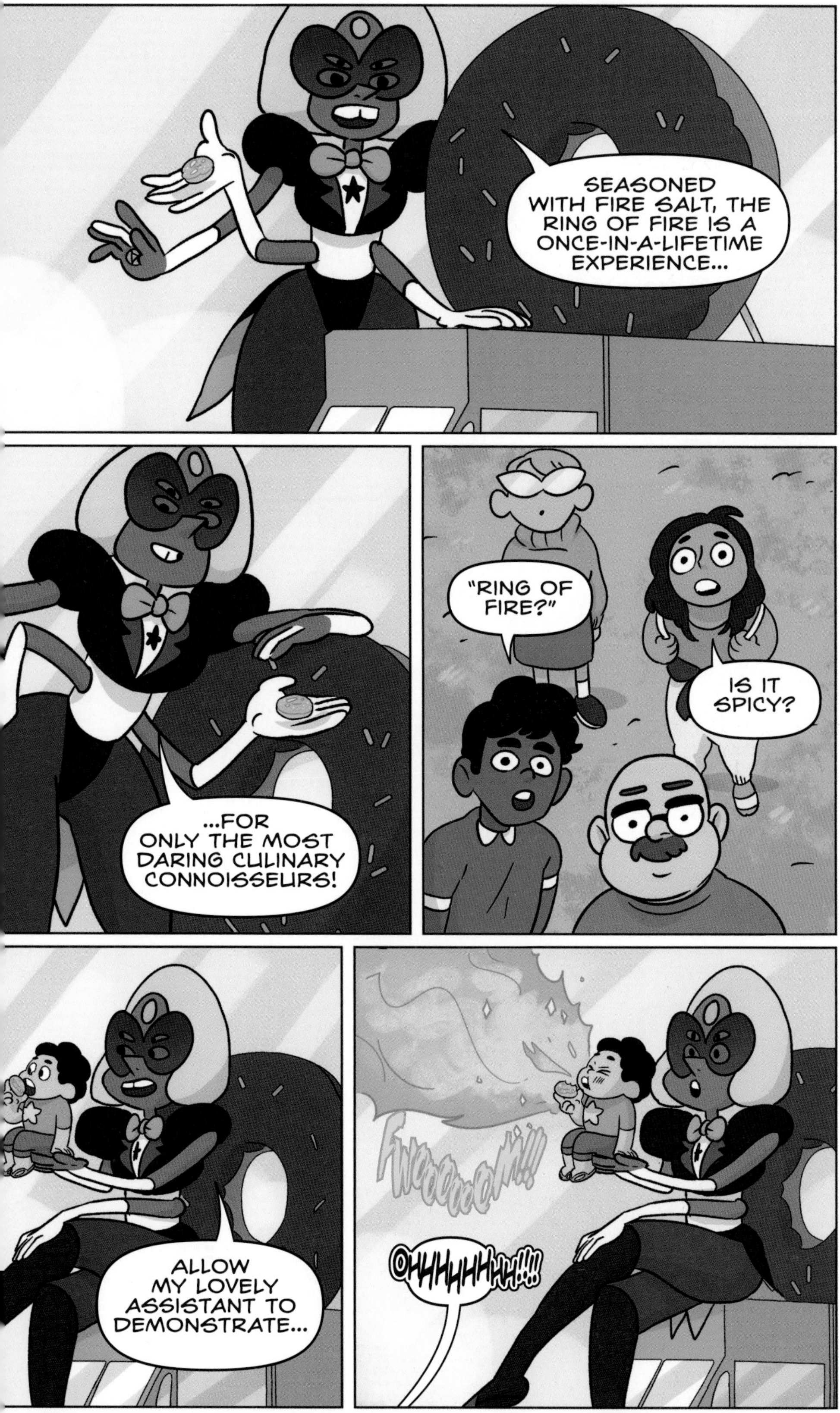
SEASONED WITH FIRE SALT, THE RING OF FIRE IS A ONCE-IN-A-LIFETIME EXPERIENCE...
...FOR ONLY THE MOST DARING CULINARY CONNOISSEURS!
"RING OF FIRE?"
IS IT SPICY?
ALLOW MY LOVELY ASSISTANT TO DEMONSTRATE...
FWOOOOOOM!!!
OHHHHHHHH!!!

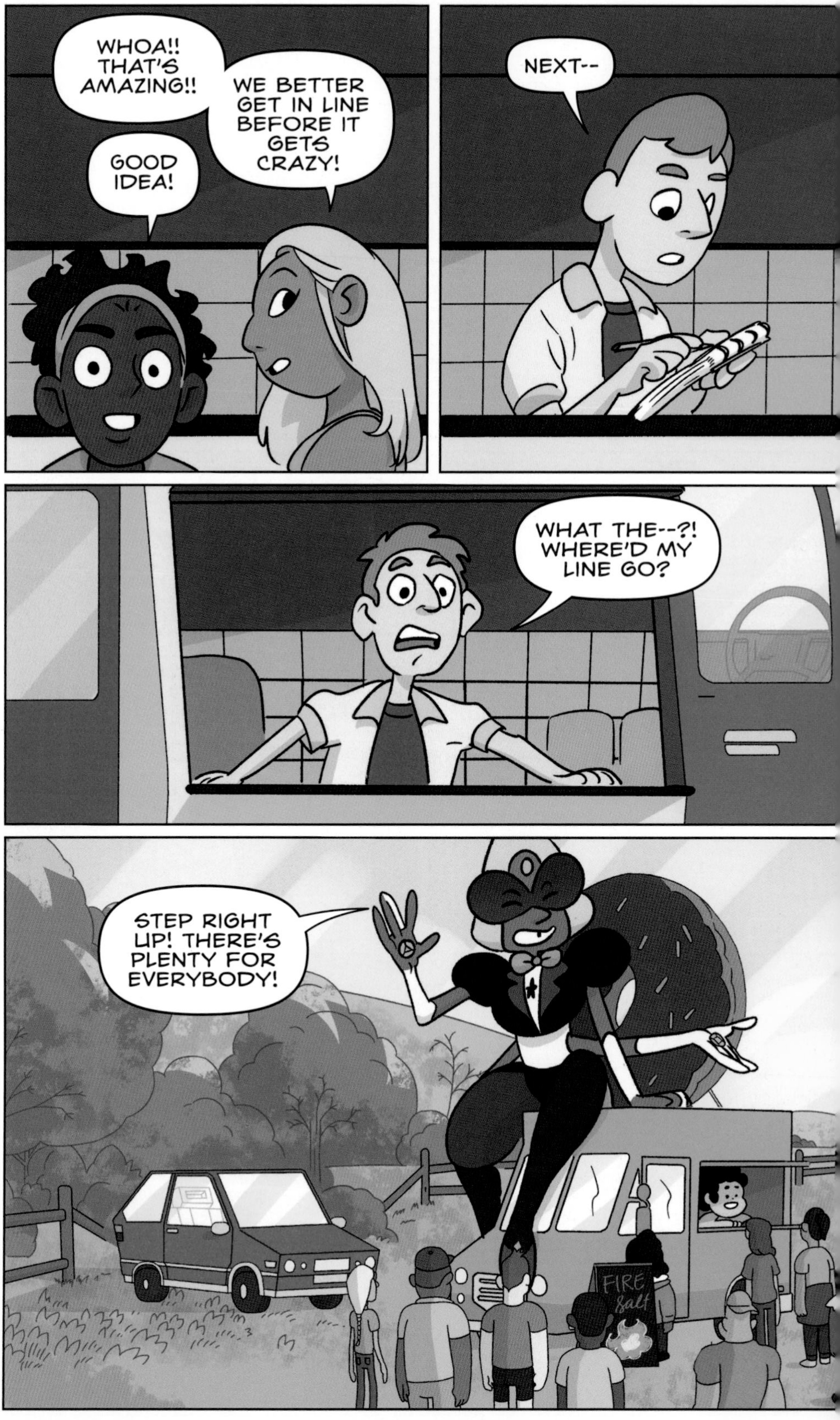
WHOA!! THAT'S AMAZING!!
WE BETTER GET IN LINE BEFORE IT GETS CRAZY!
GOOD IDEA!
NEXT--
WHAT THE--?! WHERE'D MY LINE GO?
STEP RIGHT UP! THERE'S PLENTY FOR EVERYBODY!
FIRE Salt

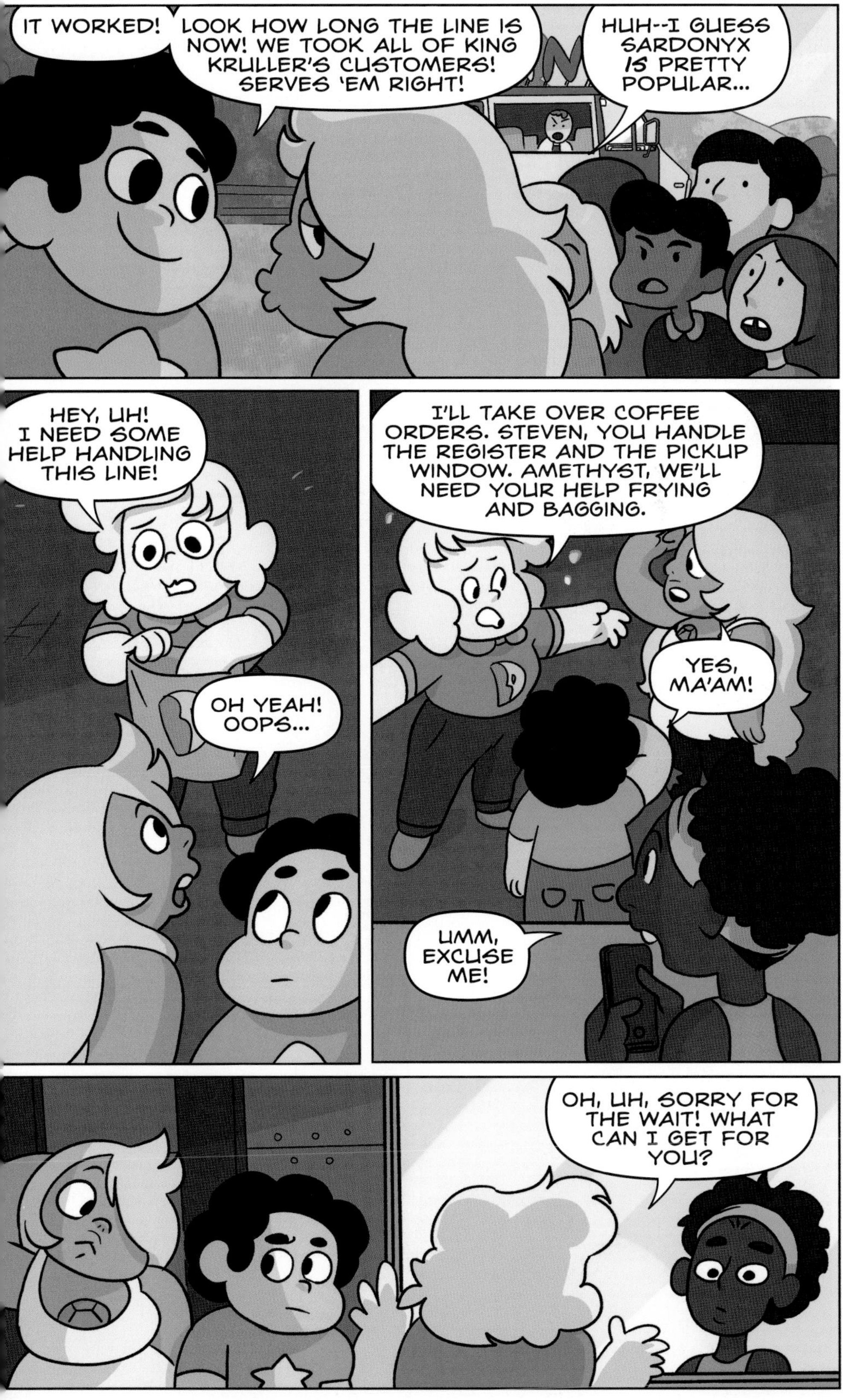
IT WORKED!
LOOK HOW LONG THE LINE IS NOW! WE TOOK ALL OF KING KRULLER'S CUSTOMERS! SERVES 'EM RIGHT!
HUH--I GUESS SARDONYX *IS* PRETTY POPULAR...
HEY, UH! I NEED SOME HELP HANDLING THIS LINE!
OH YEAH! OOPS...
I'LL TAKE OVER COFFEE ORDERS. STEVEN, YOU HANDLE THE REGISTER AND THE PICKUP WINDOW. AMETHYST, WE'LL NEED YOUR HELP FRYING AND BAGGING.
YES, MA'AM!
UMM, EXCUSE ME!
OH, UH, SORRY FOR THE WAIT! WHAT CAN I GET FOR YOU?

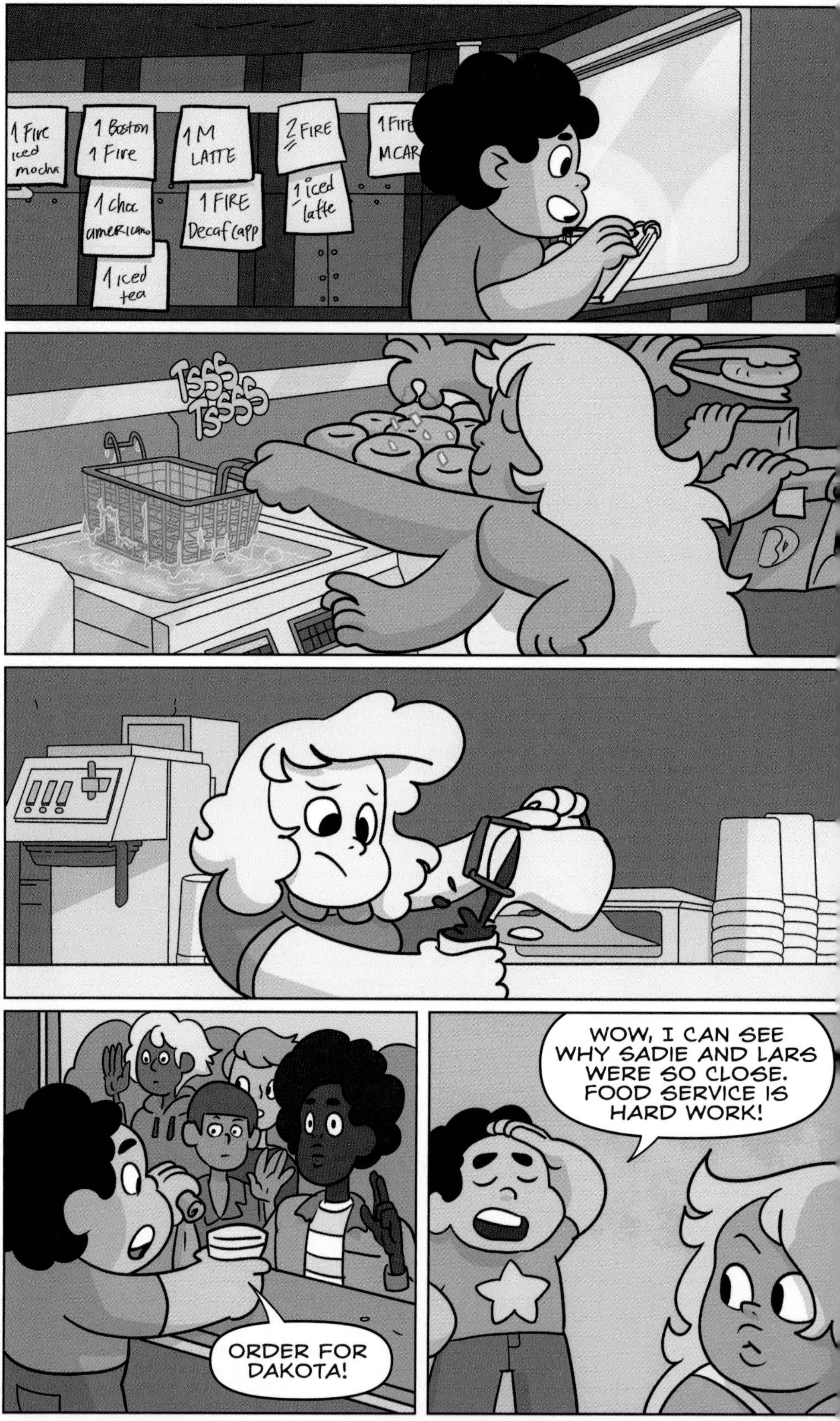
1 Fire iced mocha
1 Boston 1 Fire
1 M LATTE
2 FIRE
1 Fire MCAR
1 choc americano
1 FIRE Decaf Capp
1 iced latte
1 iced tea
TSSS TSSSS
ORDER FOR DAKOTA!
WOW, I CAN SEE WHY SADIE AND LARS WERE SO CLOSE. FOOD SERVICE IS HARD WORK!

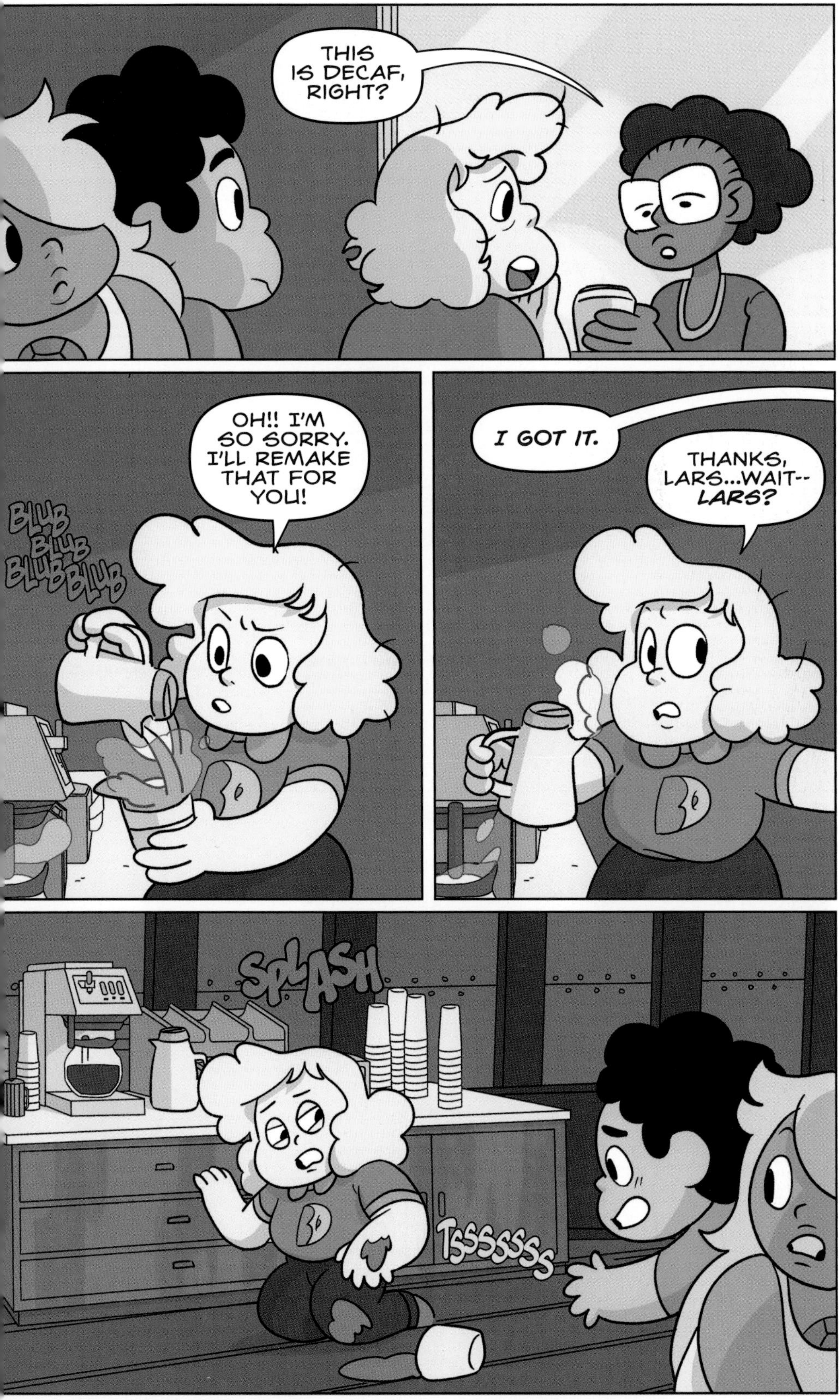
THIS IS DECAF, RIGHT?
OH!! I'M SO SORRY. I'LL REMAKE THAT FOR YOU!
BLUB BLUB BLUB BLUB
I GOT IT.
THANKS, LARS...WAIT-- LARS?
SPLASH
TSSSSSSS

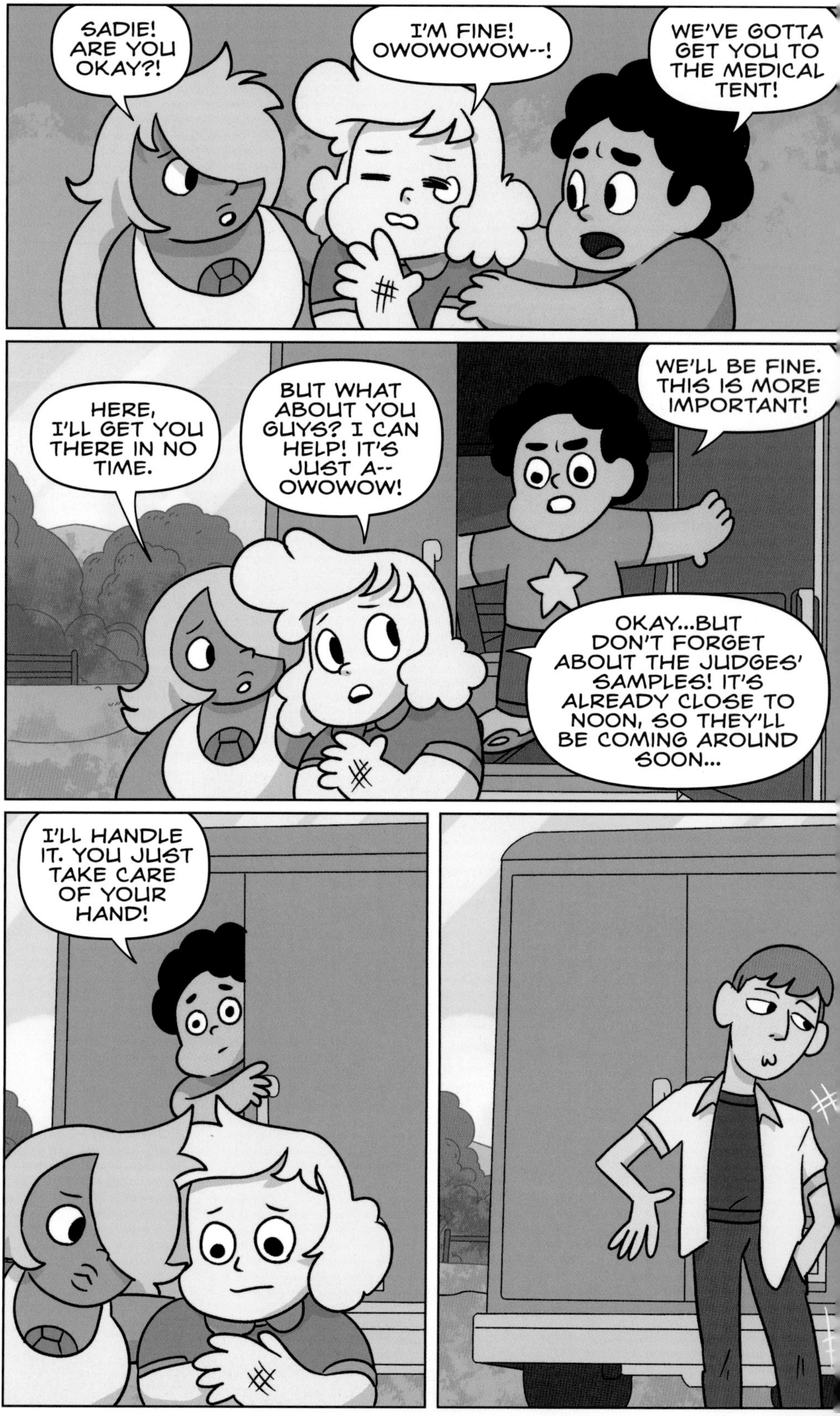
SADIE! ARE YOU OKAY?!
I'M FINE! OWOWOWOW--!
WE'VE GOTTA GET YOU TO THE MEDICAL TENT!
HERE, I'LL GET YOU THERE IN NO TIME.
BUT WHAT ABOUT YOU GUYS? I CAN HELP! IT'S JUST A-- OWOWOW!
WE'LL BE FINE. THIS IS MORE IMPORTANT!
OKAY...BUT DON'T FORGET ABOUT THE JUDGES' SAMPLES! IT'S ALREADY CLOSE TO NOON, SO THEY'LL BE COMING AROUND SOON...
I'LL HANDLE IT. YOU JUST TAKE CARE OF YOUR HAND!

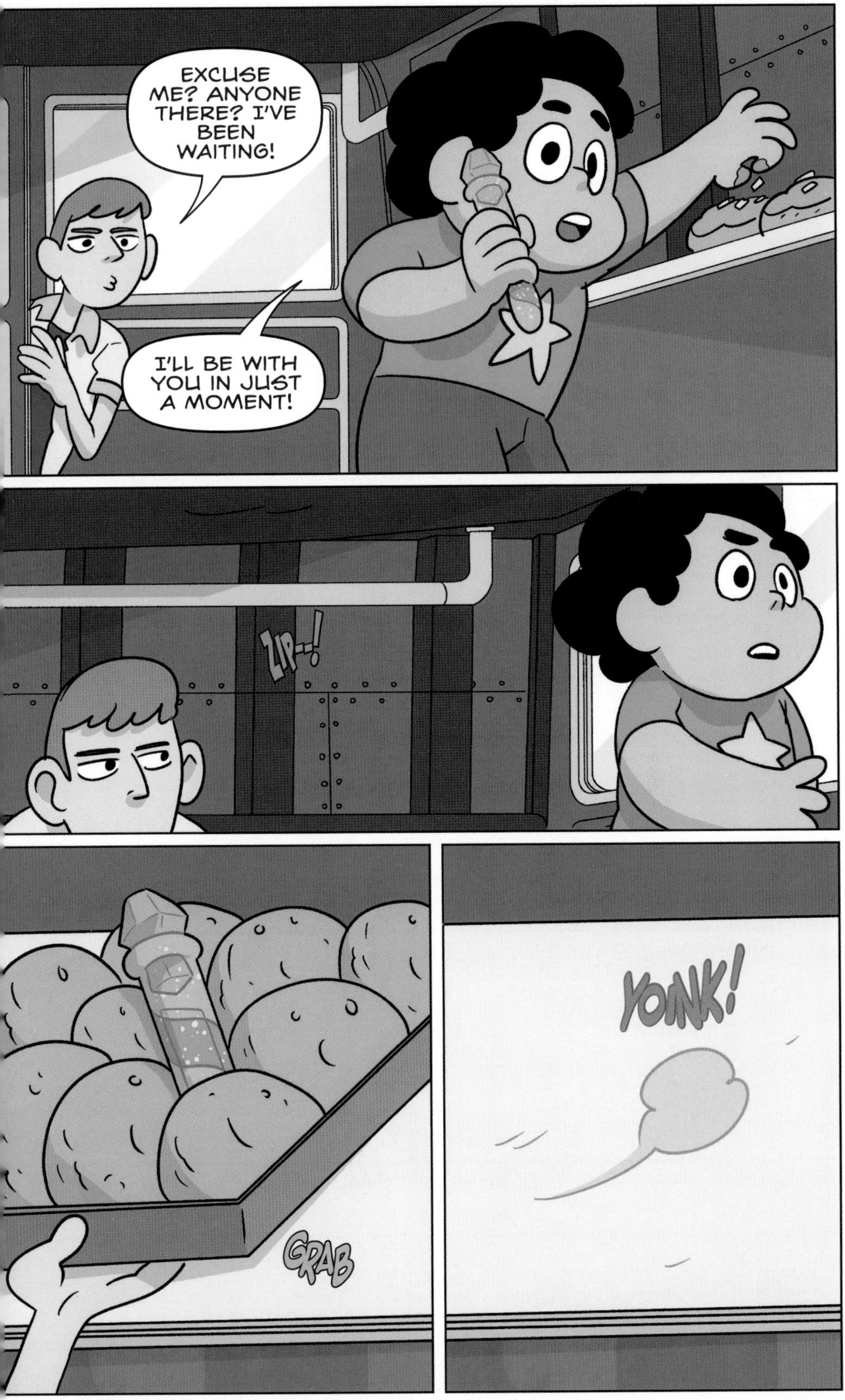
EXCUSE ME? ANYONE THERE? I'VE BEEN WAITING!
I'LL BE WITH YOU IN JUST A MOMENT!
ZIP--!
GRAB
YOINK!

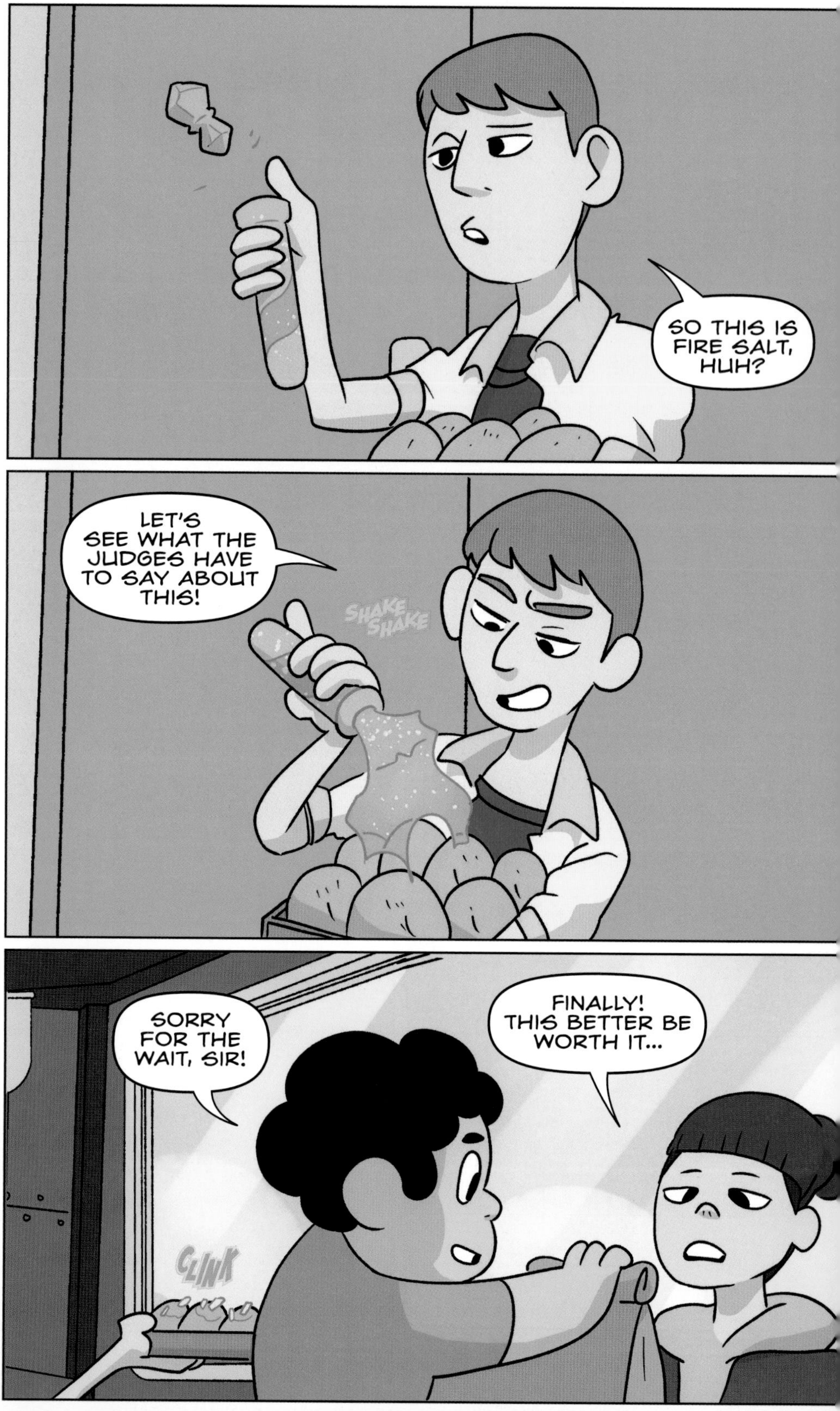
SO THIS IS FIRE SALT, HUH?
LET'S SEE WHAT THE JUDGES HAVE TO SAY ABOUT THIS!
SHAKE SHAKE
SORRY FOR THE WAIT, SIR!
FINALLY! THIS BETTER BE WORTH IT...
CLINK

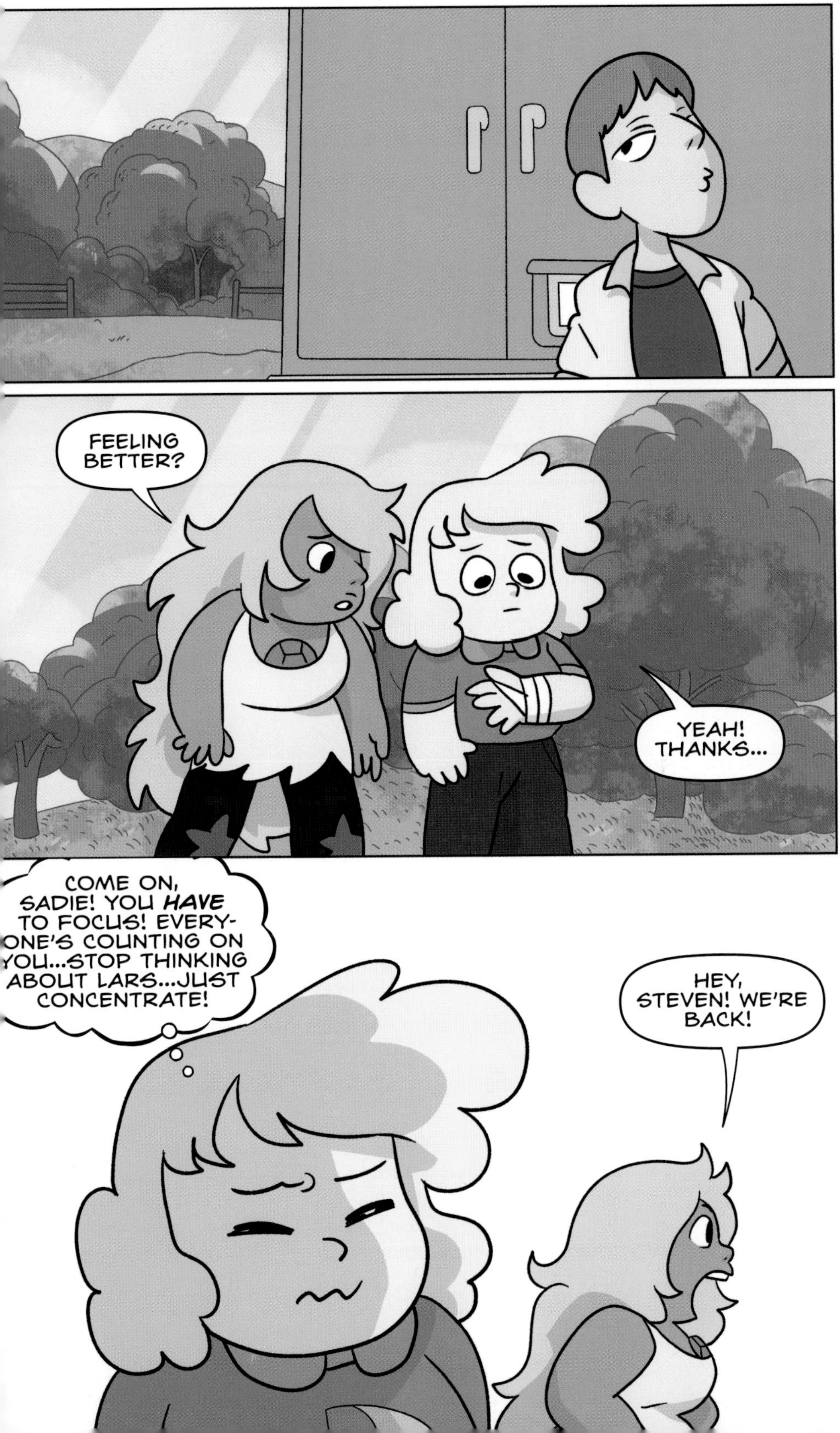
FEELING BETTER?
YEAH! THANKS...
COME ON, SADIE! YOU *HAVE* TO FOCUS! EVERY-ONE'S COUNTING ON YOU...STOP THINKING ABOUT LARS...JUST CONCENTRATE!
HEY, STEVEN! WE'RE BACK!

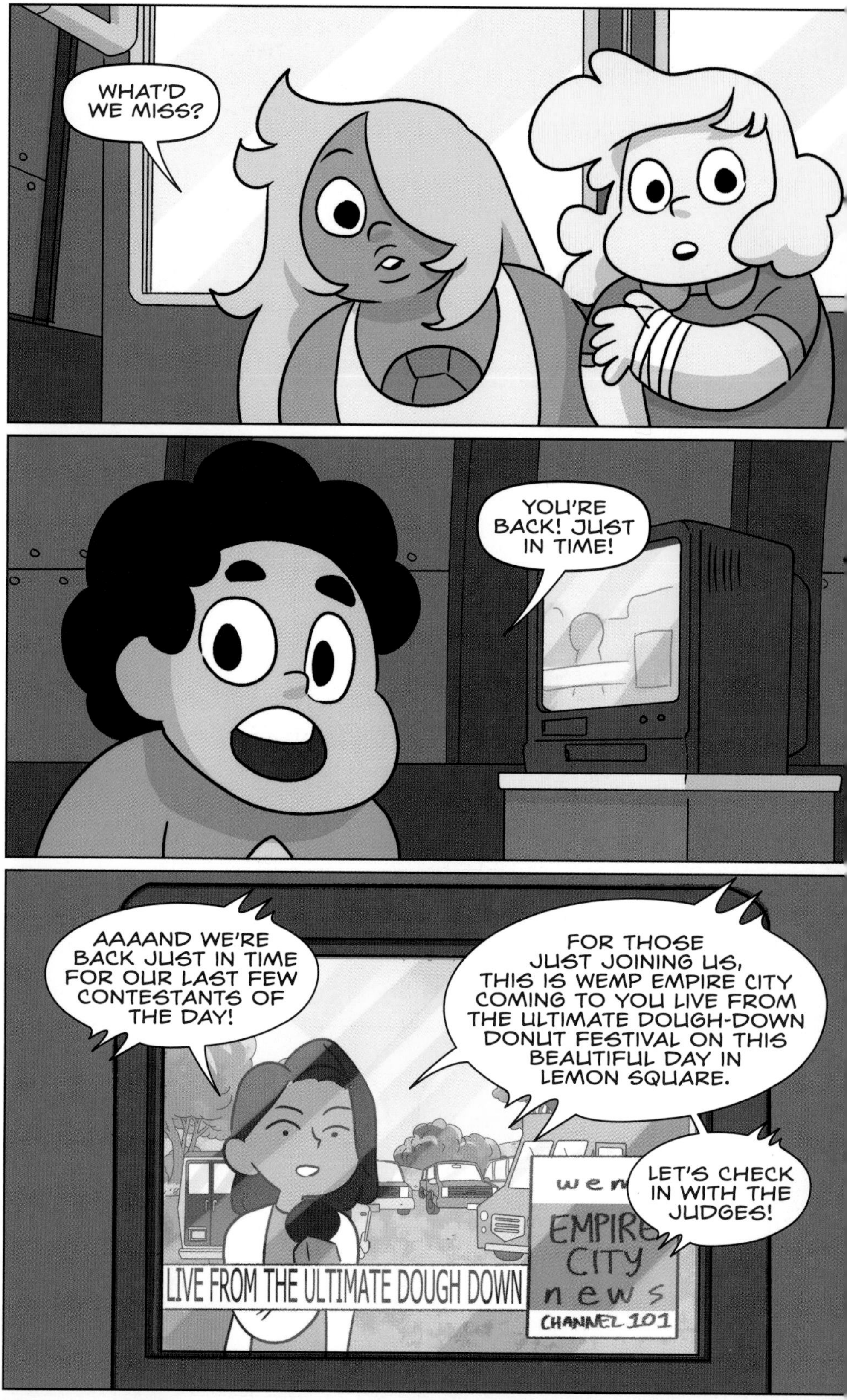
WHAT'D WE MISS?
YOU'RE BACK! JUST IN TIME!
AAAAND WE'RE BACK JUST IN TIME FOR OUR LAST FEW CONTESTANTS OF THE DAY!
FOR THOSE JUST JOINING US, THIS IS WEMP EMPIRE CITY COMING TO YOU LIVE FROM THE ULTIMATE DOUGH-DOWN DONUT FESTIVAL ON THIS BEAUTIFUL DAY IN LEMON SQUARE.
LET'S CHECK IN WITH THE JUDGES!
LIVE FROM THE ULTIMATE DOUGH DOWN
EMPIRE CITY news
CHANNEL 101

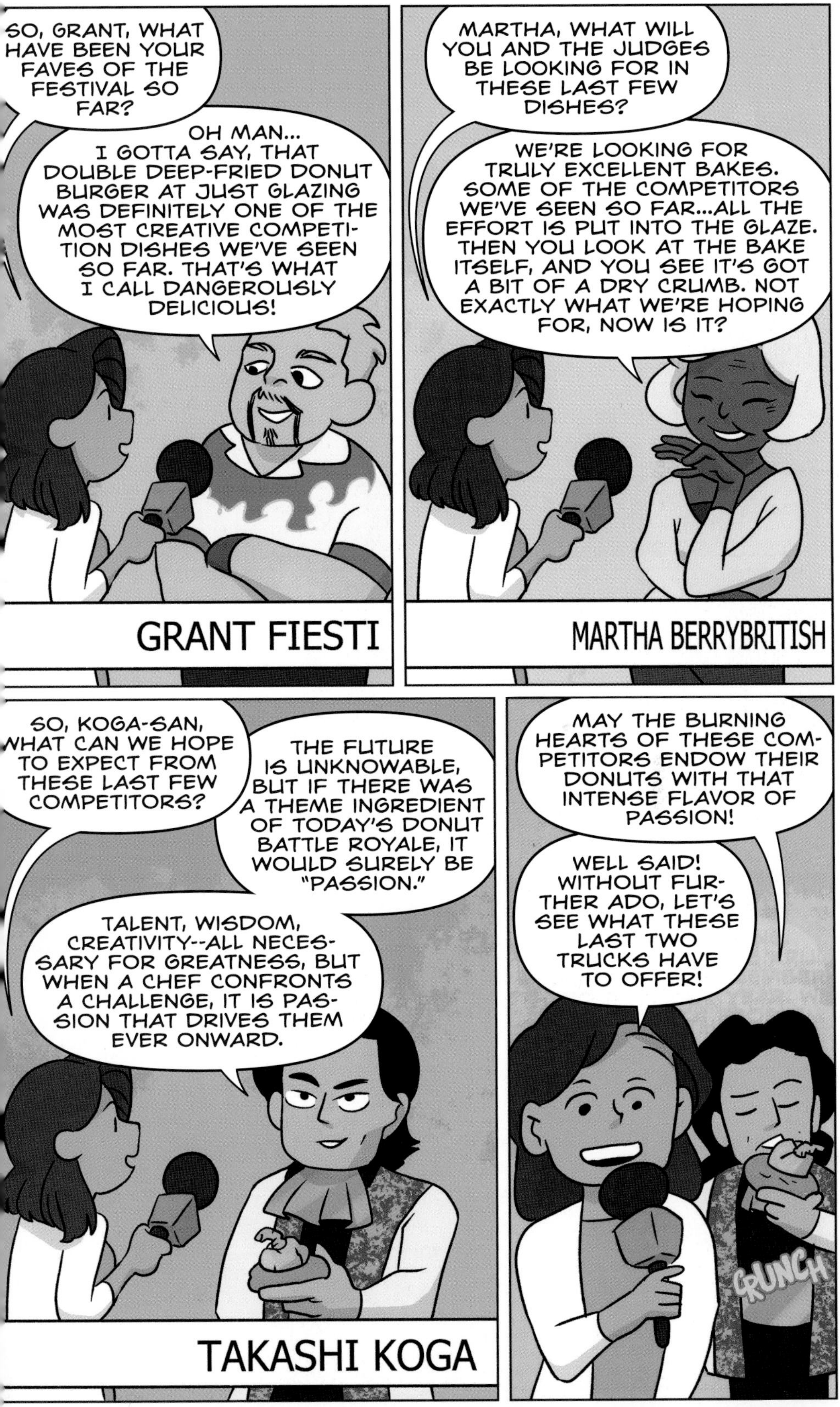
SO, GRANT, WHAT HAVE BEEN YOUR FAVES OF THE FESTIVAL SO FAR?
OH MAN... I GOTTA SAY, THAT DOUBLE DEEP-FRIED DONUT BURGER AT JUST GLAZING WAS DEFINITELY ONE OF THE MOST CREATIVE COMPETITION DISHES WE'VE SEEN SO FAR. THAT'S WHAT I CALL DANGEROUSLY DELICIOUS!
GRANT FIESTI
MARTHA, WHAT WILL YOU AND THE JUDGES BE LOOKING FOR IN THESE LAST FEW DISHES?
WE'RE LOOKING FOR TRULY EXCELLENT BAKES. SOME OF THE COMPETITORS WE'VE SEEN SO FAR...ALL THE EFFORT IS PUT INTO THE GLAZE. THEN YOU LOOK AT THE BAKE ITSELF, AND YOU SEE IT'S GOT A BIT OF A DRY CRUMB. NOT EXACTLY WHAT WE'RE HOPING FOR, NOW IS IT?
MARTHA BERRYBRITISH
SO, KOGA-SAN, WHAT CAN WE HOPE TO EXPECT FROM THESE LAST FEW COMPETITORS?
THE FUTURE IS UNKNOWABLE, BUT IF THERE WAS A THEME INGREDIENT OF TODAY'S DONUT BATTLE ROYALE, IT WOULD SURELY BE "PASSION."
TALENT, WISDOM, CREATIVITY--ALL NECESSARY FOR GREATNESS, BUT WHEN A CHEF CONFRONTS A CHALLENGE, IT IS PASSION THAT DRIVES THEM EVER ONWARD.
TAKASHI KOGA
MAY THE BURNING HEARTS OF THESE COMPETITORS ENDOW THEIR DONUTS WITH THAT INTENSE FLAVOR OF PASSION!
WELL SAID! WITHOUT FURTHER ADO, LET'S SEE WHAT THESE LAST TWO TRUCKS HAVE TO OFFER!
CRUNCH

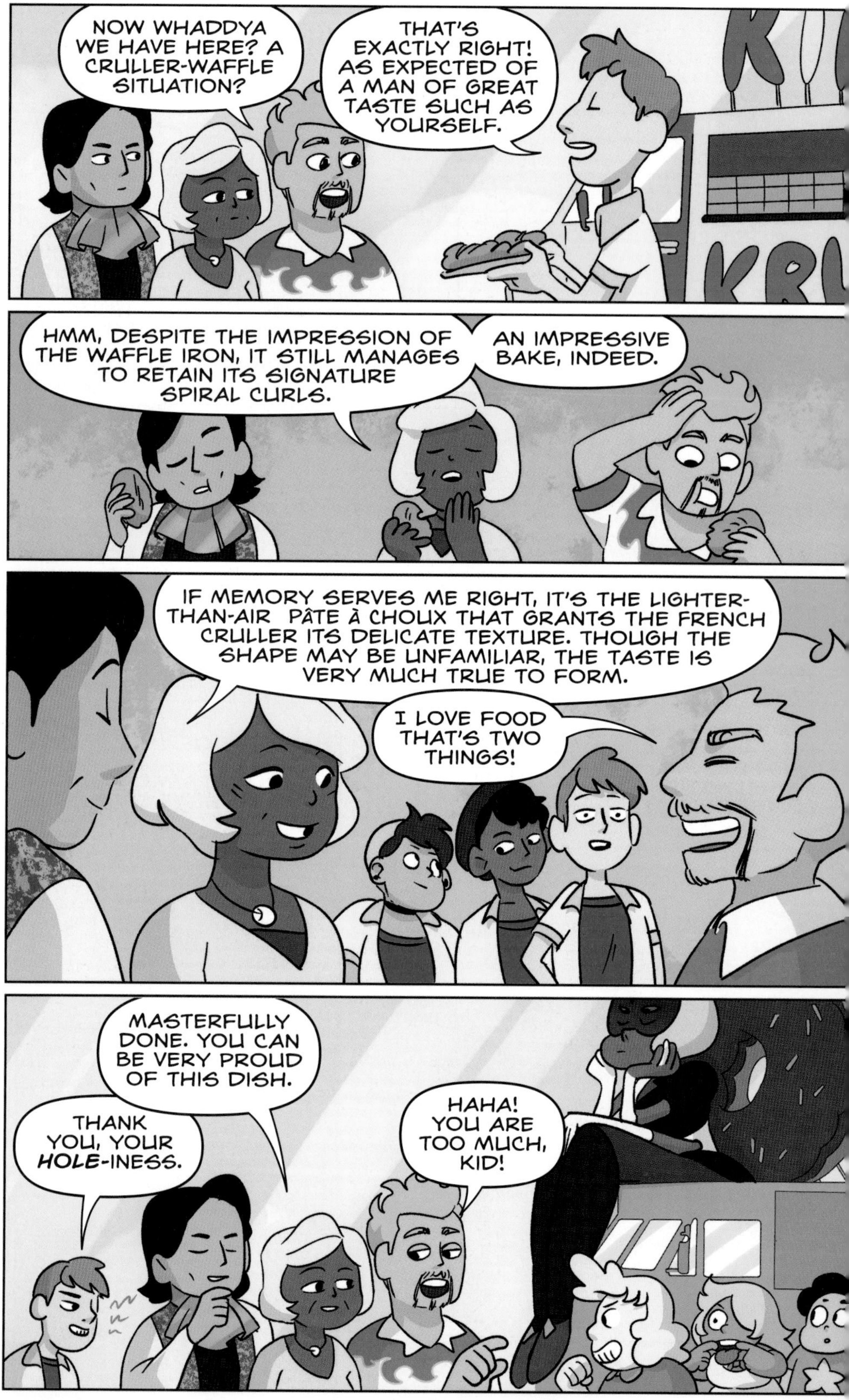
NOW WHADDYA WE HAVE HERE? A CRULLER-WAFFLE SITUATION?
THAT'S EXACTLY RIGHT! AS EXPECTED OF A MAN OF GREAT TASTE SUCH AS YOURSELF.
HMM, DESPITE THE IMPRESSION OF THE WAFFLE IRON, IT STILL MANAGES TO RETAIN ITS SIGNATURE SPIRAL CURLS.
AN IMPRESSIVE BAKE, INDEED.
IF MEMORY SERVES ME RIGHT, IT'S THE LIGHTER-THAN-AIR PÂTE À CHOUX THAT GRANTS THE FRENCH CRULLER ITS DELICATE TEXTURE. THOUGH THE SHAPE MAY BE UNFAMILIAR, THE TASTE IS VERY MUCH TRUE TO FORM.
I LOVE FOOD THAT'S TWO THINGS!
MASTERFULLY DONE. YOU CAN BE VERY PROUD OF THIS DISH.
THANK YOU, YOUR *HOLE*-INESS.
HAHA! YOU ARE TOO MUCH, KID!

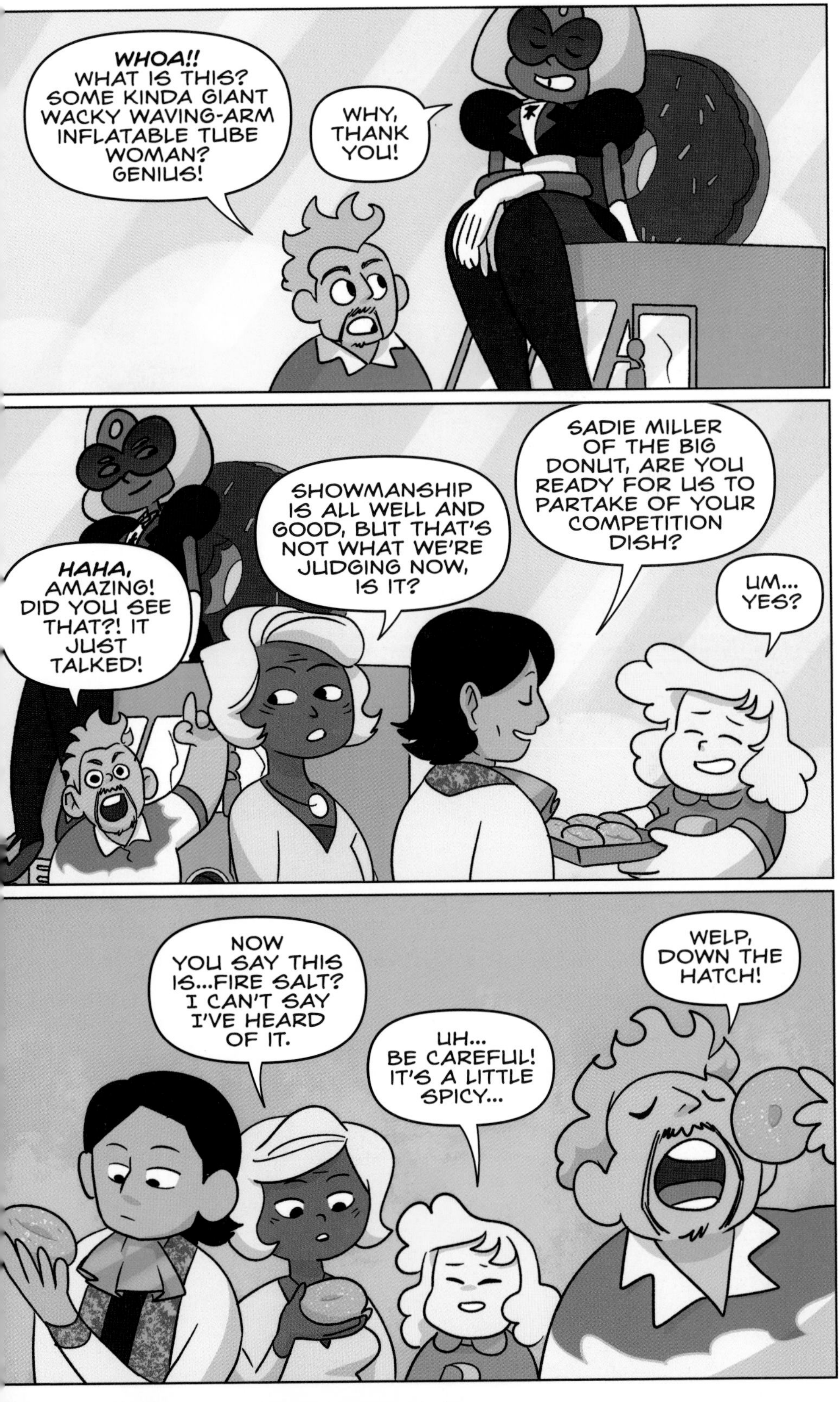
WHOA!! WHAT IS THIS? SOME KINDA GIANT WACKY WAVING-ARM INFLATABLE TUBE WOMAN? GENIUS!
WHY, THANK YOU!
HAHA, AMAZING! DID YOU SEE THAT?! IT JUST TALKED!
SHOWMANSHIP IS ALL WELL AND GOOD, BUT THAT'S NOT WHAT WE'RE JUDGING NOW, IS IT?
SADIE MILLER OF THE BIG DONUT, ARE YOU READY FOR US TO PARTAKE OF YOUR COMPETITION DISH?
UM... YES?
NOW YOU SAY THIS IS...FIRE SALT? I CAN'T SAY I'VE HEARD OF IT.
UH... BE CAREFUL! IT'S A LITTLE SPICY...
WELP, DOWN THE HATCH!

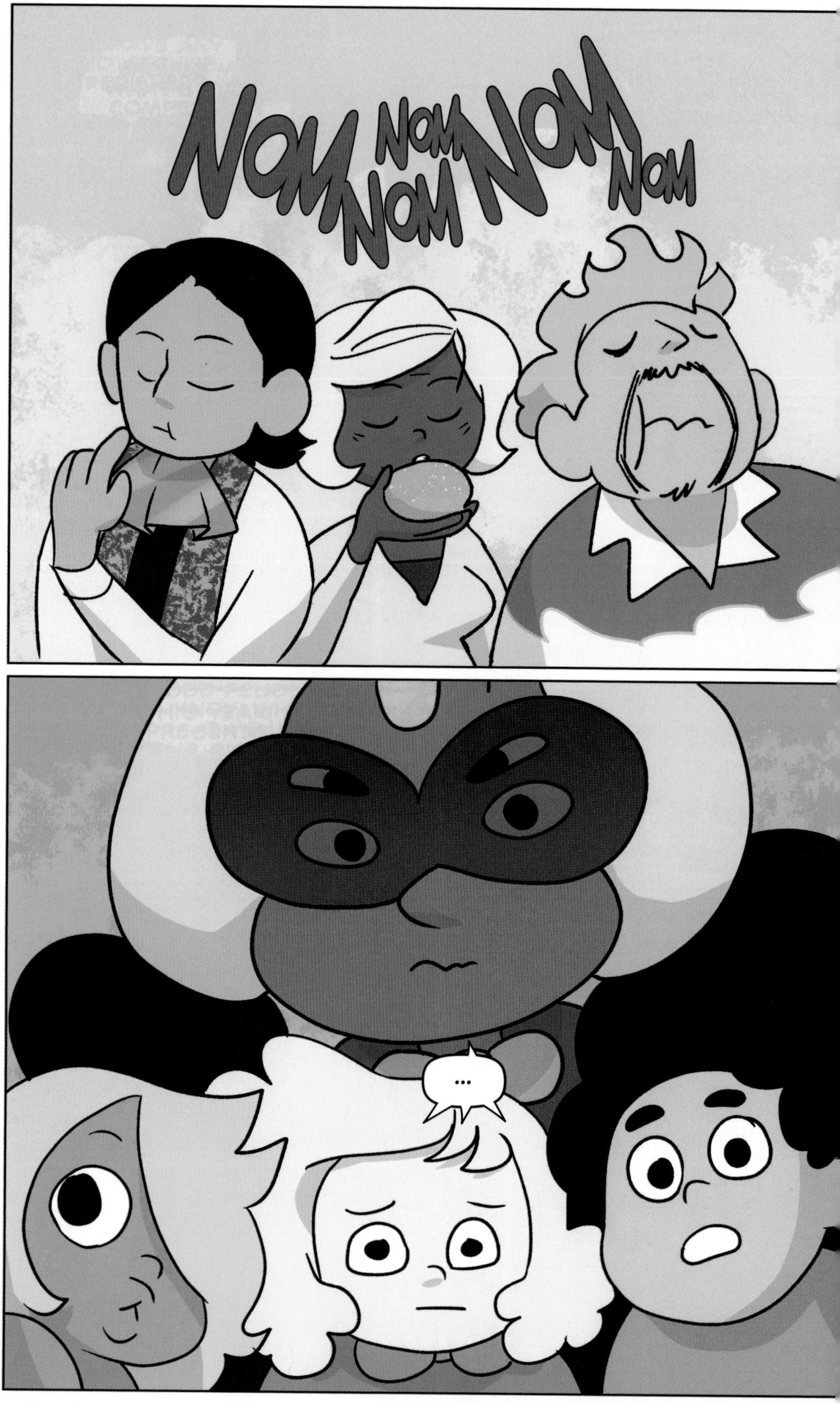
NOM NOM NOM NOM NOM NOM
...

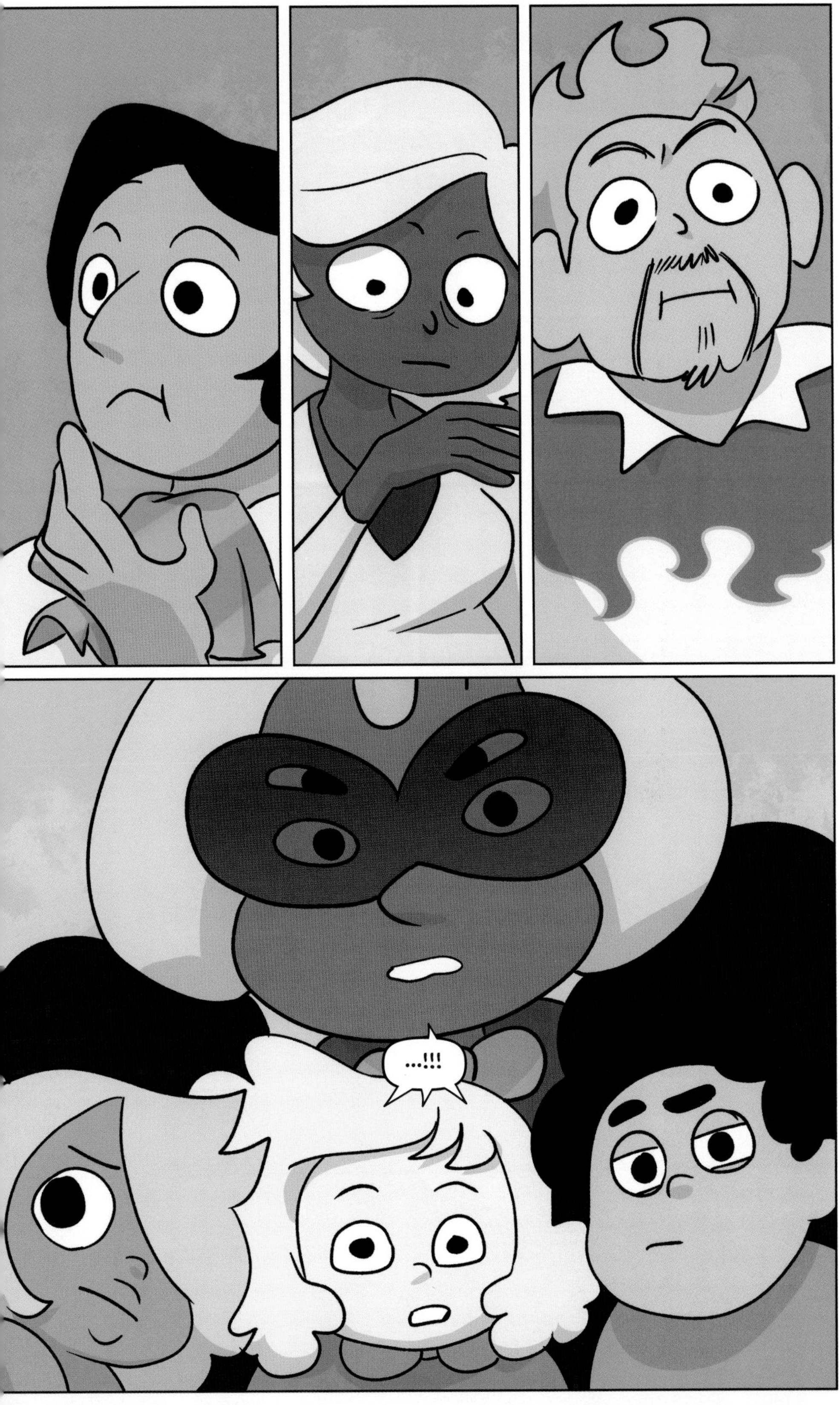
...!!!

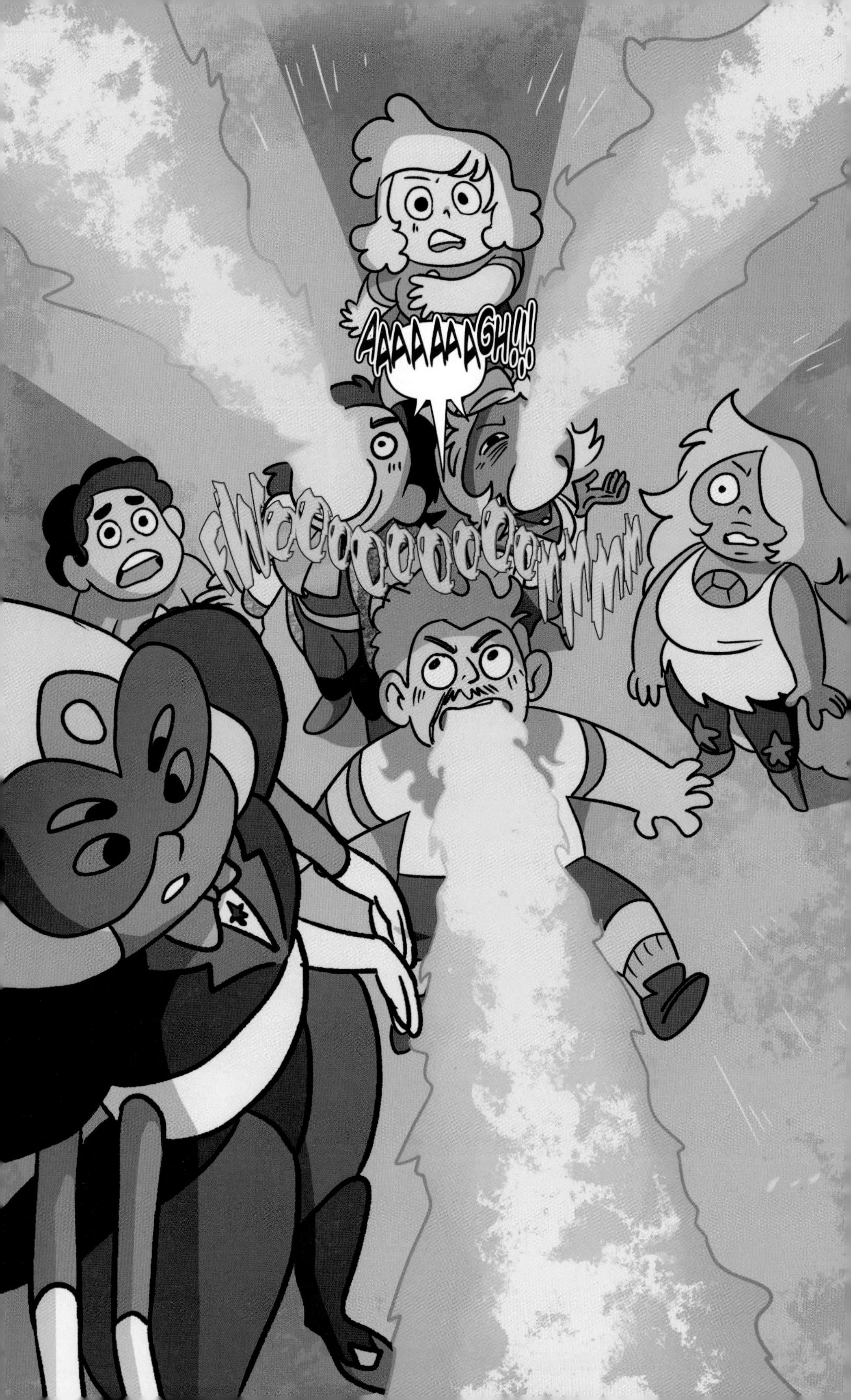
AAAAAAAGH!!!
FWOOOOOOOOOMMMMM

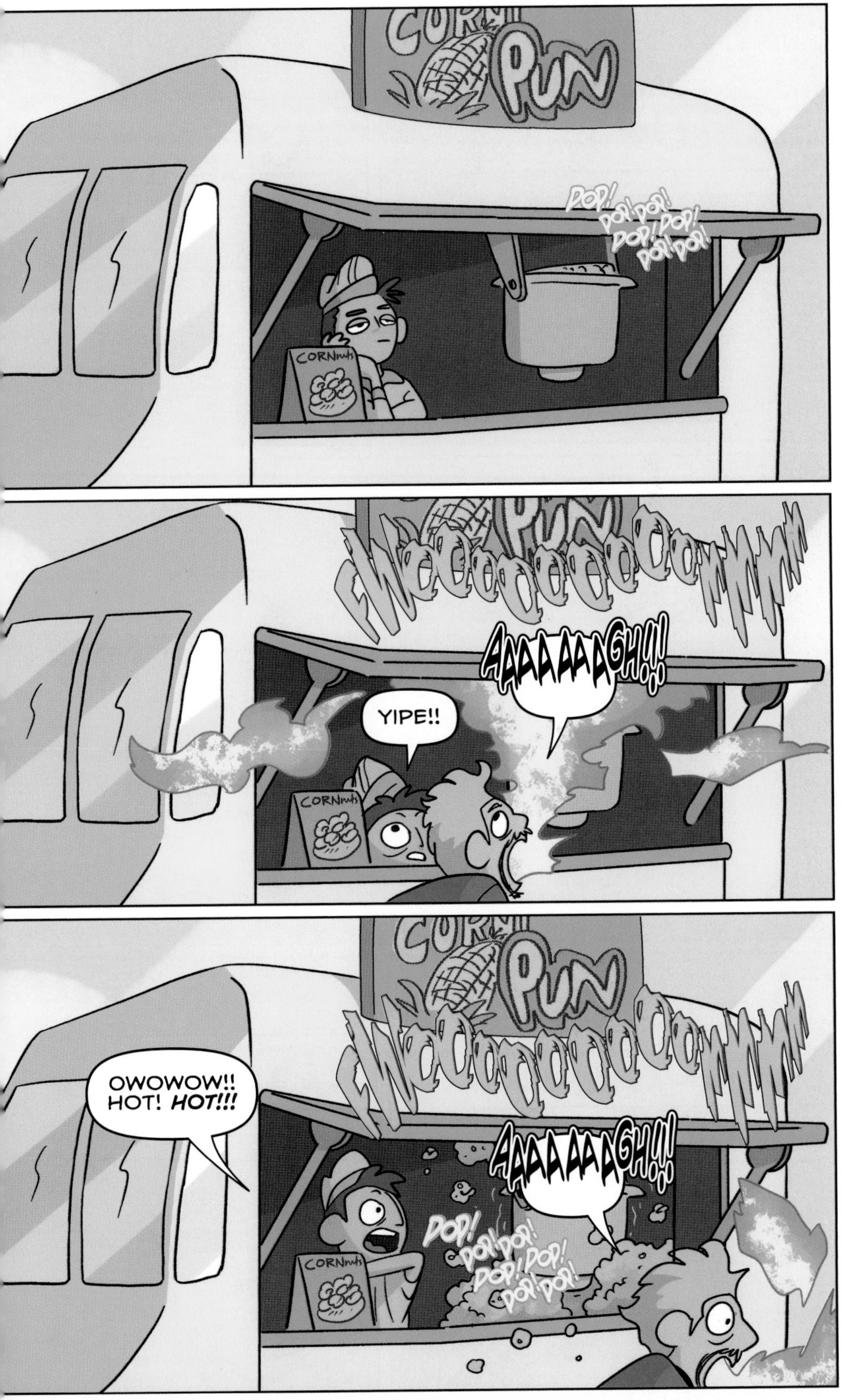
CORN PUN
POP! POP! POP! POP! POP! POP! POP!
CORNnuts
WHOOOOOOOOOMMM
AAAAAAAGH!!!
YIPE!!
CORNnuts
CORN PUN
WHOOOOOOOOOMMM
OWOWOW!! HOT! *HOT!!!*
AAAAAAAGH!!!
POP! POP! POP! POP! POP! POP! POP!
CORNnuts

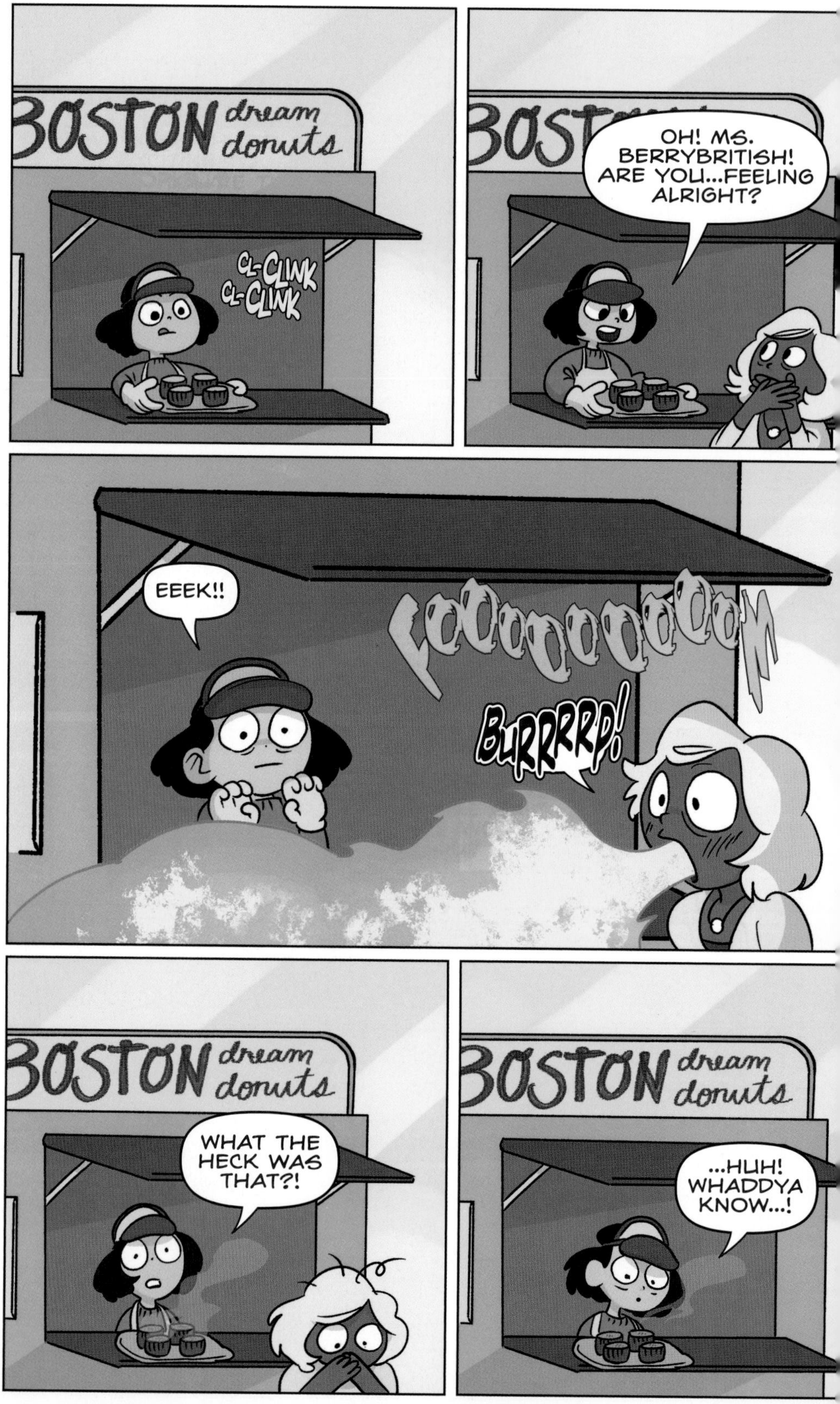
BOSTON dream donuts
CL-CLINK
CL-CLINK
BOST
OH! MS. BERRYBRITISH! ARE YOU...FEELING ALRIGHT?
EEEK!!
FOOOOOOOOOOM
BLRRRRP!
BOSTON dream donuts
WHAT THE HECK WAS THAT?!
BOSTON dream donuts
...HUH! WHADDYA KNOW...!

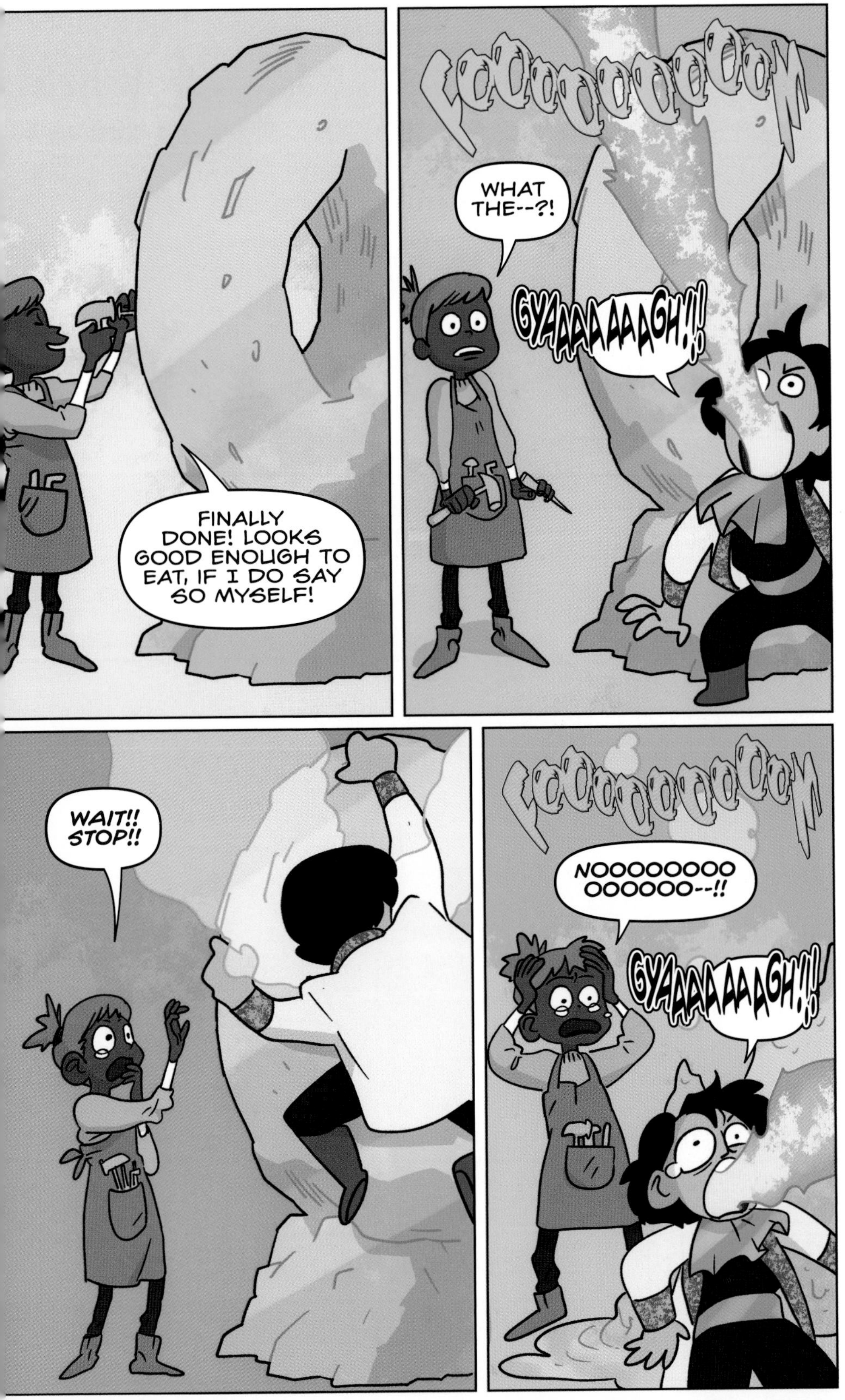

FINALLY DONE! LOOKS GOOD ENOUGH TO EAT, IF I DO SAY SO MYSELF!
FOOOOOOOOOOM
WHAT THE--?!
GYAAAAAAAGH!!!
WAIT!! STOP!!
FOOOOOOOOOOM
NOOOOOOOOOOOOOOO--!!
GYAAAAAAAGH!!!

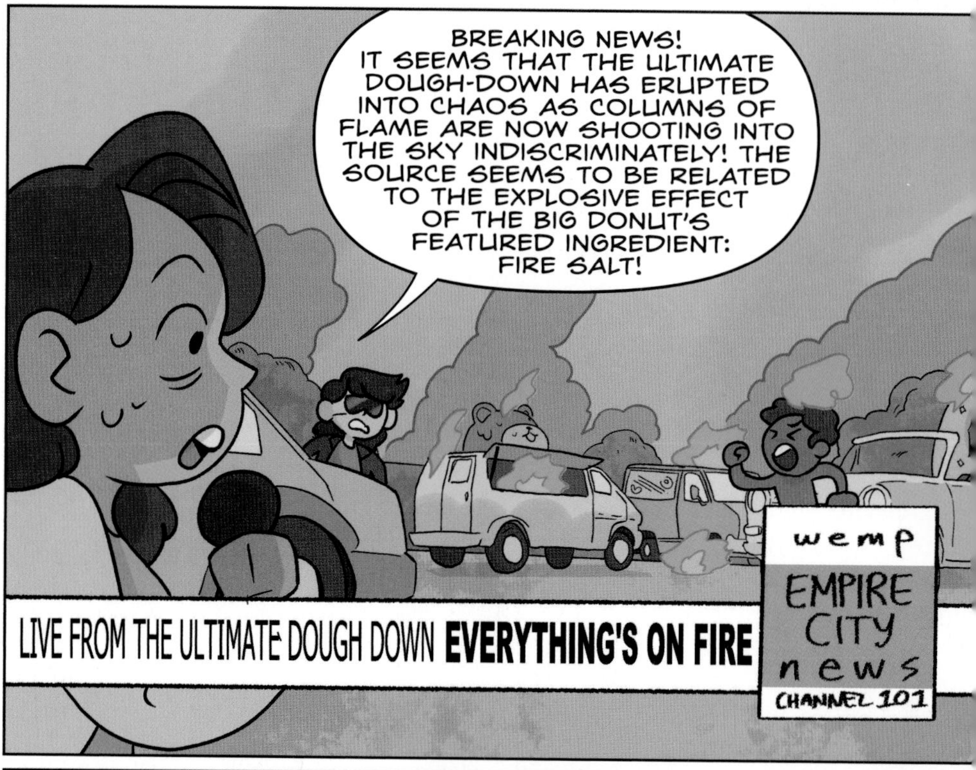
BREAKING NEWS! IT SEEMS THAT THE ULTIMATE DOUGH-DOWN HAS ERUPTED INTO CHAOS AS COLUMNS OF FLAME ARE NOW SHOOTING INTO THE SKY INDISCRIMINATELY! THE SOURCE SEEMS TO BE RELATED TO THE EXPLOSIVE EFFECT OF THE BIG DONUT'S FEATURED INGREDIENT: FIRE SALT!
LIVE FROM THE ULTIMATE DOUGH DOWN EVERYTHING'S ON FIRE
wemp
EMPIRE CITY news
CHANNEL 101

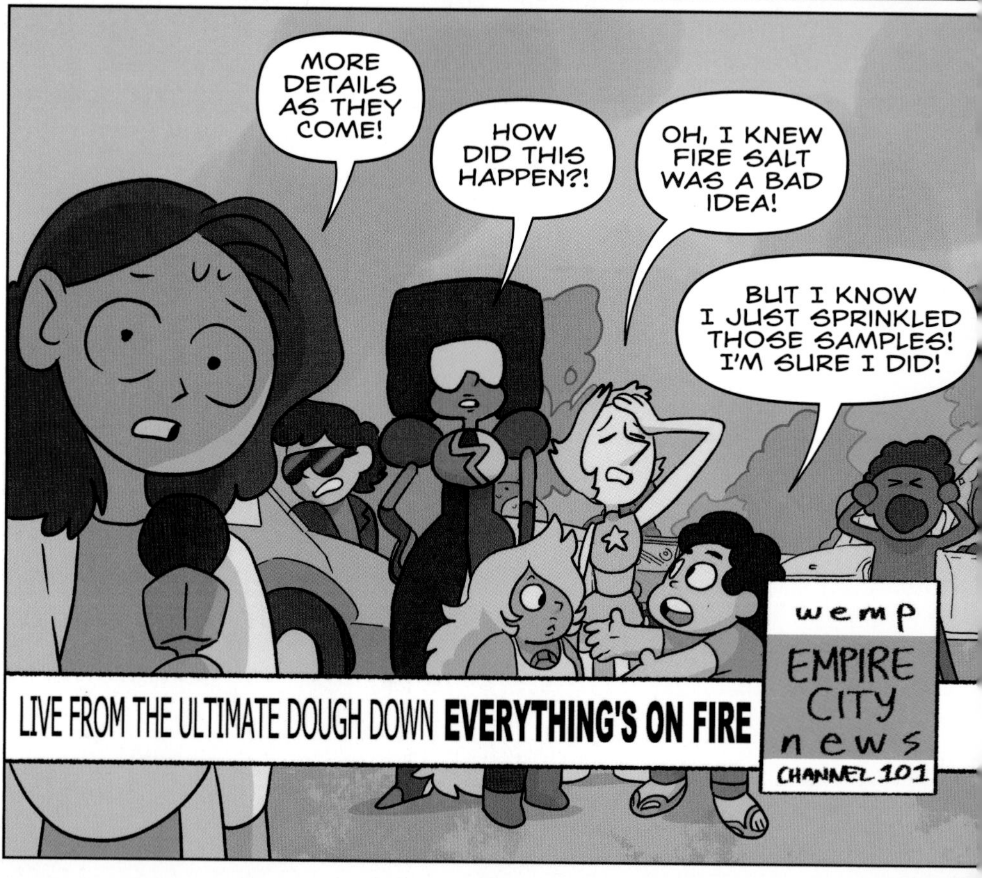
MORE DETAILS AS THEY COME!
HOW DID THIS HAPPEN?!
OH, I KNEW FIRE SALT WAS A BAD IDEA!
BUT I KNOW I JUST SPRINKLED THOSE SAMPLES! I'M SURE I DID!
LIVE FROM THE ULTIMATE DOUGH DOWN EVERYTHING'S ON FIRE
wemp
EMPIRE CITY news
CHANNEL 101

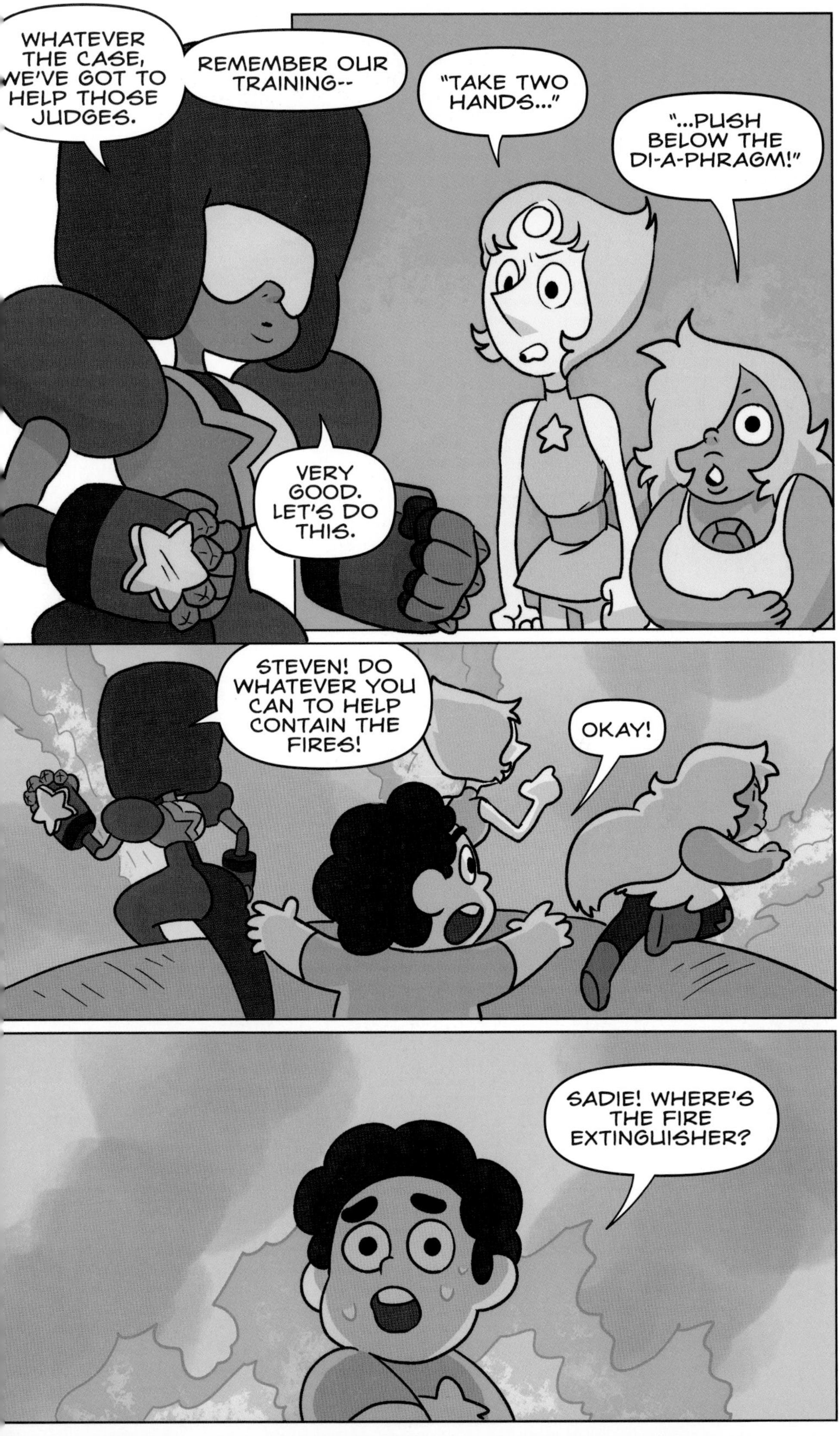
WHATEVER THE CASE, WE'VE GOT TO HELP THOSE JUDGES.
REMEMBER OUR TRAINING--
"TAKE TWO HANDS..."
"...PUSH BELOW THE DI-A-PHRAGM!"
VERY GOOD. LET'S DO THIS.
STEVEN! DO WHATEVER YOU CAN TO HELP CONTAIN THE FIRES!
OKAY!
SADIE! WHERE'S THE FIRE EXTINGUISHER?

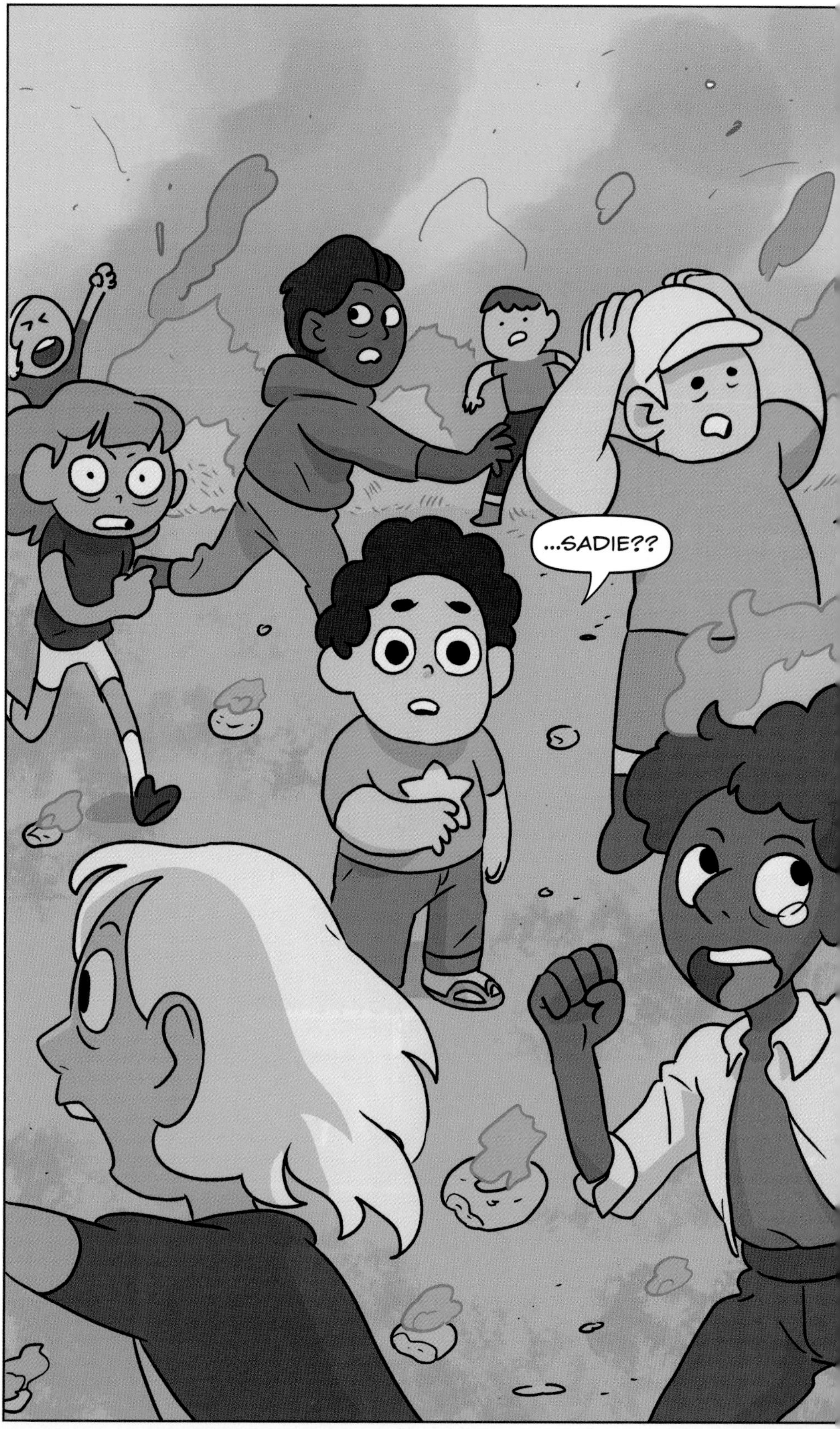
...SADIE??

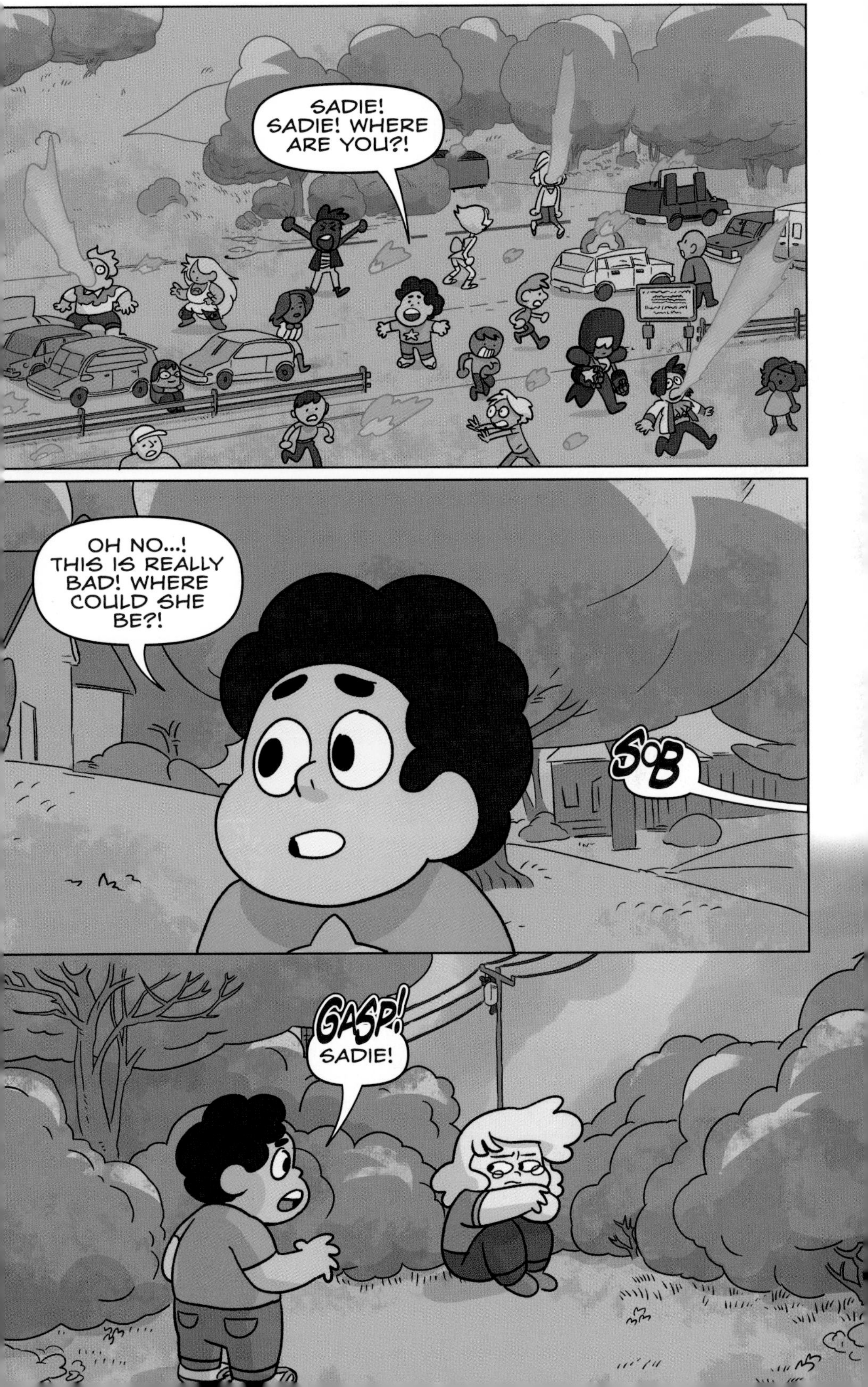
SADIE! SADIE! WHERE ARE YOU?!
OH NO...! THIS IS REALLY BAD! WHERE COULD SHE BE?!
SOB
GASP!
SADIE!

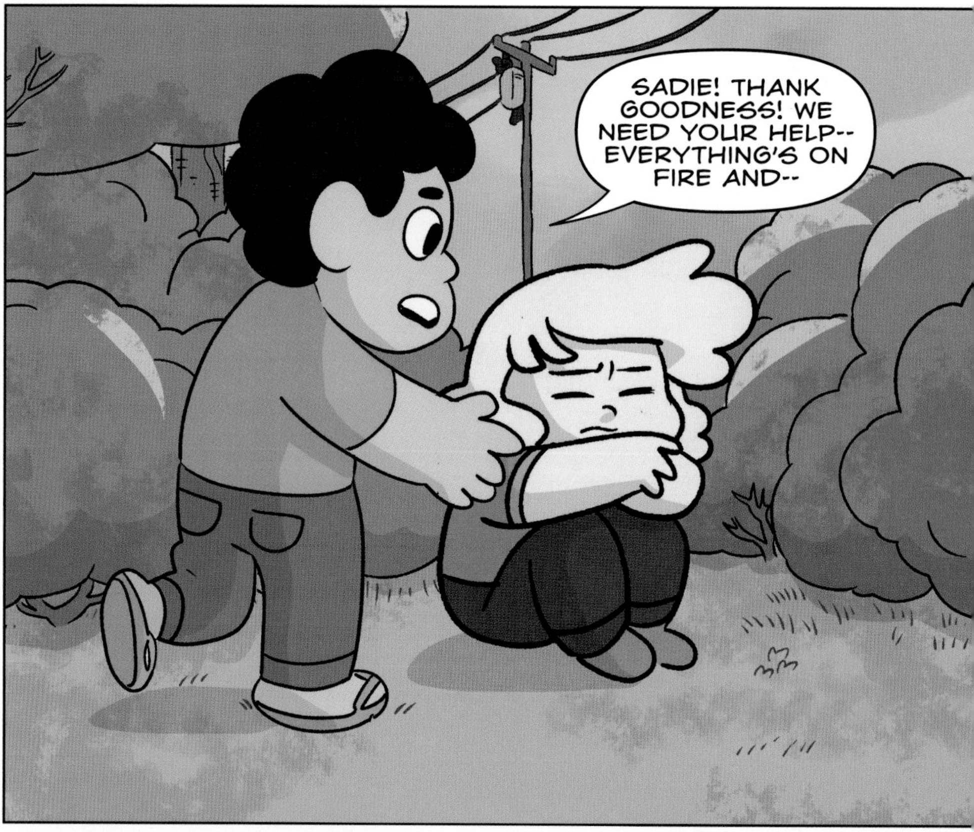
SADIE! THANK GOODNESS! WE NEED YOUR HELP--EVERYTHING'S ON FIRE AND--
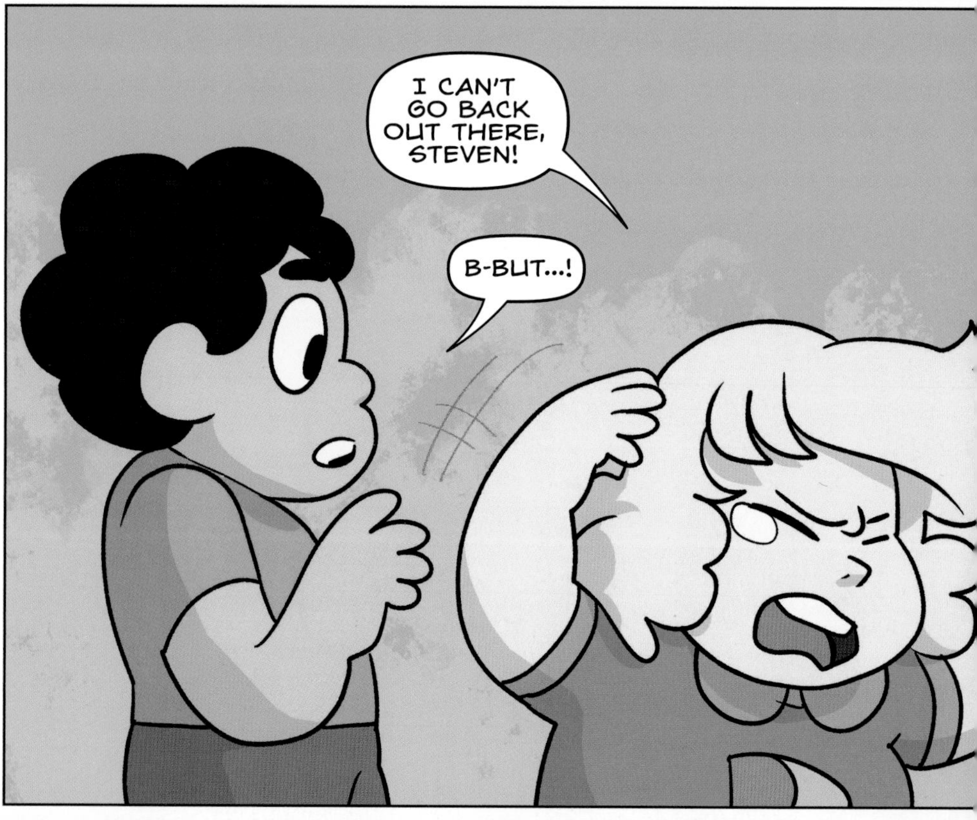
I CAN'T GO BACK OUT THERE, STEVEN!
B-BUT...!

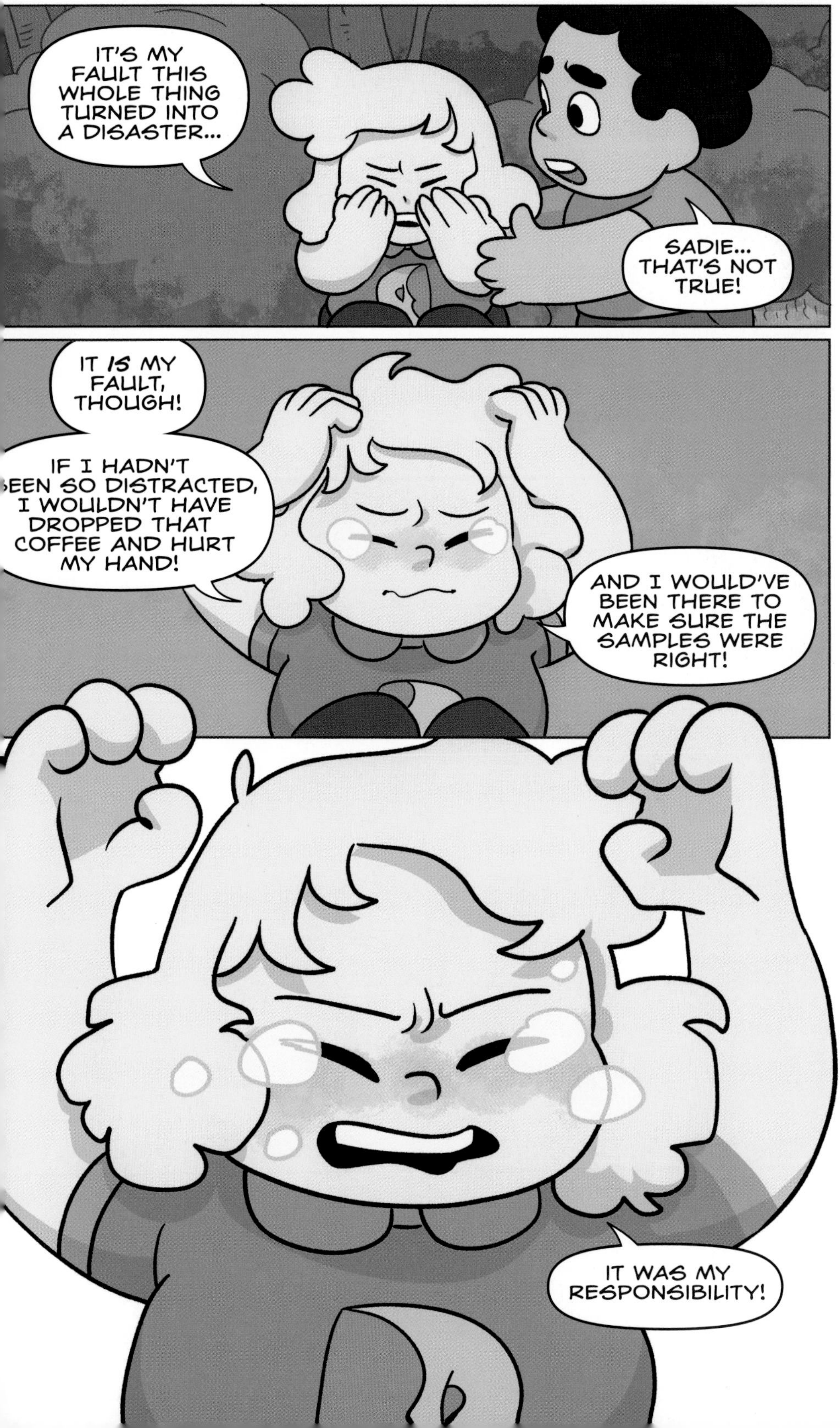
IT'S MY FAULT THIS WHOLE THING TURNED INTO A DISASTER...
SADIE... THAT'S NOT TRUE!
IT *IS* MY FAULT, THOUGH!
IF I HADN'T BEEN SO DISTRACTED, I WOULDN'T HAVE DROPPED THAT COFFEE AND HURT MY HAND!
AND I WOULD'VE BEEN THERE TO MAKE SURE THE SAMPLES WERE RIGHT!
IT WAS MY RESPONSIBILITY!

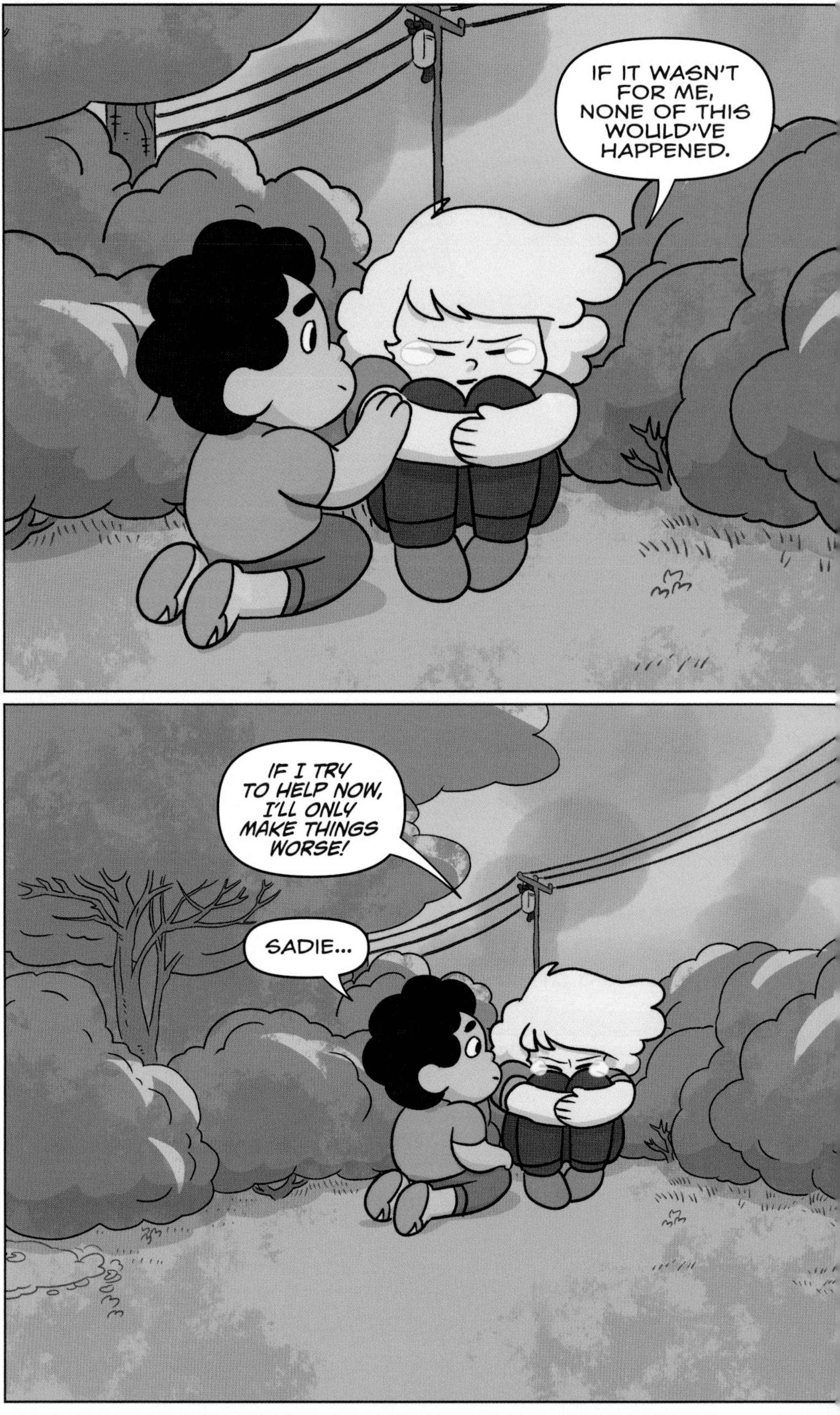
IF IT WASN'T FOR ME, NONE OF THIS WOULD'VE HAPPENED.
IF I TRY TO HELP NOW, I'LL ONLY MAKE THINGS WORSE!
SADIE...

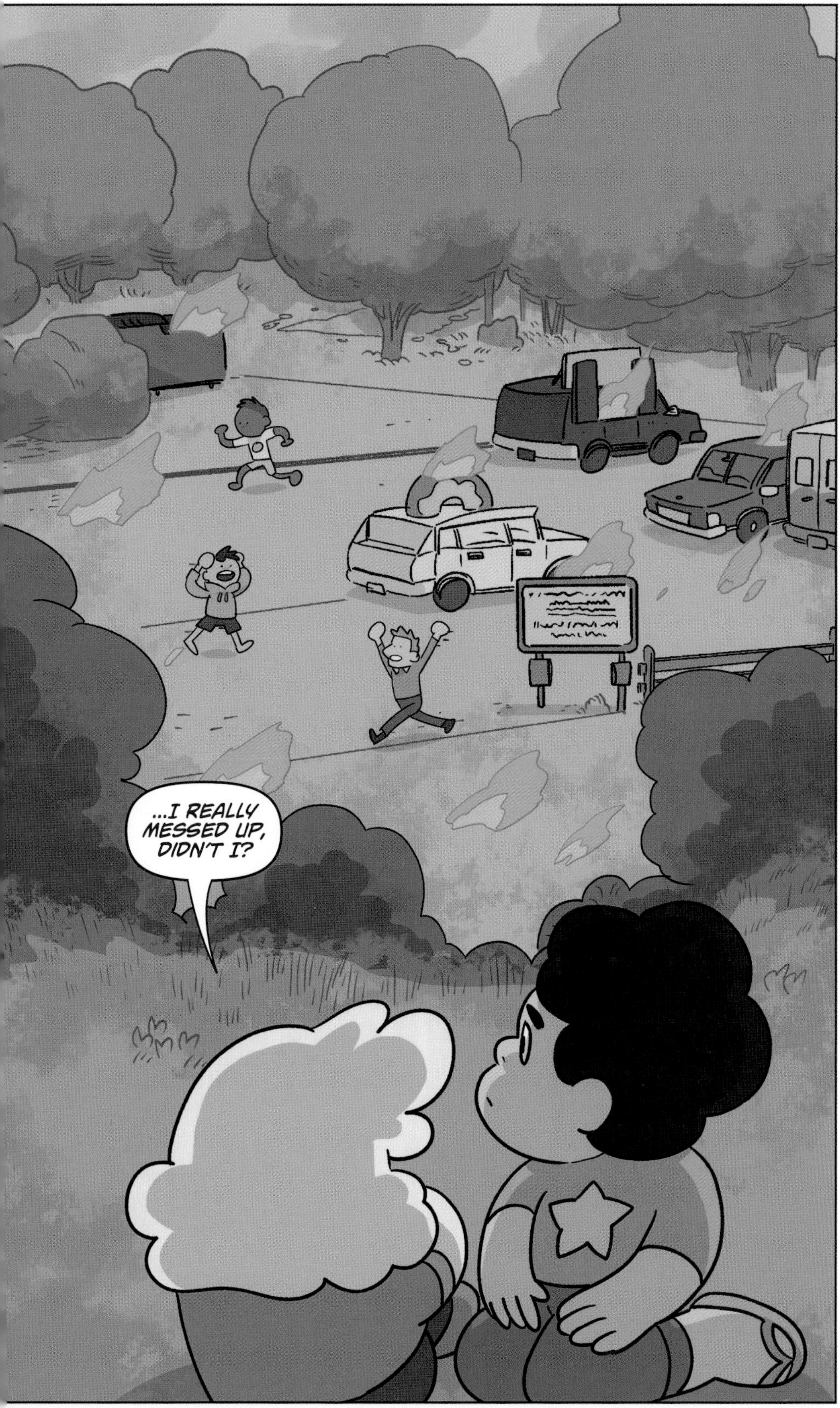
...I REALLY MESSED UP, DIDN'T I?

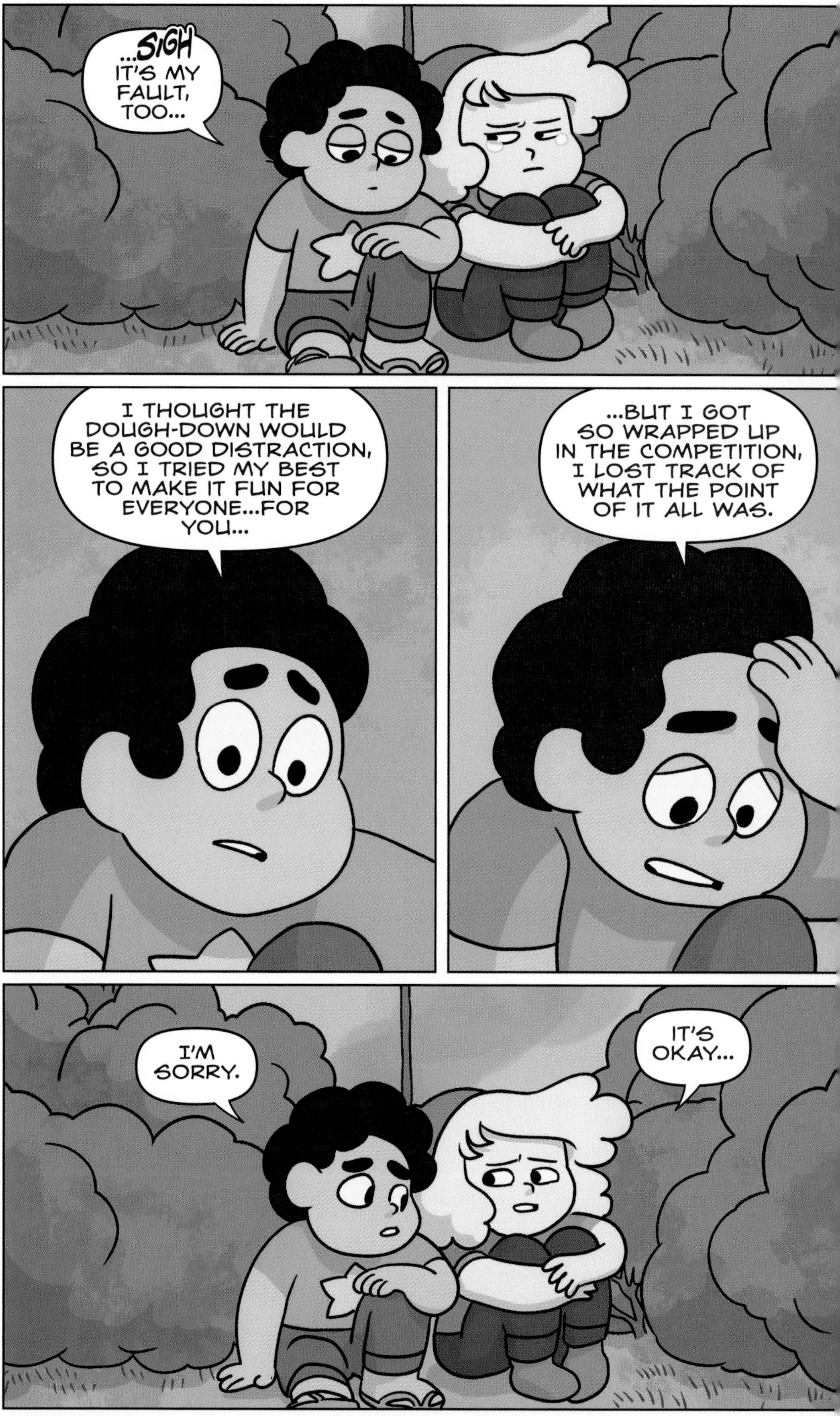
...SIGH
IT'S MY FAULT, TOO...
I THOUGHT THE DOUGH-DOWN WOULD BE A GOOD DISTRACTION, SO I TRIED MY BEST TO MAKE IT FUN FOR EVERYONE...FOR YOU...
...BUT I GOT SO WRAPPED UP IN THE COMPETITION, I LOST TRACK OF WHAT THE POINT OF IT ALL WAS.
I'M SORRY.
IT'S OKAY...

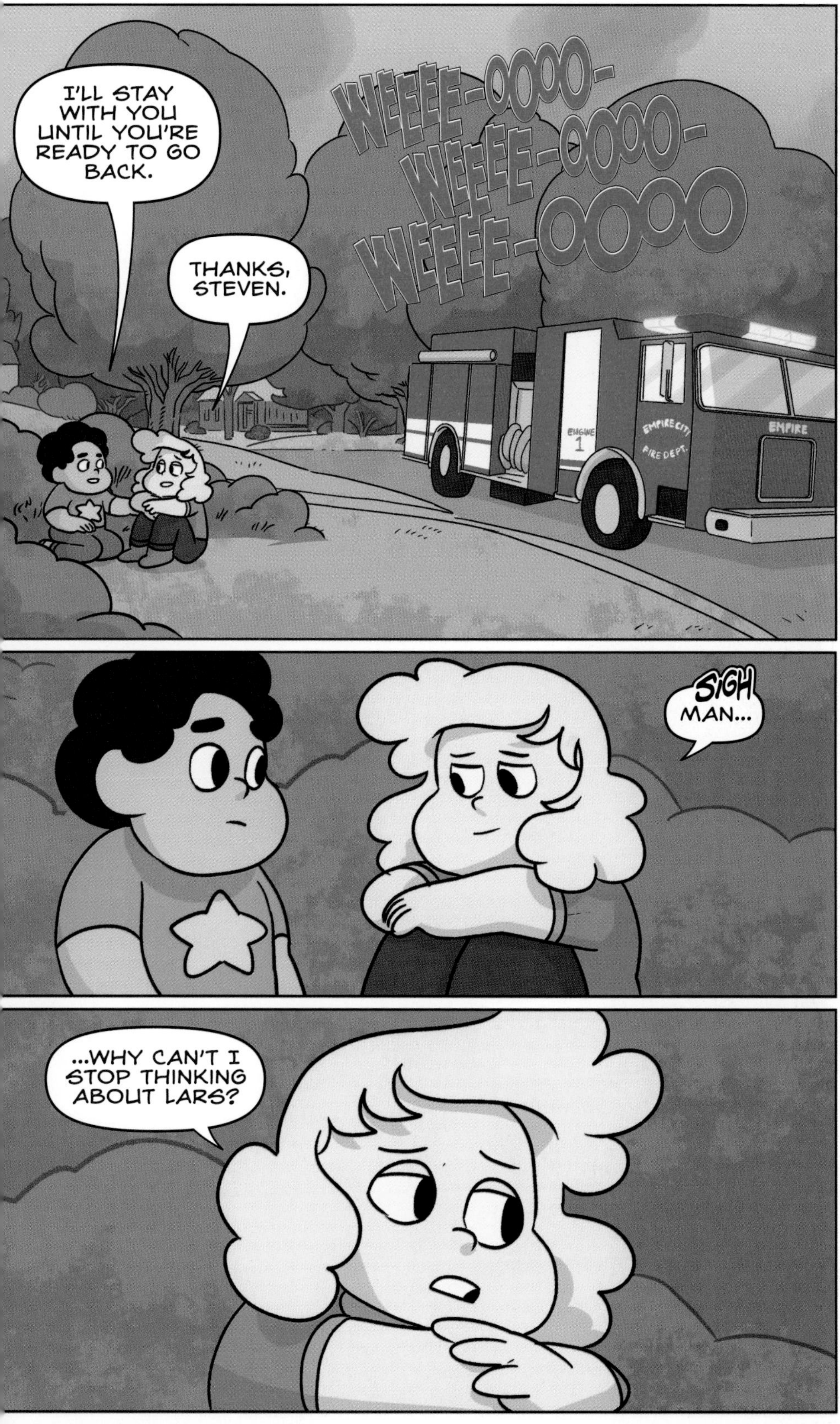
I'LL STAY WITH YOU UNTIL YOU'RE READY TO GO BACK.
WEEEE-OOOO-WEEEE-OOOO-WEEEE-OOOO
THANKS, STEVEN.
ENGINE 1
EMPIRE CITY FIRE DEPT.
EMPIRE
SIGH
MAN...
...WHY CAN'T I STOP THINKING ABOUT LARS?

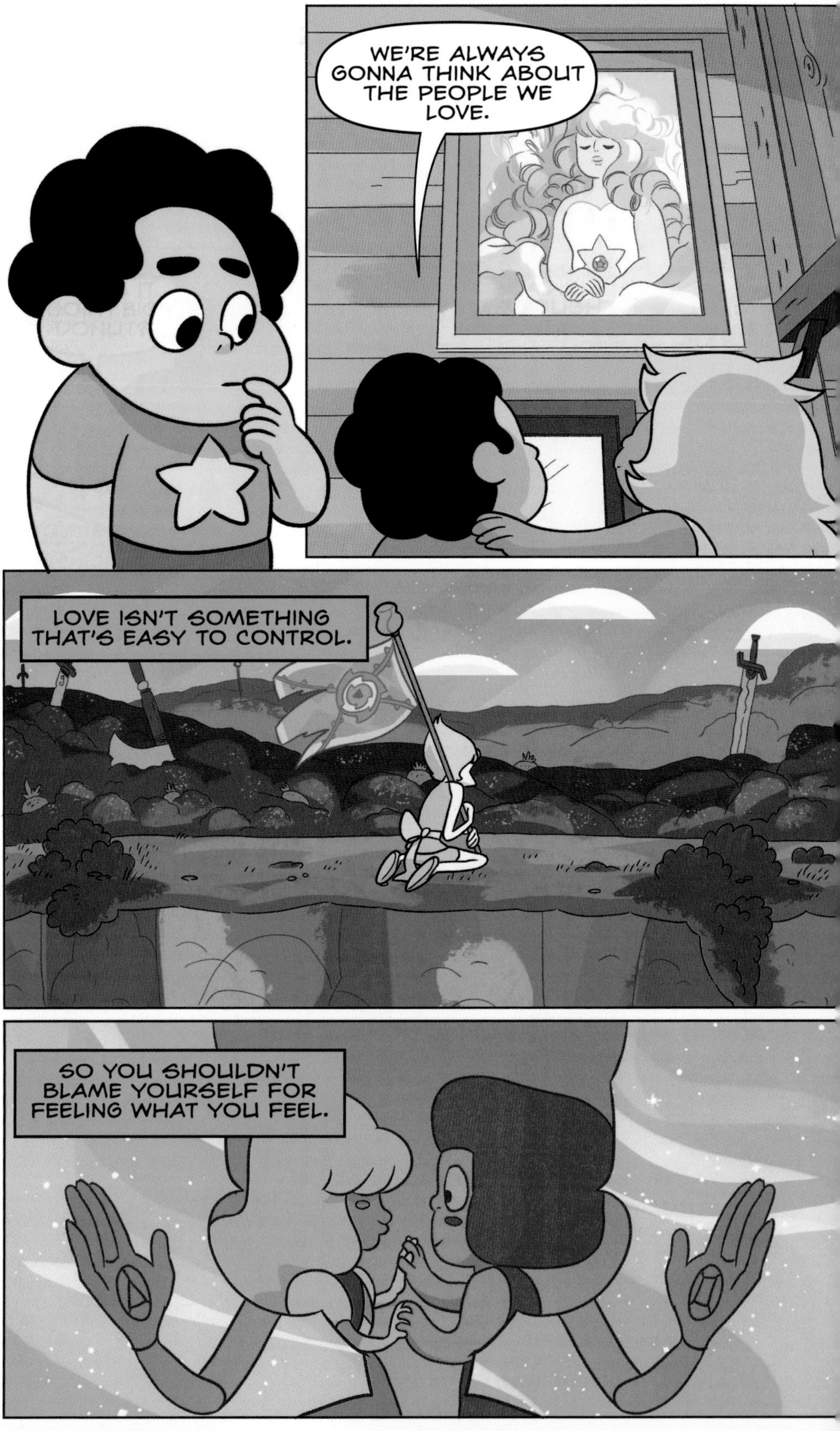
WE'RE ALWAYS GONNA THINK ABOUT THE PEOPLE WE LOVE.
LOVE ISN'T SOMETHING THAT'S EASY TO CONTROL.
SO YOU SHOULDN'T BLAME YOURSELF FOR FEELING WHAT YOU FEEL.

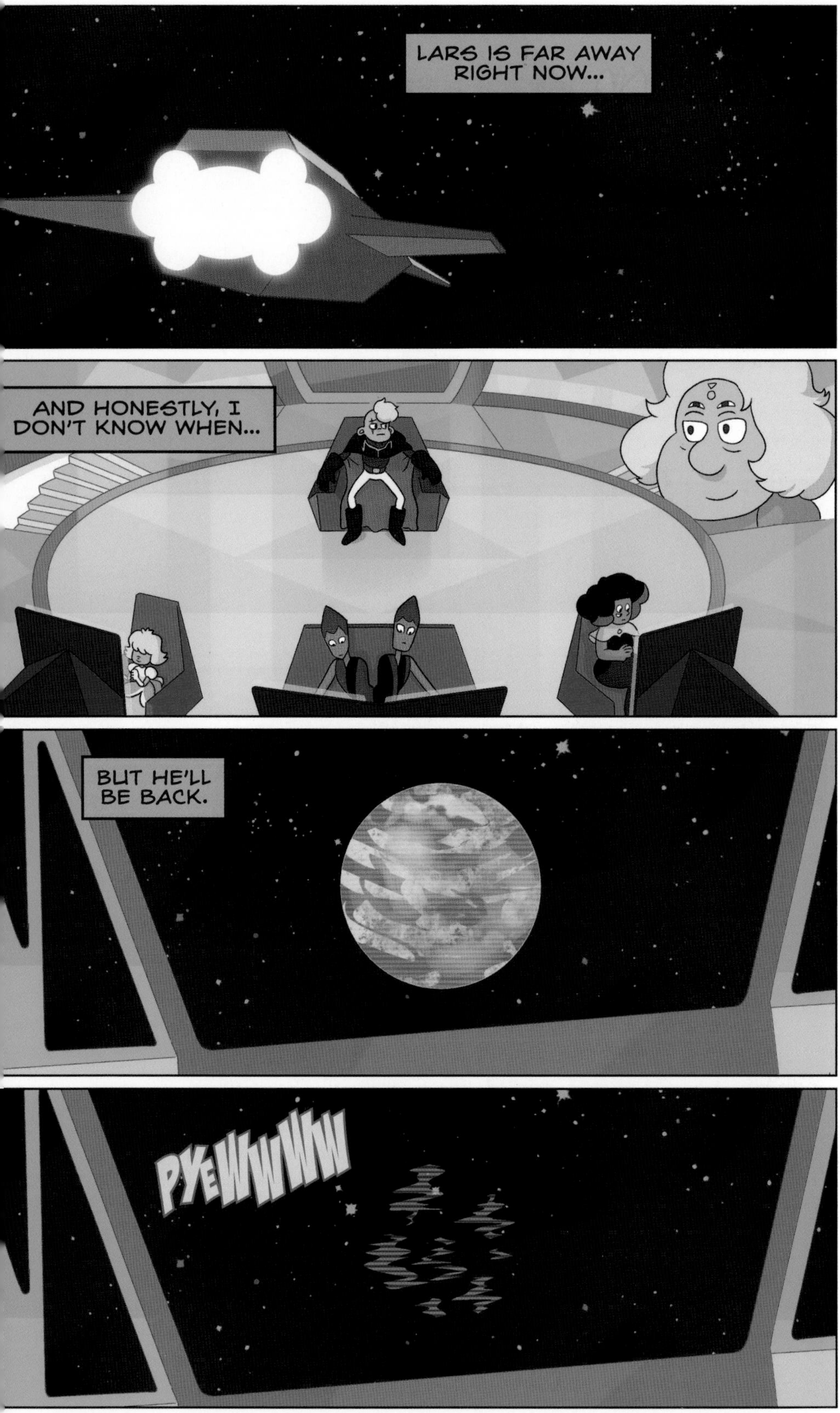
LARS IS FAR AWAY RIGHT NOW...
AND HONESTLY, I DON'T KNOW WHEN...
BUT HE'LL BE BACK.
PYEWWWW

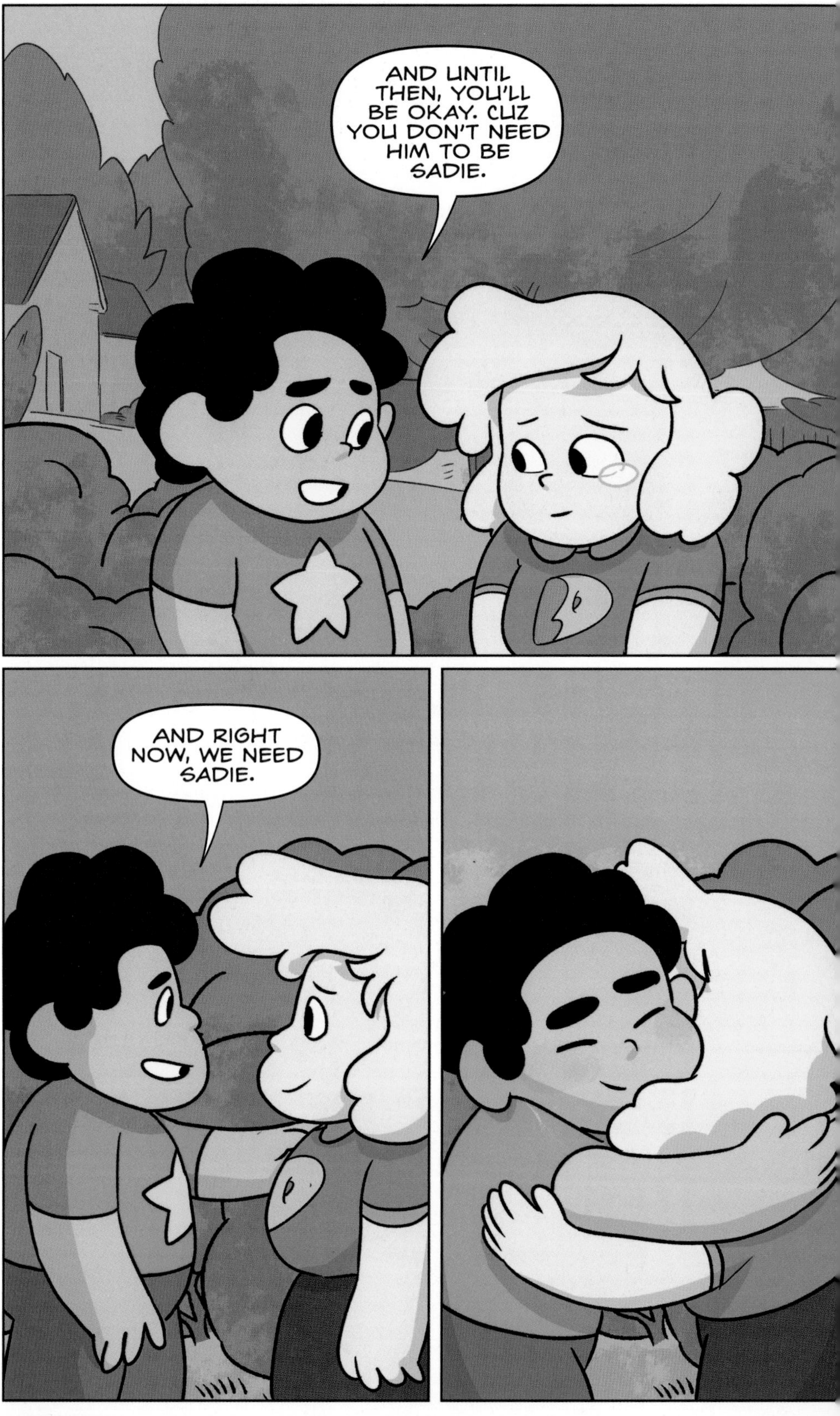
AND UNTIL THEN, YOU'LL BE OKAY. CUZ YOU DON'T NEED HIM TO BE SADIE.
AND RIGHT NOW, WE NEED SADIE.

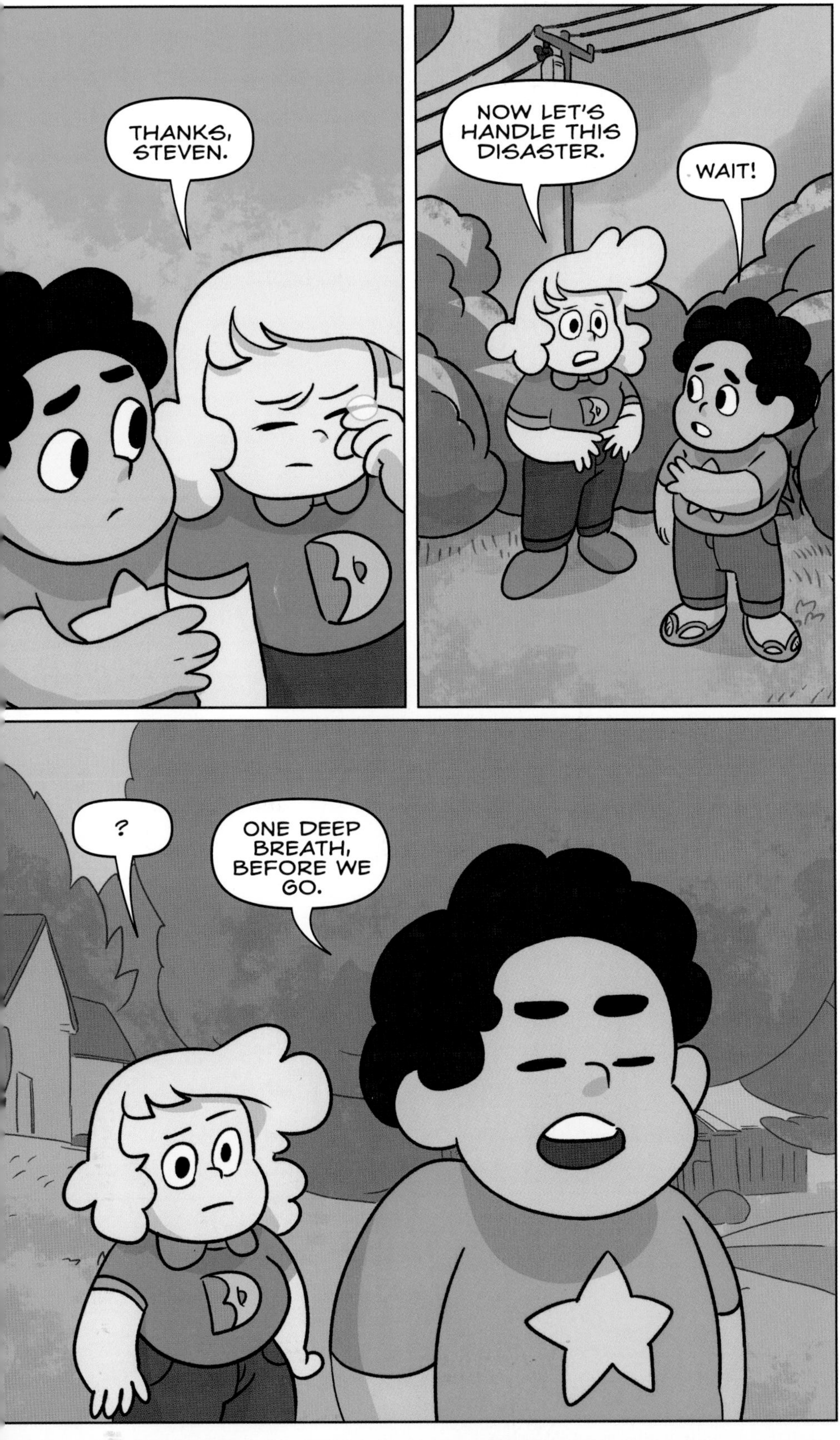
THANKS, STEVEN.
NOW LET'S HANDLE THIS DISASTER.
WAIT!
?
ONE DEEP BREATH, BEFORE WE GO.

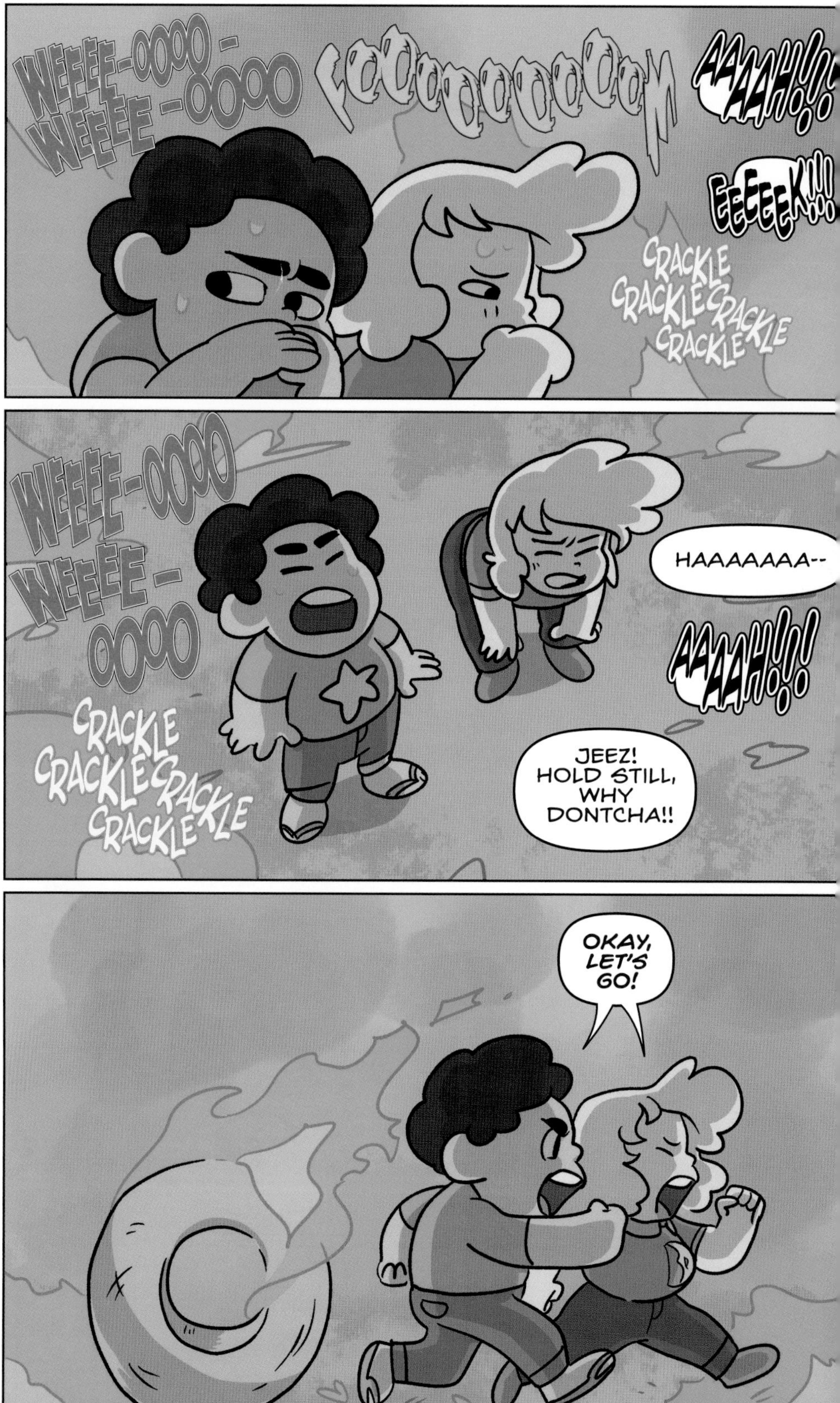
WEEEE-OOOO-
WEEEE-OOOO
FOOOOOOOOOOOM
AAAAAH!!!
EEEEEEK!!!
CRACKLE
CRACKLECRACKLE
CRACKLE
WEEEE-OOOO
WEEEE-
OOOO
CRACKLE
CRACKLECRACKLE
CRACKLE
HAAAAAAA--
AAAAH!!!
JEEZ! HOLD STILL, WHY DONTCHA!!
OKAY, LET'S GO!

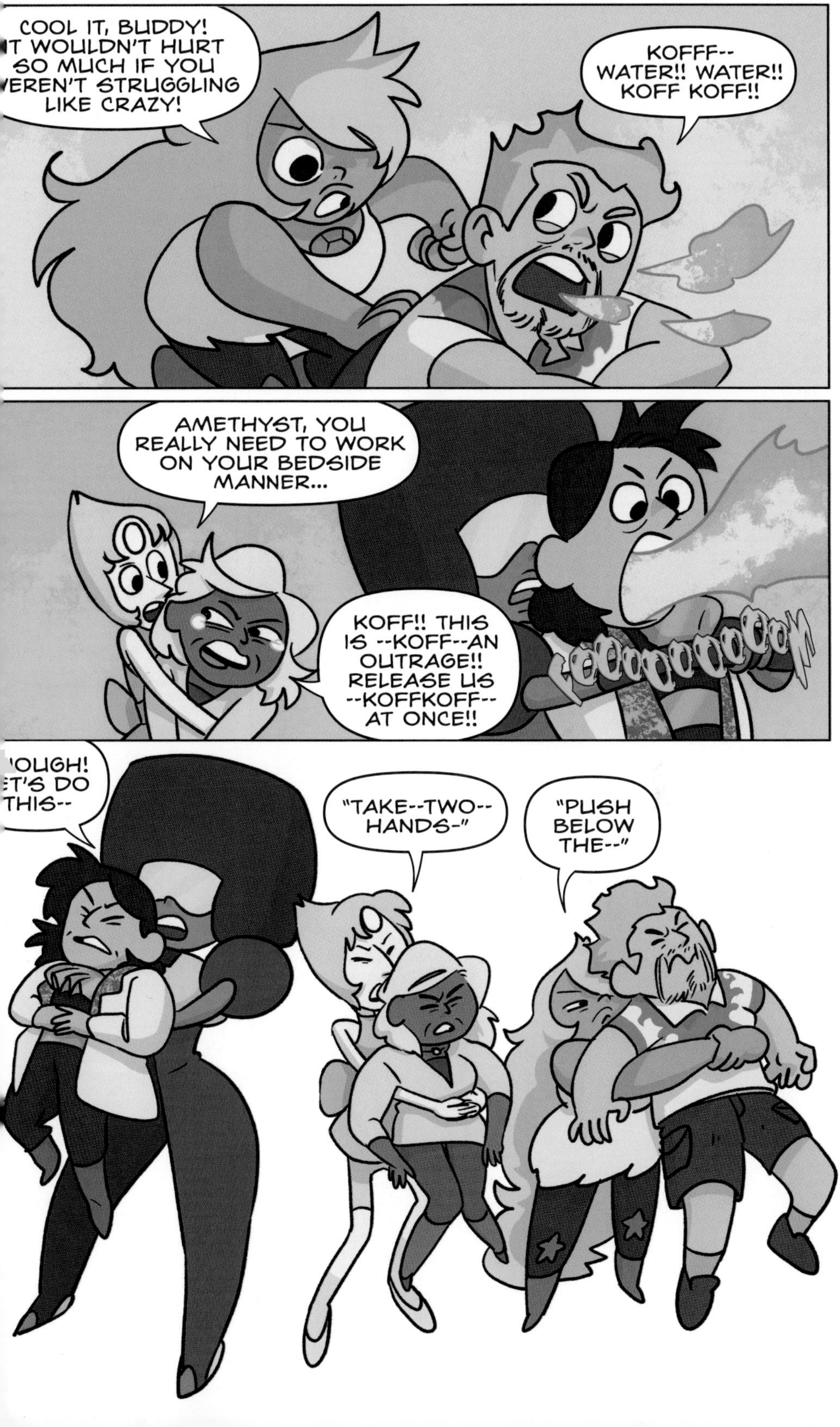

COOL IT, BUDDY! IT WOULDN'T HURT SO MUCH IF YOU WEREN'T STRUGGLING LIKE CRAZY!
KOFFF-- WATER!! WATER!! KOFF KOFF!!
AMETHYST, YOU REALLY NEED TO WORK ON YOUR BEDSIDE MANNER...
KOFF!! THIS IS --KOFF--AN OUTRAGE!! RELEASE US --KOFFKOFF-- AT ONCE!!
FOOOOOOOOOM
OUGH! ET'S DO THIS--
"TAKE--TWO--HANDS-"
"PUSH BELOW THE--"

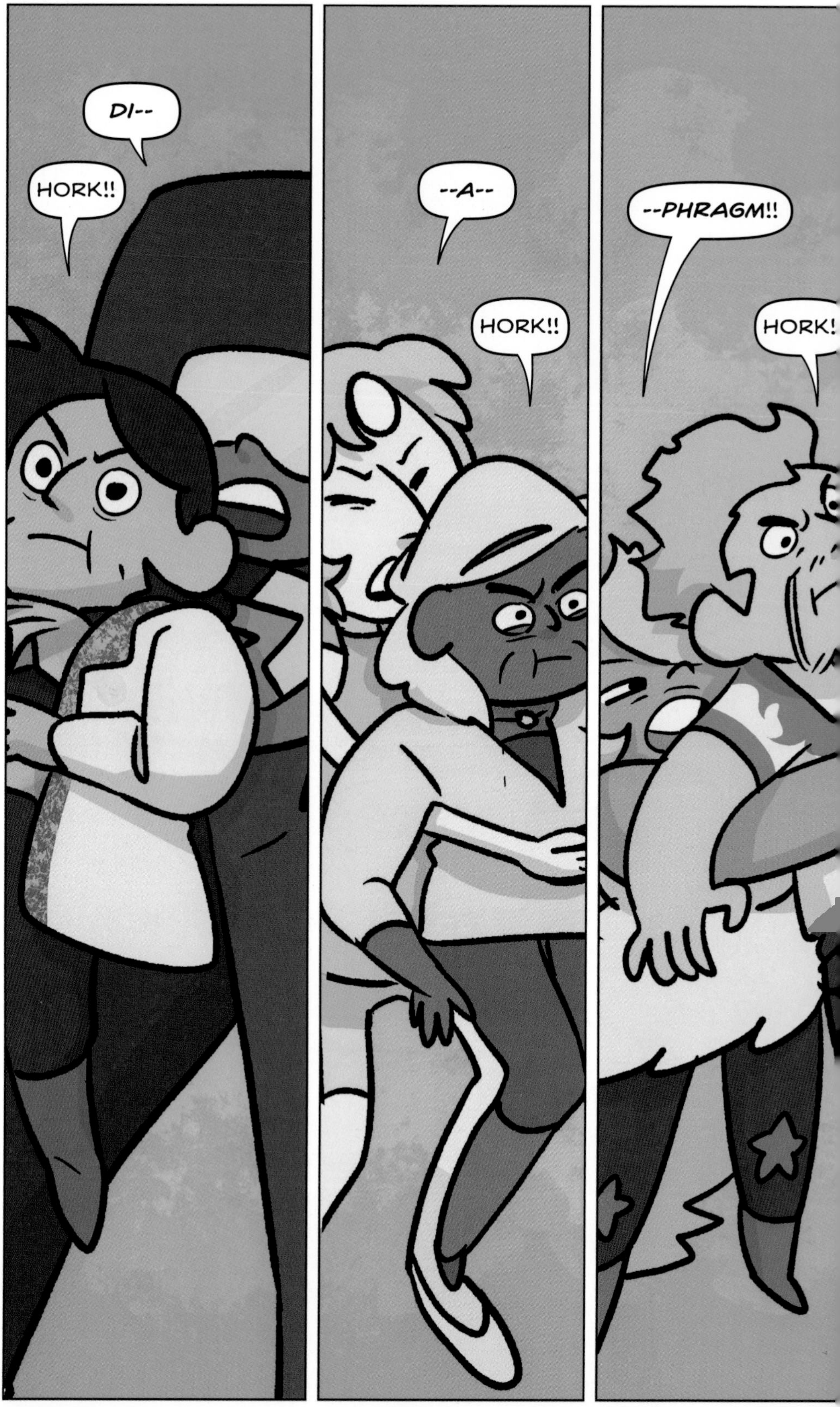
DI--
HORK!!
--A--
HORK!!
--PHRAGM!!
HORK!

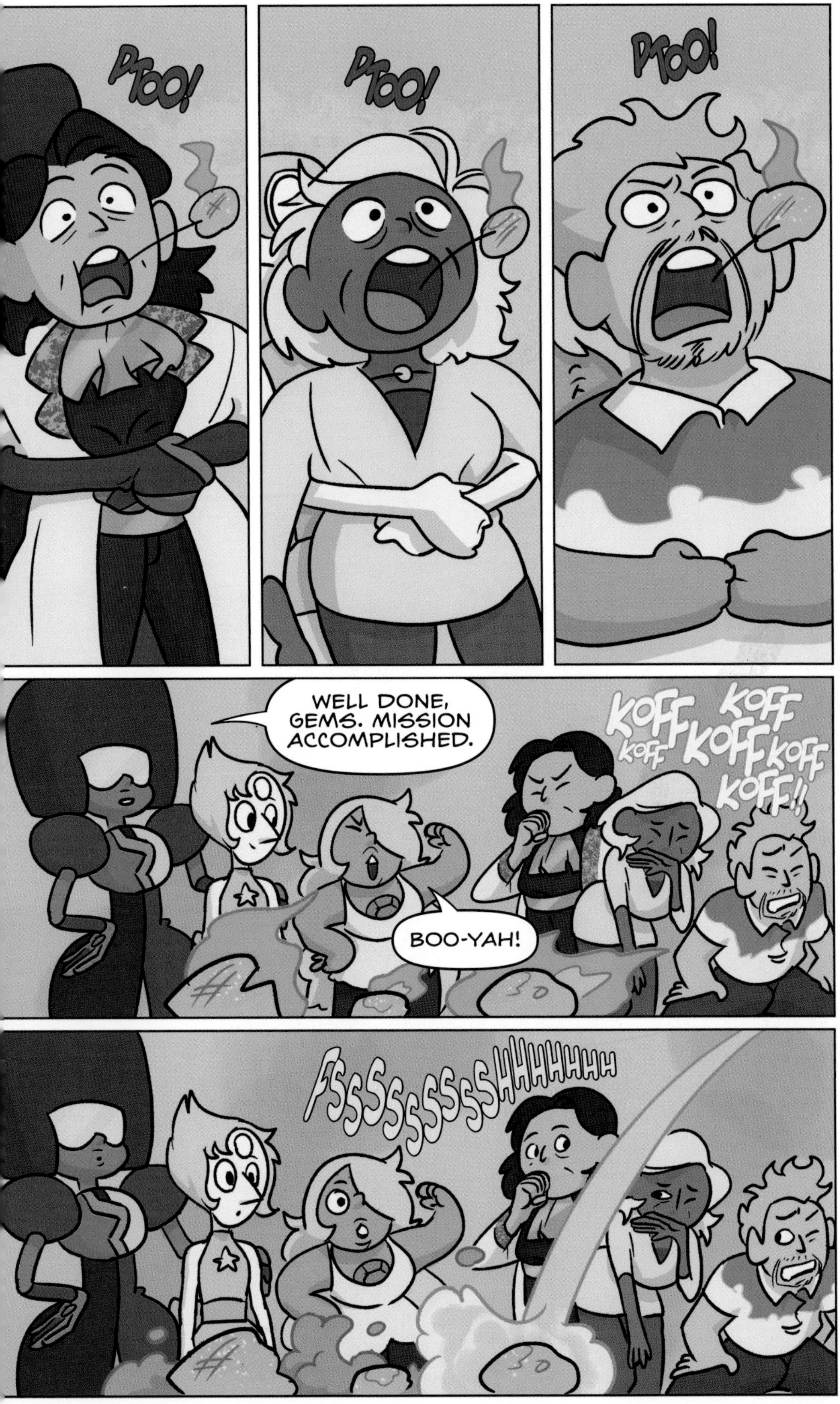
PTOO!
PTOO!
PTOO!
WELL DONE, GEMS. MISSION ACCOMPLISHED.
KOFF KOFF KOFF KOFF KOFF KOFF!!
BOO-YAH!
FSSSSSSSSSHHHHHHH

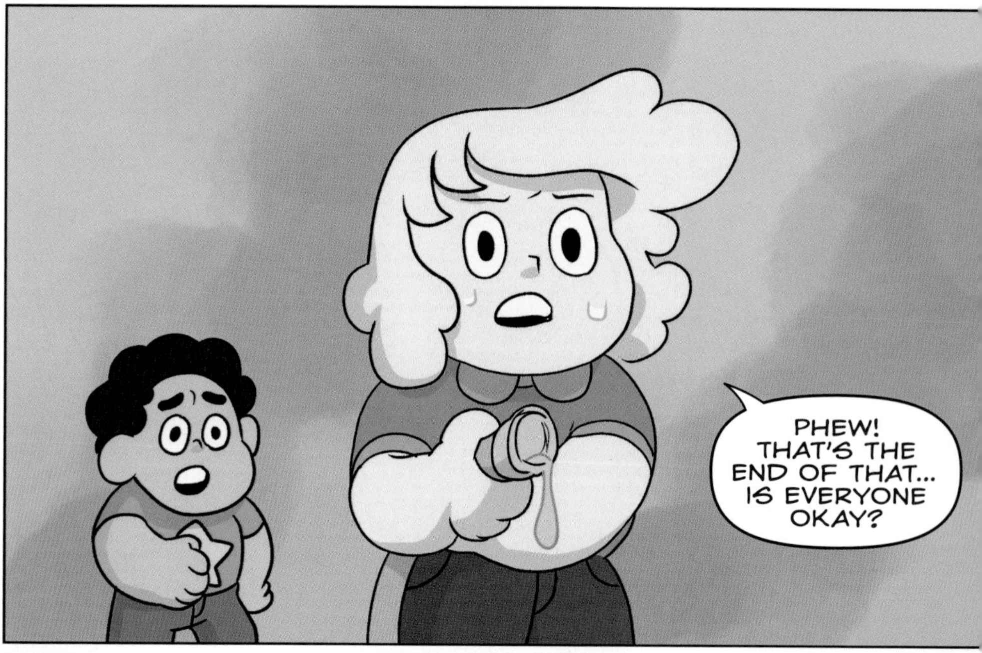
PHEW! THAT'S THE END OF THAT... IS EVERYONE OKAY?

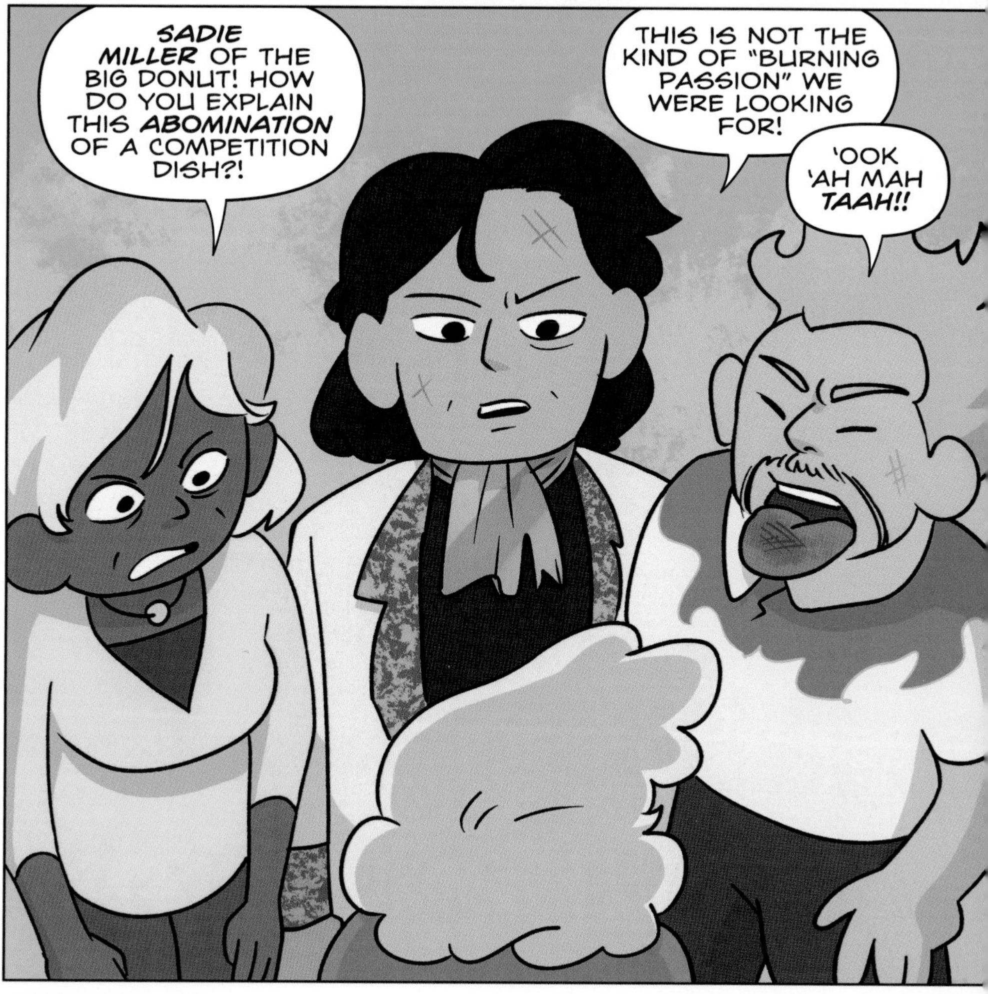
SADIE MILLER OF THE BIG DONUT! HOW DO YOU EXPLAIN THIS ABOMINATION OF A COMPETITION DISH?!
THIS IS NOT THE KIND OF "BURNING PASSION" WE WERE LOOKING FOR!
'OOK 'AH MAH TAAH!!

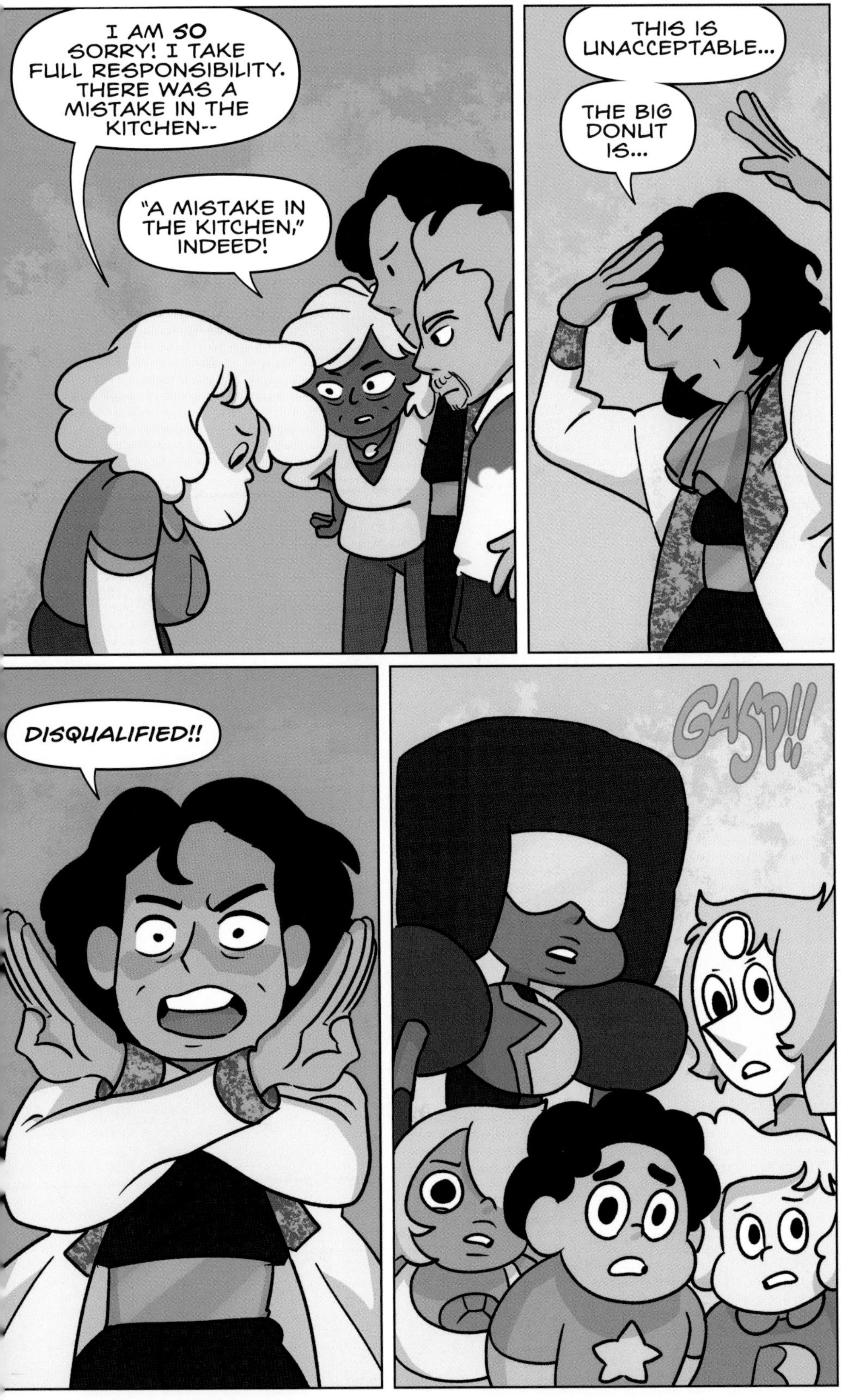
I AM SO SORRY! I TAKE FULL RESPONSIBILITY. THERE WAS A MISTAKE IN THE KITCHEN--
"A MISTAKE IN THE KITCHEN," INDEED!
THIS IS UNACCEPTABLE...
THE BIG DONUT IS...
DISQUALIFIED!!
GASP!!

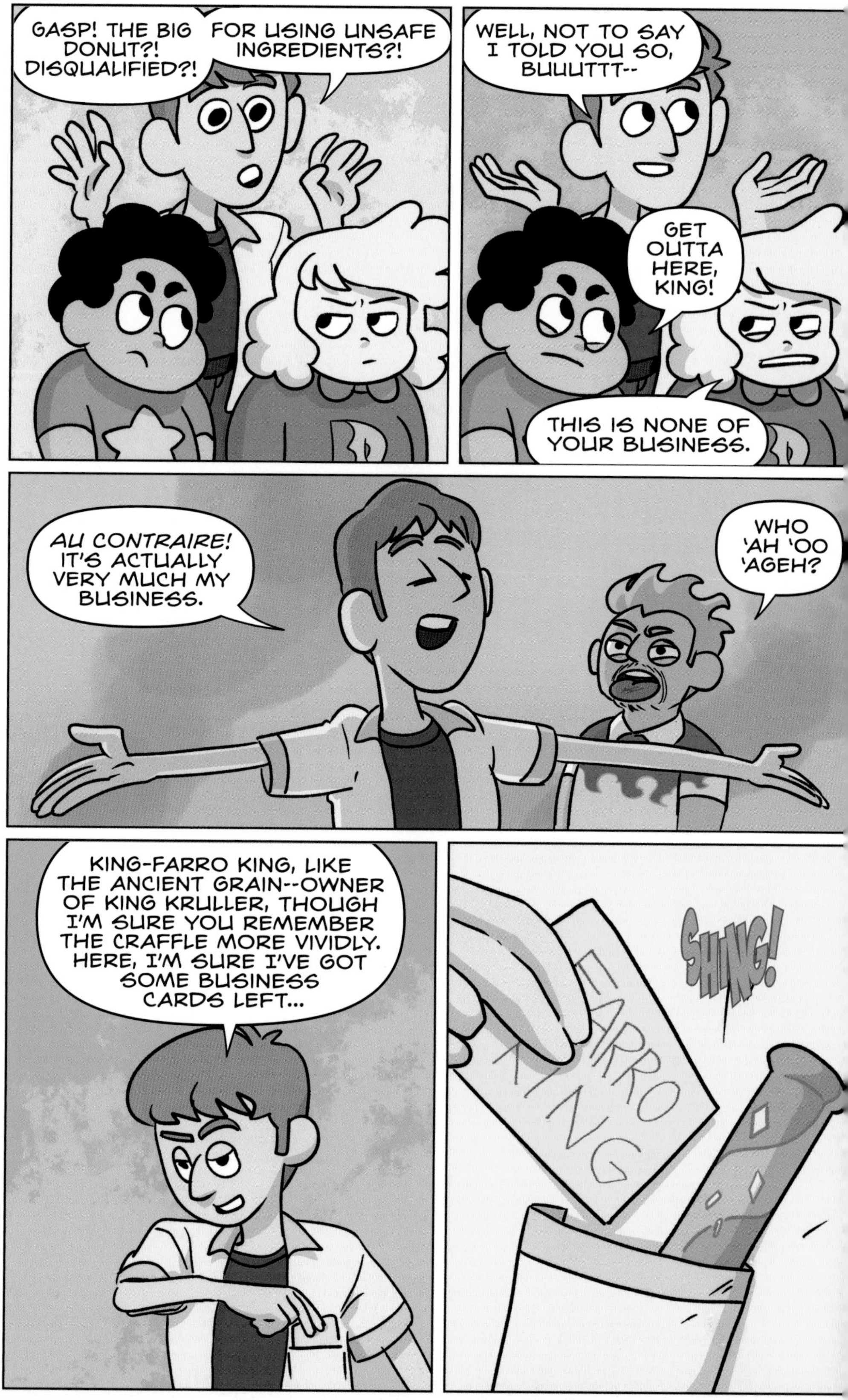
GASP! THE BIG DONUT?! DISQUALIFIED?!
FOR USING UNSAFE INGREDIENTS?!
WELL, NOT TO SAY I TOLD YOU SO, BUUUTTT--
GET OUTTA HERE, KING!
THIS IS NONE OF YOUR BUSINESS.
AU CONTRAIRE! IT'S ACTUALLY VERY MUCH MY BUSINESS.
WHO 'AH 'OO 'AGEH?
KING-FARRO KING, LIKE THE ANCIENT GRAIN--OWNER OF KING KRULLER, THOUGH I'M SURE YOU REMEMBER THE CRAFFLE MORE VIVIDLY. HERE, I'M SURE I'VE GOT SOME BUSINESS CARDS LEFT...
SHING!
FARRO KING

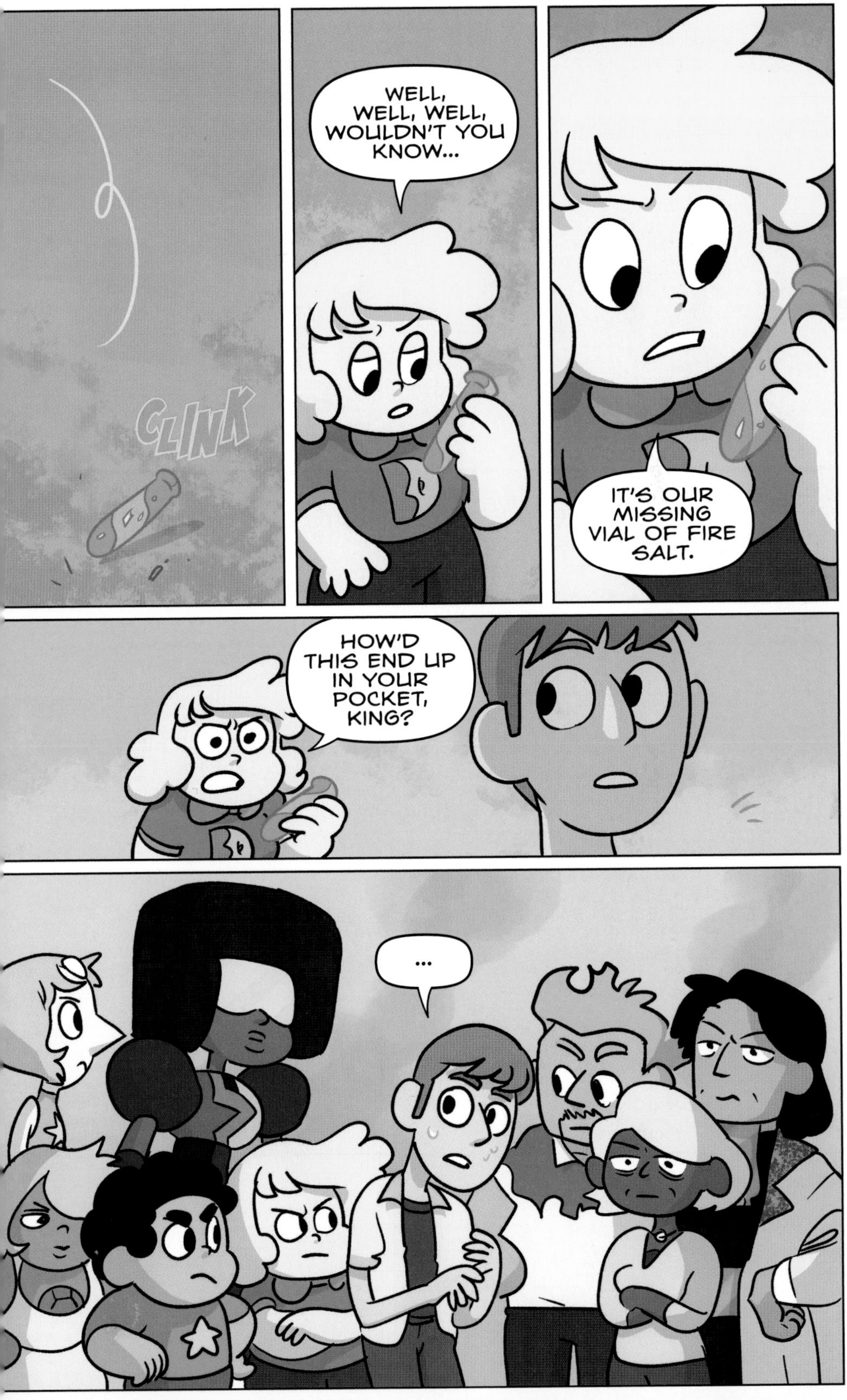
CLINK
WELL, WELL, WELL, WOULDN'T YOU KNOW...
IT'S OUR MISSING VIAL OF FIRE SALT.
HOW'D THIS END UP IN YOUR POCKET, KING?
...

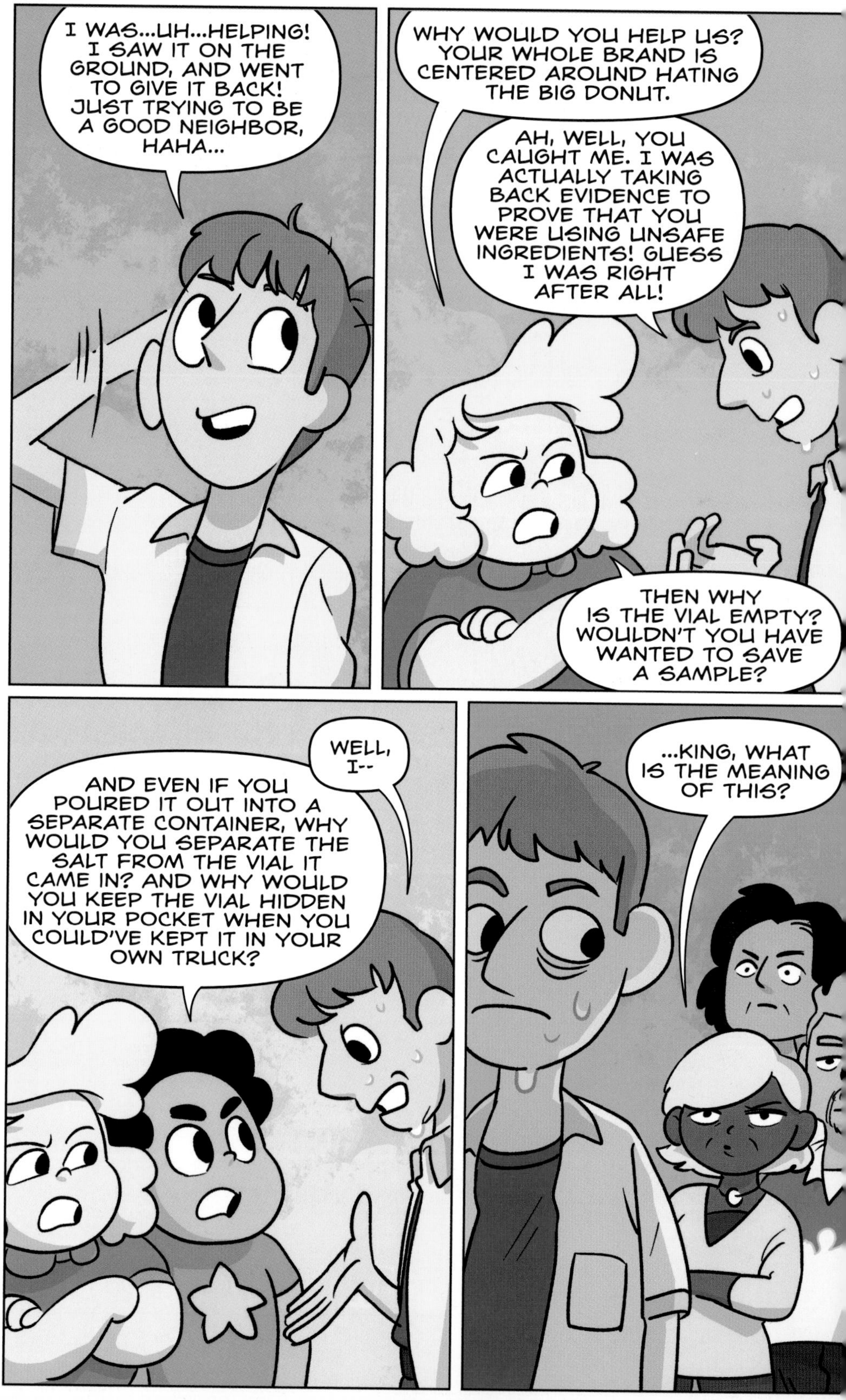
I WAS...UH...HELPING! I SAW IT ON THE GROUND, AND WENT TO GIVE IT BACK! JUST TRYING TO BE A GOOD NEIGHBOR, HAHA...
WHY WOULD YOU HELP US? YOUR WHOLE BRAND IS CENTERED AROUND HATING THE BIG DONUT.
AH, WELL, YOU CAUGHT ME. I WAS ACTUALLY TAKING BACK EVIDENCE TO PROVE THAT YOU WERE USING UNSAFE INGREDIENTS! GUESS I WAS RIGHT AFTER ALL!
THEN WHY IS THE VIAL EMPTY? WOULDN'T YOU HAVE WANTED TO SAVE A SAMPLE?
WELL, I--
AND EVEN IF YOU POURED IT OUT INTO A SEPARATE CONTAINER, WHY WOULD YOU SEPARATE THE SALT FROM THE VIAL IT CAME IN? AND WHY WOULD YOU KEEP THE VIAL HIDDEN IN YOUR POCKET WHEN YOU COULD'VE KEPT IT IN YOUR OWN TRUCK?
...KING, WHAT IS THE MEANING OF THIS?

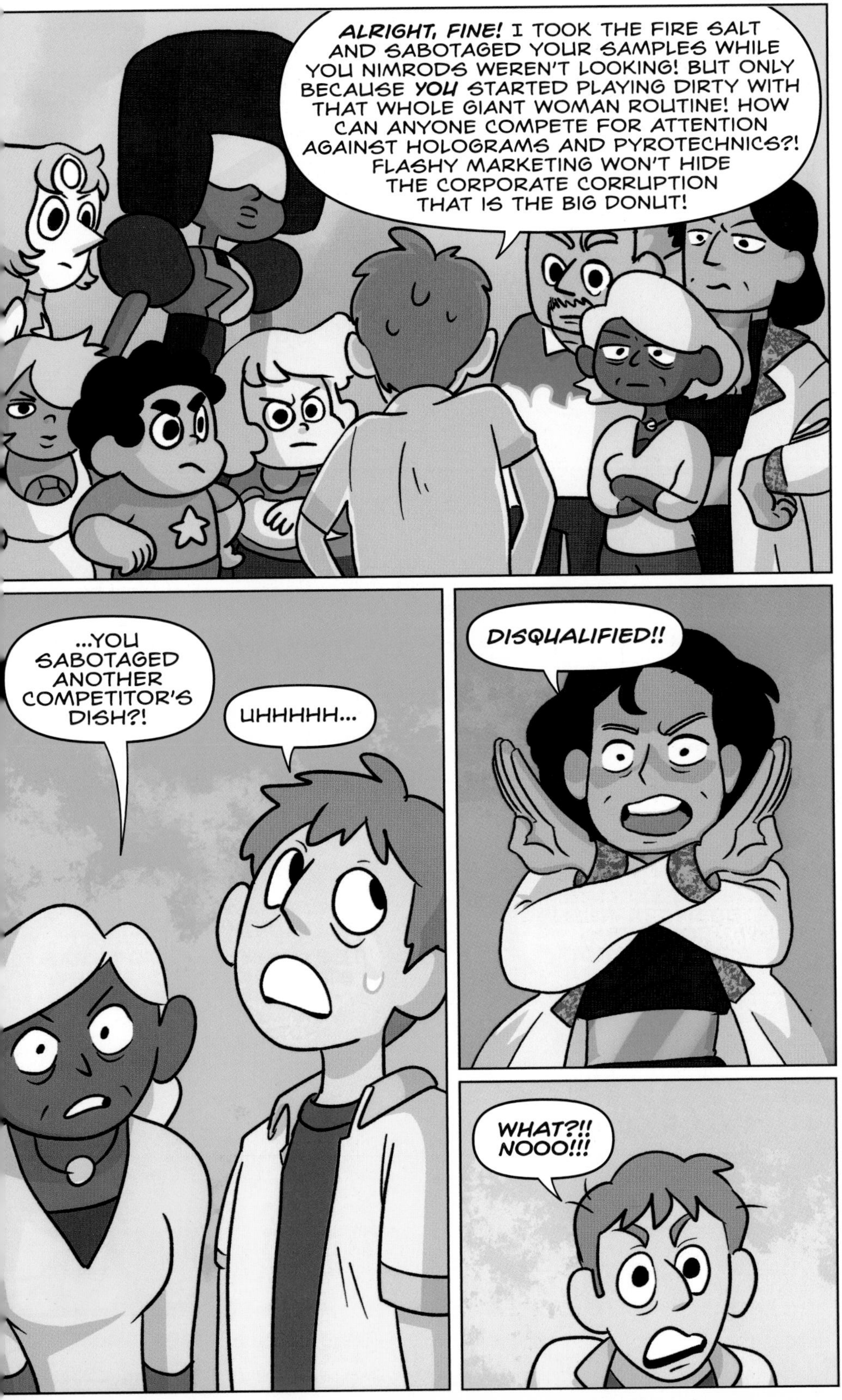
ALRIGHT, FINE! I TOOK THE FIRE SALT AND SABOTAGED YOUR SAMPLES WHILE YOU NIMRODS WEREN'T LOOKING! BUT ONLY BECAUSE YOU STARTED PLAYING DIRTY WITH THAT WHOLE GIANT WOMAN ROUTINE! HOW CAN ANYONE COMPETE FOR ATTENTION AGAINST HOLOGRAMS AND PYROTECHNICS?! FLASHY MARKETING WON'T HIDE THE CORPORATE CORRUPTION THAT IS THE BIG DONUT!
...YOU SABOTAGED ANOTHER COMPETITOR'S DISH?!
UHHHHH...
DISQUALIFIED!!
WHAT?!! NOOO!!!

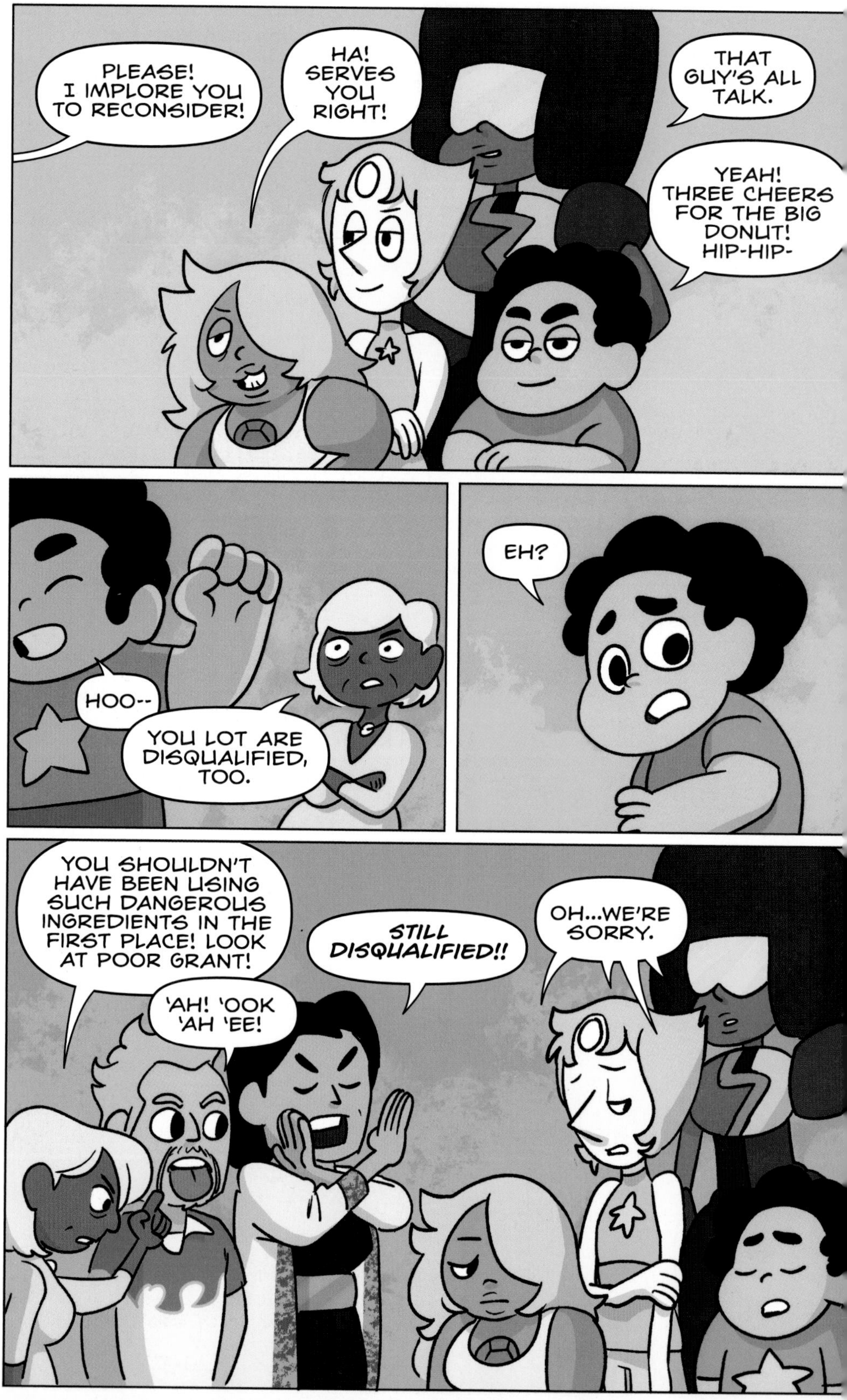
PLEASE! I IMPLORE YOU TO RECONSIDER!
HA! SERVES YOU RIGHT!
THAT GUY'S ALL TALK.
YEAH! THREE CHEERS FOR THE BIG DONUT! HIP-HIP-
HOO--
YOU LOT ARE DISQUALIFIED, TOO.
EH?
YOU SHOULDN'T HAVE BEEN USING SUCH DANGEROUS INGREDIENTS IN THE FIRST PLACE! LOOK AT POOR GRANT!
'AH! 'OOK 'AH 'EE!
STILL DISQUALIFIED!!
OH...WE'RE SORRY.

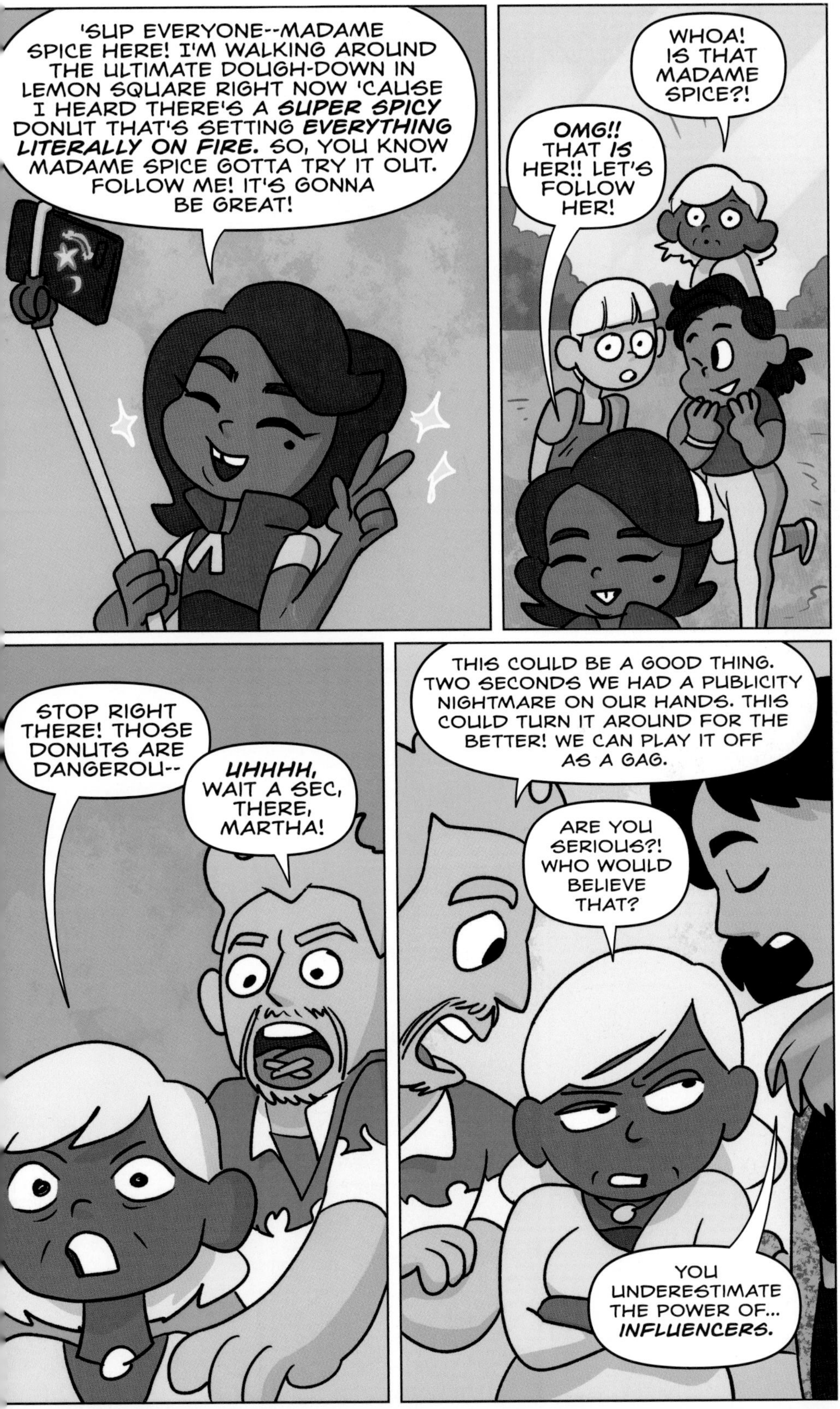
'SUP EVERYONE--MADAME SPICE HERE! I'M WALKING AROUND THE ULTIMATE DOUGH-DOWN IN LEMON SQUARE RIGHT NOW 'CAUSE I HEARD THERE'S A **SUPER SPICY** DONUT THAT'S SETTING **EVERYTHING LITERALLY ON FIRE.** SO, YOU KNOW MADAME SPICE GOTTA TRY IT OUT. FOLLOW ME! IT'S GONNA BE GREAT!
WHOA! IS THAT MADAME SPICE?!
OMG!! THAT **IS** HER!! LET'S FOLLOW HER!
STOP RIGHT THERE! THOSE DONUTS ARE DANGEROU--
UHHHH, WAIT A SEC, THERE, MARTHA!
THIS COULD BE A GOOD THING. TWO SECONDS WE HAD A PUBLICITY NIGHTMARE ON OUR HANDS. THIS COULD TURN IT AROUND FOR THE BETTER! WE CAN PLAY IT OFF AS A GAG.
ARE YOU SERIOUS?! WHO WOULD BELIEVE THAT?
YOU UNDERESTIMATE THE POWER OF... **INFLUENCERS.**

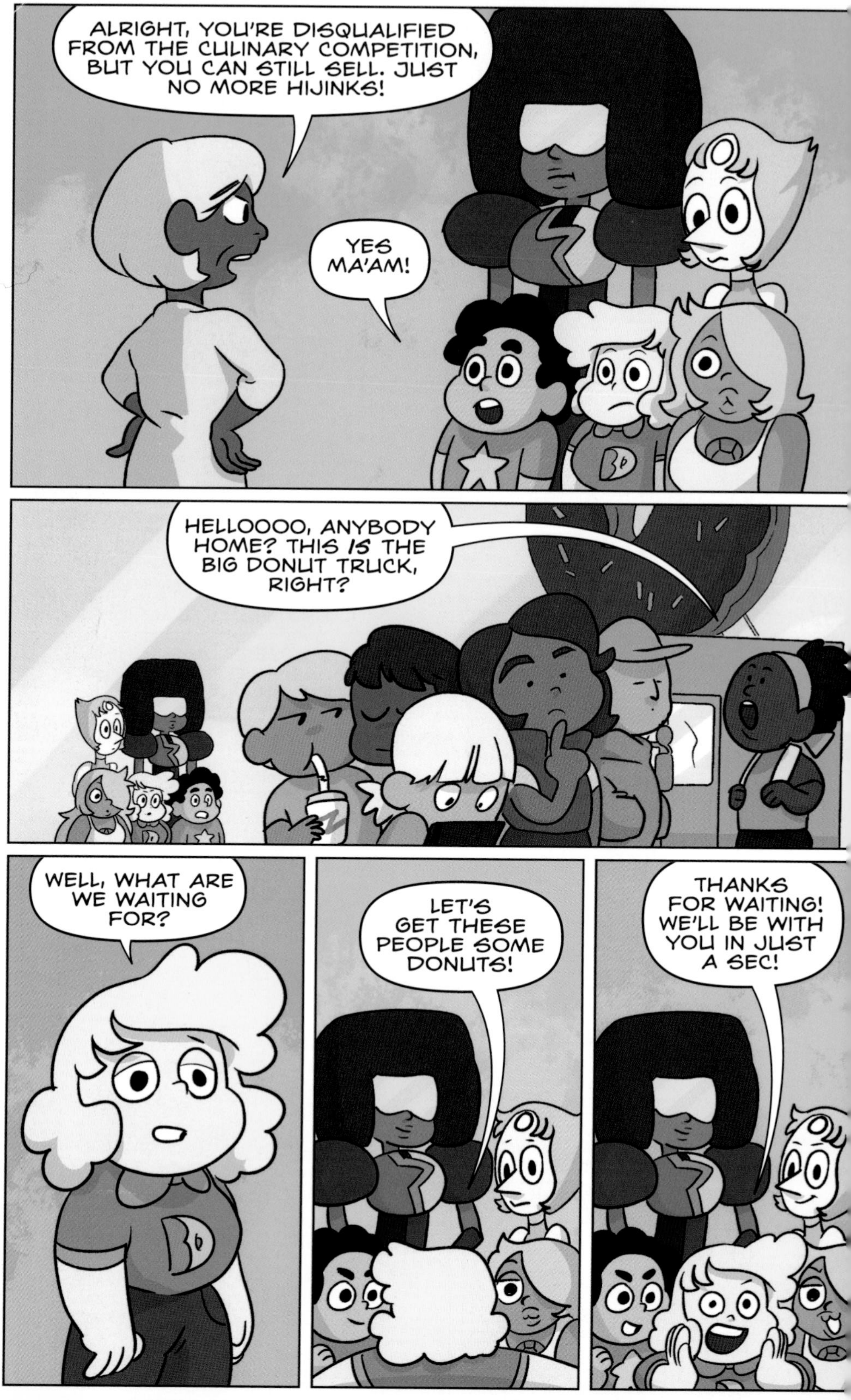
ALRIGHT, YOU'RE DISQUALIFIED FROM THE CULINARY COMPETITION, BUT YOU CAN STILL SELL. JUST NO MORE HIJINKS!
YES MA'AM!
HELLOOOO, ANYBODY HOME? THIS *IS* THE BIG DONUT TRUCK, RIGHT?
WELL, WHAT ARE WE WAITING FOR?
LET'S GET THESE PEOPLE SOME DONUTS!
THANKS FOR WAITING! WE'LL BE WITH YOU IN JUST A SEC!

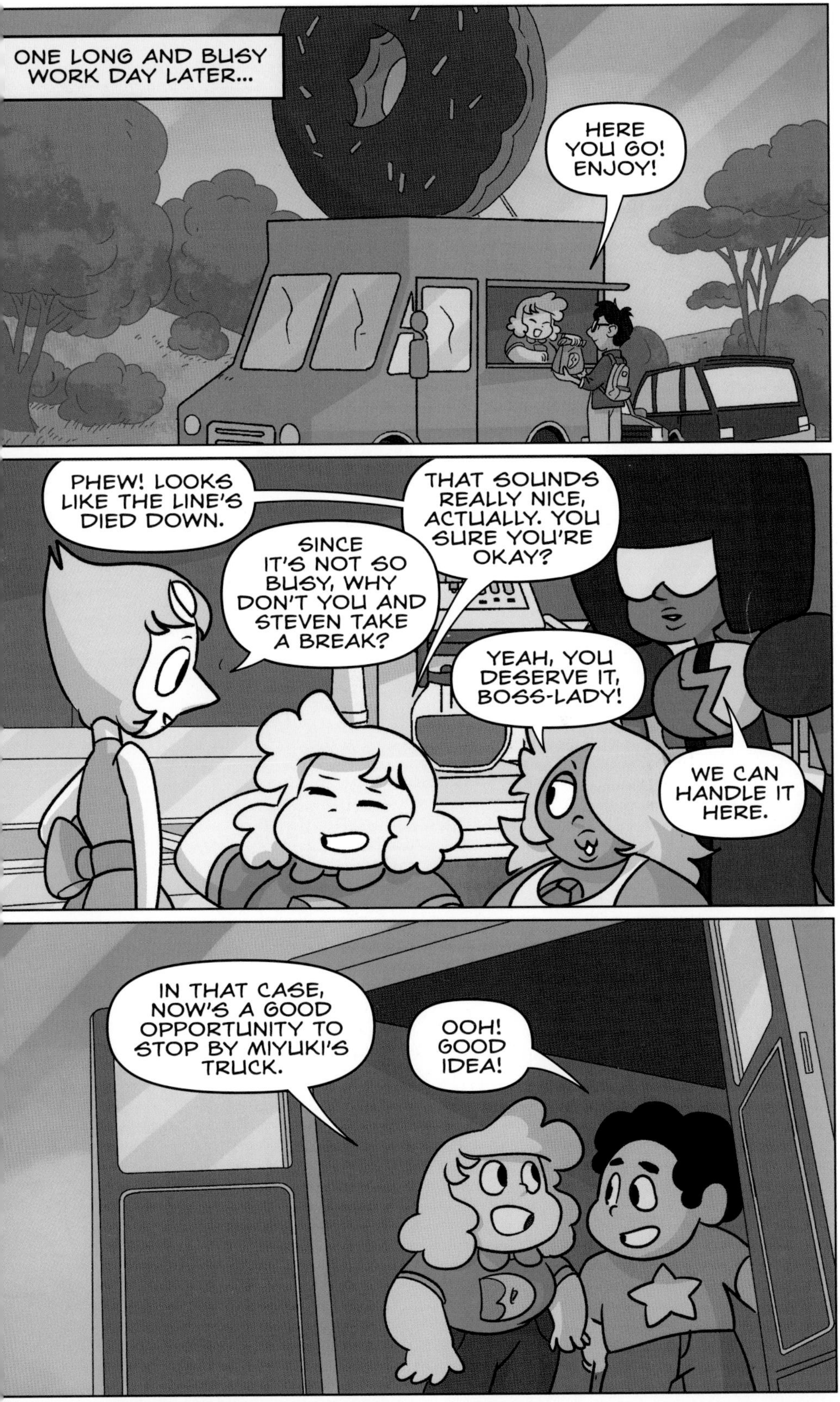
ONE LONG AND BUSY WORK DAY LATER...
HERE YOU GO! ENJOY!
PHEW! LOOKS LIKE THE LINE'S DIED DOWN.
SINCE IT'S NOT SO BUSY, WHY DON'T YOU AND STEVEN TAKE A BREAK?
THAT SOUNDS REALLY NICE, ACTUALLY. YOU SURE YOU'RE OKAY?
YEAH, YOU DESERVE IT, BOSS-LADY!
WE CAN HANDLE IT HERE.
IN THAT CASE, NOW'S A GOOD OPPORTUNITY TO STOP BY MIYUKI'S TRUCK.
OOH! GOOD IDEA!

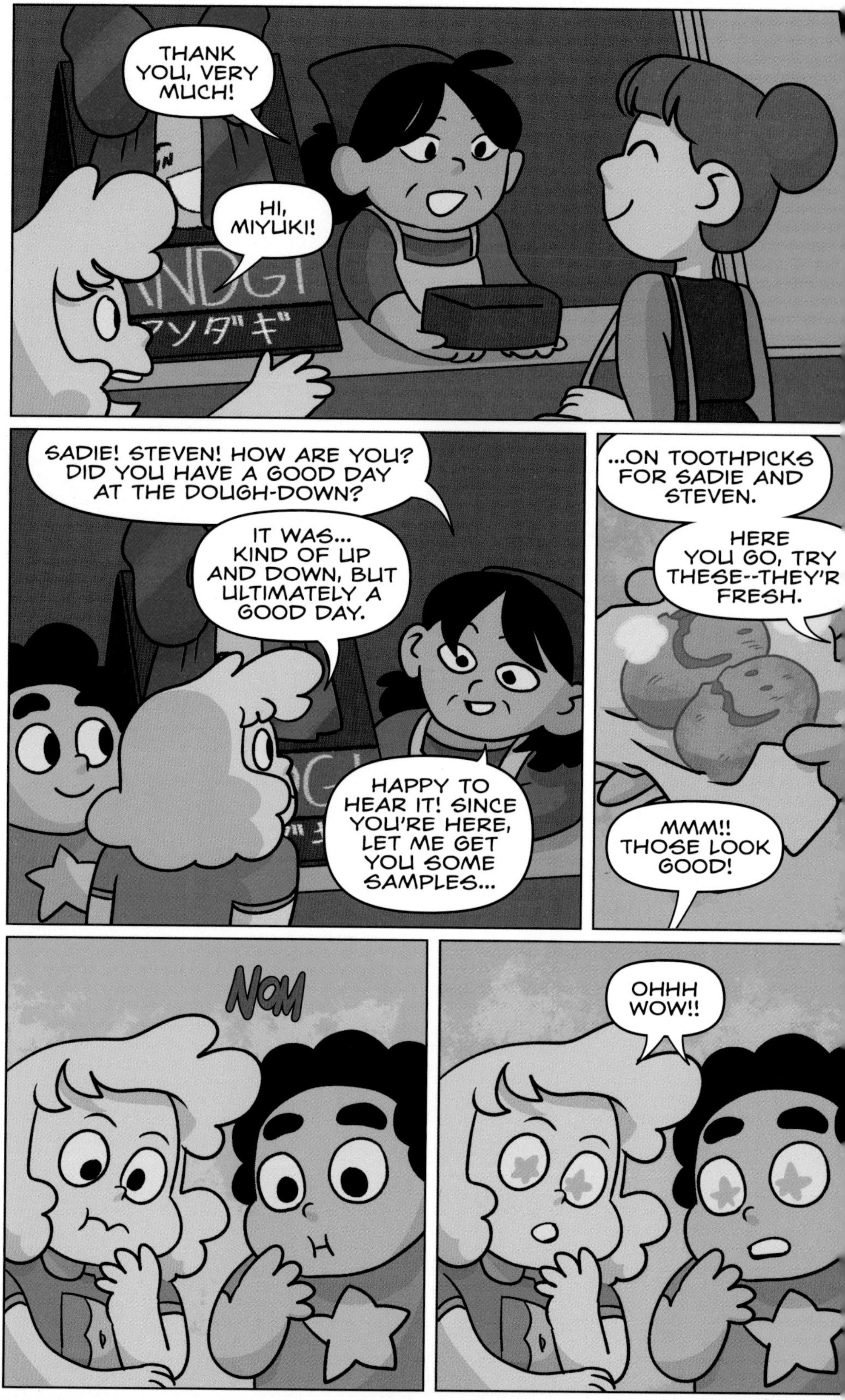
THANK YOU, VERY MUCH!
HI, MIYUKI!
SADIE! STEVEN! HOW ARE YOU? DID YOU HAVE A GOOD DAY AT THE DOUGH-DOWN?
IT WAS... KIND OF UP AND DOWN, BUT ULTIMATELY A GOOD DAY.
HAPPY TO HEAR IT! SINCE YOU'RE HERE, LET ME GET YOU SOME SAMPLES...
...ON TOOTHPICKS FOR SADIE AND STEVEN.
HERE YOU GO, TRY THESE--THEY'R FRESH.
MMM!! THOSE LOOK GOOD!
NOM
OHHH WOW!!

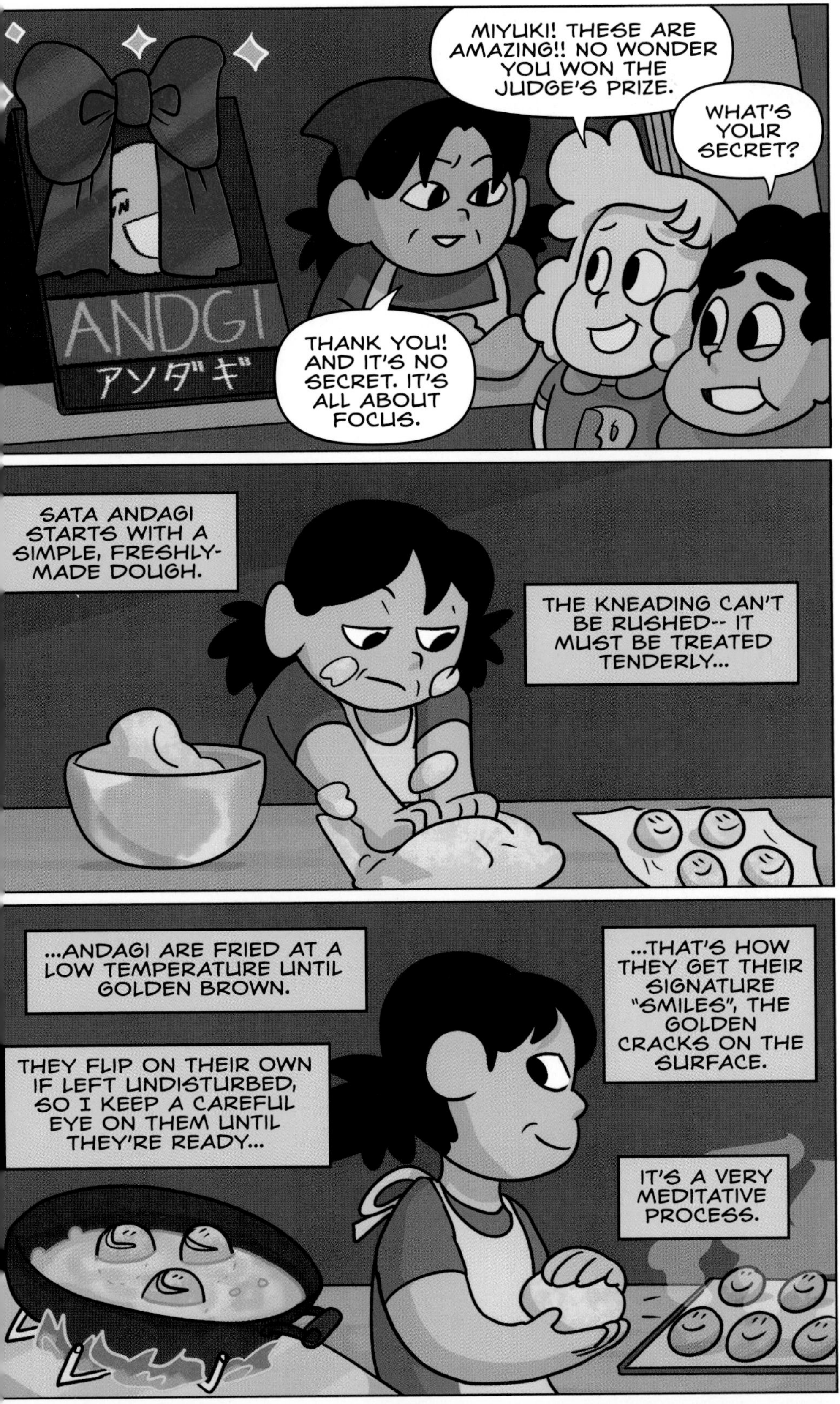
ANDGI
アンダギ
MIYUKI! THESE ARE AMAZING!! NO WONDER YOU WON THE JUDGE'S PRIZE.
WHAT'S YOUR SECRET?
THANK YOU! AND IT'S NO SECRET. IT'S ALL ABOUT FOCUS.
SATA ANDAGI STARTS WITH A SIMPLE, FRESHLY-MADE DOUGH.
THE KNEADING CAN'T BE RUSHED-- IT MUST BE TREATED TENDERLY...
...ANDAGI ARE FRIED AT A LOW TEMPERATURE UNTIL GOLDEN BROWN.
THEY FLIP ON THEIR OWN IF LEFT UNDISTURBED, SO I KEEP A CAREFUL EYE ON THEM UNTIL THEY'RE READY...
...THAT'S HOW THEY GET THEIR SIGNATURE "SMILES", THE GOLDEN CRACKS ON THE SURFACE.
IT'S A VERY MEDITATIVE PROCESS.

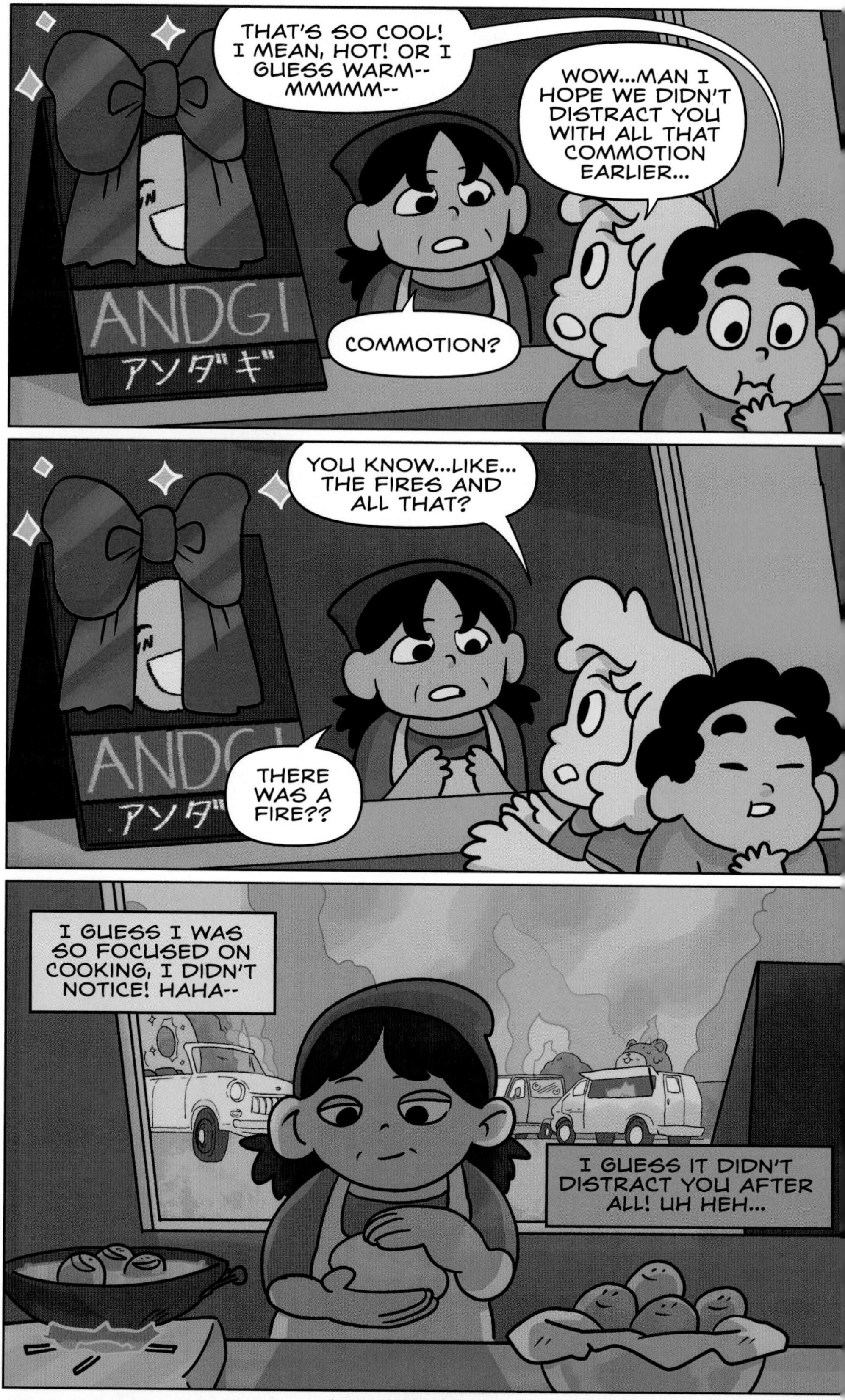
THAT'S SO COOL! I MEAN, HOT! OR I GUESS WARM-- MMMMM--
WOW...MAN I HOPE WE DIDN'T DISTRACT YOU WITH ALL THAT COMMOTION EARLIER...
ANDGI
アンダギ
COMMOTION?
YOU KNOW...LIKE... THE FIRES AND ALL THAT?
THERE WAS A FIRE??
I GUESS I WAS SO FOCUSED ON COOKING, I DIDN'T NOTICE! HAHA--
I GUESS IT DIDN'T DISTRACT YOU AFTER ALL! UH HEH...

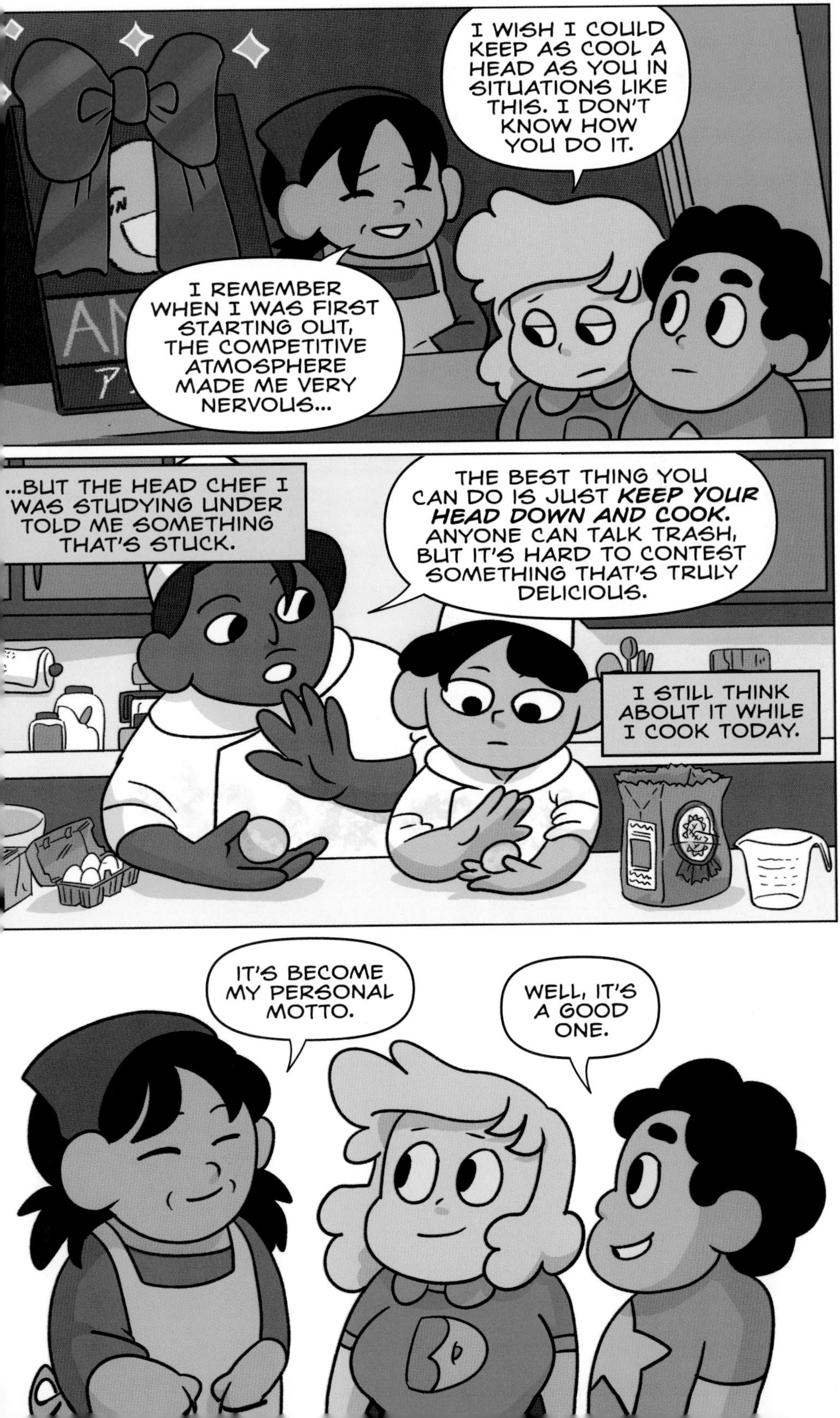
I WISH I COULD KEEP AS COOL A HEAD AS YOU IN SITUATIONS LIKE THIS. I DON'T KNOW HOW YOU DO IT.
I REMEMBER WHEN I WAS FIRST STARTING OUT, THE COMPETITIVE ATMOSPHERE MADE ME VERY NERVOUS...
...BUT THE HEAD CHEF I WAS STUDYING UNDER TOLD ME SOMETHING THAT'S STUCK.
THE BEST THING YOU CAN DO IS JUST **KEEP YOUR HEAD DOWN AND COOK.** ANYONE CAN TALK TRASH, BUT IT'S HARD TO CONTEST SOMETHING THAT'S TRULY DELICIOUS.
I STILL THINK ABOUT IT WHILE I COOK TODAY.
IT'S BECOME MY PERSONAL MOTTO.
WELL, IT'S A GOOD ONE.

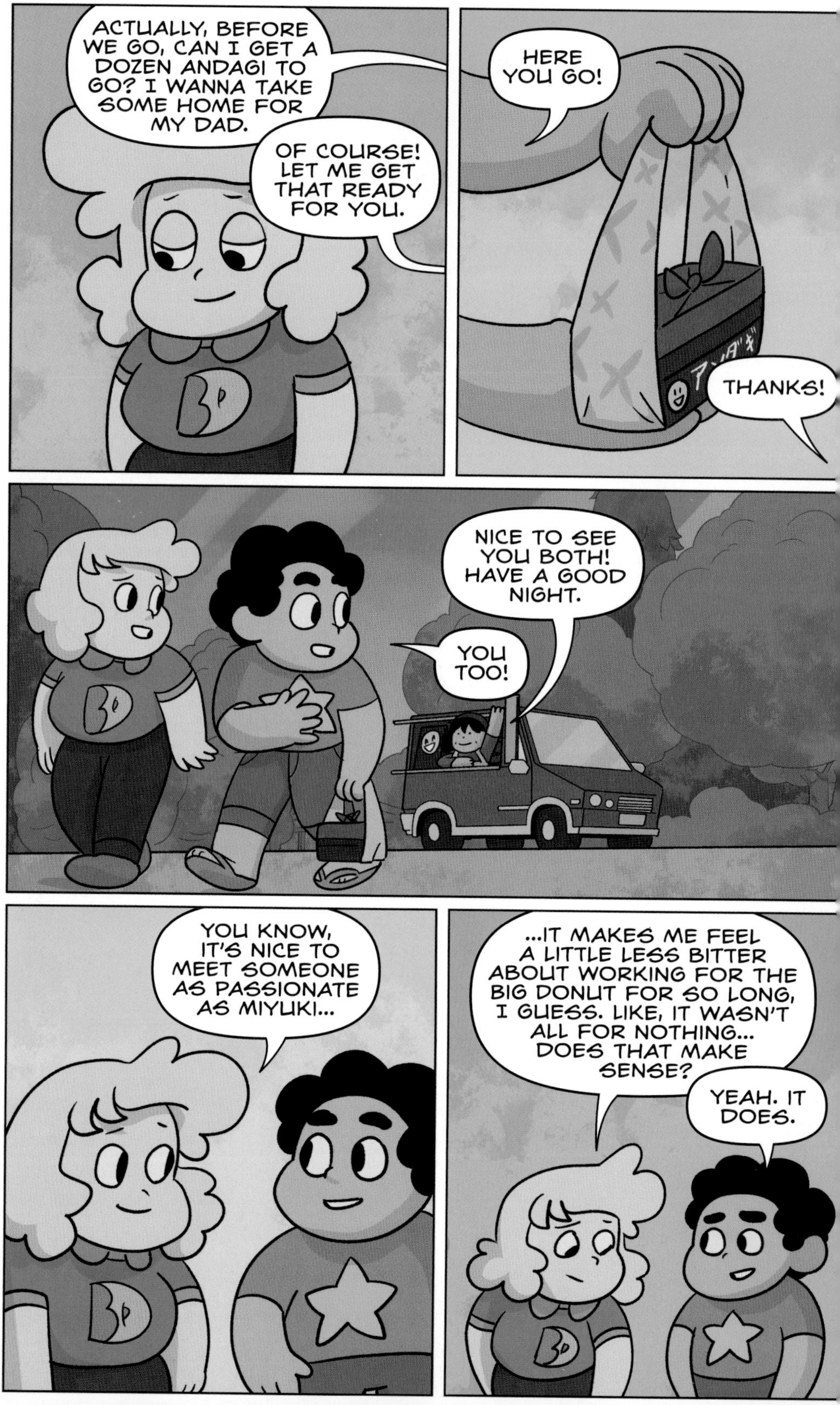
ACTUALLY, BEFORE WE GO, CAN I GET A DOZEN ANDAGI TO GO? I WANNA TAKE SOME HOME FOR MY DAD.
OF COURSE! LET ME GET THAT READY FOR YOU.
HERE YOU GO!
THANKS!
NICE TO SEE YOU BOTH! HAVE A GOOD NIGHT.
YOU TOO!
YOU KNOW, IT'S NICE TO MEET SOMEONE AS PASSIONATE AS MIYUKI...
...IT MAKES ME FEEL A LITTLE LESS BITTER ABOUT WORKING FOR THE BIG DONUT FOR SO LONG, I GUESS. LIKE, IT WASN'T ALL FOR NOTHING... DOES THAT MAKE SENSE?
YEAH. IT DOES.

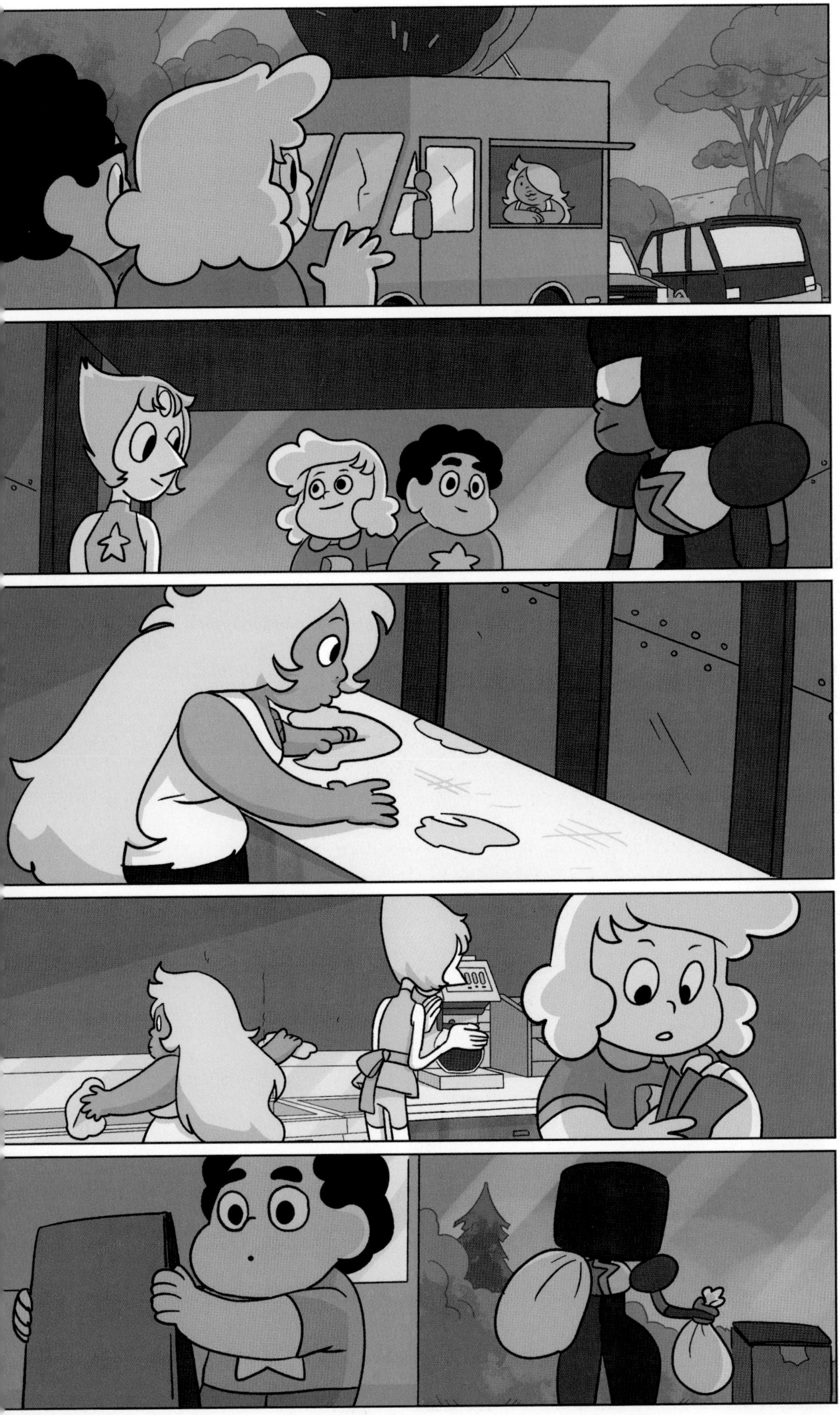

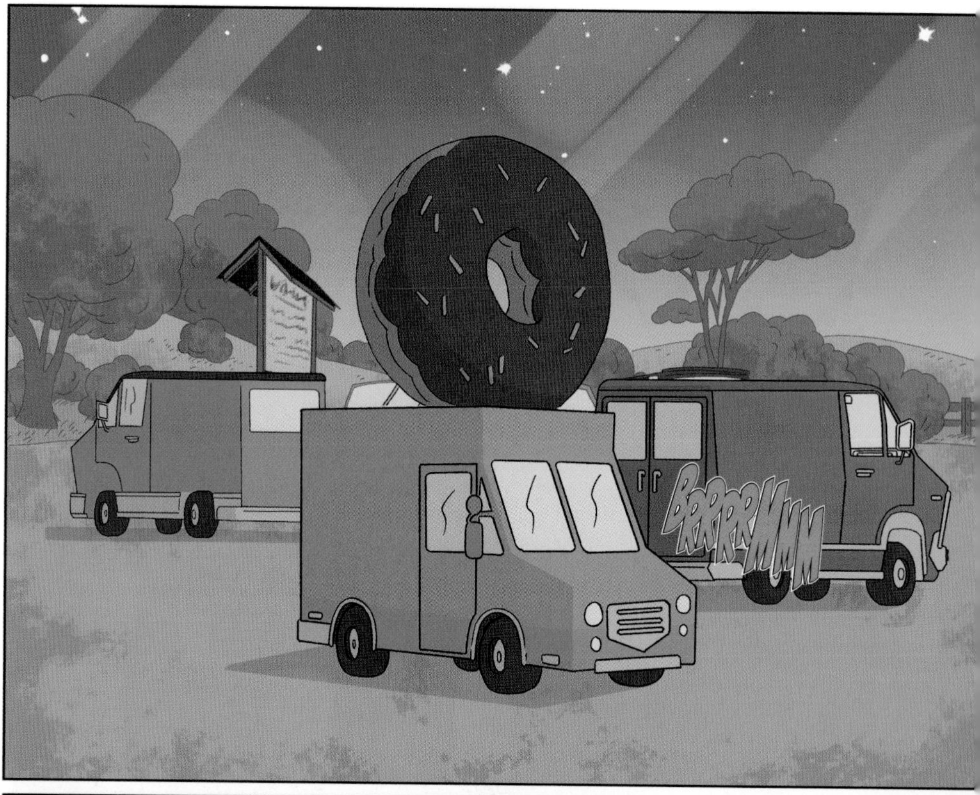
BRRRRMMM

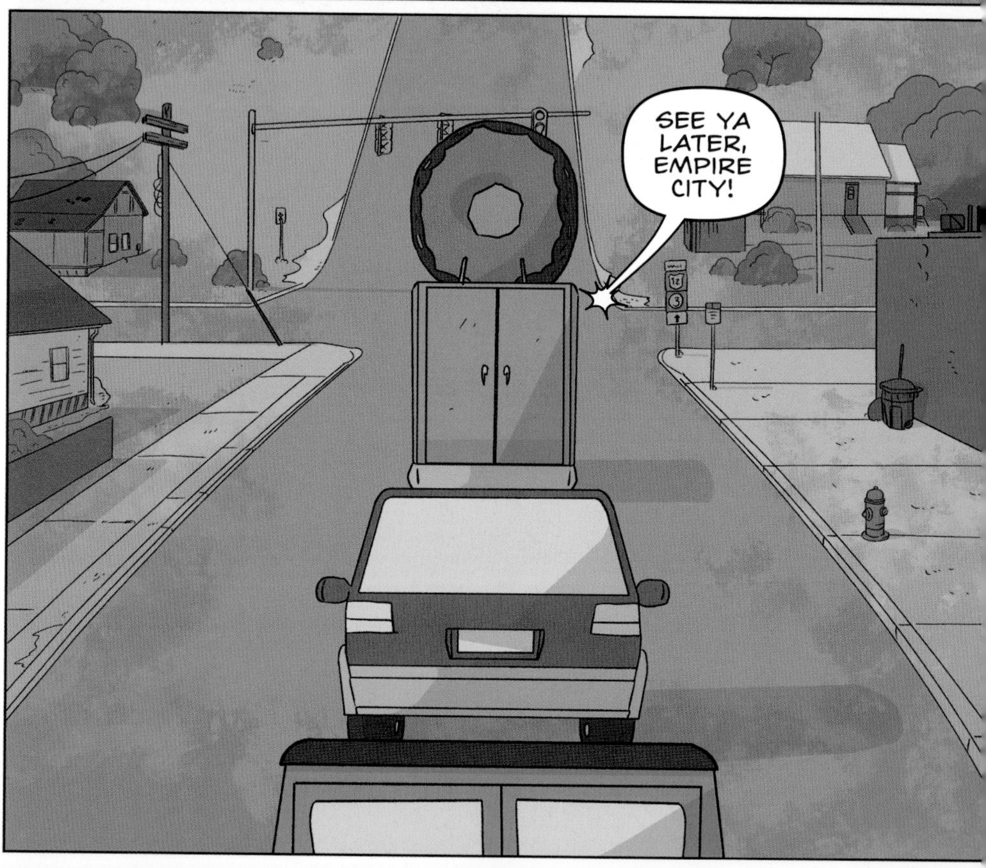
SEE YA LATER, EMPIRE CITY!

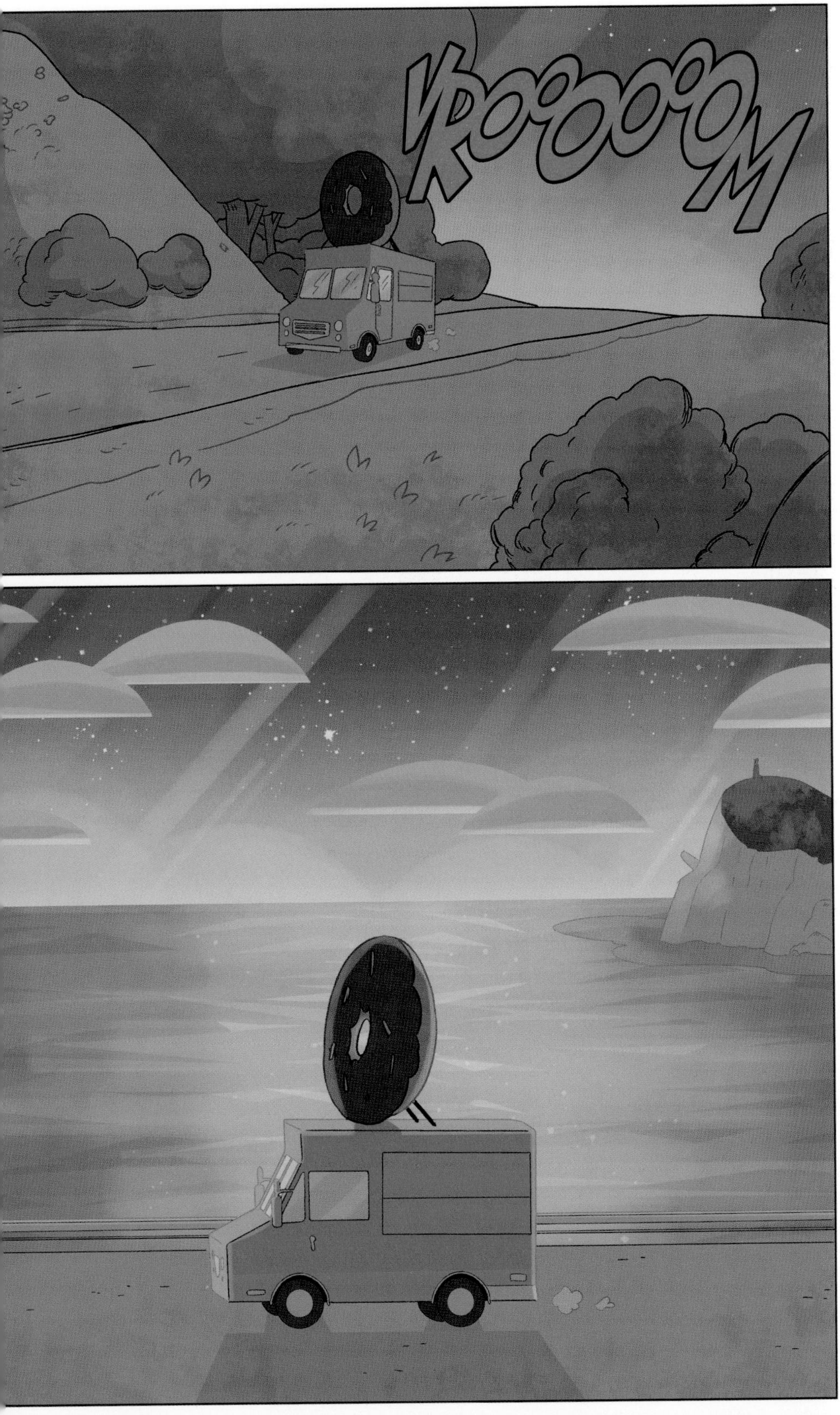
VROOOOOOM

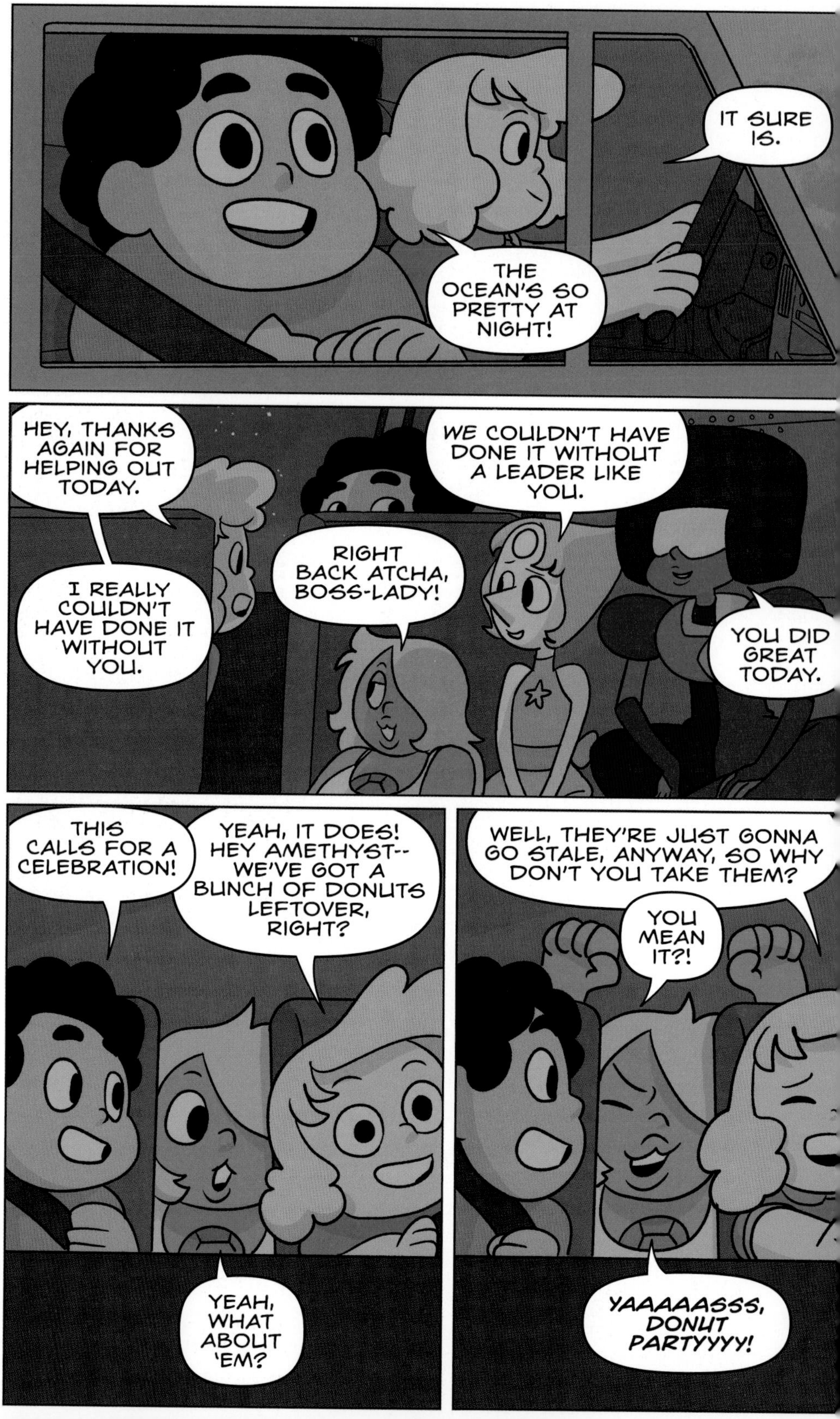
THE OCEAN'S SO PRETTY AT NIGHT!
IT SURE IS.
HEY, THANKS AGAIN FOR HELPING OUT TODAY.
I REALLY COULDN'T HAVE DONE IT WITHOUT YOU.
WE COULDN'T HAVE DONE IT WITHOUT A LEADER LIKE YOU.
RIGHT BACK ATCHA, BOSS-LADY!
YOU DID GREAT TODAY.
THIS CALLS FOR A CELEBRATION!
YEAH, IT DOES! HEY AMETHYST-- WE'VE GOT A BUNCH OF DONUTS LEFTOVER, RIGHT?
YEAH, WHAT ABOUT 'EM?
WELL, THEY'RE JUST GONNA GO STALE, ANYWAY, SO WHY DON'T YOU TAKE THEM?
YOU MEAN IT?!
YAAAAASSS, DONUT PARTYYYY!

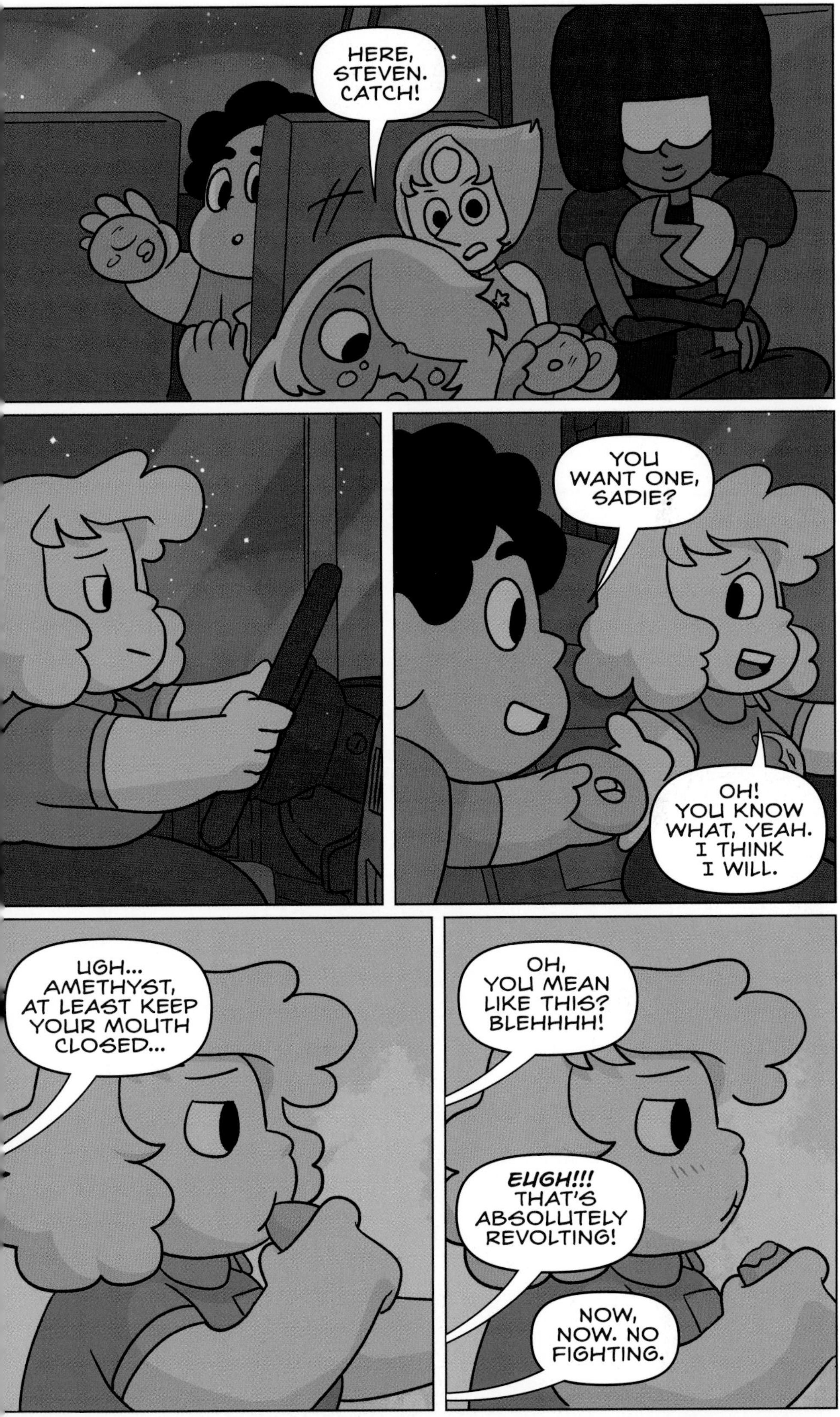
HERE, STEVEN. CATCH!
YOU WANT ONE, SADIE?
OH! YOU KNOW WHAT, YEAH. I THINK I WILL.
UGH... AMETHYST, AT LEAST KEEP YOUR MOUTH CLOSED...
OH, YOU MEAN LIKE THIS? BLEHHHH!
EUGH!!! THAT'S ABSOLUTELY REVOLTING!
NOW, NOW. NO FIGHTING.

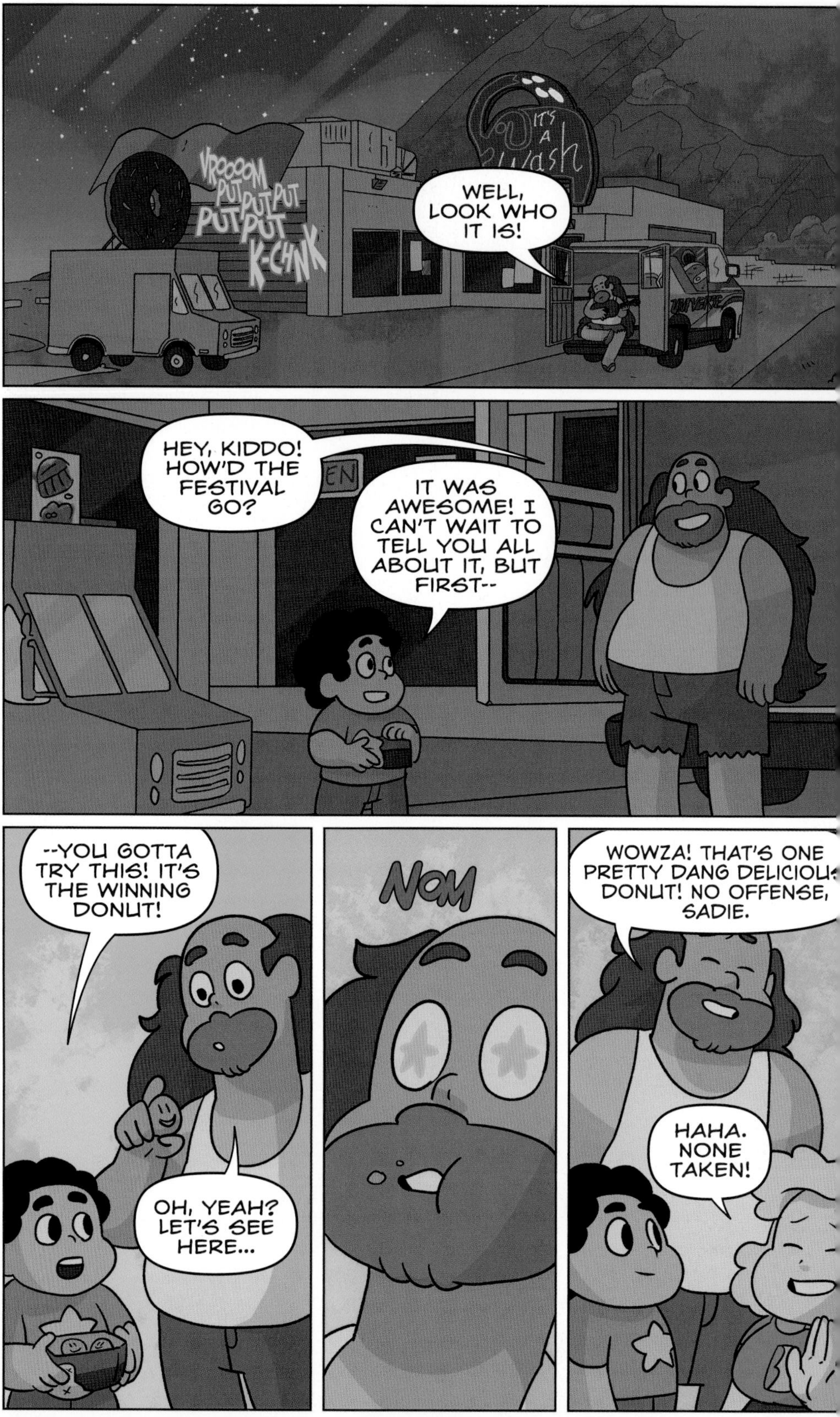
VROOOOM PUT PUT PUT PUT PUT PUT
K-CHNK
IT'S A wash
WELL, LOOK WHO IT IS!
UNIVERSE
HEY, KIDDO! HOW'D THE FESTIVAL GO?
IT WAS AWESOME! I CAN'T WAIT TO TELL YOU ALL ABOUT IT, BUT FIRST--
--YOU GOTTA TRY THIS! IT'S THE WINNING DONUT!
OH, YEAH? LET'S SEE HERE...
NOM
WOWZA! THAT'S ONE PRETTY DANG DELICIOU DONUT! NO OFFENSE, SADIE.
HAHA. NONE TAKEN!

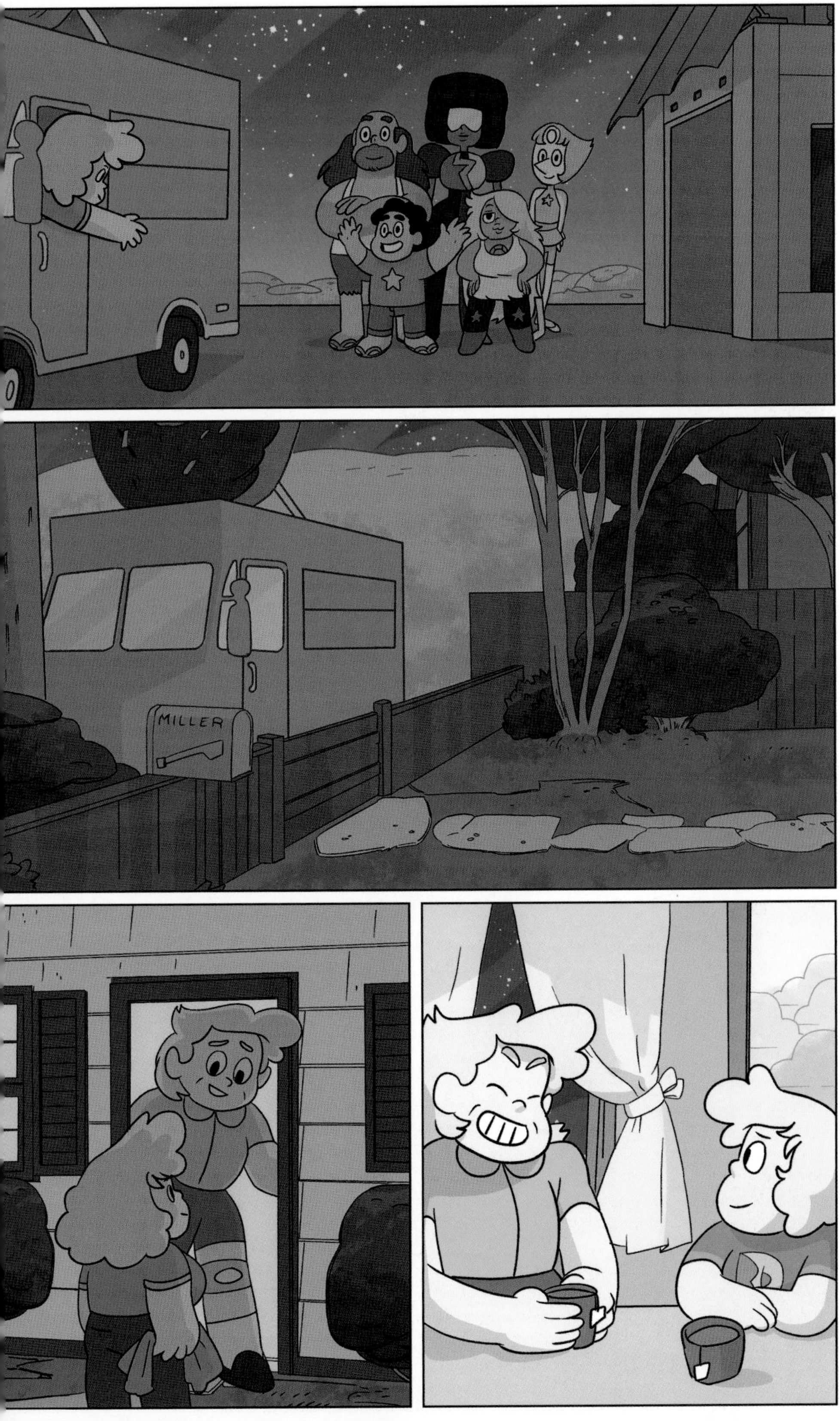
MILLER

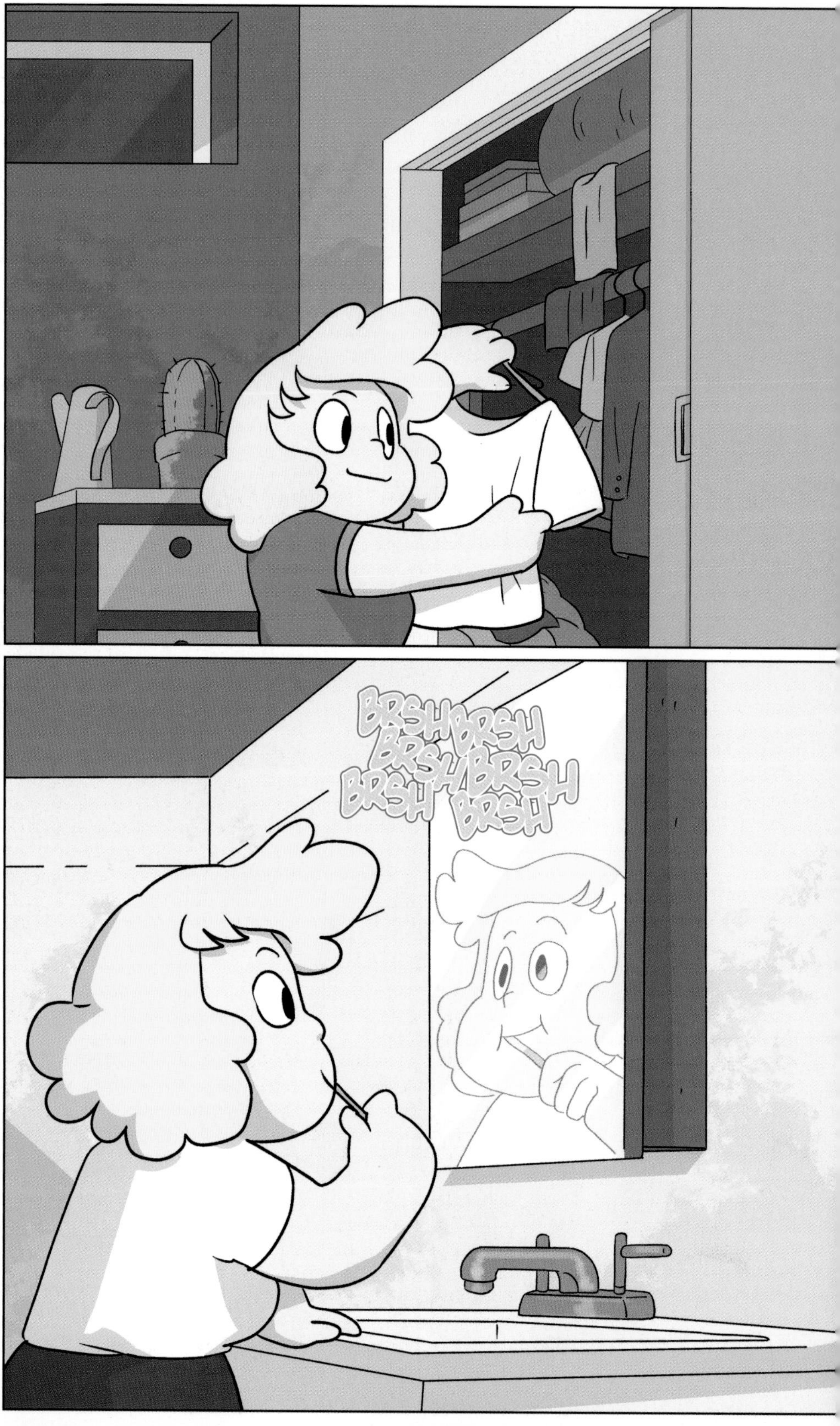
BRSH BRSH
BRSH BRSH
BRSH BRSH

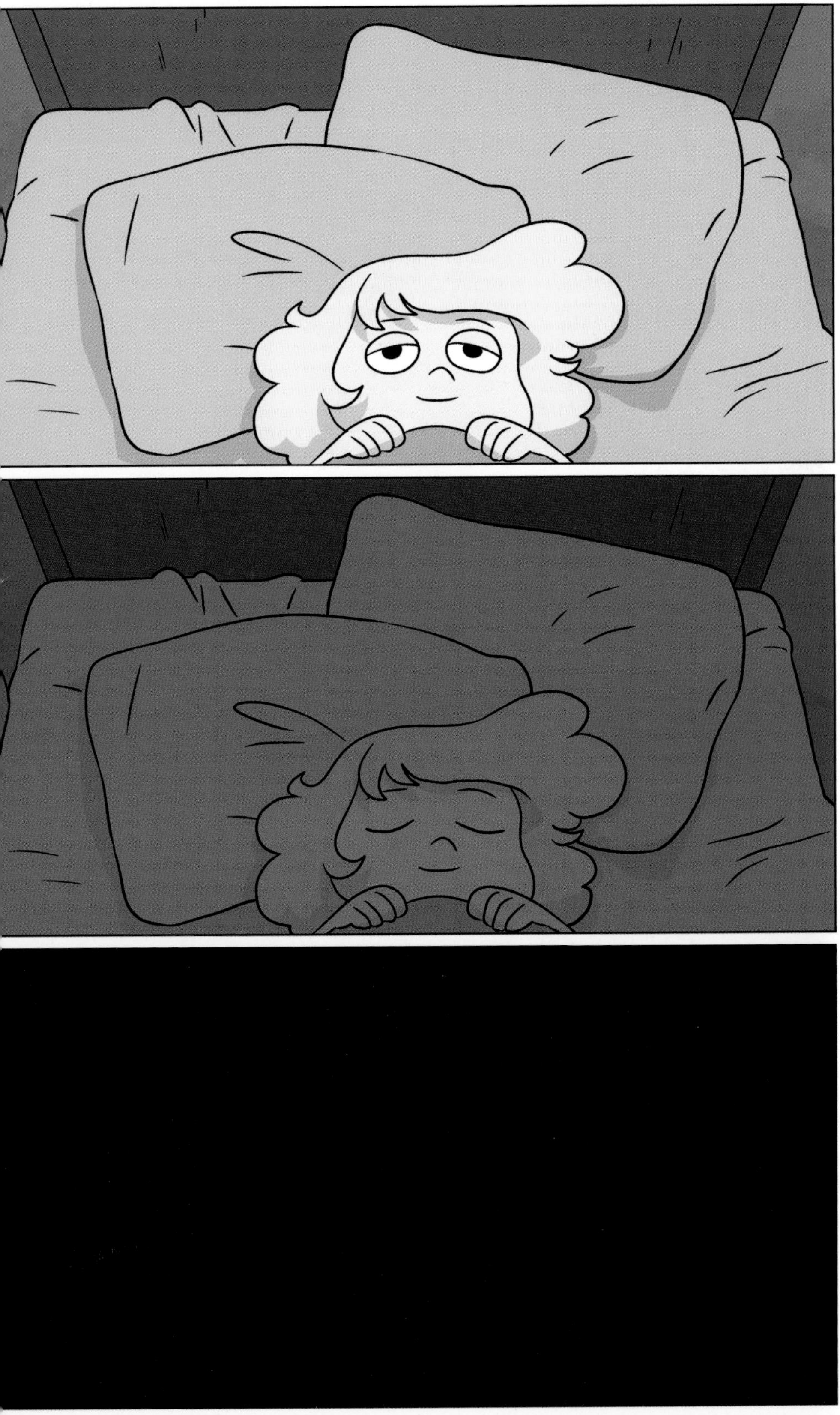

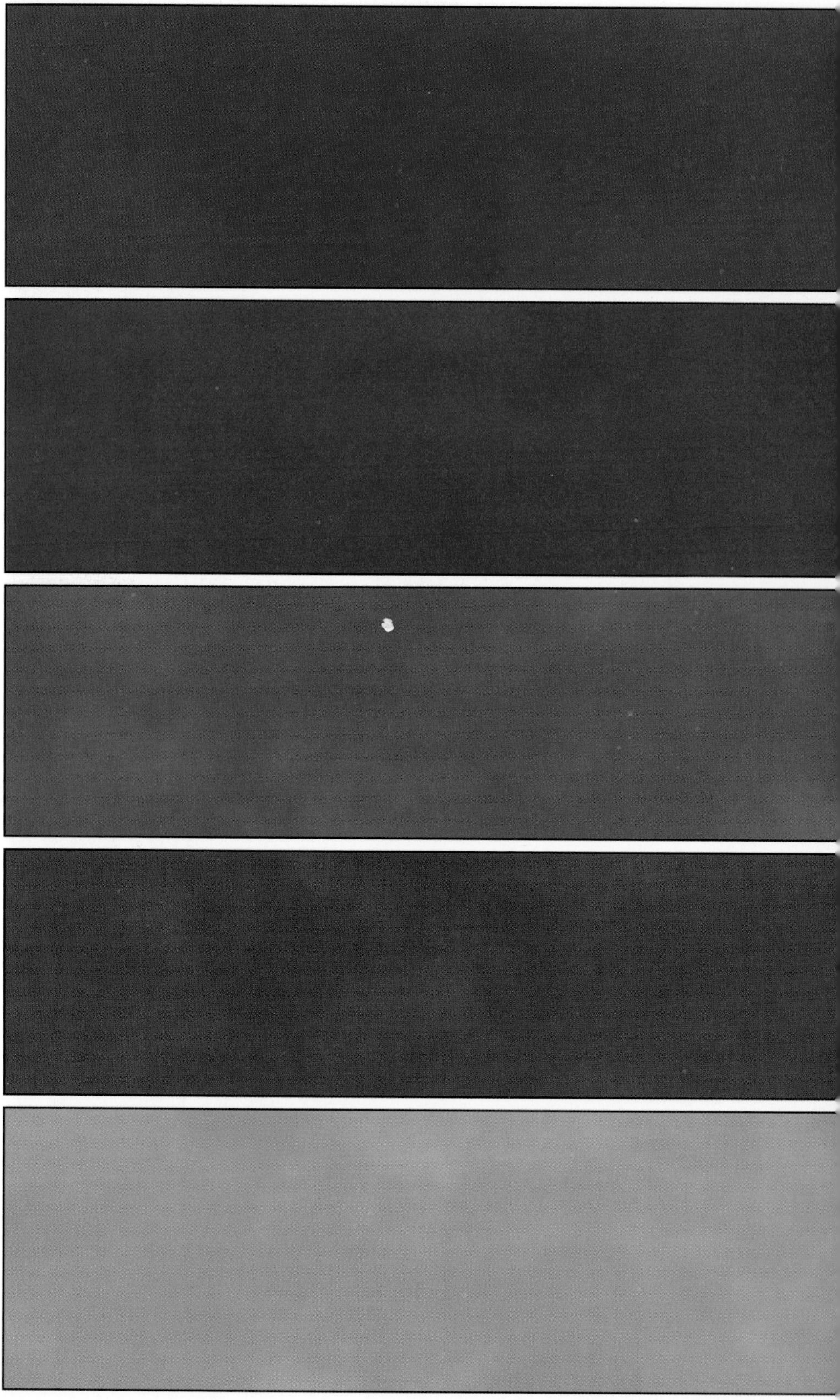

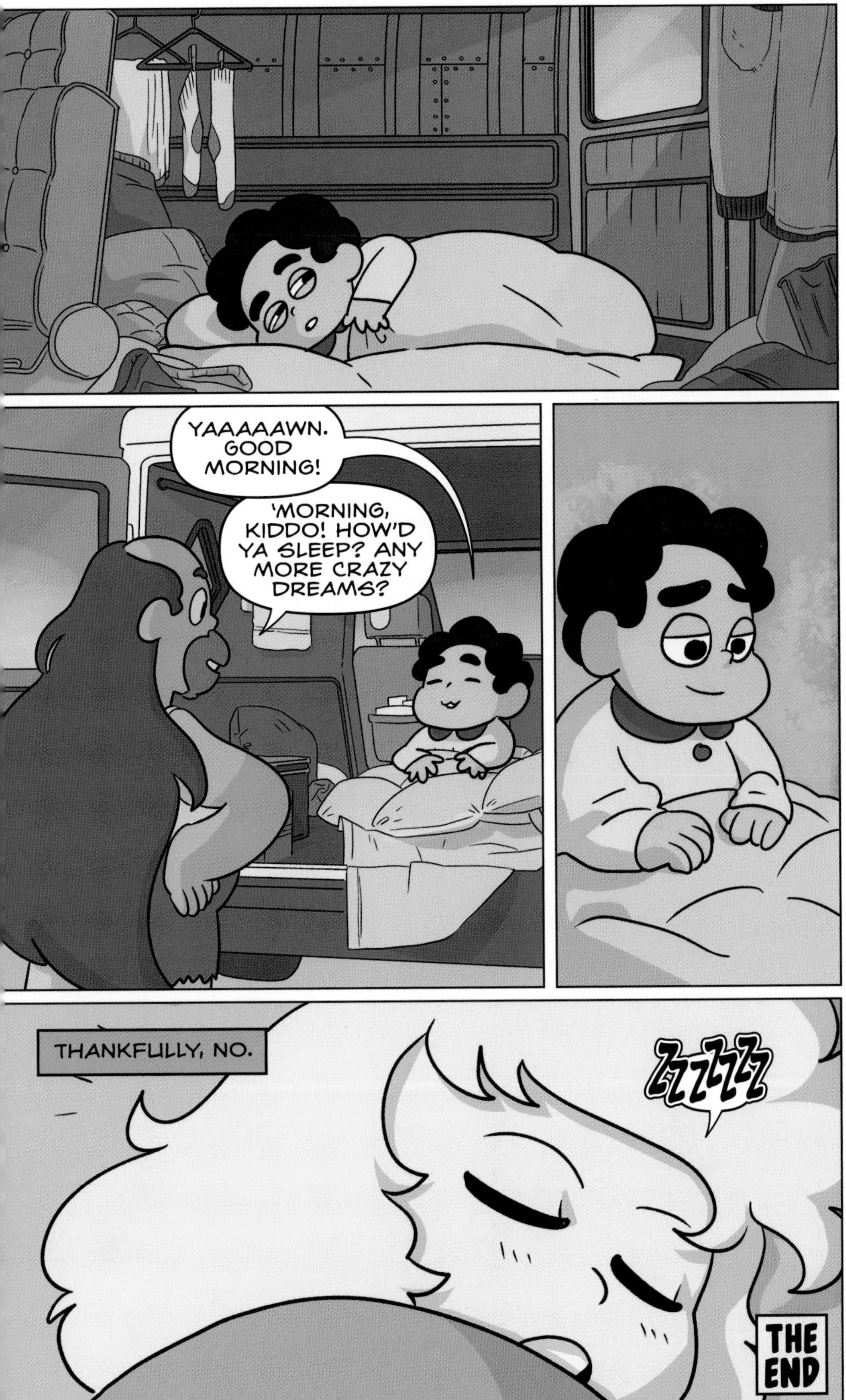
YAAAAAWN. GOOD MORNING!
'MORNING, KIDDO! HOW'D YA SLEEP? ANY MORE CRAZY DREAMS?
THANKFULLY, NO.
ZZZZZZ
THE END

DISCOVER
EXPLOSIVE NEW WORLDS

Adventure Time
Pendleton Ward and Others
Volume 1
ISBN: 978-1-60886-280-1 | $14.99 US
Volume 2
ISBN: 978-1-60886-323-5 | $14.99 US
Adventure Time: Islands
ISBN: 978-1-60886-972-5 | $9.99 US

The Amazing World of Gumball
Ben Bocquelet and Others
Volume 1
ISBN: 978-1-60886-488-1 | $14.99 US
Volume 2
ISBN: 978-1-60886-793-6 | $14.99 US

Brave Chef Brianna
Sam Sykes, Selina Espiritu
ISBN: 978-1-68415-050-2 | $14.99 US

Mega Princess
Kelly Thompson, Brianne Drouhard
ISBN: 978-1-68415-007-6 | $14.99 US

The Not-So Secret Society
Matthew Daley, Arlene Daley, Wook Jin Clark
ISBN: 978-1-60886-997-8 | $9.99 US

Over the Garden Wall
Patrick McHale, Jim Campbell and Others
Volume 1
ISBN: 978-1-60886-940-4 | $14.99 US
Volume 2
ISBN: 978-1-68415-006-9 | $14.99 US

Steven Universe
Rebecca Sugar and Others
Volume 1
ISBN: 978-1-60886-706-6 | $14.99 US
Volume 2
ISBN: 978-1-60886-796-7 | $14.99 US

Steven Universe & The Crystal Gems
ISBN: 978-1-60886-921-3 | $14.99 US

Steven Universe: Too Cool for School
ISBN: 978-1-60886-771-4 | $14.99 US

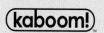

AVAILABLE AT YOUR LOCAL COMICS SHOP AND BOOKSTORE
To find a comics shop in your area, visit www.comicshoplocator.com
WWW.**BOOM-STUDIOS**.COM